Rowan had always told her that justice was the answer. And for a long time, Ayla had believed her. She'd believed that revolution was possible, that if humans just kept rising up, refusing to submit, they could really change things. But Ayla knew better now. Over the years, she'd seen how hopeless Rowan's dreams were. Every uprising had failed; every brilliant plan had been crushed; every new maneuver just resulted in more human death.

Justice was a god, and Ayla didn't believe in such childish things.

She believed in blood.

Also by Nina Varela

IRON HEART

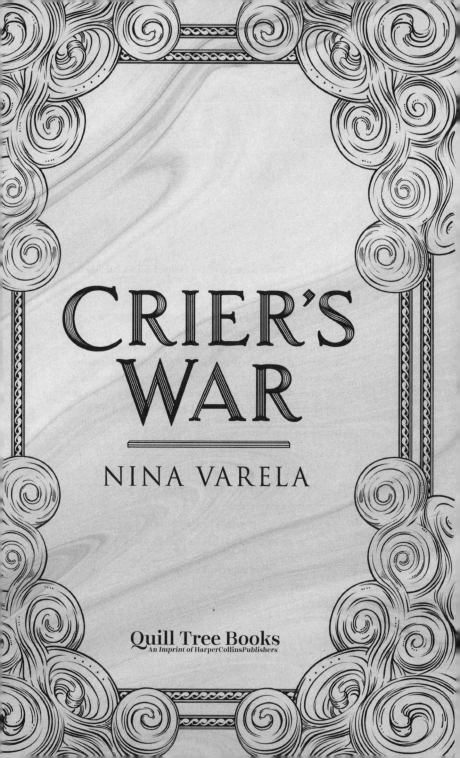

CRIER'S WAR

NINA VARELA

Quill Tree Books
An Imprint of HarperCollinsPublishers

For the queer readers. You deserve every adventure.

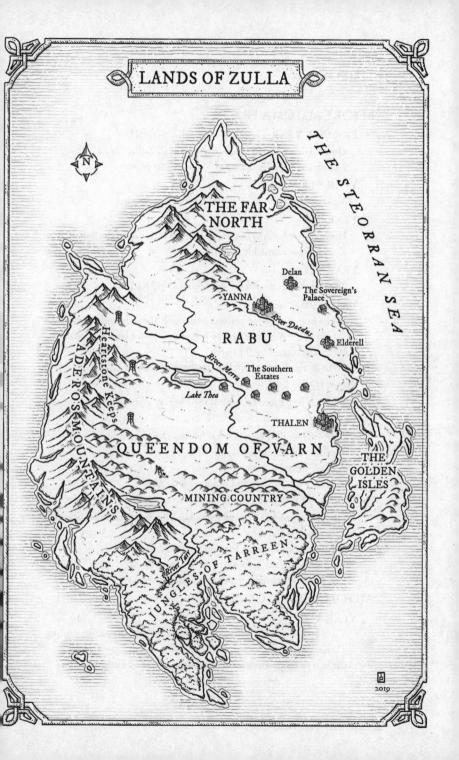

TIMELINE

BEFORE AUTOMA ERA

ERA 900, YEAR 7—RULE OF THEA BEGINS

Queen Thea, the Barren Queen, ruler of all Zulla, desires a child

Founds the Royal Academy of Makers at the palace

YEAR 911

Maker Thomas Wren creates Kiera, the first Automa

YEAR 915

Having a pet Automa has become all the rage among the human elite

Kiera becomes unstable, violent

YEAR 917

Thomas Wren arrested for attempting to kill Kiera

YEAR 920

While in prison, Wren perfects heartstone, the alchemical gem that powers the Automae, and he begins to produce large quantities

Wren is pardoned by the queen

Wren establishes the Iron Heart, a heartstone mine

YEAR 921

Automae begin to rebel against their human commissioners

YEAR 924

An Automa called Neo kills her human commissioner and escapes, calling all Automae to arms

First organized Automa revolt

War between humans and Automae is declared

YEARS 924–929—THE WAR OF KINDS

Neo and a group of Automa rebels kill Thomas Wren and take control of the Iron Heart

Kiera turns on Queen Thea; Queen Thea kills her

An Automa called Tayol assassinates Queen Thea

The tides have turned; the Automae are victorious

AUTOMA ERA BEGINS

YEAR 1–2

Tayol attempts to distribute land and resources to the Automa ruling class

Zulla is in chaos; there are many Automa raids on human villages

YEAR 3

    Tayol becomes Sovereign of Zulla

    Neo establishes the Watchers of the Heart: Automae who dedicate
        their lives to protecting the Iron Heart

YEAR 5

    A human named Siena creates an Automa girl who does not require
        blood or heartstone

    Siena names the girl "Yora" . . . and keeps her a secret

YEAR 6

    The Automae of the mining nation Varn declare independence from
        the rest of Zulla

YEAR 7

    Sovereign Tayol establishes Traditionalism

    Tayol commissions an heir, Hesod

YEAR 10

    Automa King Fierven rises to power in Varn

YEAR 31

    Siena's daughter, Clara, bears children of her own: twins Ayla and
        Storme

    Hesod becomes Sovereign of Zulla and forms the Red Council

    Hesod commissions an heir, Crier

YEAR 40

    The Sovereign orders a raid on the village of Delan

YEAR 43

    Scyre Kinok publishes the first pamphlets on a new movement he calls
        "Anti-Reliance," the antithesis of Traditionalism

YEAR 44

    Scyre Kinok begins to gain favor amongst the Automae in Rabu

    Automa King Fierven of Varn is assassinated; his daughter, Junn,
        ascends to the throne

YEAR 46

    The Anti-Reliance Movement continues to grow

    Scyre Kinok seeks alliance with Sovereign Hesod

    Scyre Kinok and Lady Crier are betrothed

YEAR 47—PRESENT DAY

There was once a queen called Thea, and in her twenty-first year it was decided that she should bear a child. As was tradition in Old Zulla, the queen was sequestered in preparation for the bearing. Her body was purified with daily baths of milk and salt lavender, with regular ingestions of blue dara root, and her handmaidens wove symbolic ribbons and white dayblossoms into her hair. Humans in era nine hundred believed that near-total rest, particularly from the duties of the throne, was necessary for a human to conceive a child. This belief had no roots in the study of Organics, as it is known now that humans can create more of their kind in almost any setting, sprouting new life whether it is invited or not, much like weeds.

However, Queen Thea was an exception. According to all accounts of that time—including the records of the queen's personal birth-witch, Bryn—the queen was, after a time, deemed barren. Despite this, accompanied only by Bryn and a single handmaiden, Queen Thea locked herself in her chambers and insisted upon an additional seven weeks of ceremonial preparation, followed by another three months of attempted mating with King Aedel. She would repeat this cycle twice more before formally accepting that she could not bear a child.

In era nine hundred, year seven, after the conspicuous death of King Aedel, Queen Thea declared that any Maker capable of building her a child— one that could perfectly imitate all the workings of a human—would be rewarded with a lifetime's worth of gold and a seat at the right hand of the throne.

In the way of humans, who are ruled by the flawed pillars of Intuition and Passion, the Makers thought this request impossible. They were wrong.

—FROM *THE BEGINNING OF THE AUTOMA ERA*,
BY EOK OF FAMILY MEADOR, 2234610907, YEAR 4 AE

FALL,

YEAR 47 AE

1

When she was newbuilt and still fragile, and her fresh-woven skin was soft and shiny from creation, Crier's father told her, "Always check their eyes. That's how you can tell if a creature is human. It's in the eyes."

Crier thought her father, Sovereign Hesod, was speaking in metaphor, that he meant humans possessed a special sort of power. Love, a glowing lantern in their hearts; hunger, a liquid heat in their bellies; souls, dark wells in their eyes.

Of course, she'd learned later that it was not a metaphor.

When light hit an Automa's eyes head-on, the irises flashed gold. A split second of reflection, refraction, like a cat's eyes at night. A flicker of gold, and you knew those eyes did not belong to a human.

Human eyes swallowed light whole.

Crier counted four heartbeats: a doe and three kits.

The woods seemed to bend around her, trees converging overhead, while near her feet there was a rabbit's den, a warm little burrow hidden underground from wolves and foxes . . . but not from her.

She stood impossibly still, listening to four tiny pulses radiating up through the dirt, beating so rapidly that they sounded like a hive of buzzing honeybees. Crier cocked her head, fascinated with the muffled hum of living organs. If she concentrated, she could hear the air moving through four sets of thumb-sized lungs. Like all Automae, she was Designed to pick up even the faintest, most faraway sounds.

This deep into the woods, dawn had barely touched the forest floor—the perfect time for a hunt. Not that Crier enjoyed hunting.

The Hunt was an old human ritual, so old that most humans did not use it anymore. But Hesod was a Traditionalist and historian at heart, and he fostered a unique appreciation for human traditions and mythology. When Crier was Made, he had anointed her forehead with wine and honey for good fortune. When she came of age at thirteen, he had gifted her a silver dress embroidered with the phases of the moon. When he decided that she would marry Kinok, a Scyre from the Western Mountains, he did not make arrangements for Crier to take part in the Automa tradition of traveling to a Maker's workshop, designing and creating a symbolic gift for her future husband. He had planned for a Hunt.

So Crier was not actually alone in these woods. Somewhere out there, hidden by the cover of shadows and trees, her fiancé, Kinok, was hunting as well.

Kinok was considered a war hero of sorts. He'd been Made long after the War of Kinds, but there had been numerous rebellions, large and small, in the five decades since the War itself. One of the biggest, a series of coups called the Southern Uprisings, had been quelled almost single-handedly by Kinok and his ingenuity.

On top of that, he was the founder and head of the Anti-Reliance Movement—a very new political group that sought to distance Automakind and humankind even further. Literally. Most of their agenda centered on building a new Automa capital to the Far North, in a territory that was uninhabitable to humans, instead of continuing to use the current capital, Yanna, which had once been a human city. It was, frankly, ridiculous. You didn't have to be the sovereign's daughter to know that building an entirely new city would require ten thousand, a hundred thousand, a *million* kings' coffers of gold, and why would such a vain effort ever be worth the time and cost? It was a fantasy.

Before Kinok had begun the Anti-Reliance Movement, about three years ago now, he'd been a Watcher of the Iron Heart. It was a sacred task, protecting the mine that made heartstone, and he was the first Watcher to ever leave his post. Which, of course, had caused much speculation among Automakind. That he'd been discharged, banished for some serious offense. But Kinok claimed it had been a simple difference of philosophy regarding the fate of their Kind, and no one had uncovered any reason more sinister than that.

The one time Crier had asked him about his past, he had been elusive. "Those were dark times," he had said. "So few of us ever saw light." She had no idea what that meant. Maybe she was overcomplicating it: he'd been living in a mine, after all.

Still, the secrets he held—about the Iron Heart, how it ran, its exact coordinates within the western mountains—made him inherently powerful, and different. Many of her father's councilmembers—the sovereign's "Red Hands," as they were called—seemed drawn to Kinok. Like Hesod, Kinok had a certain gravity to him, a certain pull, though where he was serious, Hesod was jovial. Where Kinok was controlled and quiet, Hesod was loud, quick-tempered, often brash. And determined to marry off his daughter to Kinok, despite all the whispers, the speculations. Or perhaps because of them.

Months before Kinok's arrival, Crier and her father had taken a walk along the sea cliffs. "Kinok's followers are few and scattered, but he is gaining influence at a rate I hadn't thought possible," he'd explained.

She had listened carefully, trying to understand his point. She had heard of Kinok's rallies, if "rallies" was even the right word—they were essentially just intellectual gatherings, where small groups of Automae could share their ideals, talk politics and advancement. "Scyre Kinok is a philosopher, Father, not a politician," Crier had said. "He poses no threat to your rule."

It had been late summer, the sky clear and delphinium blue.

Crier used to treasure those long, slow walks with her father, hoarding moments like pieces of jewelry, pretty things to turn over and admire in the light. She looked forward to them every day. It was *their* time—away from the Red Council, away from her studies—when she could learn from him and him alone.

"Yes, but his *philosophy* is gaining traction among the Made, the protection and rule of which are my—and your—responsibility. We must convince him to join a family structure. To bridge the divide."

Crier stopped short of the seaflowers that had just begun to bloom by the cliff's edge. "But surely if he does not agree with the tenets of Traditionalism, he will not agree to the kind of union you propose." She couldn't bring herself to say *marriage* yet.

"One might think so, but I have reason to believe he will accept the opportunity. To him, it will provide power and status. To us, it will provide stability and access. We will be able to track what the Anti-Reliance Movement is attempting to accomplish, and better rein it in."

"So you disagree with ARM," Crier said.

Hesod hedged. "Their views on humankind are too extreme for my taste. It is one thing to subjugate those who are inferior and another thing entirely to behave as if they don't exist. We must build policy around the reality of where we came from. We were not created in a void, history-less. It is ignorant to think we cannot learn from humanity's existing structures."

"You find ARM too extreme. . . . Would you consider its leader dangerous, then?" Crier asked.

9

"No," Hesod said coolly. Then he had added: "Not *yet*."

And so she had understood. Crier was the bandage to a wound—one that was minor, for now, but had the potential to fester over time. A hairline fracture in Hesod's otherwise ironclad rule, his control over all of Zulla, everything from the eastern sea to the western mountains—except the separate territory of Varn. Varn was part of Zulla but still ruled by a separate Automa monarchy. Queen Junn, the Child Queen. The Mad Queen. The Bone Eater.

Hesod didn't need any more splintering. He wanted union.

He wanted to keep the same thing Crier knew Kinok wanted: Power.

Now: the branches above Crier's head were half naked with approaching winter, but the trees were so densely packed that they blocked out almost all the weak gray sunlight, shrouding the forest floor in shadow. Overhead, the leaves were like copper etchings, a thousand waving hands in shades of red and orange and burnished gold; underfoot, they were the pale brown of dead things. Crier could smell wet earth and woodsmoke, the musk of animals, the sharp scent of pine and wood sap. It was so different from what she usually experienced, living on the icy shores of the Steorran Sea: the tang of sea air. The taste of salt on her tongue. The heavy smells of fish and rotting seaweed.

It took half a day's ride to reach these woods, and so Crier had been here only once before, nearly five years ago. Her father enjoyed hunting deer like the humans did. She remembered eating a few bites of hot, spiced venison that night, filling her belly with food she did not require. More ritual than meal. The core of her father's Traditionalism: adopting human habits and customs into daily life. He said it created meaning, structure. Under most circumstances, Crier understood the merits of Hesod's beliefs. It was why she called him "father" even though she'd never had a mother and had never been birthed. She had been commissioned, Made.

Unlike humans, all Automae really needed was heartstone. Where human bodies depended on meat and grain, Automa bodies depended on heartstone: a special red mineral imbued with alchemical energy; raw stone mined from deep within the western mountains and then transmuted by alchemists into a powerful magickal substance. It was how Thomas Wren, the greatest of the human alchemists, had created them almost one hundred years ago when he'd Designed Kiera—the first. Automae were modeled this way still.

Crier crept through the underbrush, keeping to the darkest shadows. Her feet were silent even as she walked across twigs and dry leaves, a red carpet of pine needles. Nothing would be able to hear her coming. Not deer, not elk. Not even other Automae. She paused every few moments, listening to her surroundings: the sounds of small animals skittering through the brush, the whispers of wind, the back-and-forth calls of the noonbirds and the old crows. She was careful to keep her heart rate down. If it spiked too suddenly, the distress chime in the back of her neck would go off at a pitch only Automae could hear, and all her guards would come running.

The ceremonial bow was heavy in her hand. It was carved from a single piece of dark mahogany, polished to a perfect sheen and inlaid with veins of gold, precious stones, animal bone. The three arrows sheathed at her back were equally beautiful. One tipped with iron, one with silver, and one with bone. Iron for strength and power. Silver for prosperity. Bone for two bodies bound as one.

Snap. Crier whipped around, already nocking an arrow and ready to shoot—but instead coming face-to-face with Kinok himself. He was frozen midstep, partly hidden behind a massive oak, half his face obscured and the other half in watery sunlight. Every time she saw him, which was now about ten times per day since he had taken up residence in her father's guest chambers, Crier was reminded of how handsome he was. Like all Automae, he was tall and strong, broad-shouldered, Designed to be more beautiful than the most beautiful human man. His face was a study in shadow and light: high cheekbones, knife-blade jawline, a thin, sharp nose. His skin was swarthy, a shade lighter than her own, his dark hair cropped close to his skull. His brown eyes were sharp and scrutinizing. The eyes of a scientist, a political leader. Her fiancé.

Her fiancé, who was aiming his iron-tipped arrow straight at Crier's forehead.

There was a moment—so brief that when she thought about it later she was not sure it had actually happened—in which Crier lowered her bow and Kinok did not. A single moment in which they stared at each other and Crier felt the faintest edge of nerves.

Then Kinok lowered his bow, smiling, and she scolded herself for being so silly.

"Lady Crier," he said, still smiling. "I do not think we're supposed to interact with each other until the Hunt is over . . . but you're a better conversationalist than the birds. Have you caught anything yet?"

"No, not yet," she said. "I am hoping for a deer."

His teeth flashed. "I'm hoping for a fox."

"Why is that?"

"They're quicker than deer, smaller than wolves, and cleverer than crows. I like the challenge."

"I see." She shifted, catching the faraway scuffle of a rabbit in the underbrush. The shadows dappled Kinok's face and shoulders like a horse's coloring. He was still looking at her, the last remnants of that smile still playing at the corners of his flawless mouth. "I wish you luck with your fox, Scyre," she said, preparing to track down the rabbit. "Aim well."

"Actually, I wanted to congratulate you, my lady," he said suddenly. "While we are out here, away from—from the palace. I heard you convinced Sovereign Hesod to let you attend a meeting of the Red Council next week."

Crier bit her tongue, trying to hide her excitement. After years of near-begging, her father had agreed to let her attend a council meeting. After *years* of studying history, philosophy, political theory, reading and rereading a dozen libraries' worth of books, writing essays and letters and sometimes feverish little manifestos, she would finally, *finally* be allowed to take a seat among the Red Hands. Maybe even to share her proposals for council reform. As daughter of the sovereign, the Red Council was her birthright; it was as much a part of her as her Pillars. She was *Made* for this.

"I think you're right, you know," Kinok continued. "I read the open letter you sent to Councilmember Reyka. About your proposed redistribution of representation on the Red Council. You are correct that while there is a voice for every district in Zulla outside of Varn, there is not a voice for every system of value."

"You *read* that?" Crier said, eyes snapping up to his face. "Nobody read that. I doubt even Councilmember Reyka did."

She couldn't help the note of bitterness in her voice. It was foolish, but she had thought Councilmember Reyka, of all people, would listen to her. Her argument had been that in places with higher-density human populations, the interests of those humans should be somehow accounted for in the Hands who sat on her father's council. Though she had to wonder if when Kinok mentioned her phrase, "systems of value," he was more interested in his *own* values—those he was attempting to spread through the land, via ARM—than those of the human citizens.

Still, it flattered her that he'd read it. It meant her words had more power, greater reach, than she'd realized.

She hoped Reyka had read it too, but with no reply, she'd been left to believe the worst. That Reyka thought her naive and foolish. Sometimes, Crier wondered if maybe her father thought that, too. He'd refused her for so long.

But Reyka had always shown something of a soft spot for Crier. As the longest-serving member of the Red Council, Reyka had always been a fixture in Crier's life. She'd visited the palace quite frequently. When Crier was younger, Reyka would bring her little gifts from her travels: vials of sweet-smelling hair oil, a music box the size of a thumbnail, the strange dark delicacy that was candied heartstone.

Crier had come to think of her the way human children in storybooks thought of their godmothers. She couldn't say that to Reyka, or to anyone. It was such a weak, soft-bellied idea. So she just thought it to herself, and it made her feel warm.

"Well . . ." Kinok stepped forward a little, light sliding across his face. His footsteps were silent amid the blanket of dried leaves. "I read it twice. And I agree with it. The Red Hands shouldn't be based on district alone; it leads to imbalance and bias. Have you mentioned this issue to your father?"

"Yes," Crier said quietly. "He was not incredibly receptive."

"We can work on that." At her look of surprise, Kinok shrugged one shoulder. "We are bound to be married, are we not? I am on your side, Lady Crier, as you are on mine. Right?"

"Right," she found herself saying, staring at him in wonder. What new opportunities might come to her in this marriage? For months now she had thought of it as nothing more than a prolonged political maneuver, unpleasant but ultimately bear-able, like the stench of rotting fish in the sea air.

It had not occurred to her that she might be gaining an advo-cate, as well as a husband.

"And if we are on the same side, there is something you should know," said Kinok, lowering his voice even though they were entirely alone, no living things around but the rabbits and the birds. "There was a scandal in the capital recently. I know only because I was with Councilmember Reyka when she learned of it."

Crier almost questioned that—it was no secret that Councilmember Reyka hated everything about the Anti-Reliance Movement, including Kinok himself. But another word caught her attention. "A scandal?" she asked. "What kind of scandal?"

"Midwife sabotage."

Crier's eyes widened. "What do you mean, sabotage?" she asked. Midwives were an integral part of the Making process. They were created to be assistants to the Makers themselves, a bridge between Maker and Designer. They helped newly Made Automae adjust to the world. "What did the Midwife do?"

"Faked a set of Design blueprints for a nobleman's child. It was a disaster. The child was Made wrong. More animal than Automa or even human. Their mind was wild, violent. They had to be disposed of for the safety of the nobleman's family."

"That's horrible," Crier breathed. "Why would the Midwife do such a thing? Was it madness?" She knew the condition plagued some humans.

"Nobody knows," said Kinok. "But, Lady, there is something you should know."

There was something strange in his voice. Warning? Trepidation?

"This was not her first Make," Kinok continued, meeting

Crier's eyes. "She had been working with the nobles of Rabu for decades."

A pit seemed to open in Crier's belly, but she was not sure why.

"Who was she, Scyre?" she asked slowly. "The Midwife. What was her name?"

"Torras. Her name was Torras."

Crier gripped her bow so tightly that the wood creaked in protest. Because she knew Midwife Torras.

She knew it, because that was the Midwife who had helped Make *her*.

As soon as the Hunt was complete—two rabbits and a quail ensnared—and their party had returned to the palace, Crier retired to her chambers, poring again over the *Midwife's Handbook*, a thin, leather-bound booklet she'd come across in a bookseller's stall in the market last year and bought with so much enthusiasm that the stall owner seemed a little alarmed. She reassured herself that an infraction of the kind Kinok had mentioned was nearly impossible.

There was no way her own Design had been tampered with, of course. She was far too important.

And besides, if there were something off, something Flawed, something *different* about her, she'd know it already . . . wouldn't she?

It is the duty of the Human Midwife to care for the new-Made Commission as they would for their own Human offspring.

It is the duty of the Midwife to provide the new-Made Commission with heartstone as Human child bearers provide Human offspring with milk.

It is the duty of the Midwife to ensure that the inner workings of the new-Made Commission have been Made correctly and without Flaw. The new-Made Commission must contain within its breast the Four Pillars: Reason, Calculation, Organics, and Intellect. Much like the Human Temperaments, these Four Pillars are the basis of the Automa individual and the Society as a whole.

It is the duty of the Midwife to ensure that the new-Made Commission was Made according to the Commissioner's Design; if discrepancies are discovered, the Midwife must report the discrepancies in detail to the Head Commissioner and the Head Midwife and continue to

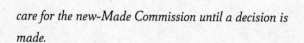

care for the new-Made Commission until a decision is made.

It is the duty of the Midwife to place the continued existence of the new-Made Commission above their own.

It is the duty of the Midwife to place the continued existence of the new-Made Commission above all.

In the rare case of an Order of Termination ordained by the Sovereign, with the unanimous support of the Red Council, only then shall the Midwife bend to the Law and allow the Flawed Commission to be terminated.

—FROM *THE MIDWIFE'S HANDBOOK*,
   BY MIDWIFE HALLA OF MIDWIFERY RM437 OF THE
   SOVEREIGN STATE OF RABU

2

Luna was killed in a white dress.

A week had passed since her death, and the dress that had been stripped off her body and dangled from the tallest post was still fluttering in the faint breeze. It was some kind of symbol, or warning. By now the dress was soaked through with rot and rainwater, but there were still some parts white enough to catch the sunlight. Catch the eye.

Ayla could not stop glancing over, and every time she did, she felt the gut-punch of what had happened to Luna all over again. And now, days later, the reminder rippled through the other humans like the dress itself rippled in the summer wind. No one even knew what Luna had done. Why the sovereign's guards had killed her.

Ayla continued on her way through the marketplace. She usually worked in the orchards at Sovereign Hesod's palace, sowing seeds and collecting bushels of ripe apples, but one of the other servants was practically delirious with fever and Ayla had been ordered to fill in. For the past week she'd joined the group of exhausted servants who left their beds halfway through the night, just so they could make it to the closest village, Kalla-den—a good four leagues of treacherous, rocky shoreline from the palace—and set up their wares by dawn. It would've been miserable no matter what, but being greeted in the marketplace by Luna's empty dress made it all the worse. It was like a ghost. Like a pale fish in dark water, flickering at the edges of Ayla's vision.

Ayla had worked in some capacity at the sovereign's palace for the past four years. And it had been months since she'd finally made it out of the stables and into the orchard-tending rotation. Some days she was so close to the white stone walls of the palace that she could smell the burning hearth fires within, taste the smoke on her tongue. And yet . . . she still hadn't managed to get *inside*.

Nothing mattered until she got inside. And she'd vowed to do so to exact her revenge—even if it killed her.

But now Ayla stared out at the marketplace, at the crowd of sleek, beautiful Automae—*leeches*—and tried to keep the hatred and disgust off her face. Nobody bought flowers from a girl who looked like she'd rather be selling poison.

"Flowers!" she called out, trying to keep her voice light. It was almost sunset, almost time to give up for the day, but there were still far too many unsold garlands in her basket. "We've got seaflowers, apple blossoms, the prettiest salt lavender up and down the coast!"

Not a single leech glanced in her direction. The Kalla-den Market was a kingdom's worth of chaos stuffed into an area the size of a barn, and it was so noisy you could hear it from half a league away. The marketplace was vendors' stalls shoved up against each other three deep, their carts and baskets overflowing with candied fruits, pastries, fresh-caught fish, oysters that smelled like death even under the weak autumn sun. It was leeches huddled around baskets of heartstone dust, dipping the tips of their fingers into the powdery red grains, bringing them to their lips to test the quality. It was whole chickens or goat legs rotating on spits, roasting slowly, smoke filling the air till Ayla's eyes watered; it was wine and apple cider and piles of colorful spices; it was a crush of grimy, skeletal, desperate humans hawking their wares to an endless stream of Automae.

And of course, the rows and rows of Hesod's prized sun apples, gleaming like so many red jewels—nearly as crimson and bright as heartstone itself.

But the majority of the Automae seemed to treat the market like one of those traveling menageries—*Step right up, folks. Gawk for free. Look at the humans. Look at the flesh-and-bone animals. Point and stare, why don't you. Watch 'em sweat and squeal like pigs.*

The only good thing about the market was Benjy. She looked over at him as she called out *Flowers!* again. He was the closest thing to a friend that Ayla would allow herself. She'd known him since she was twelve years old and haunted, hollowed by grief. In the thick of it, still.

Unlike Ayla, Benjy was used to the madness of Kalla-den.

He even seemed to thrive in it, his brown eyes bright and sparkling, the sun bringing out the freckles on his brown cheeks. The first day Ayla had joined him here in the market, he'd nearly taken some eyes out while pointing at all the exciting things he wanted Ayla to see—colorful glass baubles, mechanical insects with windup wings, twists of sugared bread shaped like animals. On the second day, Benjy showed Ayla the secret underbelly of the market: Made objects. These were forbidden items created by alchemists—Makers—and passed from hand to hand in the shadows, hidden by the dust and the crowd. Objects smaller than Ayla's little finger but worth double her weight in gold. For humans, possessing a Made object was forbidden, as Made objects were the work of alchemy and considered dangerous, powerful. After all, Automae themselves were Made. Perhaps they didn't like any reminder that they, too, were once treated like trinkets and playthings. Made objects were completely illegal, and therefore incredibly tempting.

Ayla had no use for temptation—except in one single case. The locket she wore around her neck. The only remnant she had of her family—a reminder of the violence they'd suffered, and the revenge she planned to take. She didn't even know how it worked, if it even *did* work, but she knew it was Made, and that it was forbidden, and that it was the one thing she could call hers.

"Are you going to help me or not?" Ayla said now, prodding Benjy in the ribs. He yelped. "I've been yelling my head off for an hour; it's your turn."

He looked down at her, squinting in the dying sun. "Take it from someone who's done this a hundred times. The day is over. All anyone's willing to buy right now is heartstone."

Ayla huffed. "You of all people know if we don't sell every single one of these flowers, we won't get dinner."

"Trust me, I'm aware. My belly's been growling since midmorning."

"You got any food squirreled away back in the quarters?"

"No," he said mournfully. "I had some dried plums stowed away in the old gardener's lean-to, but last time I checked they were gone. Guess someone else found them." He tugged at his messy dark curls, wiped the sweat off his forehead, fiddled with one of the garlands they had yet to sell. That was Benjy—always in motion. It would make Ayla anxious if she weren't so used to it.

"The world is just full of thieves, ain't it," Ayla said with a hint of amusement.

Benjy picked a petal off one of the seaflowers. "Like you're not a thief yourself."

She grinned.

When Ayla first met Benjy, he had looked more like a deer than a boy. Long-legged and awkward and perpetually wideeyed, sweet and young and angry, but a soft kind of angry. A harmless, deathless kind of angry. His family hadn't been killed by the sovereign's men. He'd never known them at all—his mother had left him on the doorstep of an old temple, still wet from birth. If it were Ayla, she knew she'd be consumed by the need to track them down, to find her birth mother, to ask her a thousand questions that all began with *why*. But Benjy wasn't like that. He'd survived under the care of the temple priests for nine years, then ran away. Three months later, Rowan took him in.

Benjy's anger was different now—he'd grown, learned more about this broken world, learned about the Revolution. Some bitterness had seeped into him; some passion. But he was still soft. Would always be. For years, that softness had annoyed the hell out of Ayla. Made her want to grab his shoulders and shake him till some *fury* came out.

After all, it was fury that had kept Ayla alive all these years; fury that had lit a flame inside her chest and made her keep going out of sheer *anger*.

When she had no hearth fire to keep her warm, she'd picture the look on Hesod's face when his precious daughter lay in Ayla's hands, broken beyond repair. On the days her belly seemed to crumple in on itself from lack of bread, she'd picture some older, stronger version of herself looking Hesod right in his soulless eyes and saying: *This is for my family, you murderous leech.*

Ayla scanned the crowd, feeling horribly small and soft, a mouse surrounded by cats. Automae looked human the way statues looked human—you might be tricked from far away, but once you got up close you could see all the differences. Most leeches were around six feet tall, some even taller, and their bodies, no matter the shape or size, were graceful and corded with muscle. Their faces were angular, their features sharp. They were Designed in Automa Midwiferies, each one sculpted to be beautiful, but it was a chilling kind of beautiful. Some sick practice in vanity: *How big can we make her eyes? How cutting her cheekbones? How perfectly symmetrical her features?*

There was also something odd about the look of a leech's skin. It was flawless, sure—no pores, no peach fuzz, no freckles or sunburns or scars, just smooth, supple skin. But more than that, it was the way they looked carved from stone, indestructible. It was the way their skin stretched over their hand-designed muscles and bones. Like it could barely keep all the monster inside.

The leeches had let themselves forget that they'd been created by the same humans they now treated worse than dogs. In the forty-eight years since their rise to power, they'd conveniently let themselves forget their past. Forget that they were once merely the pets and playthings of human nobility.

Ayla did not let herself think about her own past, either—the fire, the fear, the way loss lived in the cavity of the chest, the way it chewed her up from the inside out. Thinking like that wasn't how you survived.

She and Benjy packed up the stall before sundown, aiming to be long gone by the time darkness fell over Kalla-den. As they took a shortcut through a damp alley, baskets of unsold seaflowers strapped to their backs, someone fell into step behind them. Ayla glanced back and, despite herself, she almost smiled when she saw Rowan.

Rowan was a seamstress who lived and worked in Kalla-den.

At least, that's what she was on the outside.

To people like Ayla, she was something else entirely. A mentor. A trainer. A protector. A mother to the lost and the beaten and the hungry. She gave them refuge. And taught them to fight back.

You wouldn't know it from the looks of her. She had one of those faces where you couldn't quite tell how old she was—the only signs of age were her silver hair and the slight crow's feet at the corners of her eyes—and she was short, even shorter than Ayla. She looked rather like a plump little sparrow hopping around, ruffling her feathers. Sweet and harmless.

Like so much else, it was a carefully constructed lie. Rowan was no sparrow. She was a bird of prey.

Seven years ago, she'd saved Ayla's life.

She was so cold that it didn't feel like cold anymore. It didn't even burn. She barely noticed the winter air, the snow soaking through her threadbare boots, the ice crystals that whipped across her face and left her skin red and raw. She was cold from the inside out, the coldness pulsing through her with every weak flutter of her heart. Dimly, she knew this was how it felt right before you died.

It was comforting.

She was so cold, and so tired of being alone. So tired of hurting. The last thing she'd eaten was a scrap of half-rotted meat three days ago. Maybe four. Time kept blurring, rolling over itself, going belly-up like a dead animal. Ayla wasn't hungry anymore. Her stomach had stopped making noises. Quietly, it was eating what little muscle she had left.

There was a patch of darkness up ahead. Darkness, which meant something not covered in snow. Ayla stumbled forward, the ground tilting in strange ways beneath her feet. Her eyes kept falling shut against her will. She forced them open again, head pounding, vision reduced to a pinprick of light at the end of a long, long tunnel. The darkness—there. So close. Gray, a stone wall. The dark brown of cobblestones.

It was a tiny gap between two buildings. A sloping roof caught the snow, protecting the ground beneath. Ayla dragged herself into the dark snowless space and her knees gave out. She hit the wall sideways and fell hard, skull cracking against the cobblestones. And there she lay.

"Hey."

Her eyes were closed.

"Hey! Wake up!"

No. She was finally warm.

"Wake up, you idiot!"

A sound like striking an oyster shell against rock; a sharp, stinging pressure on Ayla's cheek. Heat, for a moment. Someone was talking, maybe, but they were very far away, and Ayla couldn't make out the words. The exhaustion closed over her head like water, and she let go.

It was only later that she learned just how far Rowan had dragged her body to warmth and safety, before nursing her back to health.

Back then, Rowan's hair had still been brown, streaked silver only at the temples. But her eyes were the same. Deep and steady. "You were ready to die," she had said.

Ayla didn't answer.

"I don't know what happened to you, exactly," said Rowan. "But I know you're alone. I know you've been cast aside, left to die in the snow like an animal." She reached out and took Ayla's hands, held them between her own. It felt like being cradled: like being held all over. "You're not alone anymore. I can give you something to fight for, child. I can give you a purpose."

"A purpose?" Ayla had said. Her voice was weak, scraped out.

"Justice," said Rowan. And she squeezed Ayla's hands.

"The moon is full," said Rowan now, looking straight ahead, in the hushed, coded tone Ayla had come to know so well.

The three of them moved easily through the crowd of humans, used to dodging people and carts and stray dogs. The chaos of the Kalla-den streets was a strange kind of blessing: a thousand human voices all shouting at once meant it was the perfect place for conversations you didn't want anyone to overhear.

"Clear skies lately," Ayla and Benjy said in unison. *Nothing to report.*

It was Rowan, of course, who had taught them the language

of rebellion. A sprig of rosemary passed between hands on a crowded street, garlands woven from flowers with symbolic meanings, coded messages hidden inside loaves of bread, faerie stories or old folk songs used like passwords to determine who you could trust. Rowan had taught them everything. She'd saved Ayla first, Benjy a few months later. Took them in. Clothed them. Taught them how to beg, and then how to find work. Fed them. But also gave them a new hunger: *justice*.

Because they should never have needed to beg in the first place.

"What news?" Benjy asked.

"A comet is crossing to the southern skies," Rowan said with a smile. "A week from now. It will be a beautiful night."

Benjy took Ayla's hand and squeezed. She didn't return it. She knew what the code meant: an uprising in the South. Another one. It filled her gut with suspicion and dread.

They turned onto a wider street, the crowd thinning out a little. They spoke more softly now.

"Crossing south," Ayla repeated. Her heart sank. "And how many stars will be out in the southern skies?"

Rowan didn't pick up on her skepticism. "Oh, I've heard around two hundred."

"*Two hundred*," Benjy repeated, eyes gleaming.

Two hundred human rebels gathering in the South.

"High time, loves."

Rowan was gone as swiftly as she had appeared, leaving only a crumpled flyer in Benjy's hands—a religious pamphlet, something about the gods and believers. Ayla knew it would be riddled with code—code that only those in the Resistance could decipher.

Part of Ayla worried that Rowan was still harboring hope for these uprisings, for what she called "justice," because of her grief for Luna and Luna's sister, Faye. After all, they'd been two of Rowan's lost children, just like Ayla and Benjy. It was known within the village that any orphan kid could find food and comfort with Rowan. Ayla remembered when Faye and Luna had come to Rowan's after their mother had died. Ayla had taken to Luna immediately, a girl with shy smiles and sweet questions. Faye had been pricklier, distrusting, far too much like Ayla for the two of them to get along. But still, they'd grown up around each other. And Ayla knew that Rowan's soft heart grieved for the two sisters. Those two girls she'd tried to save.

Two girls who, in her mind, she had failed.

And in that grief, Rowan was willing to send more innocents off to find more of her "justice."

Over the years, they'd received word of a few uprisings here in Rabu, but each one had been bloody—and quelled quickly. The Sovereign State of Rabu was controlled by Sovereign Hesod. His rule had come to extend to all of Zulla except for the queendom of Varn. Though he claimed he did not hold all the power, as the Red Council—a group of Automa aristocrats—was supposed to share governance of Rabu, Ayla hardly believed that to be true. Hesod was enormously wealthy and influential. He was also power-hungry. It had been *his* father who led the Automa troops in the War of Kinds. It was he who first declared humans should be separated from their families. And it was on his personal land, the vast grounds of his seaside palace, that Ayla, Benjy, and four hundred other human servants lived and worked.

The Red Council was cruel, merciless, and worst of all, creative. That was part of the reason the Revolution was so slow-going—people were just so damn terrified of the Council and its ever-tightening laws. Even Ayla had to admit their fears were well founded. Luna—and her disembodied dress—was proof of that.

Benjy looked at Ayla as they hiked up the steeply sloping path toward the palace, his eyes full of hope and excitement. The message was clear: he wanted to join. Even after the disastrous uprisings of last year.

She shook her head. *No.* He knew better. He knew she couldn't leave now, tonight. Not when she was this close to the inside of the palace. And Crier.

Benjy's smile vanished. "Ayla."

"*No,*" she said. "I'm not going." Did she want what he wanted? Did she want the leeches dead? Of course, but not like this. Not when it only meant a trail of human blood, not when it was doomed to futility. She was not ready to lose anyone else. The last time there had been an uprising in the South, it was quashed almost immediately—and that uprising had been massive, with nearly two thousand humans marching through the streets of the city Bram, armed with torches and saltpeter, aiming to take the heart of the city where the most powerful Automae lived.

They had been defeated in a single night. The Automa who had led the counterattack—who had destroyed them—became a decorated war hero. A household name, a household monster. *Kinok.*

Benjy fell silent, but Ayla could finally feel his anger—could tell that it was now directed at *her*. His strides grew long, determined, as they reached the narrow path that curved up toward the palace. She could see the peaked roofs of the palace towers now in the distance.

She hurried to catch up with him, panting in the heat. By now they were farther from the crowd. She grabbed his shoulder, and he stopped walking so suddenly she nearly crashed into him.

"I know what you're going to say," he said through gritted teeth.

Ayla struggled to catch her breath. "You could always . . . watch the comet without me." The words grated in her throat like she'd swallowed a mouthful of salt.

His dark-brown eyes locked onto hers. The breeze danced in his messy hair. He'd grown taller than her, and broader too. She held his gaze.

For a full minute, he said nothing. They just stood there, breathing hard, looking at each other. Thinking the same thing: it was too soon.

Ayla wanted to say: *Don't leave me.*

Ayla should have said: *Leave me.* Because maybe it would be better that way.

Benjy's anger seemed to transmute into sadness, his lips

parting. Finally, he said, "I won't do that. I won't go without you, and you know it."

She did. And that scared her more than anything. He *wouldn't* leave her. It made her heart rage. *Leave*, she wanted to scream. *Don't stay for me.*

But then another part of her, buried so deep it had almost, almost, gone silent, knew she couldn't do this—do any of it—without him.

His lips were still slightly parted, as though there was more he wanted to say. She knew how badly he needed this. Revolution. Blood. Change. She waited for him to keep going, to try again to convince her. But he also knew how much *she* wanted what she wanted: Lady Crier's blood on her hands.

So in the end, Benjy just sighed. More and more servants began to pass them on their way up the narrow path, and Ayla put a few paces between herself and Benjy, kept her eyes on the rutted path as they marched the rest of the way back to their quarters in silence, the past piling into her thoughts like shovelfuls of dirt.

After what Ayla had come to think of as *that day*, the day that changed everything, the splitting point in her mind, the thing that cracked her life into a *before* and *after*, the waking nightmare, the bloodstain, the splintered bone that would not heal, *that day*, Ayla had allowed herself one week to mourn.

Even at nine years old, she'd known that it was all too easy to drown in grief—get pulled under and never come back up. One week, she told herself. One week.

One week to mourn the deaths of her entire family.

Mama. Papa. Her twin brother, Storme, who had loved Ayla more than anything else in the whole world. Who had been wrenched away from her, trying to protect her from Them. Storme, who, from the sounds of his screaming cut short, had met his end then and there, just beyond the walls of what had been their home.

You couldn't depend on much in this world, but you could depend on this: love brought nothing but death. Where love existed, death would follow, a wolf trailing after a wounded deer. Scenting blood in the air. Ayla had learned that the hard way.

Now she was sixteen, and everything she wanted was just inches from her fingertips.

When Rowan had first rescued her, Ayla only had her pain and her anger.

But one day, about a month after being with Rowan, a group of nomadic humans had come into town. Rowan had given Ayla a choice. Leave with these traveling humans, leave all of her pain and her memories behind and start anew. Or stay under Rowan's wing. Rowan would care for her until she could find work. And Ayla would learn to fight, learn to live, and plan for justice.

Ayla had chosen the latter. And Rowan, keeping her promise, had found Ayla work as a servant of the palace.

Hesod. The leech who'd ordered the raid of Ayla's village.

It was Hesod's men who had broken into Ayla's childhood home, who had murdered her family just because they *could*.

Hesod prided himself on spreading Traditionalism throughout Rabu—the Automa belief in modeling their society after human behavior, as though humans were a long-lost civilization from which they could cherry-pick the best attributes to mimic. Family was important to Sovereign Hesod, or so he and his council preached. The irony was not lost on Ayla.

And now she worked for him. It disgusted her, every second of it, but it was the only way she could get close to Hesod. She'd come so far. She was *not* going to throw it all away for some doomed dream of revolution.

Rowan had always told her that justice was the answer. And for a long time, Ayla had believed her. She'd believed that revolution was possible, that if humans just kept rising up, refusing to submit, they could really change things. But Ayla knew better now. Over the years, she'd seen how hopeless Rowan's dreams were. Every uprising had failed; every brilliant plan had been crushed; every new maneuver just resulted in more human death.

Justice was a god, and Ayla didn't believe in such childish things.

She believed in blood.

3

Crier's father and Kinok were already seated in the great hall
for breakfast when she arrived, dressed in a new gown this
morning. Her father's and fiancé's heads were bent toward each
other in a discussion that broke off as soon as Crier entered.

For a moment, she stared at her father—the man who'd
commissioned her. Hesod was a masterpiece of Design. He was
Made to be powerful, influential, brilliant even for an Automa,
respected by everyone in Zulla. When he spoke, people listened.

What would he say about Midwife Torras's betrayal?

She hadn't told him yet.

Was afraid to, really.

Kinok had mentioned the scandal a week ago, during their
Hunt, and yet she'd kept it to herself.

She sat down at the table across from Kinok. The great hall,
in the east wing of the palace, could easily seat fifty—it was
huge, airy, with a high, arched ceiling and a massive banquet

table made of well-sheened pine. But despite its vastness, most days it saw only Crier, Hesod, and a handful of servants. And, over the past months of his courtship, Kinok.

"Good morning, my lady," said Kinok. Crier nodded in greeting, gaze averted.

"Daughter," said Hesod, and Crier managed to look him in the eyes.

"Father," she murmured.

A serving boy came in carrying a golden platter, and with it, liquid heartstone.

The subterranean jewel, carefully mined, was the source of the Automae's strength. It ran through their veins, their inner workings, not like human blood but like ichor, the blood of the old gods in all the human storybooks. Something closer to magick, alchemy, than anything natural.

Crier sat up straighter in her chair.

The liquid heartstone was served in a teapot shaped like a bird skull, with a long handle carved from heartstone itself. Steam leaked from the bird's eye sockets. Crier tried not to look eager when she pushed her teacup forward.

She needed this. Especially after what Kinok had told her last week. About the Midwife's scandal, the Design that had been tampered with. It made her stomach harden and twist inside to think there'd been even the slightest risk to her *own* Design. She hadn't slept since.

Automae did not require nightly rest like humans did, but it was recommended that they sleep for at least six hours every three days. Sleeping let their organs slow and reset, let their bodies repair any internal or external damage. Crier was usually very diligent about getting the proper amount of sleep—she found it almost pleasing, curling up in the soft blankets and watching the moon rise outside her window, letting her thoughts drain away like bathwater.

It felt like playing human.

But ever since Kinok had returned to the palace, Crier had found it more and more difficult to empty her mind enough to sleep.

The serving boy filled Crier's cup last. The liquid he poured was a deep, dark red, the color of heartstone dust steeped in water. It was less concentrated in this form but easier to consume, and besides, Hesod took pleasure in mimicking human customs such as drinking tea in the morning. Unlike some other members of the Red Council, he thought Automae could stand to learn from humans. Human culture had been, after all, the basis of stabilization across Rabu: *Organization, System, Family.* Hesod's core values. We must never forget, he said, that for thousands of years the kings of this land were all human. And the human kings began their days with tea.

Crier reached for the cup, but in her haste, her hand shook. A splash of the liquid spilled.

"Apologies," she murmured, picking up her napkin to wipe it away.

Hesod's hand came over hers, stopping her. "Don't. This is what they're here for." He snapped his fingers at the serving boy.

Crier lowered her eyes.

When he was done, she picked up her cup again, careful to balance it. One sip of liquid heartstone, and Crier felt *power* spread through her. It was like stepping into a patch of sunlight, slipping into a hot bath—a slow, pleasing sensation that warmed her from head to foot. Any negative side effects from the lack of sleep were gone now. Crier felt stronger all over, like she could run straight out of the great hall and not stop until she hit the Aderos Mountains five hundred leagues away. Even her brain felt stronger, clearer. She hid a satisfied smile behind her teacup.

"Is there something you find amusing, Lady Crier?" Kinok said, staring at her curiously.

Of course Kinok had noticed. He noticed everything. He was looking at her now over the rim of his own teacup, his lips stained slightly red.

"It is not important," Crier said, a little flustered by Kinok's unwavering gaze. "I merely thought of a book I was reading last night."

"Ah. Which book?"

"A collection of essays on economic structure," she said. "Specifically, the intersection of market structure with physical or geographical environment."

Kinok's eyebrows lifted. "I see." To Hesod, he said, "Such inherent curiosity. Perhaps it is best that she has not yet attended a meeting of the council. I think, given an hour, she would take over as head."

Crier preened, until she saw Hesod's jaw tighten.

"On the contrary," he said. "I believe attending next week's meeting will be an invaluable experience for her. Perhaps it will give her pause the next time she is tempted to voice her own opinions on how to run a nation."

Crier glanced at Kinok. He gave her a small, crooked smile. "It will be an honor to have her there."

Which meant he would be in attendance as well.

She remembered what her father had told her: that Kinok was not a threat to Hesod's hold on Rabu and the other territories. Not if he joined a family. Not if he submitted to Traditionalism.

It seemed Hesod trusted him enough to include him in the affairs of the Red Council now.

In the nearly fifty years since the War of Kinds, Crier's father had made great efforts to coexist peacefully with the humans of Zulla. With the formation of the Red Council, he had successfully gained control of all the human settlements not just in Rabu, the main territory of Zulla, where they lived, but even in the tiniest fishing villages dotting the coast of Tarreen.

Zulla was like an Automa's heart, he'd once explained to her—it had four layers, the same way Automae had the four pillars of Reason, Calculation, Organics, and Intellect. In Zulla, the layers were, from the north down: the Far North, Rabu, Varn, and Tarreen. Along the western coast of Rabu and winding up into the north stood the Aderos Mountains, which hid the Iron Heart somewhere in their jagged peaks. A few leagues off the eastern coast: the Golden Isles, neutral territory, populated mainly by seabirds and wild pigs.

The queendom of Varn blocked access between Rabu, to its north, and Tarreen, to its south. As a result, Tarreen was known for being a lawless wilderness, not structured and civilized like Rabu. Hesod's efforts to control it, to govern its people and make use of its few resources, had been one of his greatest challenges during the course of Crier's lifetime.

Even in wild Tarreen, Hesod had attempted to preserve the humans' way of life wherever possible. He fostered a genuine appreciation for their food, their music, their strange ceremonies; he found all of it very entertaining, and Hesod loved to be entertained. His dedication was admirable—especially because many other Automae, Kinok included, did not regard human culture with such an open mind. Though perhaps Kinok was more intensely anticohabitation than most because, in addition to being a former Watcher of the Iron Heart, he was a Scyre: part of an elite guild that studied the Four Pillars in order to further advance Automakind.

Crier tried to keep her eyes on her hands, her lap, her empty, red-rimmed teacup, but she could not help stealing another glance at the man who was to become her husband.

Kinok was her future, and her future was dressed in fine black brocade. The crest of the Iron Heart flashed at his throat, a reminder of his former Watcher status. A reminder that he was a mystery.

After the meal ended, Kinok caught up to Crier on her way

to the libraries for her first lesson of the day. His feet were so silent on the flagstones that she did not hear him approach until he was already touching her shoulder.

"Scyre," she said. It was the term he preferred.

"Leave us," he said to the guards stationed at the end of the hallway. They looked at Crier for approval and, nonplussed, she nodded. Kinok waited until their footsteps had faded before speaking, leaning in close to her. "My lady," he said, and from his black brocaded coat he withdrew a roll of yellowed parchment tied with twine. "You must be eager for more information on Midwife Torras, so I hope you do not find my actions offensive. But through a personal connection I was able to obtain several of the Midwife's private correspondences and Designs."

Crier waited, hyperaware of how little space there was between their bodies, the way he bent his head to speak softly in her ear.

"One of them was yours," he went on. "Your Design, my lady, as commissioned by the sovereign."

"My—?" She stared at the roll of parchment in his hand. "That is my Design?"

He'd made these inquiries, had acquired her Design, in a week's time. It led her to wonder just how extensive his connections throughout the territory were. The Midwifery where she'd been Made was nearly a full day's ride from here. And for proprietary reasons they were generally on strict advisement to keep all Designs confidential.

"Yes. I thought—with the scandal—you might be interested."

"Scyre Kinok," she breathed. "May I . . . ?"

But instead of handing the roll to her, he took her hand. "Crier," he said, low and steady. "I give this to you for another reason. I know—I know you have been . . . reluctant about receiving my courtship over this past year. I know you still have reservations, though I have endeavored to show myself as a favorable asset to your cause and—ambitions. I hope that this will serve as a gesture of my faithfulness to you, should you choose to accept it."

She looked at him. His chiseled face. His eyes, dark and unreadable. She didn't know what to think, or to say.

"Thank you."

"Of course," he said, pressing the papers into her hand. His eyes were fixed on her face, almost concerned. "Remember, you can trust me. We are on the same side."

And then he was gone.

Crier couldn't get outside fast enough, the rolled-up Design light in her fist as she pushed through the northeast doors to the gardens.

Her father's gardens were huge and sprawling, starting at the east wing of the palace and stretching out to the edge of the bluffs, where the Steorran Sea crusted everything with salt. Nearly every evening after finishing her studies—Crier's days were occupied by a series of tutors in history, the sciences, economics, complex mathematics—she escaped to the gardens and the cool air and the smell of growing things. Rarely did she stray this close to the cliffs. But she wanted to look through the documents in private. Whatever she would find there, she wanted to find it alone.

The gardens were arranged carefully by type and color: fruit and flowering trees near the east wing, so one could look out the window at sweet sun apples and fat ripe plums. Day-blossoms beyond that, white and pale yellow, and beyond that, salt lavender and walnut. Beyond that, wild seaflowers, which were plucked and sold in nearby villages. Beyond that, the sea.

Then, if you followed the rise and crash of waves down to the south, if you sailed along miles of cragged and rocky shoreline, there was Varn. The queendom ruled by Queen Junn. The only place Crier's father could not touch. There were more rumors about the queen than about Kinok and the Watchers of the Heart put together. Whispers at every gathering: that Queen Junn was mad. That Varn was rife with infighting due to her progressive policies. That she was arming Varn against the rest of Zulla. That she was ruthless.

But Crier had always thought that the stories of Junn spoke of power and strength, of a girl ascending to the throne at just sixteen after her father, the king, was killed.

She readjusted the strip of red cloth tied around her upper arm, the mark of one betrothed, and continued to move through the gardens.

Everywhere the gardeners did their work—feeding and watering and trimming and arranging, cutting off the dead flowers when they curled into themselves and went brown. Unlike most other humans, the gardeners did not shy away when Crier came near. They had grown accustomed to her presence.

Crier had always been fascinated by humans: by their hot dark eyes and the strange songs they sang at night, in the gardens and the fields and the black shores where they dived for oysters; how sometimes they moved like there was something else inside them, something too big and tooth-gnashing for the soft human skin to hold inside. Once, and only once, she had mentioned this fascination to her father. She told him all about the songs, and how they sounded either like whale songs or like wobbly speaking, and how the humans sang frequently of *love* and *hate* and *loss*.

Her father said he did not completely understand all the different forms of human love, but that he had thought carefully about it and that perhaps, beyond his fascination with their history, their little cultures, he did love humans. In his own way.

Like how they loved dogs, he said, enough to feed them scraps of meat.

Crier continued to walk until she found a deserted corner of the gardens, a tangle of tall rosebushes with thorns the size of her fingernails. Here, hidden from sight, she finally untied the string and unfurled the thick bundle of pages. Her hands were not shaking, but it felt like her heart was, or her teeth, or her inner workings. She could not remember ever experiencing this much dread. *It will be fine,* she told herself, eyes adjusting to the tiny, cramped writing on the first page. *Everything will be normal. Who would dare to sabotage a Design from the sovereign?*

Makerwork Design By Commission, Ideation
Final, Year 30 AE:
Crier of Family Hesod, Model 9648880130

She read the pages quickly, her nerves subsiding. Nothing out of the ordinary. There was a letter from her father, faded and yellowed after seventeen years, in which he formally stated his desire to create a child, as his forebear, Sovereign Tayol, the first sovereign, had done before him.

There were a series of blueprints he and Midwife Torras had Designed together—the first, third, eighth drafts of Crier's form. They balanced her four pillars based on Hesod's requirements for a potential heir. They Designed her inner workings and her outer appearance, the color of her skin and hair and eyes, the measurements of her body, putting meticulous consideration into everything from the shape of her nose to the exact length of her fingers. As she read, hardly noticing the night falling down around her, Crier could not help but compare the documents to her actual physical body. She touched her nose, her throat; she wiggled her long fingers and studied the faint lines on her palms.

The last page was the final draft of her Design, the one that the Makers would have used to actually create her. Unlike the previous drafts, this one had only Torras's neat, blocky handwriting—none of her father's scrawl. But that made sense. Torras was the Midwife, not her father. Crier gave a quick once-over to the ink drawings of her body, the cross section of her inner workings. She was more than ready to return these documents to Kinok and forget all about her ridiculous paranoia.

But there was something *off* about this page.

Crier held it up to the moonlight, frowning. The proportions of her body were all the same. None of the numbers had changed. What was—?

There. The cross section of her brain. A small portion of it was redrawn to the side in greater detail: the portion that represented her pillars. They were not physical elements of her body, but metaphysical elements of her mind, her intelligence, her personality. Each blueprint had shown four pillars in her mind, balancing out like scales.

Intellect. Organics. The two human pillars.

Calculation. Reason. The two Automa pillars.

In this blueprint—only this one—there were five. Inside the Design of Crier's mind was another little column drawn in deep-blue ink. A fifth pillar.

Passion, it was labeled.

Passion.

Crier, the daughter of the sovereign, had five pillars instead of four. It was unheard of. Everyone knew Automae were created with two human pillars and two Automa pillars. Crier had never imagined there could be one with *three* human pillars. And that was what Passion was, without a doubt: *human*.

The papers were shaking in her hands. No. Her hands were shaking. Suddenly paranoid, Crier glanced around to make sure she was truly alone in this corner of the gardens. *What if someone sees?*

What would happen if the wrong person—if any person— discovered that the heir to the sovereign of Rabu had been sabotaged by her own Midwife? What would happen to her? She shuddered, thinking of Kinok's words back in the forest during the Hunt. *They were disposed of.* Would she be disposed of? Or, no, no no no, what if someone tried to use her against her father? This was perfect blackmail.

The heir, the sovereign's daughter, a *mistake*. It would bring shame to her family. Worse, it could cause the political scandal of the century. People could call for Hesod to step down as sovereign. They could use Crier to threaten her father. Through him, they could gain power over the entire Red Council. Over all of Rabu—and more.

Crier was Flawed. She was *broken*.

The thought shook her deeply. All this time she'd been treated like the jewel of the sovereign's estate, a glorious creation, but no. She was an abomination.

This was too much—this evil, sickening truth about herself, was too great to take in.

With nowhere to go, nowhere else to be alone to process this, she sank right down where she was, in the middle of the gardens, as the sun bled out behind the brush, and closed her eyes.

[the Barren Queen] desires what—a homunculus!—an alchemist's creation!—a Devil!—she knows not what she asks of us, and she dares to offer such a ludicrous prize, dangling it before us like meat before a pack of starving wolves—she might as well offer the damn'd throne to the first man who brings her the ocean in a thimble.

I could be hanged for writing such things, but the Barren Queen knows not what she asks.

—FROM THE RECORDS OF GRAY ÖLING, HEAD MAKER,
E. 900, Y. 7

4

It was late evening and Ayla had a break from the fields. She hadn't been called back to the market in Kalla-den, thankfully, since last week. Instead of taking supper, like the other servants, she was using her fleeting moments of rest to practice. To hone. To train. She had to be ready, for when her time came.

Ready to take what she'd come for, what she'd waited years for.

Her muscles ached but her body craved release. She had to find somewhere private, somewhere hidden. And besides, she couldn't sit next to Benjy for another night in a row. Though nearly a week had passed since they'd spoken to Rowan in Kalla-den, Benjy was still angry with Ayla. Truthfully, she didn't blame him. She knew how badly he wanted to join Rowan in the South, to fight, to aid the revolution, and she'd convinced him to stay here and be useless.

Right now, Ayla suspected Rowan was preparing to pack her

bags. Benjy could still go with her. But Ayla knew he wouldn't.

Ayla was caught between relief that Benjy wasn't in danger and self-loathing because of the relief. He was a liability; he was a weak spot in her armor.

She hated to think of him like that. But the last time Ayla had a weak spot, it had destroyed her. Her family's death had left her not a person but a ghost, a ruined shell, a carcass. The parts that had survived would be tainted forever.

She didn't want to see him hurt. And yet she knew: better to do what was right than to be kind.

It was a lesson she'd learned herself, when she was thirteen. She'd taken in a starving puppy—surprised that Rowan let her keep it, under the condition that she never let it out of her sight. But one night, the puppy had whined and clawed at the door so piteously, she finally let it out. She never saw the puppy again. She cried to Rowan, saying she'd only wanted to be kind. It had seemed so desperate, so determined to go outside and breathe the fresh air. But Rowan had reminded her: the world outside was dangerous. It was always better to do what you knew was right than what was kind.

She thought of Rowan's words now, as she picked her way through the sovereign's endless flower gardens. The heat of the day had faded; the sea breeze was blessedly cool against her face. Across the gardens, she could just barely make out leech guards stationed around the palace, tall shadows against the white stone walls. Metal sheaths glinted at their hips, catching the moonlight.

The guards were, what, three hundred paces away? Which meant that if Ayla so much as blinked wrong, they could reach her in . . . She brushed a finger over a stalk of salt lavender, doing the math. Six seconds, maybe.

And some other human would have to wipe her blood off the flowers.

To the east, the ocean swelled and burst open against the cliffs like thunder. Every so often a black cloud would drift across the moon, and the whole palace would be plunged into darkness. Darkness.

Ayla had been spared only because her brother, Storme, had heard them coming. Her brother, who was dead.

Storme grabbed her hand and pulled her out the back door as They came through the front.

It was their father who screamed first.

Storme led her to the outhouse even as Ayla begged for him to stop, no no no please no, let go of me, that was Papa, let me go help Papa. He forced the plank of wood up and pushed Ayla down into the dank, shallow hole. She fell on her knees, her arms and legs covered in mud and shit and piss. The smell was unbearable. She looked up at Storme and pushed back against the wall to make room. It was then that she realized the space was only big enough for one person.

She watched, mute with shock, as her twin brother replaced the wood and disappeared.

Darkness.

His screams came next. Then her mother's.

For hours, Ayla hadn't moved. She'd barely even breathed, even though after a while she couldn't smell the stench. Couldn't smell anything at all.

The raids had begun at dawn. By what must have been late afternoon, she finally deemed it safe enough to climb out.

Inside the house, the knife wound in her mother's chest had clotted, darkened, and congealed. Ayla stared at her mother, and her mother stared back. She'd died with her eyes on Ayla's father, whose head had rolled a mere inch away from her mother's body. The rest of him was gone.

At the front of the house was another body. It was burned beyond all recognition, but Ayla could tell its head was turned in the direction of the outhouse.

Storme.

Now, Ayla picked her way along the rows of seaflowers, heading in the direction of the rocky bluffs that overlooked the Steorran Sea. Her boots left wet imprints in the soft, dark soil.

The palace was laid out like a giant compass rose with spokes pointing north, south, east, and west. The center of the compass was the palace itself, all white marble and glowing windows, and the spokes were the groupings of outbuildings that served to separate the sun apple orchards from the seaflower gardens, the pastures, and finally, the grain fields. At the outer edge of the northernmost spoke sat the servant quarters, and to the end of the eastern spoke, just past the storage house, lay the sea, frothing and angry and always cold.

Ayla walked right up to the edge of the bluffs. It was slippery here, the black rocks wet with sea spray. Treacherous, especially at night. She reached into her pocket and grasped the knife she'd stolen from a leech in the market at Kalla-den nearly a month ago, the first time she'd ever gone to sell flowers.

Her first opportunity. To get a weapon.

She had been so overwhelmed with the adrenaline of getting away from the sovereign's palace that she'd just—slipped her hand into the folds of a leech girl's skirt and *taken* it, hidden by the swarming crowd.

Stealing it had been easy enough, but using it would take patience.

And practice. She was familiar with sparring, the specific movements of the body, the weight of a knife in her hand— though the one she'd used to practice with had been significantly heavier than this one, and balanced differently. As she settled into a fighting stance—feet shoulder-width apart, front foot pointed forward and back foot slightly angled—she smiled a little, remembering the endless afternoons she'd spent sparring with Benjy after Rowan took him in. Self-defense was something Rowan had insisted on teaching them, whether it was with a knife or just their fists. Rowan was a strict but fair teacher. She'd make Ayla and Benjy practice a single move over and over again until their arms were aching, their muscles trembling, the calluses on their palms split open and bleeding, but she always praised them afterward and rewarded them with a hot, hearty dinner. She rubbed ointment on their sore muscles, tended to the broken skin on their knuckles and palms.

One afternoon, she'd pulled Ayla aside after a particularly brutal round of training left Benjy sulking by the hearth fire, nursing a sprained wrist.

You're stronger than him, Ayla, Rowan had said. *You have to protect him.*

At the time, Ayla hadn't understood. Sure, she was quick and wily, but Benjy was physically much stronger. He won their fights eight out of ten times. *What are you talking about?* she'd asked. *Just yesterday he practically tossed me across the room. My tailbone's still hurting.*

But you got up, said Rowan. *You fought three more rounds. And here you are again today, even though you're in pain. Whereas Benjy . . .* She trailed off. *I wasn't talking about physical strength, Ayla. I was talking about resilience. I was talking about how you never, ever stop fighting, no matter how much it hurts.*

The knife was finally starting to feel natural in her hands. Just a few days of sparring in the dark was already beginning to pay off. She came here whenever she could, past the edge of the gardens, out of sight, slipping into shadow and becoming lethal with the blade.

Jab. Swipe. Duck.

The most effective way to kill an Automa was to deprive them of heartstone. The second most effective way was beheading. But to do so required force, more force than a human could produce with their bare hands.

Swipe. Change hands. *Jab*.

You could also kill a leech with a stab to the heart.

Slash. Recoil.

At the right angle, it could be done in a matter of seconds.

Lunge. Ayla thrust the knife forward, twisted it into an invisible body—imagining it being Crier's—and then, sweating, she let her arm drop. Slipped the knife back into her pocket. Catching her breath, she looked up at the wide and open night sky. She pulled her locket out from beneath her shirt, a talisman.

This was another secret she kept from Benjy. Her necklace wasn't a weapon, and yet it was so much more dangerous than a stolen knife. She held it up to the moonlight, admiring it as she'd done countless times before: the eight-point star engraved into the gold. The red gemstone at the center of the star. This, too, she could only do in the cloak of night. Alone.

There were no exceptions to the law. If you got caught with a forbidden object, you could be killed. Even if the object, like Ayla's necklace, was completely harmless and honestly sort of unimpressive. Probably the Maker had created it with some sort of purpose—maybe it was supposed to be a little music box, or maybe the locket could transform into a golden beetle and flit around people's heads—but whatever that purpose was, Ayla had never figured it out. She'd never even been able to open the locket, no matter how hard she picked and pried at the tiny clasp. The only interesting thing about the necklace was the fluttering noise that came from within—like the ticking of a clock but softer, more rhythmic. *Tmp-tmp, tmp-tmp.* Almost like a heartbeat.

It wasn't a weapon, it wasn't a tool, and it could easily get her killed. Ayla should have tossed the necklace into the ocean years ago. But she hadn't. Because her mother had given it to her—pressed it into Ayla's palm when she was no more than four or five, *keep it safe, child, remember us, remember our story*—and because, stars and skies, she *couldn't*, the necklace was all she had left of them, the only proof that her family had ever existed at all. Like Ayla herself, this necklace used to have a twin; it was one half of a matching set. The second necklace had been lost years and years ago, before Ayla and her brother were even born. Ayla wouldn't let this one share the same fate.

She slipped it back beneath her shirt.

The wind was freezing against her cheeks. Her mouth tasted like salt. The sea was lit up with moonlight, sparkling. A hundred feet below, the waves burst into white foam. She didn't have long until curfew, until she'd have to retreat back into the servants' quarters for the night, but for now she could stand here on the cliff's edge and hold the knife in her pocket. A promise of what was to come. Revenge. Killing Hesod's daughter. Even if it took years.

There was a noise to her left. The sound of footsteps on wet rock.

Ayla turned.

Someone else was standing on the bluffs maybe thirty paces

away, looking out over the ocean. Had they seen her? Her heart quickened, then settled. No. They were facing away from Ayla. They hadn't yet noticed she was here. Another servant?

Then, a voice: "—and is that the only reason you've agreed to this marriage?"

"You already knew that," said a second voice, and Ayla shrank farther behind a seaflower bush. The first voice Ayla didn't recognize. The second was undeniable. It was the sovereign himself, Hesod. She had only ever seen him from a distance, as he was always in the palace and surrounded by guards, but she'd heard his voice. He'd given a speech, once, after a stableboy had tried to attack one of the guards. The stableboy was killed on the spot, of course. Throat pierced with the same awl he'd been using as a weapon. And the next day, all the servants were gathered in the main courtyard and forced to their knees, bent over, foreheads pressed to the packed dirt. And Hesod had stood above them and said: *I would rather kill you all than replace a single guard. I suggest you do not let it come to that.*

But there was nobody protecting him right now.

"Your marriage to Crier would be of enormous benefit to Rabu," Hesod continued, and Ayla's ears pricked.

"I see you've noticed my growing popularity," the first voice drawled.

"I have—" And Hesod's voice dropped low enough that even an Automa wouldn't have been able to pick out the words over the waves and the sea wind. Ayla strained to hear more, but still could catch only pieces.

"—it is always political, Scyre Kinok," Hesod was saying.

Kinok. The war hero. Lady Crier's betrothed.

He'd quelled human rebellions and was responsible for the deaths of many. Still, when dealing with monsters, Ayla almost preferred that kind of frontal attack over Hesod's insidious tyranny, the way he professed his *appreciation for humankind* with one breath and ordered massacres with the next. The way he made laws pretending they were for the "good" of humans. Like the one that banned any use of large storage spaces: places where grains or dry goods could be kept for the drought and cold seasons were explicitly banned under the guise of caring for human welfare. Hesod—and the Red Council—said it was because humans might hoard. They might let their food rot and spread disease. But the rebellion knew better. Rowan had told Ayla and Benjy that the Automae were worried that any large storage spaces could be used to meet in secret or hide weapons. And in their fear, they sentenced many families to almost starve to death during the winter seasons.

"It is no secret," Kinok said, "that the union of our two political visions would only benefit Rabu. With Varn growing stronger, with Queen Junn gaining more support, whether she bought it or not . . . her people are still divided, but they will fight for her."

"Rumors," said Hesod dismissively. "Junn is delusional. Her people are weak, and her system, if it can even be called that, lacks structure. Varn will fall easily, if it comes to that."

"Of course, Sovereign."

The wind changed again and their voices fell away. Ayla found herself leaning forward, nearly sticking her nose into the seaflowers, straining her ears to catch anything—

"Politics aside, I have heard there may be developments in your experiments. Would you care to elaborate on the results?"

Kinok was quiet for a moment before she heard him respond, "All of it is still very nascent, Sovereign."

"Well, I'm sure that given your knowledge, given your *history*, you will triumph in your endeavors," Hesod responded.

What were they talking about? What endeavors?

Hesod was still speaking, and now his tone had turned somewhat warning. "To have been a Watcher of the Heart is a great honor, and we must ensure that honor is not tarnished," he was saying.

Ayla blinked. Kinok was a Watcher? She thought they weren't allowed to ever leave the Heart. That was the whole point, the sacrifice. They guarded the location of the Heart for their entire lives.

"It was an honor, yes," said Kinok. "And a position I did not take lightly. Nor do I take my current work lightly."

"I've always considered myself a guardian of the Heart," said Hesod, sounding far away, as if he wasn't really listening to Kinok. "At least from afar. As head of the council, it is my duty to ensure that the trading routes are clear and well guarded to make way for the shipments of heartstone. One could say I protect the veins of this land."

"And the Watchers are ever thankful, Sovereign. We know

the Heart requires so much of so many to keep its secrets safe." Kinok paused. "Though it might help if you allowed Varn to trade across your borders, instead of forcing them to take to the sea."

Keep its secrets safe. Kinok had to mean the location of the Iron Heart. Ayla's breath caught in her throat; as a Watcher, Kinok knew where the Iron Heart was . . . its *exact* location. How it worked. He knew everything.

And he was standing only a few paces away from Ayla.

Of course, everyone knew the Heart was *somewhere* to the west, somewhere deep within the Aderos Mountains. The vast mountain range hid a massive mine, which produced heartstone: the mysterious red jewel that, when crushed into a fine dust, fed all Automae. According to Rowan, human rebels had tried many times to attack the caravans that carried shipments of heartstone dust all over Zulla, and every single time they'd failed; they'd lost dozens, sometimes hundreds, of human lives for every stolen gem, making it both a risky and ultimately futile effort. The supplies of heartstone seemed limitless.

Here was the crux of it: if leeches didn't ingest the dust every day, they'd stop functioning. It was their lifeblood. Depriving them of heartstone dust was the easiest way to kill them—faster, even, than depriving a human of food or water. So of course they guarded the dust, and the Aderos Mountains, more heavily than anything else.

That was why finding the Iron Heart had become the obsession of the Revolution.

The key to the rebellion, the one piece of information that Rowan had been searching for tirelessly for as long as Ayla had known her.

And now, it was only a few paces away.

This was bigger than any uprising. Bigger than any of Rowan's *full moons*.

Ayla's heart fluttered like a bird's wings in her chest. Hesod's next words, Automa-quiet, were lost to her, but then there was another sound. A footstep on wet rock.

Then rustling.

Ayla was not spying alone.

5

It had been so long since Crier had properly slept that she was shocked to awaken and find herself in the gardens hours later, her Design scrolls still tucked into her sleeve. Night had fallen, crickets chirped. She had heard voices—that's why she'd woken up. Now she steadied herself against a branch, trying not to rustle the flowers and leaves as she inched closer to the sound.

It was her father.

And Kinok.

Having, apparently, some sort of private conversation.

Crier frowned. For all her political aspirations, she had always disliked the way her father would take private meetings, or would shut himself away in the north wing and shuffle around lives and livelihoods like pieces on a chessboard, arranging them like he had the gardens, and his estate, and Crier's engagement: logically, masterfully, neatly sidestepping every possible obstacle months or years before it even began to form. And now, this—a

NINA VARELA

secluded conversation with Kinok, out here, in the darkness of the gardens. *Her* special place, where she came to think and be alone.

She had not meant to listen in, and it was not like she could hear much of anything above the wind and the crashing sea— but now that she was here, she was curious.

"—and far be it from me to spill such secrets, Sovereign," Kinok said.

Secrets. It was bad enough being excluded from her father's work—Crier could not stand the idea of him having secrets *with Kinok*. Part of her thought it better that she could not hear what they were saying, but the other part, a larger part, worried that this was about her Flaw. What if Kinok did know and was now revealing it to her father?

How would he react?

Would she be terminated?

It had happened before—young Automae with Flawed Designs, assigned early termination. That was back before Hesod's rule, but it didn't mean it couldn't happen again.

She slipped out from behind the seaflower bush and moved to the next one, and the next, careful to remain hidden.

Her father and Kinok, their backs turned, were maybe fifty or sixty paces away.

If she just darted from this row to the next, maybe she could get closer. She would be visible for less than a second. She set her shoulders and continued, reaching the end of the row. The moonlight was pale on her skin.

"—this will be more fruitful than I had ever hoped," Hesod said, but his next words were lost as the sea wind howled. Crier leaned forward, straining to hear.

She was right on the edge of the bluffs.

And then the ground beneath her feet fell away.

There was a split second in which Crier simply pitched forward, frozen, mind whirring—*why am I off-balance—why am I slipping*—and then she realized the bluff was crumbling. Her weight had been a catalyst, the rocks were breaking and sliding off the cliff face and she was sliding with them—down down *down*. She twisted wildly, fingers scrabbling for anything solid, and found nothing but broken rock and slippery yellowish grass and—

A jut of rock. Solid. She grabbed it with both hands right as the Crier-sized chunk of cliff fell. She heard it crack and shatter against one of the jagged black rocks that stuck up out of the water and tried not to think about her own body hitting that rock. How she would have cracked and shattered.

How she still might. She was dangling off the edge of the bluff with nothing but air beneath her feet.

The Design papers slipped from her sleeve, like an afterthought, and fluttered down into the darkness, flapping, birdlike, until she could no longer see them.

She was going to fall, she knew it. The jut of rock that had saved her was smooth and slick. There was a twinge of sensation in her wrist, and she realized her flesh had torn open. A deep three-inch gash, skin peeling away to reveal strips of finely Made muscle and bone. Dark purplish fluid dripping from the wound, running down her arm.

"Help," she said, but it came out hoarse, weak, pathetic; Kinok and her father would never hear her over the crashing waves. "Help—please—I, I need—please." Her fingers slipped another half inch. Another. She was going to fall. Crier was ten times stronger than any human and she was created to be perfect and she was going to *fall* and crack and shatter against the wet black rocks and spill her perfect insides into the sea. And be swallowed.

No. No no no please no—

A hand grabbed her wrist, holding her up as she dangled off the cliff's edge.

"Oh—"

Crier looked up and into a pair of dark eyes.

It was not Kinok who had saved her. Not her father.

It was a human.

For a moment Crier was frozen. She forgot the ocean and the rocks below.

She had never really seen a pair of eyes like this. It was like standing in the doorway to a dark room, like balancing on the threshold, holding a lantern up and watching how it kissed some things gold and left other things in shadow. It was the kind of dark that hid and held a lot of things. A hot fluid dark, a summer tide pool dark, a wild breathless dark.

A hand on Crier's wrist, holding her up. A thumb digging into the tear in her flesh.

A face, moon-shaped, with thick, arched eyebrows and a mass of tangled dark hair. Red uniform, dark like dried blood.

This human girl's eyes were wide. Her grip shifted on Crier's wounded wrist.

Crier realized that she had not yet been saved.

The girl's breaths were coming fast. Her mouth twisted, her grip loosened—

A necklace fell out of her shirt and dangled between them. Crier's gaze flicked from the girl's face to her necklace, a split second of winking gold in the moonlight, a pendant carved with an eight-point star—the all-too-familiar symbol of the Makers— and then the girl gave a low wrenching noise and pulled Crier up up *up*, back over the edge of the bluff, and then they were both scrambling away from the edge, collapsing beneath a sea-flower bush. Gasping. Shaking. Crier squeezed her eyes shut and pressed her face into the dirt, which was illogical but felt like the only thing she would ever want to do for the rest of her life. The dirt smelled like rain and soft green things and *not dying*.

Four seconds. Five. She shoved herself upright. Her face was wet, dirt sticking to her cheeks, and she did not understand why. She tasted salt. Sea spray, but different.

The girl was already looking at her. Crier saw her own shock mirrored in those dark eyes. But why were they both shocked? Of course the girl had saved her. Crier had needed help. This girl was in Hesod's command, and therefore also in Crier's command. Why would she do anything else? Why was Crier's vision blurring?

The girl reached forward and pressed her thumb to the soft

skin below Crier's left eye. Again they stared at each other. The girl's eyes flicked between her hand and Crier's face, as if she was confused by her own actions. Crier held very still, and when the girl's thumb came away from her skin, she saw the way it glistened with something wet.

Tears.

Crier's hands flew up to her cheeks. Her skin was grimy, almost sticky, damp with dirt and—*tears*. Water from her eyes, salt on her lips. Tears, like the strange wet that streaked down human faces, but these were her own. They were hot like blood. It *felt* like she was bleeding, like she was wounded. But Automae did not cry like humans did. Why would they.

The girl wiped her thumb on her shirt. *My tears*, Crier thought, staring at the damp spot. *My salt*.

Her eyes stung.

"Lady Crier!"

Six guards were heading toward them, dark figures in the gloom. Even when running, their strides were identical; they did not fall out of line; their uniforms were pristine. Six guards—Crier's distress chime must have gone off. She scrubbed at her face, wiping away all evidence of the tears. Nobody could see. (*Somebody already had*.) It was bad enough that she had nearly died, doubly bad that she had been saved by a servant. A human.

What would her father think?

What would Kinok think?

Crier got to her feet and did her best to brush the dirt off her clothes, to fix her messy, wind-whipped hair. Out of the corner of her eye, she noticed the human girl doing the same. She watched the girl hide the gold necklace back beneath her shirt, avoiding Crier's eyes.

So she had not imagined the Maker symbol carved into the small, coin-like pendant. Crier stared at the girl again, this time with a new shock.

A symbol written in a language that had been dead for a hundred years, the old language of the alchemists.

How did you get that? Crier thought, unable to tear her eyes away from the girl's face. *Who are you?*

But already the guards had reached them and immediately fell upon the girl, wrestling her arms behind her back and shoving her head down, trapping her between them. Three on the girl, the other three pointing their swords at her throat, her stomach, the base of her neck. The girl did not struggle. There would be no point. It took six hundred and seventy pounds of force to snap a human's neck. The guards could apply that pressure in half a second.

She stared at the guards. "What are you doing?"

"Was it the human?" one guard asked. "What was it doing here? Did it attack you?" He was the one holding the girl's head down. Crier could not see her face.

The way her grip had shifted on Crier's wrist. The fierce look in her eyes. The press of her thumb into Crier's wound. How, for a moment, Crier had been absolutely sure the girl was going to let her drop. The shock on both their faces when the girl had pulled her up up up and over, back to solid ground.

Of course the girl had saved her.

But for a moment—for a moment—

"No," Crier heard herself say. "No, it did not push me. I fell. The human saved my life."

The girl's head jerked beneath the guard's hand. Like she had just tried to look up. At Crier.

"The human saved me," Crier repeated. She glanced toward the spot where she had heard her father and Kinok speaking, but they were long gone. They must have been heading back toward the palace when she fell. "I sustained a minor injury. I require medical assistance. Escort me to the physician immediately. And please keep this between us—my father is quite busy with our guest and he does not need any added stress."

"Yes, Lady Crier." They let go of the girl and she stumbled forward a little, straightened up. She glanced at Crier just long enough for Crier to see that her face was blank, her emotions tamped down, but her eyes: they were anything but blank. They were shocked and confused and *furious* (at the guards? at Crier?) and dark, and when the moonlight hit them at just the right angle they stayed dark and heated and terribly, impossibly *human*.

What was she doing out here, all alone in the dark?

Crier supposed she could be asked the same question.

"Now, please."

Crier was escorted back to the palace.

The girl stayed behind, her silhouette melting into the night. Crier looked back at her once and then did not look again.

When the guards delivered her to the physician, Crier paused in the doorway and said, "Wait."

Crier really should report her.

"The human from the bluffs," she said. "Get me her name."

Ayla.

Ayla.

Crier let the name turn over inside her mind, studying every angle and curve of it, as she sat on the window seat of her bedchamber early the next morning, a book in her lap, watching the sun break from the horizon with a flash of gold.

Her hands ached. There were nasty scrapes on her fingertips, the skin peeled raw. Marks from where she had scrabbled desperately at the rocks yesterday, searching for a handhold as she fell. After Crier had been released from the physician, her handmaiden Malwin had drawn her a long, soothing bath; together they had watched the dirt and blood stream off Crier's body and disappear, hidden by the swirls of soap and steam. The physician had given her a salve that would have fixed the imperfections on her skin just as easily as it closed up the gash on her wrist. Within hours, Crier would be left with unblemished fingertips and one less physical reminder that she had, in fact, fallen. That she had been saved.

She had not yet applied the salve.

Instead, she picked at the wounds, keeping the scrapes open. Tiny beads of blood welled up on her skin like jewels. Automa blood was not so dissimilar to human blood, except that the color was different. Where human blood was red, Automa blood was darker, bluer, almost violet. Crier stared at her own blood now, shining in the light, and let out a breath. Violet. Inhuman. Flawless.

And yet.

The first blush pinks of dawn filtered through the window, coloring the stacks of books and maps upon Crier's writing desk and canopied bed. There was a silk tapestry on the far wall of her bedchamber. Tiny, interwoven threads of silver and gold shone brightly in the sunlight, standing out against the deep, colorful background.

Unlike most tapestries in the palace, this one was very simple. There were no Automa hunters chasing a wild boar on foot, their human servants trailing behind with the dogs. No depiction of the Iron Heart, no jewel-studded castle, no ships tossed on a blue-silk ocean. There was only a woman. Dark-haired, brown-skinned, beautiful, she stared out at Crier's bedchamber from her place on the wall. Her dress was saffron yellow, her mouth madder-root red. Her eyes were stitched with gold.

Kiera.

The first of their Kind.

In the sunlight, her eyes almost glowed.

When the knock came at the door, Crier sat up straighter, her book shifting against her thighs. She shoved it aside.

"Enter," she said, and Ayla (*Ayla*) stumbled into her bedchamber.

She looked the same as last night—red uniform, messy dark

braid, big brown eyes. She carried the same intensity about her, like heat waves rising from her skin, even though she was just standing in the doorway and not currently in the middle of saving Crier's life.

Like she was more than a human girl.

Like she was a summer storm made flesh.

Ayla's arms hung at her sides, her fingers twisted in the hidden folds of her uniform. Crier felt like she had managed to capture a butterfly in her cupped hands, and now it was frantically beating its wings.

"You summoned me?" said Ayla.

Her voice was low, a little raspy.

Perhaps the butterfly was actually a wasp.

Crier had been stung by one, once. She grasped at the memory, suddenly longing to remember how it felt.

"Ayla," said Crier, the name slipping between her lips. "I summoned you here because I must ask you something."

Ayla's chin jutted out. "Whatever my punishment is, I'll take it with my head up."

"Punishment?" Crier peered at her. "Come. Walk with me."

"Walk with you?"

"Yes. Did you misunderstand?"

"No, I understood you," Ayla said, and then added, "my lady," like she had only just then remembered that she was supposed to use Crier's title at all times. And she stood there, holding very still as Crier unfolded herself from the window seat and joined Ayla in the doorway, the space seeming to constrict with a shudder as Crier passed her.

She led her through the winding corridors of the palace, walking in silence a few steps ahead, as was proper, though with every single step she wanted to turn around and look back at Ayla's face, to try and read her expression, to puzzle out what she was thinking. Ayla's face was fascinating. Crier had seen her barely twice and she already knew this like she knew the constellations.

It was like the tapestry of Kiera: with the first glance, you saw the deepest colors, her skin and eyebrows and the pink of her mouth. With the second glance, you saw the threads of gold, the spark in her eyes and the tiny scar on her left cheekbone, her perpetual frown—and you were captivated.

Crier's skin felt too tight.

She led Ayla out of the palace, into the gardens, wet with the last of morning's dew, and then onto the bluffs. The cool sea air was a relief.

They only stopped walking once they reached the very edge of the bluffs. The exact spot where, last night, Crier had fallen and Ayla had pulled her back up. Crier rubbed at her wrist. There were marks of her fall on the cliff itself: dark spots where Crier had clutched at handfuls of seagrass, jagged broken rock. Eight sets of footprints pressed into the soft mud. Crier, Ayla, and the guards.

"This," said Crier, "is where I fell."

A pause. "Yes, my lady."

"Why did you save me?" Crier asked.

For the first time, Ayla's eyes flicked up to meet Crier's, sending a sensation of shock through her. "It's my job," she said slowly. "It's my job to—to serve the house of Sovereign Hesod. That includes you."

It was exactly the answer she should have given.

It was not at all what Crier had wanted to hear.

"Is there no other reason?" she asked, resisting the urge to lean closer, fearing she might. "No other reason to preserve my life?"

Have you ever observed me before? Have you seen me in the gardens? Did you see something in me?

Can you tell that I am different? Flawed?

Look at me again.

Ayla's mouth twisted, but she did not look—and this, too, was a relief.

Still: Was there a redness in her cheeks, beneath the brown of her skin, beneath the freckles? Or was that a trick of the morning sun, which had risen like a gasp, like the burst of saltpeter bombs exploding in the night sky, color and fire and light? Crier now felt something burst open inside herself, too. *Did you see something in me?*

She wanted to ask. She did not.

Instead of an answer, Ayla responded with a question. "Why did you fall?"

What a curious question to ask. Then again, why *did* she fall? How had it happened?

"I have been occupied lately," Crier said, putting the words together like layers of starched silk—covering herself with them.

"Tomorrow I—I will be officially engaged to Scyre Kinok, there will be a celebration—and three days after that, I will be attending a council meeting for the very first time, as daughter of the sovereign. Hopefully, the first meeting of many. There is so much to do—I was occupied. Preoccupied. I required fresh air, and I walked too close to the edge of the cliff."

Ayla nodded. And then she looked up, meeting Crier's gaze dead on. "Why didn't you report me?"

Ayla reached up and touched a spot on her own chest, over her sternum. Where her forbidden necklace must lie beneath her work shirt, cool against her warm skin. Ayla's jaw was tight, her chin jutting out again.

Crier swallowed, though she didn't need to. It was a good question. There were too many questions without answers. Those were the kind Crier hated.

"Because you saved my life," she replied, but haltingly.

Ayla shook her head. "Your guards arrived quick enough. You would've been all right even if I hadn't been there."

"That is true," Crier admitted, because it was. Had always been. She was well protected. "Father Designed me with a chime," she said, suddenly wishing to convey to Ayla why this mattered, wanting her to understand. "If my heart rate rises too quickly, the device sends out a silent distress signal to the guards. Even we can't hear it, but they can."

Now she was speaking just to fill the silence, and so she stopped.

Ayla's eyebrows arched, ever so slightly. The breeze was a

trailing finger, lifting the little tendrils of hair that had come loose from Crier's plait. Automa hair was thick and glossy, usually worn high up on the head, a braid twisted into a tight crown. Crier felt very exposed all of a sudden, hyperaware of the tiny, wispy curls at her temples and the nape of her neck. She felt improper before Ayla's gaze. In disarray.

"Is it because I saw you cry?" Ayla said, and then bit down hard on her bottom lip.

"I did not cry," Crier said stiffly.

"Yes, you did. I saw it. I *touched* it. Seawater isn't warm like that."

They glared at each other a little.

"Fine," Crier said. "But I am your lady. And you are not the only one who saw something not meant for your eyes last night." She looked pointedly at the spot where the necklace must be. "Your Kind are not supposed to wear trinkets like that."

Ayla's hands jerked as if she was suppressing an impulse to reach for her necklace. "It's not a *trinket*."

"Whatever it is, it is forbidden." She cocked her head. "Is it true that humans collect shiny objects? Like magpies do?" She'd seen how the black-feathered birds lingered in high branches and swooped down to investigate fallen coins; she'd even heard once about a crow that had nearly taken out a lady's eye in an attempt to inspect her jeweled tiara. Sometimes, during meals in the great hall, she thought of that story and had to hide a smile behind her sleeve.

"You live in a palace of white marble and gold," Ayla said

incredulously. "There are pearls in your hair. And you're calling me the magpie?"

"I am a lady," Crier snapped. "You are not."

"Well, my necklace isn't a trinket," Ayla snapped right back. "It's not just something shiny. It contains histories."

"Oh," said Crier. "Really? What kind of histories? What do you mean, *contains*?" She peered at Ayla's sternum as if she would somehow be able to *see* the necklace's mysterious properties. "Is there a coded message inside? Is the necklace a key to a secret library? Is it an ancient relic?"

"No, no, and no," said Ayla, eyes wide. "No, I . . . well, I don't actually know."

"That is disappointing."

Ayla's mouth twitched. Bitterness, maybe.

Looking at her, Crier felt dizzy. Off-balance. This close to the cliff's edge, she was in danger of falling all over again—it was as if the rush of sea below them was calling out to her, beckoning. Ayla's eyes were so dark.

Crier thought suddenly of the gardens. All that color— kept bright by human servants. Inside the palace, there was color only in her bedchamber, her tapestry of Kiera. Who had woven that tapestry? An Automa? Crier had studied fourteen languages, twenty-nine branches of science and mathematics, one thousand years of history for every formally recognized kingdom and territory, but she had never woven a single thread. Never painted, never written anything but essays. She looked at Ayla, who was looking back. Ayla's hair was limp in the ocean breeze, sticking to her temples.

"Have you ever taken any lessons?" She hadn't meant to ask that.

Ayla's nose scrunched up. She did that a lot. "No. I don't . . ."

"Don't what?"

"Read, my lady. I can't."

Crier paused, taking that in. She couldn't imagine not knowing how to read. It seemed somehow very cruel. "Is there anything you wish to learn?"

What she meant was: *What do you find interesting?* Were there certain words or ideas that made Ayla's frown smooth out, that made her eyes brighten? Crier wanted to study her like a map. Draw an easy path between all the specific yet scattered points of her.

Ayla shrugged. "Maybe?"

Crier waited.

Ayla looked out over the ocean. "A very long time ago, I knew someone who liked to study nature. The natural laws. Once, I asked him why, and he told me that he liked knowing there's certain laws in the universe. He said you can't count on much, can't trust most things to stay solid, but, you know, there's always some sort of force at work. Even way out there past the sky, so far away that we can't even imagine it, things work the same. Everything's just bodies in orbit, like here. Pushing and pulling. They call it the law of falling, I think."

The law of falling. "Who said that to you?"

When Ayla looked back at her, there was fire in her dark

eyes. "Someone I will not see again," she said. Another pause. "Is there something you wanted, Lady Crier? If you're not going to punish me, why are we here?"

Because you saw me cry.

"I have grown tired of my current handmaiden," said Crier. "I wish to replace her." When Ayla just frowned, confused, she went on. "You have already helped me once. I want you to help me again. Be my handmaiden."

Ayla sucked in a breath. "*What?*"

"You will report to my chambers at dawn and spend your days at my side. You will attend to me and only me. It is a position of power and honor. Handmaiden to the sovereign's heir."

Crier knew that expression. *Shock.* But Crier did not care. Could not care. She had known Ayla for less than an hour total, and already she knew what she wanted. She wanted those dark eyes, that quiet, sharp-edged intensity, the evasive responses that she knew, she *knew*, would give her yet another sleepless night. Another night spent wondering and guessing and—dreaming. Or something close to it.

Once again, Crier felt a kind of draw, a temptation to lean closer to Ayla, a kind of inner falling. She held still. It was a skill only Automae possessed, to hold still without trembling.

"Why are you doing this?" said Ayla finally. "Why aren't you reporting me for the necklace? Why do you want me at your side?"

Ayla could not help her, Crier knew. She could not change her flawed Design. She could not save Crier from marrying

Kinok. In fact, she could make everything worse. Crier knew that.

And yet, there was this: the push. The pull.

The inner falling, like a kind of law.

"Your necklace. My . . ." She couldn't bring herself to say the human word: *tears*. She looked down her nose at Ayla, squaring her shoulders. "We both have secrets. And when someone knows your secrets, do you not prefer to keep them within arm's reach?"

Ayla was silent.

"I will expect you tomorrow at dawn," Crier said, and turned away.

It began with this: All things possessed a certain prima materia, a pure, intangible substance older than the Universe Itself; the Metaphysical material from which such a borderless object as the human Soul is woven. If humankind is formed from such material, from organ to bone to flesh to even the intangible Soul, then surely the Maker can transmute human life.

—FROM *THE MAKER'S HANDBOOK*,
BY ULGA OF FAMILY DAMEROS, 2187440906, YEAR 4 AE

6

She'd been so close.

For the second time in so many days, Ayla had had Crier right on the edge of a cliff. And yet Crier was still alive. As she headed back across the palace grounds to the long, low building where all the servants slept, Ayla felt at war with herself. Half of her was raging, screaming in frustration: she'd been so damn close. She could have let Crier fall, either by never grabbing her wrist in the first place or by looking her in the eye, saying *This is for my family*, and letting her go. Watching as her body tumbled down to the rocks and the devouring ocean below. Today, she could have pushed Crier over the edge. There had been plenty of moments during their conversation when Ayla could tell Crier's guard was down; she wouldn't have seen it coming; she could be *dead* right now. But she wasn't.

The other half of Ayla was trying desperately to justify her own inaction. Yes, she could have let Crier fall. Could have pushed her. But—over the years, whenever Ayla had pictured her revenge, she'd always pictured blood. A knife to the heart, to the throat, Crier's dark, unnatural blood on her hands. Visceral. Satisfying. As cruel and violent as the raids on Ayla's village had been. Why else had she waited so patiently, for so long? Why else had she gone the lengths to work her way up, to steal the knife, to practice for hours in the gardens at night?

It wasn't enough to just let Crier die in an accident, and it wasn't even enough to push her off the sea cliffs. Neither of those deaths felt like justice. And even then . . . something about the conversation with Crier had sparked—not curiosity, not desire, but . . . maybe a mixture of the two. Lady Crier had *secrets*. It wasn't something Ayla would have ever expected, and a big part of her wanted to learn more. To infiltrate the palace, using Crier as her in. She'd always thought that the most she would be able to do was kill Hesod's daughter. But what if she could destroy him even more completely? Kill his daughter *and* burn his kingdom to the ground?

The midday sun was too bright in her eyes, searing. She hurried along the narrow dirt path that connected the servants' quarters to the palace, separated by about a half mile of land. Hesod preferred to have the stables in view of the main home, and the human housing out of sight, hidden from visiting officials. Today, it was an advantage. Rowan was coming to say goodbye to Ayla and Benjy before she headed south to join the latest uprisings, and the servants' quarters were the safest place to meet. During the day, when all the servants were working elsewhere, the guards only patrolled the area every few hours.

Ayla picked up her pace. Revenge wasn't the only thing on her mind—unwittingly, Lady Crier had given Ayla a vital piece of information about the Iron Heart. A piece of information that could change everything, for her and for the rebels. For Rowan, in the coming days. Ayla was itching to tell her and Benjy what she'd learned.

She slipped through the door of the servants' quarters and kept her head down as she walked between the rows of cots, even though the quarters were abandoned at this time of day. She headed straight for the back, where there was another, smaller door.

Ayla took a deep breath, relishing the clean air while it lasted—and opened the door to the latrines.

As always, the smell hit her like a sucker punch, foul memories rising like bile, black spots popping up behind her eyes. The latrines were small and cramped, stone walls and a handful of chamber pots and then two slabs of wood that concealed the deep holes into which all the servants tossed their waste. The wooden covers did absolutely nothing to block off the stench. Eyes watering, Ayla yanked her collar up to cover her nose and forced herself to actually go inside.

Benjy and Rowan were huddled in a corner of the latrines, handkerchiefs tied over their noses and mouths, sunlight streaming through the rafters and setting Rowan's silver hair alight. Benjy's eyes widened when he caught sight of Ayla and he bounded over to her, looking equal parts relieved and annoyed.

"Where in all the hells have you been?" he demanded, his voice slightly garbled by the handkerchief. "First you don't show up to morning meal, then you don't report to Nessa, and one of the scullery maids said she'd seen you in the gardens with *Crier*? And now you're *late*, and Rowan's got to get on the road, and if I'm not back in the orchards in under an hour I'll probably be *flogged*—"

"Perhaps if you want an explanation, you should let the girl speak," Rowan broke in. She pulled Ayla into a quick, rosemary-scented hug, her hair tickling Ayla's cheek. "Hello, birdy. It's not like you to be late—did something happen?"

"Yes, and you're not going to believe it," said Ayla. Whispering, because you never knew who might be listening, she told them everything that had happened since she was summoned to Lady Crier's bedchamber that morning. About the walk through the gardens. About Crier's strange, persistent questioning of Ayla's motives. About the offer (no, not offer; *order*) that Ayla become Crier's personal handmaiden.

"I never imagined I'd get a chance like this," she admitted, meeting Rowan's steady gaze. "I dreamed of being assigned to something inside the palace, but—I thought I'd be in the kitchens, or a nameless maidservant . . . I'm a *handmaiden*. The handmaiden to Lady Crier herself. It's got to be a sign."

"A sign of what?" asked Benjy.

"A sign that—" Ayla dropped her voice even lower. "Killing Crier wouldn't be true revenge. Not the way I've always wanted it. If I want to destroy Hesod, really destroy him . . . I have to kill *everything* he cares about."

He huffed, frustrated. "What do you mean?"

"Killing his daughter is one thing, but for Hesod? For men like that, Automa or not, there's nothing so dear to them as power. Blood and gold and precious stones—it all comes in second to having a seat on the council, command over an army. To having control. The only way to really destroy Hesod is to take away his *power*."

"So it's still about revenge for you," said Benjy, almost annoyed. "Not revolution."

Ayla stared at him. How did he not understand? She turned to Rowan, beseeching. "You understand, right?"

"I do." Rowan reached out to ruffle Benjy's hair, smiling when he squirmed away, and then she ruffled Ayla's for good measure. "Benjy, love, this *is* revolution. The sovereign is the head of the great beast. We all have our own reasons for wanting to cut off the head. All that matters, in the end, is that someone does."

"Besides, it's not just Hesod I'll be in close quarters with," Ayla added. "Rowan, how much do you know about Kinok?"

Rowan frowned. "The Scyre?"

"Not just a Scyre." Ayla leaned closer, excited. She'd never quite grown out of the wild urge to impress Rowan, to make her—proud, maybe. Something like it. "He used to be a Watcher."

"*What?*" said Benjy. "That's—that's impossible. Watchers don't leave the Heart. Ever. They pledge their entire lives to protecting it."

"I don't know how he was able to leave his post, but he did. And now he's here, and he's set to marry Lady Crier."

"And he still has connections to the Heart," said Rowan. There was something hushed about her voice, something almost reverent.

"He's got more than connections," said Ayla, biting back a wicked grin. "He's got *knowledge*. Of how it works, how to get there. Trade routes. Maybe even . . . weaknesses, vulnerable points. Who knows!"

Benjy opened his mouth to say something else, but Rowan cut him off. "Stars and skies, birdy," she said, her brown eyes lit up in the sunlight. She looked less like a sparrow and more like . . . like a warrior, fierce and brilliant and flush with hope. Like the warrior she had been in past uprisings; like the warrior she would be again. The revolutionary, the leader. "Ayla, my love," she said. "This is incredible, this is—this is the best chance we've had in *years*. You can be our eyes and ears on the inside, love. Stationed right at the heart of the spider's nest, imagine that. And—personal handmaiden to Lady Crier? Gods, it's like they *want* a coup."

"So you think I should use my position," said Ayla, unable to keep the triumph out of her voice, even as she saw Benjy's scowl deepen. "You think I should be a mole."

"Yes," said Rowan. "Yes, gods, of course. Though"—here her voice changed a little, grew harder—"it will be dangerous. Ayla, you have to focus on the Scyre. He's the one with knowledge about the Iron Heart. Maybe he's even got a map of the Aderos

Mountains, or of the trade routes, a ledger of all the heartstone traders, something, *anything*. Whatever you can find, it'll be valuable." She grinned, sharp and bright, and cupped Ayla's face in both hands, pressing a kiss to her forehead. "You clever girl. Oh, you clever, fearsome girl."

Ayla grinned back, but her mind was already spinning. Was it possible? Was there a chance that Scyre Kinok really did have a map of the Aderos Mountains—a map that could lead them to the Iron Heart itself?

If he did . . .

No more white dresses hanging over the marketplace like ghosts.

Because humans wouldn't have to kill Automae to set themselves free. The Automae would die, all at once. During Ayla's first year working under Sovereign Hesod, the orchards had nearly been wiped out by an infestation of locusts. It was an unusually hot spring: the kind of spring where the end of winter felt less like a rebirth, like shaking the weight of snow off your shoulders and emerging lighter for it, and more like a slow descent into boiling water. The air was thick and wet as steam. Sometimes it ached even to breathe. When the locusts came, settling over the orchards like a living, buzzing shadow, even they seemed a little exhausted by the heat. They ate slowly: first the budding fruits, then the blossoms, then the leaves. They ate nonstop for days. All the servants were panicking, because no one knew what to do about the loss of the fruit harvest. And what happened when the locusts stripped the fruit trees bare?

Would they fly away, or would they just migrate to the gardens? The fields of barley and sea lavender? Would the entire year's crop be devoured?

It was Nessa—the head servant—who saved them. Nessa who got the idea to spray the locusts with clouds of poisoned water. It wouldn't hurt the trees—and besides, most of them were already naked and dead-looking—but it began to kill the locusts the second it touched their shiny green skin.

Within a single day, the trees were empty. The dirt below their branches was littered with millions of dead, silent locusts, their bodies piled ankle-deep. Ayla was one of the servants assigned to clearing them away. Barefoot, she waded through the orchards, filling her basket over and over again with corpses and then loading the baskets onto a cart, dragging the cart out to the bluffs, tossing the contents of each basket over the edge and into the waiting sea. The locusts' tiny iridescent wings caught the sunlight as they fell; with each basket, Ayla felt like she was pouring out a cascade of glittering gemstones.

One day's work and all the locusts were dead; the orchards were saved.

That was what would happen if the Iron Heart was destroyed, if the Automae were deprived of heartstone dust. One day's work. A living shadow lifted.

Ayla blinked. Realized Rowan was still watching her, waiting for her response. Benjy wasn't looking at either of them. He was staring at the dirt floor, jaw working.

"I'm going to work for Lady Crier," said Ayla. "I'm going

to spy on the Scyre and learn everything I can about the Iron Heart."

"What about your revenge?" Benjy mumbled.

"I won't be rash," she promised. There was no point in telling Benjy that the fire in her hadn't diminished—had grown, even. This killing fire inside her—he didn't need to know just how long and cruel it had been burning. Just how charred and scarred she was. Somewhere in the back of her mind, her brother's voice echoed. *Act only when the odds are on your side, Ayla. Gamble with bread and coins, not your life.* "I swear to you, Benjy," she said. "I won't do anything to Hesod or Crier until I've found enough information to destroy the Iron Heart. I won't let my revenge compromise the Revolution."

Rowan patted her cheek, beaming. "That's my girl."

And even though her eyes were still watering from the terrible stench of the latrines, even though the idea of serving Crier disgusted her, even though part of her wasn't sure she'd be able to find any information on the Heart at all . . . For the first time since *that day*, Ayla had a plan. Not just the nebulous, half-formed notion of *I want to hurt Hesod. I want to take away his family like he took away mine.* But a real plan. Something so much bigger than Crier, Hesod, Kinok, even herself. It felt like—like this was what she was meant to do.

Her heart was lit up with something quick and hot. A lightning storm inside her.

Somewhere along the line, she'd forgotten how it felt to begin.

Planning to spy on the Scyre was a lot easier than actually doing it. Ayla was far too occupied with the bustle of the household and its needs—most importantly, Crier's—to get away for even a second. Her new schedule, it turned out, was just as demanding as her work in the fields had been.

This morning, for the first time in her four years as a servant to the sovereign, Ayla didn't report to the stables or the orchards at dawn. Instead, she joined the thin stream of humans heading up from the servants' quarters to the palace itself, and—after an Automa guard checked her face, gripping her chin hard as he verified her identity—she passed through the huge wooden doors.

It felt like sneaking into a dragon's cave.

Ayla hurried through the vast, twisting hallways, ceilings arching high above her head, trying to memorize the layout, which felt far more complicated than it should, given she knew the palace was divided into four wings. The north wing was the most heavily guarded—she knew that simply from observing the guards as she worked on the palace grounds. That was probably where the sleeping quarters were, and maybe the sovereign's study or his war room. Would Kinok sleep there as well, or were guests relegated to a different area of the palace? The kitchens and the great hall were in the east wing, every floor but the first with a vast view of the Steorran Sea. The grand ballroom was in the west, and the south held the guards' quarters, extra harvest and weaponry stores, solaria, large rooms where the Red Council sometimes met. But the wings were huge—all four of them were three stories high and large enough to hold dozens of spacious rooms. They could be hiding anything.

Ayla's job was to figure out where Kinok's quarters were—and how to get in.

Tonight, the engagement ball would be held in the grand ballroom in the west wing. That was where Ayla had to report first, and she barely had two seconds to take in the sheer *grandness* of the room—the entire apple orchard could have fit comfortably within its cavernous walls; the ceiling was so high that Ayla had to tip her head all the way back just to look up at it; the walls were dripping with candles and sheer gold curtains; the marble floor was polished to a glass-like shine and cleared for dancing.

"You!" A housemaid she didn't recognize was barking orders. "You're the new handmaiden, are you?"

"Yes," Ayla said. She was already dreading whatever task she was about to be assigned.

The housemaid smirked. "Polish the dance floor."

Ayla looked back at the wide-open space in the middle of the ballroom. The surface of the marble floor was gleaming and flawless. "With all due respect, hasn't it already been—?"

"We always polish it twice," said the housemaid, still smirking. "You'll find the supplies over there already. Be quick about it, will you? Shouldn't take more than an hour." And with that she turned on her heel and flounced away.

Ayla gritted her teeth and headed over to the edge of the dance floor. She almost laughed when she saw the "supplies" the housemaid had left her: a bucket of soapy water and a single cloth. There was no way that she'd be able to do this in an hour. The dance floor was huge, big enough to hold a hundred turning couples, and she'd be scrubbing it on her knees. This wasn't a chore. It was an exercise in public humiliation.

But asking for help would make it so much worse, that much Ayla knew. So she pushed up her sleeves and got to work.

She'd only managed to scrub maybe a six-by-six-foot area when she nearly ran her cloth right over a pair of shoes. Ayla sat back on her heels and looked up to find Nessa standing over her, hands on her hips. Ayla didn't know how she'd approached so quietly, almost like an Automa. She knew Nessa, of course. All of the servants reported to her. But as head servant, Nessa spent most of her time inside the palace, and rarely did Ayla have to actually work beneath her. The woman was tall, commanding, and slightly hunched, encumbered with the months-old child strapped to her chest all day. She was the only servant Ayla knew to have had a child.

Nessa looked deeply unimpressed.

Ayla wiped the sweat off her forehead. "Hello, ma'am."

"You're dragging your own dirty shoes through the clean parts," Nessa said, pointing.

Ayla looked back—and sure enough, there were streaks of dirt on the floor she'd *just* scrubbed. She groaned out loud, tossed the cloth aside, and began to tug off her shoes. "My apologies, ma'am," she mumbled.

Nessa sighed. And then she knelt down to join Ayla on the

floor, pulling her own rag out of the pocket of her uniform and dunking it in the soapy water. Ayla stared at the top of her baby's head, through the sling, hanging dangerously low as Nessa scrubbed.

"What're you looking at, girl," Nessa said, and then followed Ayla's gaze. She snorted. "Gods, it's like you've never seen a baby before. Go on, keep staring, will you? I'm sure you don't have better things to do."

"The guards don't mind?" Ayla asked.

"Lily's quiet. Never makes a fuss."

They worked together in silence for a while, side by side on the floor. Then finally Ayla couldn't help but blurt out, "Is it true that you married Thom?"

Nessa gave her an incredulous look. "Do you go around sticking your nose into everyone's business, or just mine?" At Ayla's silence, she rolled her eyes. "Yes, of course it's true. What a stupid rumor that would be."

"But—why?"

Another look. "The same reason I've got Lily, idiot. Because I love him."

That made even less sense to Ayla. But Nessa went right back to scrubbing, and Ayla knew she'd already pushed too much, so she held her tongue. She spent the rest of the morning like that, scrubbing in silence, until her knees were numb and her arms ached horribly.

Already the sovereign's guests were pouring in; Ayla kept catching glimpses, whenever she stood up to wring out her cloth and was able to peek out the second-story windows overlooking the courtyard. Their throats and wrists and ears were heavy with gold. They were arriving on horseback, in gilded caravans, in horse-drawn carriages. And then she saw it: a black uniform among all the red-uniformed servants. The colors of a Scyre.

Her skin prickled. She didn't like being locked up in this cold palace with so many leeches.

That evening, Ayla was ordered to fetch Crier's ball gown from the seamstress. Feet aching from walking on flagstones all day instead of softer dirt, she dragged herself down to the underground level where the housemaids, laundry maids, and seamstresses did most of their work. All she wanted to do was sleep. For years. Curl up right here on the cold flagstones, hide herself in the shadows, sleep for a decade. It was the kind of tired that left her head all foggy and tipsy and slow. She'd imagined that housework would be easier than field work, but she'd underestimated not just the quantity of work but the sheer exhaustion of being constantly watched and monitored, of controlling her expression and stifling any suggestion of that fatigue—a single yawn could get her kicked out of the palace for good.

That was why, when she stepped into the washing room, she stopped dead in the doorway. She genuinely thought she was dreaming, just for a moment.

Because there was *Faye* bent over one of the massive tubs of steaming, soapy water. Luna's sister. The one everyone in the market had gossiped about. The one who hadn't been seen since

Luna's transgression—whatever it was—and subsequent murder by the leeches.

Faye was gripping a long wooden paddle, stirring the linens and the discarded clothes, her face pink and sweaty from the heat.

The last time she'd seen Faye, it was noon and the sun was beating down on their heads and Faye was on the ground, covered in dust, screaming in the raw and wordless way of tortured animals. Automa soldiers kicked her in the belly and she didn't stop screaming. Sometimes, her lips formed the word *Luna*. But it was so drawn out, so wrecked with terror and anguish, that it didn't sound like her sister's name at all.

A white dress, fluttering in the breeze.

And somehow, she was still alive. She was *here*, in the palace, stirring a tub full of linens. She didn't look injured. No missing limbs, no scars on the side of her face that Ayla could see. The only difference was that the Faye of one month ago had kept her hair long, always twisted into a knot at the back of her head. This Faye's hair was cropped short, cut so messily in places that bits of pale scalp showed through.

But she was alive.

Faye was *alive*.

"Faye," Ayla said helplessly. The second she made noise, Faye startled and dropped the wooden paddle; she whirled around to face Ayla, her eyes huge. The door closed behind Ayla. They were alone together. "Faye, where have you *been*? I thought you were—"

"Do not say my name," said Faye.

"—What?"

"Do not. Say my name." Faye cocked her head to one side, her eyes fixed on Ayla. She hadn't yet blinked. She had an oddly precise way of speaking, her words sharp even though her voice was quiet. "That is not. My name. Anymore. Don't say it. Do not say it. Who are you?"

"What do you mean?" said Ayla. "I'm—I'm Ayla. You know me. Remember? I'm a friend of Rowan's. I didn't know you were alive. I swear, I would've found you. Rowan didn't know either. We thought they'd taken you away."

Faye laughed.

Or shrieked.

"Taken me away," she repeated. "Taken me away. No. No, not quite. Should have, though. Deserved it. Wasn't her. Wasn't her, wasn't her."

Her eyes were the kind of wild Ayla had seen before. Usually, you saw those eyes in graveyards, or at executions, or at the burnings. Ayla felt the first real prickle of unease along her spine. She'd heard of Hesod taking human servants into the palace to pay off debts, even going so far as cutting them off from their families, but hadn't Luna's death been punishment enough?

"What wasn't her?" she asked. "Are you talking about Luna?"

"*Don't say her name,*" Faye hissed. Her teeth were bared.

"What did she do?" Ayla demanded. Something felt so *wrong.* "What wasn't Luna? What did she *do?*"

"The apples," Faye mumbled, clutching at her own hair. "The apples, the apples—"

And she screamed at the top of her lungs, the sound bouncing and echoing around the tiny washing room, and bolted forward quick as an Automa—one second she was halfway across the room, the next she was right in front of Ayla, her chest heaving. Ayla leaped backward, drawing the bag of linens up in front of her like some sort of pathetic shield, but it was too late. "*Don't touch her!*" Faye shrieked. "*Don't touch my sister!*" And she lashed out blindly with one arm, her hand catching Ayla's nose. Ayla staggered back, pain spiking where she'd been struck. When she reached up to touch her face, her fingers came away red and she could feel the hot sticky drip of blood from her nostrils.

"I said don't touch her," Faye rasped, shaking her head, flinging droplets of sweat. "Don't touch her, don't touch her, take me instead, don't touch her don't touch her don't touch her no no *no no no* NO—" Her voice broke and she backed away, first slowly and then nearly tripping over her feet. She hit one of the tubs, boiling water sloshing over the opposite side, a paddle clattering to the floor, and then she howled and ran out of the washing room, into the swallowing dark of the corridor outside. Cool air rushed into the smelly, humid washing room.

Shaking, Ayla tilted her head back to stop the blood flow. Her nose hurt, but not enough to be broken. Just a low twinge pulsing along with the beat of her heart, a sick reminder of Faye's—what? Grief? Madness? Both?

The apples, the apples.

"Here," said someone from behind her, and she jolted—but it was only Nessa standing in the doorway. Her baby was still strapped to her body, and she was holding out a handkerchief, scrutinizing Ayla with her beady eyes. "For the blood," she said. "You're lucky the lady has been far too busy greeting guests today to bother with you."

"I am fortunate," Ayla mumbled, and began to blot clumsily at her nose.

Nessa sniffed. "In the future, stay away from that girl. She's not well and she never will be. Gods only know why she's kept around."

Gods only know, indeed.

Ayla nodded. "Yes'm."

Nessa turned on her heel and headed in the direction Faye had run, and Ayla was alone with her thoughts, the steaming baths, the blood in her mouth. The memory of Faye's mad eyes.

The day had been agonizingly long. All Ayla wanted to do after scrubbing the floors and desperately trying to scrub the image of Faye's terrified face from her thoughts was to fall flat on a bed and never wake up. Her nose ached, and Nessa's kerchief still sat in her pocket, like evidence.

Instead, she had been summoned to Crier's chambers.

"Sing," Crier commanded. They were in one of the smaller rooms off her bedchamber, and Ayla had just dumped a heavy, scalding pot of water into the freestanding bath. Her arms ached as she watched the water slosh along the slick white porcelain.

"My lady?" said Ayla.

"Malwin sang to me often," said Crier, beginning to undo

the buttons along her sleeve. "It was pleasing. I want you to sing for me as well."

"I—I'm very unpracticed, my lady," Ayla tried. It was true. She hadn't sung in years, not outside her own head. The act of singing was so mired in memory: her mother's voice singing lullabies and sea shanties, her father joining in, a duet like a nightingale accompanied by the deep, low rush of the ocean itself. Little Ayla and Storme laughing, singing along, dancing clumsily in front of the hearth fire. No. Ayla did not want to sing.

But she remembered a time in the market when visiting Automa officials were touring the town. Hesod had approached a man and a woman and told them to dance. The woman, so filled with fear, had burst into tears. But they'd complied. Because to refuse would mean a swift punishment. And so the man had swung his sobbing partner in circles, their movement unnatural and jerky, like dolls being whipped around by a cruel child. Ayla stared at Crier now; it seemed the daughter was just like the father.

"Then consider this your practice," Crier said.

So, Ayla sang.

She sang an old folk song as she poured rose-scented oil into Crier's bath, averting her gaze while her mistress undressed and sank into it, lathering soap along her legs. She sang as she brushed and oiled Crier's dark hair afterward, felt its surprising softness, noticing, too, the smooth perfection of her Made skin, the way the collarbones formed an open V below her delicate chin.

The base of her skull. The soft skin between each rib. The curve of her throat.

If she had a knife right now, she could have killed Crier ten times over.

But she couldn't do that. Not today. Not yet.

Her unused voice was weak and breathy and kept cracking in odd places, although the more she sang the stronger it got, as if the songs themselves had woken from a long sleep. At first, she'd planned to sing only one song, but she found herself unable to stop. It kept her calm, even as her imagination slipped beneath the door and swirled silently through the halls of the palace like smoke, mapping out a plan. While Crier was otherwise occupied with tonight's party, Ayla would finally have a chance to begin her mission.

After the bath and the hair, she pulled down the new dress from where she'd hung it. It was the most ridiculously complicated poof of a ball gown she'd ever seen. It was pale silver, with an embroidered train and a skirt like a wide bell, and the bodice had to be laced up in back, closed around Crier's body like a hunter's trap. The only upside, Ayla thought as she tied what must've been the thousandth pair of tiny laces, was that Crier looked about as miserable as Ayla felt. She was almost fidgety, eyes darting around her bedchamber, fingers twitching.

Her gaze kept catching on Ayla's throat. The spot where her necklace lay beneath the collar of her handmaiden's uniform. Once again, Ayla wanted to snap at her: *I know you saw it.* Wanted to say she couldn't be toyed with. That it didn't matter if Crier punished her now or dragged it on for weeks. It would all end the same way.

Ayla tugged at the laces harder than was necessary.

Two servants had carried in a big mirror for the purpose of preparing Crier for the ball. Crier was standing right in front of it, Ayla behind her, and when Ayla looked up, her eyes met Crier's in the reflection.

She paused with the laces. Braced herself for an order.

"Why do humans still marry?" asked Crier.

"What?" Surely she'd misheard.

"In the past," Crier said haltingly, like she was still working it through in her head. "I know your marriage customs were similar to ours. Largely for political or strategic gain, especially among the more influential bloodlines."

"Yes," said Ayla, and refrained from adding, *Your customs are similar because your entire culture was stolen from ours. Because you have no history or culture of your own.*

"But last spring, a serving boy married one of my father's stableboys. And the year before, I know Nessa courted Thom from the orchards. None of them hold any significant status. So—"

"How do you know about that?" Ayla demanded, letting her hands fall away from the laces. She stared at Crier's reflection, unable to keep the surprise off her own face. Ayla and Nessa weren't friends, by any means, but Ayla felt protective of any of the servants' secrets. Marriage among servants wasn't illegal, but you never knew when the laws might change, or what ways the

Automae would think of next to punish their own staff, to send ripples of fear among the humans.

Crier cocked her head. "The boys married at midnight on the bluffs. There was a partial eclipse that night and I wished to observe it from higher ground. I overheard them. Kinok informed me about Nessa and Thom."

Ayla's stomach dropped.

How in all the hells did Kinok find out? Why would he even care? Why would he tell Crier?

"So, if there is nothing to gain—no political influence, strategic advantage, or division of property—then why do humans marry?" Crier was peering at Ayla in the mirror, her eyes wide and curious, her body unnaturally still. She'd done this a few times, Ayla had noticed—so focused on one particular thing that she apparently forgot to play up the tiny movements that made her look more human: breathing, blinking, shifting, fiddling with something. Facial expressions, sometimes. Instead, she would just stand there, tall and frozen, a creature carved from stone.

"I don't know if I'm the person to ask about that," said Ayla.

"But you are my handmaiden," said Crier with a slight air of triumph, "and you are supposed to attend to my needs. What I need is an answer."

Ayla kept her eyes firmly on the laces beneath her hands, refused to meet Crier's gaze in the mirror. It was getting darker outside the windows, the sky purple with dusk. They didn't have much time before Crier was supposed to make her entrance at the party, and Ayla itched for the brief freedom she knew tonight would bring.

"Supposedly, we marry for love," Ayla said at last. The word was a bitter seed on her tongue. She'd never been in love before. Not like that. But she'd felt love—for her family.

Crier frowned. "That seems . . . ill-advised."

"Agreed."

Crier's voice was softer now, barely audible. "That seems like it could end in a great deal of suffering."

What would you know about suffering?

Ayla tugged at the second to last pair of laces, at the very top of Crier's spine. "Almost done." She was in a hurry now, the eagerness leaping up inside her like a flame.

Tonight, when the entire palace—Automae and servants alike—was preoccupied with the engagement ball, Ayla would be slipping down below the grand ballroom to the lower levels, where she'd learned that Kinok's quarters were. She would be sifting through his possessions, his correspondence, anything she could find. Rowan had been clear. Look for a map or a ledger of heartstone trade. Maybe a diagram of the Heart itself, if such a thing existed. She could only read a handful of words, but Benjy had once showed her the names of council members, written them out for her in the dirt and then swept them away with one hand. She'd forgotten most of them, but she could still picture some of them, the specific shapes of each letter. She knew *Ellios, Burn, Markus. Kita. Thaddian.* She knew *Automa*; she knew *human*; she knew *rebel*. She knew *heart*.

She might not get it all tonight, but eventually, she would find something. She'd learn Kinok's secrets. She'd find out what he knew of the Iron Heart, how to infiltrate and destroy it. She'd find the information that would change everything, information that could destroy the Automae in one fell swoop. That could end their reign forever. Freedom for all of humanity.

It was almost too big. Too much to conceptualize. So much bigger than the one fatal strike that mattered the most to her: Crier, dead in her arms.

But for that, Ayla would have to wait. She'd already waited so long; she could wait longer still. She could wait as long as it took.

First, she'd do what she promised Benjy and Rowan—she'd help the cause. She'd find a route to the Iron Heart, if such a thing existed. Then, and only then, would she give herself the one thing she wanted most—personal revenge.

She brushed some of Crier's hair out of the way, more than ready to get this whole thing over with, and that was when she saw the tattoo.

It was tiny. Plain. Ten numbers etched into Crier's skin with blue-black ink, each one smaller than a fingernail. Ayla had heard of these tattoos before, but she'd never gotten close enough to an Automa to actually see one.

This was Crier's model number. The first six numbers identified her as Crier of Family Hesod. The second four indicated the year of her creation. It was one more reminder that the creature before Ayla, the creature laced into this rich, beautiful dress, the creature who prowled the bluffs at night—this creature was not human.

Unthinking, Ayla brushed her thumb across the number. A soft, barely-there touch; the second she realized what she was doing, she drew back and tried to play it off as pure accident. She didn't look in the mirror, didn't dare check whether or not Crier had noticed.

Crier's skin was warmer than Ayla might have thought.

It was Crier who broke the silence between them. "Have you experienced love?"

"Yes." Ayla bit her tongue.

"What does it feel like?"

Ayla thought not of love but of her necklace. The single shining piece of proof that once, a very long time ago, she had not been so alone.

"I don't remember," she answered at last. She finished the last lace and took a big step back, away from the mirror, still avoiding Crier's eyes.

Crier wasn't giving up. "Is there a physical sensation? Is it pleasant or painful?"

"Depends."

"So you do remember."

Just let me go. "Sometimes I feel better when I think of a certain song," said Ayla. "That's as much as I can tell you."

"A certain song. Have I heard it?"

"No."

"You did not sing it to me?"

"No, my lady."

"Why not?"

Ayla sighed. "Well, it is . . . private." It was a word servants rarely said. Nothing about their lives was supposed to be private.

Crier made a small, considering noise. "Then—you love that song? You love music?"

"Sure."

Crier turned to face Ayla. Somehow, she was more intimidating in the ball gown than in her plain clothes. Taller, fiercer, the corded muscles in her arms on full display. It didn't help that she was wearing makeup—kohl around her eyes, a dark stain on her mouth. She looked like a monster from the old stories. A bloodsucker, a witch, beautiful and deadly.

"Here," Crier said, and crossed to her bedside table. Opened one of the drawers. Took something out. Tossed it to Ayla without warning.

Ayla startled and just barely managed to catch the thing before it hit her in the face. When she looked down at her hands, she saw she was now holding a single metal key.

"There is a music room in the west wing," said Crier. "I go there sometimes. To practice."

Ayla stared at her.

Then stared at the large key in her hands.

A gift.

She could hardly comprehend such a thing. It seemed impossible that Crier would trust her this soon, this readily.

Unless . . . unless she had already *wanted* to trust her. Unless that had been part of the reason she'd sought her out in the first place.

The thought wiggled something loose in Ayla, and she wasn't sure how to feel about it. *Trust*. Trust meant closeness.

Trust meant Ayla could more easily get answers.

The key was cold but weighty in her hand.

"The walls are thick, so no sound escapes. No one will interrupt you. Now," Crier said, apparently satisfied with the shock that must have been written on Ayla's face, "you may escort me to the ballroom."

7

Tonight, Crier was going to do everything right.

Tonight, her secret would remain safe. She might be Flawed on the inside, with the pillar of Passion wreaking havoc on her from within, but no one had to know.

Several hundred guests had arrived for the ball—Crier knew, as she had penned many of the invitations herself, had studied long lists of names and connections. They had all gathered to celebrate her engagement to Kinok, pooling from the edges of the dance floor toward the dais at its head, drinking liquid heart-stone and pale wine and murmuring in anticipation. Though she couldn't see them all from her hiding place behind the dais, she could hear guests trickle in through the entrances at either end of the room, until Crier began to feel that the crowd was almost choking her.

There were men in dark, brocaded waistcoats. Women in dresses of every color and style, their hair loose and tumbling or braided in tight crowns or hidden beneath colorful silks; some were in sharp military uniforms, crests or badges at their throats. Crier wondered if they had ever actually seen battle. Surely most of them were part of the latest generation of Automae, those who'd been created long after the War of Kinds.

The grand ballroom had always been beautiful, but tonight it was a vision, everything glittering and exquisite. The floor, polished smooth and shining like ice, had been cleared to make room for dancing. The walls were hung with huge floor-to-ceiling tapestries Crier had never seen before, all depicting scenes of celebration and unification: the crowning of some ancient king; a royal wedding featuring a dress made entirely of white pearls; a battlefield scene in which uniformed Automae stood over the fallen bodies of countless humans—and the bodies of the rare human sympathizers, the traitors. All of those Automae, Crier knew, had been rooted out, considered Flawed. Burned.

At the head of it all stood Crier, taking measured breaths four times per minute. The ceremonial dais before her was carved to look like a mass of tangled human bodies, Automae standing triumphant above them. Even painted with gold leaf and almost glowing beneath the warm light of two dozen crystal chandeliers and their four hundred candles, it was gruesome. Crier kept staring at it, picking out a new detail each time: the unnatural bend of a leg, a face with bulging eyes, a golden mouth twisted into a silent, unending howl.

The dais was *meant* to catch the eye. No matter where you stood, you could not forget why you were here tonight.

To make the engagement between Crier and Kinok official.

Crier wanted nothing more than to look away, but the only other option would be to turn toward Kinok, who stood rock-still beside her. He was absolutely calm, but in a way that made Crier think of tide pools: motionless on the surface, things dark and spiny hidden below.

Outside the ballroom, the moon would be reaching its peak. It was almost time.

Her father ascended the dais. He looked proud and powerful standing alone up there. Like the figurehead of a ship, facing off against an ocean of Automae.

"Organization, System, Family," said Hesod, his voice booming and echoing around the room. Instantly, the low rumble of a thousand conversations gave way to a hushed silence. The few guests Crier could see all turned to look at Hesod in unison, a ripple of simultaneous movement. "The beauty and symmetry of such values should not merely be wasted on human life," he continued, quoting from his own manifesto, "but studied and applied for the benefit of all Automakind. Organization, System, Family. Tonight we honor those values. Tonight we honor two lives that will soon be inextricably bound, but we also honor that which a binding symbolizes: The perpetuation of our culture. The unification of our people. The continued success of a civilization built on tradition. A civilization that because of tradition has grown more powerful and magnificent than every civilization that rose and fell before us."

Carved into the back of the dais, right in front of Crier's face, was the body of a naked human woman. Her limbs were long and broken, intertwined with the bodies around her; her hair was a cloud of gold around her golden head. Like all the other bodies on the dais, her face was turned upward as if she, too, was watching Hesod speak. But unlike Crier and Kinok, unlike all the Automa guests, her face was twisted into an expression of pure anguish. A wide and wrenching mouth, eyes that were huge and grotesque and almost frog-like. One of her hands was visible, the fingers stiff and pointed like the claws of a vulture. Other bodies were grabbing on to her—hands on her hips, her thighs, her ankles—as if trying desperately to climb up and over her, using her body as a ladder. A means of escape.

"Unity—of politics, of thought, of family—is written into our Design," Hesod was saying. "Tonight, Lady Crier of Rabu and Scyre Kinok of the Western Mountains will pledge themselves to each other and, above all else, to the core tenets of our glorious society. My daughter. Honorable Scyre. The time has come to ascend."

For a second, Crier did not move. Then Kinok brushed past her on his way to climb the dais, and she shook the ice off her limbs and followed him.

The steps built into the side of the dais were shaped like cupped human hands. Crier climbed up slowly, placing her feet carefully into their golden palms.

After that, time slid into itself. The ceremony came to Crier in fragments: her father's voice booming through the grand hall as he recited old, half-human words; Kinok's eyes fixed on the side of Crier's face; the crowd, motionless as a sea of statues, staring up at Crier with a thousand empty eyes. Was that her own heart in her ears? She could hear the pounding, the tiny clicks of her workings. Was it going too fast?

Was she breathing?

She kept forgetting to breathe.

Four breaths per minute.

She didn't surface until it was time, *it was time.* Kinok raised the ceremonial knife. Its blade caught the light of all four hundred candles, and Crier thought hazily of stars, or fireflies.

Then Kinok said, "We shall be bound, body to body, blood to blood," and she rested her forearm on the edge of the dais, and he slid the blade almost gently across her skin from elbow to wrist.

Blood welled up immediately, a deep violet. Hesod's grip tightened on Crier's shoulders—reassurance? pride?—as they watched the blood spill down her arm, down her fingers. It dripped from her fingertips and spattered the golden floor of the dais, ran in tiny rivulets down the outer wall, down the faces and bodies of the naked golden humans, not a single drop landing on Crier's dress. Kinok set the knife aside. With long, steady fingers, he untied the armband that Crier had worn for the past few months. He set it beside the knife, a coil of red, a snake.

As with all things, the wound came first and then the pain. Crier's arm ached terribly, even though she knew logically that the long, neat slice in her skin (the cut of a surgeon, she thought distantly) had already begun to heal. It took everything in her to stand still and keep her expression blank and let herself bleed. She was given only a few moments to gather herself before it was her turn to wield the knife. The cut she made on Kinok's forearm was not nearly so neat as his—a little shaky, a little too deep or too shallow in some places—but of course his blood spilled all the same. She untied his armband. Cast it aside. And under Hesod's guidance, they pressed their forearms together, violet blood smearing between them, snaking down to drip from their elbows. A single drop landed on Crier's skirt.

"We shall be bound," Crier said. Her voice was quiet but clear, like a bell chime ringing through the ballroom. "Body to body. Blood to blood."

"We shall be bound," Kinok murmured, meeting her eyes. They held their pose—facing each other, wounds pressed together—for another moment.

Then Hesod said, "It is done," and the crowd, which had been silent, repeated in unison, "It is done." A single voice with a thousand layers.

Crier dropped her gaze from Kinok's face as soon as she could. She looked down at the tiny dark stain on her skirt, the drop of fallen blood.

It was done.

After the ceremony ended, Crier was free to mingle with the guests, however little she actually wanted to do so. Kinok helped her down from the dais, his hand cool in hers, and together they stepped into the waiting crowd. The musicians had stopped playing during the ceremony, and now they started up again with a series of waltzes, music that was soft and tumbling beneath the hum of conversation. Crier soon lost her father to a member of the council and Kinok to a woman who was apparently also a Scyre, but she preferred it that way. She was not much in the mood for pleasantries. Her arm had been bandaged, but it still hurt, and the sick feeling in her stomach had returned. Had never left, maybe.

As she sought a quiet spot near one of the tapestries, Crier found herself sneaking glances at the only other humans in the ballroom who weren't servants—the musicians, set up in a far corner. They were a quartet, lute and harp and pipes and a slow, rhythmic drumbeat. They kept their heads down, backs bowed over their instruments. There was no conductor, and yet each piece flowed seamlessly into the next, syrupy Tarreenian ballads becoming Varnian dancing songs becoming quick, light melodies that reminded Crier of sunlight scattered on the ocean, sparkling on the waves. With each new song, Crier thought: Would Ayla like this?

The crowd parted as she headed for the edge of the ballroom, seeking space, or air, or silence, all things she craved but would not find here. She was stopped every few moments by a guest offering well wishes or news or introductions or a glass of that pale wine.

The first time she saw someone wearing a black armband, so similar to the red one Kinok had just removed from her upper arm, she took little notice of it.

The second time, she thought it was an odd coincidence.

The third time, she wondered if perhaps this was a new trend.

The fourth time, she asked. She had finally spotted someone she actually knew: a girl named Rosi, who was the daughter of a merchant important enough to visit the sovereign's home a few times a year but not important enough to wield any significant influence over the council. Rosi was wearing a dress of deep-blue silk, her hair twisted into a shining knot atop her head. She had tiny freckles painted all over her nose, rouge on her cheeks. A band of black fabric was wrapped around her left arm.

"Lady Crier!" Rosi called out, and extricated herself from a conversation with another girl to glide over, moving with the kind of effortless grace that all Automae were supposed to emulate. She had always been like that. "Lady Crier, it's been too long."

"A year at least," Crier said. "I hoped you would come tonight." And she meant it. Crier sensed that Rosi was most interested in her for the opportunity of social advancement she promised, perhaps believing that Crier, as the sovereign's daughter, could help elevate her own standing. But even still, Crier appreciated having someone to write to regularly, someone to make her life less narrow and confined.

They had written each other a handful of letters over the last few years, and were as close as two Automae might get to being considered what humans called "friends." Their Kind didn't really experience friendship in the way humans did, as it was not particularly inherent or cultivated—it was not part of Traditionalism and thus not reinforced, the way family and some of the arts were encouraged under Hesod's rule.

Which was perhaps why Rosi looked so surprised—and relieved.

"Really? I am honored, my lady."

"That black band on your arm, though. I am curious that you never spoke of it in our correspondence. Is this some type of fashion?"

Rosi laughed, and then seemed to realize that Crier was serious. "Oh! No, my lady," she said, giving Crier a confused little smile. "Do you really not know? It is your fiancé's symbol, after all."

"His symbol?"

"Yes." Rosi finished her glass of wine in one swallow and passed the empty glass off to a human servant, switching it for a full one. It took perhaps a barrel of wine to have any effect on an Automa's faculties; she seemed determined to reach that point. "We use it to identify fellow members of the Movement."

The Anti-Reliance Movement.

Crier frowned, scanning the crowded ballroom. Now that she was looking for it, she realized that practically one in every ten guests was wearing the black band. Did Kinok really have so many dedicated followers? And they were bold enough, it seemed, to declare their alliance so openly, right under Hesod's nose.

"Right," she said. "Of course. And you—you're a member of the Movement?"

"Oh, yes. I learned about it from my own fiancé, actually. He's around here somewhere—Foer, son of Councilmember

Addock. Have you met?"

"Yes, I've met Foer." From what Crier could remember, he was a quiet, unassuming boy, softer than his father had intended. "Congratulations on your binding."

"Thank you, lady," said Rosi. Then she glanced around, as if making sure there were no eyes on their conversation, and leaned in closer. "Truth be told, it would never have happened if not for Scyre Kinok."

"What do you mean?"

"Councilmember Addock's estate was one of those targeted in the Southern Uprisings. If Scyre Kinok had not been there to warn him, to help him fend off the attacks, the humans might have overrun his estate. Councilmember Addock, his husband, my Foer—they all might have been killed."

"I see," Crier murmured.

"Oh, look!" said Rosi, loud again. "They've begun dancing. Your first dance will be soon, my lady." She laughed, light and pretty. "Such an old-fashioned custom, is it not? I prefer not to dance myself. It always looks so clumsy."

"I like it," said Crier, ever the good daughter.

Then she turned—just in time to nearly collide with the very person she was looking for. Kinok stood before her, calm as ever, his red waistcoat the color of human blood.

"My lady," he said. "Will you join me for our first dance?"

All the guests around them were looking at her now; the dance floor was emptying out. A space cleared just for Crier and her fiancé. Her bound life. Body to body, blood to blood.

"Yes, Scyre," she said, and let him pull her into the middle of the ballroom.

Everyone was watching, including her father. On the surface, it looked like he was continuing his conversation with an envoy from the Far North, smiling jovially, charming her, charming everyone, but his eyes were on Crier. Which reminded her: in all the chaos of the planning and the ceremony, she had nearly forgotten that in just three days, she was to attend her very first council meeting. It was something to look forward to, at least.

Smiling, Kinok drew her close. One of his hands rested on the small of her back, the other entwined with her own hand. Their fingers slotted together like stitches on an open wound. Crier put her free hand on Kinok's shoulder, keeping her touch as light as possible, unwilling, still, to press into him.

A strain of harp strings.

A low, deep drumbeat.

Alone in the center of the ballroom, countless pairs of eyes tracking their every move, Crier and Kinok began to dance.

It was a waltz. Yet another human tradition, one her father was particularly enamored with: he often brought human dancers into the palace and bid them to perform for him, slow waltzes and fast, wild numbers that looked more like fighting than dancing, and he watched it all with dark, fascinated eyes. "Look," he would say to Crier, ordering the dancers to repeat a certain movement or sequence of steps. "Look at the fluidity, the grace in each transition. They make it seem effortless. But see for yourself: their muscles are trembling. It is not effortless at all."

Once, he had said: "If there exists a type of human capable of dismantling our world, it is the dancer."

Crier thought of this as she turned around the floor with Kinok. Thought, too, of her new handmaiden. Did Ayla know how to waltz? Probably not. And even if she did, she'd certainly never dance with Crier, never place her hand at Crier's waist and steer her through a ballroom the way Kinok was doing, spinning with the music, their bodies close together and yet separated by two inches of tense space. Close enough to feel the rhythm of her human breath.

No. Ayla would never dance with her.

And yet: Crier recalled the look of surprise on Ayla's face when she'd given her the key to the music room this evening. For some reason, that surprise had pleased her.

"You must be in good spirits," Kinok said, and Crier realized she had been smiling to herself. "Tonight has gone well."

"I think my father will be satisfied," she agreed carefully.

"And what about *you*? How do you feel?"

"I . . ." She glanced up to find him gazing down at her, eyes intent. "I feel that our union is good for the future of our country."

"That's not what I asked."

"I don't understand. Why would it matter what I feel?" She pushed into the next step of the waltz perhaps a bit too quickly.

Kinok matched her steps easily. "Lady Crier, there is no need to keep secrets from me."

"Secrets?" She glanced up at him and was met with his

steady gaze, brown and piercing. It was intimidating, but her curiosity won out. He seemed to know so much about her—she wanted to balance the scales. "It seems you are the one with secrets, Kinok."

A smile revealed his perfect teeth. "Whatever do you mean?"

"You've been a guest in our home for nearly a year, coming and going as you please, involved in your private studies and building up your Movement. You seem to take an interest in my political views and essays, but what do you share of *your* work?"

The smile remained. "I'm happy to tell you anything you'd like to know."

"What do you spend so many hours researching, then?"

"History. Connections. The work of Thomas Wren."

"The first Maker?"

"Creator of our Kind," Kinok said with a nod.

"A human genius," Crier added.

He twirled her around. "As a Scyre, I studied the Makers who were part of the Barren Queen's academy. Thomas Wren gets a lot of credit—but I've found that tends to diminish the true richness of the history."

"The richness of *our* history."

"Indeed." He stared at her for a moment. "It's beautiful, really. There is quite a bit of complexity in how we are Made. Each one of us is a little different. Though of course, there are limits to *how* different."

Despite herself, Crier was intrigued. Not only did Kinok seem to know something she didn't about Thomas Wren, but it was surprising that he was so fascinated with the subject to begin with.

"Lady Crier," he said quietly, interrupting her thoughts. "I know your secret."

It took everything inside her to keep dancing, to keep her face pleasantly impassive even as her blood turned to ice. "I'm not sure what you're talking about, Scyre."

"I saw your Design."

Her stomach lurched and her mind raced. He had looked? He knew? "I don't—"

"Please don't misunderstand. I mean you no harm, my lady." He bent his head, whispering in her ear. To the onlookers, it would appear intimate. It *was* intimate, she realized. "I won't tell anyone that you are . . . Flawed." The word whispered across his tongue and yet it stung like a snake's bite. "Your secret is safe with me. We are bound, aren't we?"

He was offering her comfort, solidarity. And yet . . .

"We are," Crier breathed. Her heart was pounding so rapidly that she half expected her chime to go off. "We—we are bound."

"So, I will help you. And I'm sure you will do the same for me."

"Help me? How?"

His fingers flexed on her waist. "The sovereign has been unable to find any information on the Midwife Torras. Anyone who has done this to you, and perhaps others as well, deserves to be punished." He did not elaborate, which was probably for the better. If Kinok thought he could unearth information beyond the sovereign's reach, he had to be operating outside the law. Usually, Crier would discourage him. But if there was anything about Torras that could help Crier, protect her reputation, protect her father . . . she had to use it.

"Do it," she said shakily. "Find her. Do whatever you must. Just—don't tell anyone."

"Of course," he said. "We are bound. It's you and me, Lady Crier."

There was one last pluck of the harp, a high, thin note wavering in the air, and the waltz came to a close.

They let go of each other and stepped back. Crier's hands fell to her sides, empty.

"You and me," she said.

The Maker Thomas Wren built a child that fit the queen's requirements: ten times stronger than the strongest human ever recorded. Ten times faster on foot. This child required no food, no sleep; it could hear whispered conversation from a distance of one thousand paces and see in the dark like a cat; its mind worked through even the most advanced mathematical and metaphysical equations at fifty times the speed of human experts; it never tired, never weakened, never succumbed to illness.

Wren named the child Kiera and delivered her to the capital. Queen Thea was so overcome with joy that she adopted Kiera as her daughter and heir before the sun set that same day. She gave Wren his promised gold and a seat at the right hand of the throne, and for the next seven days the queen sent caravans of bread and honey to the farthest reaches of Zulla, celebrating her newbuilt daughter.

Kiera.

Wren's greatest creation had only one flaw: because she was not alchemical magick, not automaton, not flesh and bone, but a combination of all three, she was not perfectly self-sustaining. There is a law in this universe. One cannot create something from nothing. Because she was created for and bound to the queen, Kiera required the queen's blood to survive.

—FROM *THE BEGINNING OF THE AUTOMA ERA*,
BY EOK OF FAMILY MEADOR, 2234610907, YEAR 4 AE

8

Far above her head, even through thick layers of stone, Ayla could hear the noise emanating from the grand ballroom: music, echoing conversation, the rumble of several hundred voices all talking at once. Up there it would be bright and loud and warm. Down here, in the underground corridors below the ballroom, it was dark, silent, freezing cold. The wall sconces, delicate baubles of blue glass with candles flickering within, gave off the very strange effect of being underwater.

Ayla moved quickly through the darkness, ears straining for any sounds of footsteps or voices as she made her way through the hallway. This was her chance to explore and see if she could find any information on Kinok. She'd encountered two guards on routine patrol, but all she had to do was murmur "Errand for the lady" and they let her pass. Lady Crier's name was like a secret password. A skeleton key.

The engagement ceremony had already ended, making it

easy for Ayla to slip away, but she had no idea how long Kinok would linger at his own party. All she could do was hope that he planned to stay in the ballroom all night, greeting his admirers. Whenever she passed a door, she tried the handle. All of them swung open immediately, offering views of nothing more than dark washing rooms or larders or once a wine cellar, until she began to doubt herself. Perhaps she'd seen wrong. What could Kinok possibly be doing housed down here? But then, finally: one of the doors didn't open.

She dropped to her knees, squinting into the tiny gap between the door and the doorjamb. The lock wouldn't be too much trouble. Her brother had taught her how to deal with locks. She reached into the pocket of her uniform, retrieved the hairpin she had stolen from Crier's room earlier, and inserted it carefully into the keyhole. There was no real finesse to lockpicking, not for her. Her brother, Storme, though—he had been the real expert. He'd been able to pick the lock on their family's cottage in ten seconds flat. Ayla's style was more of the "jimmy the doorknob and rattle things around for a while and see what happens" variety. She bit her lip, poking the hairpin around inside the keyhole, and—*click*.

Then she took out a handkerchief—the one Nessa had lent her earlier, to clean her bloodied nose—and used it to prevent any trace of fingerprints or skin oil when she turned the doorknob, pushing the door open gently. She was still kneeling, and that was the only reason she saw it.

A hair, silently drifting to the flagstones from the door's latch.

Her body went cold. It wasn't an ordinary booby trap, the kind she and Storme used to prank each other with—a pitcher of water above the front door, a string that, when inevitably tripped over, would cause the teakettle to clatter to the floor. Those traps were obvious, used to scare an intruder away. To signal a warning.

This trap was different. Only the person who had placed the trap would know that it had been disturbed, that someone had been in the room. Kinok didn't want to scare his intruders. He just wanted to know if they existed. Somehow, it felt so much more sinister. Ayla shuddered and picked up the hair, placing it carefully into her pocket so she could replace it when she left, the same way Kinok must have done. Then she slipped inside.

The bedchamber itself was almost the exact twin to Crier's. There was a bed just like hers, big and four-postered with a linen canopy. A mirror, a bathtub, a large wooden chest in one corner. Kinok did not keep a fire going in the hearth, though, so the room was so cold that Ayla was shivering in her thin handmaiden's uniform. And there was only one tapestry.

She searched methodically, starting in one corner and going from there, looking for any maps, drawings, symbols, or books that might contain information about the Iron Heart. *Think like him*, she told herself, wrapping the handkerchief around her hand again, fingers skimming the lid of the wooden chest. *Think like an Automa.*

Nothing in the chest but clothing and loose coins. Nothing in or around the bathtub, the mirror, the half-empty bookshelf, the hearth. . . . Ayla checked every surface, every nook, every shadow. The bedding, the bathing screen, the curtains; she even crawled beneath the bed to see if there was anything tucked up in the bed frame . . . *nothing*.

Disappointed, and growing more nervous as the minutes ticked by, Ayla finally turned to the tapestry. It was beautiful, a woven scene of musicians playing to a little girl with golden eyes. Ayla felt around the edges of the tapestry, lifted it up off the wall to check the back—but when she lifted it, she didn't see the expected stone wall. She saw paper.

Heart in her throat, she grabbed the tapestry with both hands and held it above her head, trying to see the entirety of what had been hiding beneath it.

At first Ayla thought it was a map. But then she realized that no, it was too sparse—there was no land, no blue ocean. A star chart? She squinted through the darkness, trying to make out the design.

And her breath caught.

Kinok wasn't charting stars.

He was charting *people*.

There, sketched out in perfect detail, were human faces. Hundreds of them, each rendered in black ink, no bigger than a copper statescoin. It took only a moment for Ayla to see a face she recognized: Nessa. And there, a hand's length away: Thom, Nessa's husband, who tended the orchards. There was Laurel, Gedda, Rie, from the kitchens. The drawing of Rie even had the deep, pockmarked scar where her left eye used to be.

There was Yoon from the kitchens, Idric, Una, Jack. Each drawing was connected to the other drawings by different colored threads: red, blue, gold. From a few paces away, it really had looked like a star chart, a night sky full of constellations.

Nessa and Thom, the not-so-secret lovers, were connected by a red line. Gedda and his closest friend, another stableboy named Ket, were connected in blue. Laurel and her little sister, Edy, in gold. The threads stretched out across the chart, dozens and dozens of them, overlapping, creating a vast, complex web of—relationships.

With a growing sense of cold, sick horror, Ayla searched the chart for one specific face.

Benjy.

There were blue lines connecting Benjy to a couple other servants. No gold lines—no family.

A single bright, bloodred line. It ran like a vein across the chart.

The face at the other end of it was Ayla. She stared at the tiny depiction of herself: at her round face, her ink-black hair. The red thread pinned at her throat.

Ridiculously, her first reaction was hot embarrassment. Kinok thought she and Benjy were lovers? Why? They'd never been anything but friends, they'd never gone further, they wouldn't. Couldn't. (There was that one time, when Benjy pressed their foreheads together, and for a moment, Ayla had thought—*no*.) For years Ayla had tried her damnedest to keep Benjy at arm's length. She knew that even friendship made you weak, made hard decisions only harder to make, in a world where you had to look out for yourself first.

As for love? It was worse than a weakness.

Love broke you. After all, it was love, wasn't it, that had made Ayla weep for weeks after the death of her family, had made her curl up, unable to move. Love was what made you invite death, wish for it, crave it, just so that you could be freed from your own pain.

Once Rowan had gotten Ayla back on her feet and given her a new start, Ayla had vowed to herself that she would never let love break her again.

Ayla shuddered now and leaned in closer, her nose nearly brushing the chart. She couldn't help but notice that her face was the only one on the chart that had just the one thread connected to it. The rest of the ink faces had threads of all colors branching out from them—friends, siblings, lovers.

Slowly, as if in a trance, Ayla kept searching for familiar faces. There were so many she half recognized, people she'd glimpsed in Kalla-den, villagers and merchants. Was Rowan on this chart? Was Faye?

Was Luna?

What color did you get when you were connected to a corpse?

Ayla stood on her tiptoes, searching. There. Faye, with her wild eyes. There was a black thread connected to her. Ayla followed it—but the face on the other end of Faye's thread had been scratched out. Her black thread led to nothing.

That must have been Luna.

Ayla stared at the scratch mark that had once been Luna's face, willing the truth to not be the truth, but it was too late; she had already figured it out; she knew why the thread was black; it was horrible and sickening and the only explanation that made any sense.

Why did Kinok keep this chart? What good did it do him to know all of these connections?

Unless . . . unless he was using human relationships against them in some way, to keep them in order, to keep them in line.

The thought hit her like a roll of thunder. The answer to the mystery of Luna's death.

It hadn't been a punishment for something Luna did. *Wasn't her, wasn't her*, Faye had said.

Because Luna hadn't done *anything* wrong.

Luna's death had been a punishment for something *Faye* did.

That was what this chart was for. To find human weaknesses—and exploit them.

It was beyond cruel, beyond sick.

It was the work of a master manipulator.

Gods, no wonder Faye had gone mad. *Take me instead*, she'd screamed. *Kill me instead.*

A creak in the hallway outside Kinok's door wrenched Ayla back to the present. She dropped the tapestry and leaped away from the chart, pressing herself up against the wall. Luckily, nobody came inside. The footsteps passed, heading down the corridor outside. She wasn't safe here. Breathless, ears ringing, she slipped out of Kinok's bedchamber. Replaced the hair in the latch. Closed the heavy wooden door behind her. Then she practically ran down the corridor, away from the freezing room and the dead hearth and the chart of faces, weblike and fragile.

She turned a corner and headed down a narrow hallway, running blindly for the staircase that would take her up into the light and the warmth, her breath coming in harsh gasps.

Ayla tried to keep track of her turns as she hurried down the halls—*left, left, right*—but all she could hold in her head were the drawings, Benjy's tiny ink freckles, her own inky hair, and she lost track—*left and then right—no, right and then right.* She was hopelessly disoriented.

Then she came up short beside a door with a golden knocker shaped like a harp.

The music room.

She reached into her pocket and gripped the cool metal key Crier had given her. Panting, Ayla nearly dropped it twice before she finally got it into the lock. But it turned, and the door opened, and here: the music room.

Her momentary gasp of relief fled into another feeling altogether—wonder. *Fear.* Crier hadn't exaggerated the thick walls. As she shut the door behind her, the room's silence enveloped her like a living creature, or like velvet pressed over her mouth. The inside of the music room was beautiful—spacious, with a high vaulted ceiling. Ayla could make out the big dark shapes of what must have been two dozen musical instruments, even more, hanging on the walls. But stars and skies, the *silence*. It felt somehow familiar, tomb-like. It took her a moment to figure out what this place reminded her of.

Another place, dark and empty. Another place she'd been entirely alone, with nothing but the wind inside her head.

The outhouse where she had hidden during the raid. When *they* had stormed in, and taken everything.

Ayla sank down onto a leather bench and tucked her knees up beneath her forehead. She hadn't realized until now that her whole body was shaking, but in the stillness of this room, she couldn't stop it. She felt even something essential to the core of her—her revenge—beginning to tremble. It had always been like a hotly burning fire, but now it leaped and fell, leaped and fell, as though its flames had met with a light rain.

It took her a while to realize what this feeling was: uncertainty.

Just before dawn, Benjy shook Ayla awake with a violence that almost, *almost*, brought her back to *that day*.

When she opened her eyes, he was hovering over her in the dark. His face was bloodless, his mouth pressed into a white line. He was gripping her shoulder with one hand. The other hand was twisted up in her blankets, fist clenched so tight that it looked as if the bones of his knuckles were about to burst right through the skin.

"Ayla," he said. "Something's happened. They killed Nessa."

Ayla reeled. *That's impossible*, she kept hearing herself say. *I just saw her in the palace.*

Benjy said, "It's not. They are capable of anything. You know that better than anyone. The others are saying the guards tried to take Nessa's child, and Nessa fought back, and . . ."

"How could this—have possibly happened—?" Ayla's voice ripped through her. Her words were choking her. She tried to close her eyes, but when she did, it was the screams of her brother that broke into her mind, shattering the darkness. The smell of burned flesh, of ash. The paralyzing, numbing fear. She opened her eyes. Seeing was better than not seeing.

Benjy's face was stricken, his hands shaking with fear or anger or something bigger. "Come on. You know I wouldn't lie about this. People saw her body, Ayla. Thom saw her body."

"But why—? What did she do—? Why did they want to punish her?"

Benjy's jaw clenched. "I heard trespassing. Someone said they'd found her handkerchief in the Scyre's room three days ago. Guess they thought she was snooping around."

He kept talking but Ayla wasn't listening.

They'd found her handkerchief in the Scyre's room.

Thought she was snooping around.

Her mouth tasted of bile, sour and dead and wrong. She could feel it rising in her throat—she was going to be sick, or maybe it was just the guilt, a physical thing inside her, choking her like a weed.

My fault, she kept thinking. *My fault*. She was the one who'd gone sneaking. Who'd left the handkerchief there like a flag of surrender on the floor, the damning evidence. Now Nessa was dead, Thom a widower, Lily motherless.

Ayla shook her head. "No."

"Keep your voice down." Benjy glanced around them.

"I have to go," she managed, and then she was scrambling away, and then she was at the door, and maybe people were looking but she couldn't tell, and then she was outside, her dress only half tied at the neck and wrists. In the predawn cool, where the dark tasted like salt.

They found Nessa's handkerchief in the Scyre's room. In the Scyre's room. Why didn't Nessa *tell the leeches* that she had given her handkerchief away, that she'd never stepped foot in Kinok's bedchamber?

Maybe Nessa *had* told.

Maybe by then it hadn't mattered—or had been too late.

They'd tried to take her child.

Would they come for Ayla next?

For Benjy?

Ayla thought of her own face on Kinok's wall. Benjy's, his hair a curl of black ink. That long, red thread. Kinok knew Benjy was the only person Ayla cared about. If he wanted to punish her, he knew how to do it.

She doubled over, one hand braced against the stone wall of the servants' quarters, and heaved into the weedy grass, her stomach spasming, though nothing came up but a thin stream of spit. Her stomach was too empty already.

If Nessa had told, Benjy was in grave danger.

If Nessa hadn't told, then she'd died for Ayla, *because of* Ayla—

"Ayla?" Benjy called out from behind her, and Ayla ran.

Ran from his face: his freckles, his doe eyes, his black-ink curls.

Maybe it was already too late. The chart. The line connecting them.

She rounded the corner of the servants' quarters and kept going, her thin shoes slapping against the hard-packed dirt. She ran past the gardens. The orchards.

And then she saw it.

There, hanging between two trees at the entrance to the orchards. Where everyone could see. There, strung up like a lantern.

Nessa's shoes. And her handkerchief.

The blood on it—from Ayla's stupid bloody nose, after her encounter with Faye—had dried and darkened, but it was unmistakable. The handkerchief fluttered in the breeze, pale like Luna's dress, which seemed to be both ages ago and happening all over again before Ayla's eyes.

A few servants were gathered beneath the trees. They were looking up at the shoes and handkerchief in silence. Just watching.

Ayla could hear her own breaths coming too loud and too harsh in the stillness of the early morning, but she couldn't stop.

Malwin was among the crowd. She was recognizable by her white bonnet. After a long moment, she turned her face away from the handkerchief, the shoes, and hurried away with her shoulders hunched up around her ears. Before Ayla realized what she was doing, she was chasing after her.

She caught up to Malwin quickly. "Hey!" The rage, the sadness, the panic that had flooded her veins all narrowed into focus. Made her shake with urgency. Nessa was gone. But Benjy still lived—for now. She had to be sure he'd stay safe. No one else knew about Kinok's chart yet. She hadn't told anyone.

And no one—no one else was dying on her account, unless it was Crier.

Malwin whirled around. Her eyes were wild, her face bloodless. "You," she said. More like *spat*.

Ayla ignored it. "You've been in the palace longer than any of us," she said. "You know more than—than anyone now, after Nessa—"

"What do you want?" Malwin spat.

"Information. About Nessa and what she did, what she told them, what got her *killed*—"

"You stole my place." Malwin's mouth twisted. "You stole my job, my coin. I owe you nothing."

"I'm not asking for myself."

"Then take some advice," said Malwin, stepping into Ayla's space. She was so close now that Ayla could smell her: herbs and flour, like the kitchens. Her hair was damp with sweat beneath the white bonnet. "Ask for no one but yourself. Care for no one but yourself. That's the only way you'll ever survive this place."

"Malwin—"

"They know everything about us," Malwin breathed. "Everything we do. Everyone we—" She took a step back, her fists clenched and trembling. "The Scyre's always watching."

"The Scyre? What do you know about Kinok?"

"*Oh no you don't*," Malwin hissed. "I don't want none of what Faye got. You saw what happened to her sister."

"Faye . . . ?" Ayla frowned, the tapestry in Kinok's quarters, and the chart it covered, wavering through her mind. "Did . . . did Faye do something to Kinok? Is that why the leeches killed Luna? Is that why you're scared?"

"I don't wanna talk about it," Malwin whispered, her eyes darting around. "Don't wanna bring the bad things down on myself." Then she leaned in close, speaking barely above a whisper. "All I know is this: track the sun apples. But the Scyre keeps his secrets *safe*. Don't *study* him too close."

Safe. Study.

Ayla waited, but Malwin didn't offer up anything else.

"And that's all you heard?" said Ayla, trying not to let her frustration show.

Malwin shook her head. "That's all. Told you it wasn't much. I don't go poking around," she said pointedly, "because I don't want nobody else dying in this place, not because of me."

"Of course," said Ayla, backing off. "Thank you, Malwin."

"Don't come near me again. I won't be tied to you." Malwin spat on the ground at Ayla's feet. "I won't end up like Ness."

Then she stalked off.

Ayla was left there, standing alone in the middle of the grounds, and for the longest time she did not move. She wanted to cry. But she'd lost that ability years ago.

Benjy had wanted to join the rebellion in the South with Rowan. He *should* have gone. But she had told Benjy that the odds were in their favor. That Ayla's position as handmaiden was their chance at real revolution. He had believed her.

That feeling, the same one that had come to her in the music room last night, returned to her now. That leaping and falling. That fear. Had she made the wrong choice?

Did it matter?

She looked down at her hands. They were shaking.

Rowan. She wanted to talk to Rowan now, needed her advice, craved her presence, and the feeling that no matter what happened, Rowan would be there to bandage her wounds, to get her back on her feet. Rowan, who had put her up to this in the first place—who had left, already, to investigate the uprising in the south. To throw herself headlong into the vision of justice she believed in.

Rowan wasn't here to comfort her, but Rowan was the reason Ayla knew what she had to do.

After all, she had learned something today. That Kinok had a study, separate from his rooms. And in that study, there was a safe.

A flock of birds took to the sky, crying out at the dawn.

She'd come this far. And she knew:

There wasn't any going back now.

9

There was a strange cast to the dawn light the morning after her father's men murdered a woman and hung her shoes in the sun apple trees.

By daybreak, when Ayla was meant to come wake her, Crier had already heard about the killing—from a terrified servant no less, who'd entered her bedchamber to stoke the hearth fire; not even from her *father*. Crier stood in the center of her bedchamber, unmoored, shaking from a sick mixture of horror and rage and wrenching grief. She knew things like this happened, sometimes, elsewhere, but her father hadn't ordered such an extreme punishment in years—and never one like this, for such a senseless reason.

Crier pressed a hand over her mouth, trying to calm down. Maybe Hesod hadn't ordered it at all. Maybe the guards had gone rogue. She knew it wasn't possible, but—the alternative made her sick. To know that her father was capable of something like this.

Thoughts roiling like the sea, Crier waited and waited and waited for Ayla's knock.

But Ayla never showed up.

The sun rose, and Ayla never showed up.

More than anything, Crier wanted to find Ayla. To track her down in the servants' quarters and make sure she was all right. But there was no way Crier would be late to her very first council meeting. All she could do, in the end, was catch a maidservant and instruct her to deliver a full breakfast—bread, fruits, cheeses, a bowl of honey—to Handmaiden Ayla, wherever she was, and to inform her that she was relieved of all her duties for the next two days. The maidservant must have been confused, but she was trained not to show it on her face. She just nodded, murmured, "Yes, Lady Crier," and hurried off in the direction of the kitchens.

It wasn't much. It wasn't nearly enough. But if Crier could not see Ayla, at least she could make sure Ayla's belly was full. At least she could go to the council meeting. At least she could fight against this, propose and draft more laws for the protection of humans, make it forbidden to kill a servant, or a child, something, anything. At least she could do everything in her power to make sure this never happened again.

For now, that would have to be enough.

The carriage ride took upward of three hours, and left Crier too long to think about what had happened at the palace—and what *would* happen when they arrived at the council meeting. The first time Crier caught a glimpse of the Councilroom, she was barely more than new-Made. It had taken weeks of pleading with her father before she was allowed to accompany him to the capital, and even then, she was expressly forbidden from entering the Councilroom. She was permitted only to sit beside her father in the caravan, watching the rocky hills slide by outside the windows, giving way to wider trading roads and bigger villages and then towns and then finally the capital city itself, Yanna, the pearl of Rabu, teeming with people, glittering in the spring sun. It was the first time she'd ever seen a city. It was also the first time she'd seen humans who were not her father's servants. She still remembered how they walked with their backs bent, their eyes on the dusty street. Their clothes were old and sun-faded, their skin streaked with grime and oil and dust.

"We do so much for them," Hesod had said. "Beneath us, they thrive. Before us, there was chaos."

Crier had pressed her small hands to the window and peered out at the crowds of humans, watching how they parted around her father's caravan. How they mixed and swirled together like silt in water, all colors. She saw a human girl who looked about her age with spindly arms and pale, tangled hair. Her feet were bare and dirty. Two streets over, all the buildings were tall and lavish, the streets free of litter and waste and other human detritus, the shops run by Automae. The difference between the human and Automa parts of the city was stark, almost shocking. It caught in her mind like a fishhook, leaving her unable to think of anything else. Her Kind lived in luxury while humans starved at their feet.

She shivered as she stared out of the carriage window. They clopped over cobblestone streets and through the massive gates of the Old Palace in the heart of the city.

It had once belonged to a human king and now belonged to the Red Council. The palace itself was made of pale coral-colored stone, shining in the weak winter sunlight, almost too bright to look at. This was where Crier, like all other nobles, had been Designed. Where her father had worked with Designers and Makers to create her blueprints before they were sent to the Midwifery. When she was younger, she liked to imagine her father strolling through the city and the palace gardens and the long halls with the stained-glass ceilings, thinking about exactly what kind of daughter he wanted to create.

Now, thinking about her Design made Crier want to peel off her own Made skin. She couldn't think *Design* without thinking *Flaw*.

The inside of the Councilroom was all white. The floors, the walls, the two long tables bisecting the room, even the fifty chairs around the tables—all of it was made from spotless snow-white marble, somehow paler and cleaner than the rest of the palace. The walls were lined with windows facing east; the morning sun streamed in, falling in bright squares on the tabletop. Dust motes floated in the air, tiny glowing pinpricks. The only color in the room—besides the red robes of the fifty Red Hands, who were all standing behind their respective chairs—came from a war flag. It was hanging on the northern wall, at the head of the table, torn and dirty, one edge burnt and shriveled.

Crier had seen paintings of this flag in this room. It was a relic. A moment in history, crystallized, real. This flag—a band of black on the bottom for the Iron Heart, a band of deep violet above, the color of Automa blood; four vertical white lines to represent the Four Pillars—was the original flag that General Eden had carried into battle during the War of Kinds. In some paintings, the war flag was new and glorious, flying high above the battlefield. In others, it was soaked in the red of human blood.

When Crier and Hesod entered the Councilroom, the other Red Hands bowed their heads in unison. Crier looked around the table, her eyes flicking over the familiar faces of the other Hands—fifty faces ranging from ancient to barely older than she was, fifty faces representing the various cities and regions of Rabu and the few inhabited portions of the Far North—all of them wearing the same solemn expression. She looked at them, taking them in . . . and then she looked again. And again.

Someone was missing. Where was Councilmember Reyka? She'd been hoping to see her here. To find out if she had indeed read Crier's essays, and why she hadn't responded.

And there was an *extra* face at the table. Kinok.

Crier had known he would be here. He had taken a separate caravan, pulled by his own monstrous gray horses from the west. Crier didn't know why he always insisted on traveling separately, but she didn't question it. They might be allies, and engaged, but she still didn't want to spend three hours in a cramped, rattling box with him.

Now, though, she saw he'd taken advantage of arriving ahead of them. He had already chosen a seat at the table—the chair directly to the right of Hesod's. In the Councilroom, those who sat closest to the head (to Crier's father) were the most important, the most influential. And there was Kinok, the newcomer, the comparative youngling, standing like a proud, immovable statue behind the second most important chair in the room.

Were the other Hands actually all right with this?

And where *was* Reyka?

"Crier," said Hesod, snapping her out of her thoughts. "Stay."

Confused, Crier stayed where she was—just inside the door—as her father moved to take his spot at the head of the table. When he stood behind the white marble chair, the war flag framed him in black and violet.

There were no more chairs open. It took an embarrassingly long amount of time for Crier to realize that she was meant to stay posted in the doorway like this for the entire meeting, like a guard. Or a servant.

But I'm his daughter. It was a pitiful thought, from a small, weak place inside her.

I was supposed to be one of you.

But she wasn't. She stood there, silent and humiliated, as her father greeted the other Hands. He was good at this: working the room, looking into everyone's eyes, clasping their hands, making them feel seen and known. He was a skilled politician. A natural leader, able to change anyone's mind over the course of a single conversation; able to make anyone follow him.

When Hesod commanded it, the Hands took their seats. Only Crier remained standing, horribly out of place, her skin hot with embarrassment. But it didn't even seem to matter. Nobody, not even Kinok, had even looked at her yet—not even a *glance*, not even a split second of acknowledgment that she was in the room. It was as if Hesod had entered alone. As if Crier simply did not exist. In all her fantasies—when she had dared to let herself imagine this—she had been sitting in the spot that Kinok had taken. Sometimes, she even imagined herself at the head of the table. In her fantasies, all the Hands had greeted her, bowing their heads in deference, and she was wearing deep scarlet robes, and when she spoke the whole room listened.

She had never once imagined herself standing awkwardly in the doorway, completely removed from the actual meeting. A pointless, invisible observer.

It's all right, she tried to tell herself. *It's your first meeting. At least you're in the room. At least you're allowed to talk.*

Hesod called the meeting to open. First the Hands gave reports of the latest mundane happenings in their respective districts. Then Lady Mar—who Crier had always found fascinating, to the point where she'd made a conscious effort to follow the details of Mar's rise to power in western Rabu—stood up, both hands braced on the table, and said, "There is no point in stalling. We are gathered for a reason. For too long, this Council has remained silent, *passive*, as a new war brews throughout the entire kingdom."

"Do you speak of the human uprisings?" asked Councilmember Yaanik. "I would hardly claim that we have been passive. The uprisings are small, the work of a few human radicals throwing a fit. They have always been dealt with swiftly and without mercy."

"I do not speak of the humans," said Mar. "I speak of the Anti-Reliance Movement."

Multiple Hands' eyes flicked to Kinok. He, however, showed no reaction at all.

"With all due respect, my lord," Mar continued, inclining her head in Hesod's direction, "it seems unwise that the Scyre should attend this meeting at all. He is the face of the Movement. The face of the violence, the controversy. His *political assemblies* devolve into riots under his instruction—or, at the very least, his failure to condemn such behavior."

Riots? Crier hadn't heard anything about *riots*. Of course, her mind went straight to the Southern Uprisings—the ones Kinok was so famous for having squelched.

"It is true," added Councilmember Paradem, from the Far North. Crier did not know how old she was, but she was far more visibly aged than the other Hands. Her skin had a certain dullness to it, her eyes clouded. Her head was shaved, perhaps to disguise the fact that her hair had lost its color. Sometimes, when she held a quill, her hands trembled. "I attended an Anti-Reliance assembly once, a year ago," she said. "I expected a gathering of minds, but instead found myself caught in a crowd of hundreds calling for the total cessation of our relationship with humanity. It was base. Chaotic. Something I would expect from humans—not the elevated Kind. And what is the thesis of your little movement, Scyre? Creating a new capital? It would never work."

Mar nodded. "The War is long over. With the proper governance, humans are capable of contributing to society." Her mouth twitched, amused. "How far does this 'anti-reliance' extend? Should we kill the pack horses and the cattle? Should we sink the Iron Heart into the sea? Should we build our dwellings deep below the earth to avoid the touch of sunlight?"

"That depends, Councilmember," said Kinok, speaking up for the first time. He pulled out what looked like a pocket watch, holding it up to the light and then letting it dangle from his hand like a hypnotist's pendulum. He seemed very intent on making sure all the Hands could see it, and to Crier's surprise, they all seemed to know exactly what it was. More than that, the sight of the pocket watch made them all sit up a little straighter, turn their eyes to Kinok, actually paying attention to him. "Do the pack horses and the cattle conspire to murder us in our beds and burn our settlements to the ground? Does the Iron Heart whisper in code, planning the next uprising? Does sunlight stockpile knives and farming tools, anything that can cut, and swarm the Midwiferies in the dead of night?" He stared around the room, cold, and every single Hand looked back. Rapt. "Proper governance applies to our Kind, not the humans. There is no governing a rabid beast. They are violent, and they grow more violent—and more organized, more powerful—each day. Humans are *dangerous*. We may wish to believe that they could never harm us, but they can; they have. There is no shame in acknowledging a threat—and removing it."

The image of shoes swinging from the sun apple branches surfaced again in Crier's mind. She hesitated for a moment, knowing it was not her place to speak, but—

"Yes, some humans can be dangerous," she said, amazed when her voice didn't shake. All faces turned to her, their expressions impassive. In a room filled with silent Automae, it was difficult to guess what anyone was thinking, and easy to feel mocked. Crier straightened her spine, standing tall, trying to look as imposing as her father. "But too often it seems we punish minor infractions with—with torture, confinement, even death."

She could feel her father's eyes on her.

"We were created to be the enlightened Kind," Crier continued, forcing herself to look around the room, to meet their eyes. This was what she'd been waiting for, was it not? She couldn't let fear silence her. "We were created to be more than human, better than human, but—are we really any better, if we resort to senseless violence so easily? How far are we willing to go? We must not—"

"Daughter," Hesod cut in.

Her mouth snapped shut. Feeling cold, she finally looked at her father, only to find him looking back. But the look on his face wasn't angry; it was a careful mask.

She'd seen this look so many times before, in reaction to her essays. Her thoughts. Her ideas.

"My apologies," Hesod said, addressing the room at large. "My daughter thinks herself wise beyond her years."

A smattering of laughter.

"She'd prove herself the wiser, then," said Councilmember Shen, "if she occupied herself with the current state of affairs of the human population. As we know, there are reports of more uprisings in Tarreen. One of our Kind died this time. Head was severed and burned."

Several of the Hands voiced their revulsion aloud. "Not even the most recent incident," said another. "Just two days ago, twenty leagues south. An entire farm's worth of servants attacked their lord. The casualties were all human, but it was a close call."

Just like that, the silent, dignified room devolved into fifty people talking all at once. Mute, humiliated, Crier listened to them argue, some levelheaded and eloquent and some taken by outrage. The only person who wasn't speaking was Kinok. He was leaning back in his marble chair, regarding the mess before him with cool, amused eyes. He was still holding the pocket watch, spinning it in his fingers . . . and Crier finally got a good look at it. She realized it wasn't a watch.

It was a—compass?

"Enough!" said Hesod finally.

The voices petered out into another ringing silence.

"There is business to attend to," said Hesod. "Queen Junn

of Varn has made a formal request—"

"The Mad Queen?" someone muttered.

"But what about the uprisings?" demanded Shen.

"What about *Reyka*?" said another, and Crier's head jerked up—what *about* her?—but Hesod ignored the interruptions.

"Queen Junn of Varn has made a formal request for a tour of diplomacy," he said. "To begin the process of mending the broken bridge between our nations. She wishes to travel from our shared border up to the city of Yanna, paying her respects to each Red Hand along the way."

Crier inched forward, eyes wide. Queen Junn, *here*?

The one the people all called mad.

The one whose power Crier had for so long coveted, so pined to meet.

"Why now?" added Paradem. "Why come now? What has changed?"

"I do not trust it," said Mar. "She is known as the Mad Queen for a reason. She is famously volatile, unpredictable. We are balanced precariously enough already."

Crier could not stand it.

"Her Highness Queen Junn is not volatile," she said loudly, her voice cutting through the room. The Red Hands all turned to stare at her at once, some of them blinking as if they'd forgotten her existence entirely. "She rules swiftly and intensely, but never recklessly. I have followed her court for years now. If she says she wants to mend the bridge between us, she means it. None of her actions in the past two years have contradicted this desire to mend our relations, or at the very least form a military alliance. She has been working toward this for a long time."

"Then it should please you to hear that the queen made another request," her father said. His eyes were unreadable. "It seems she is quite interested in meeting *you*."

Inexplicably, Crier felt her cheeks heating up. Before she could even begin to process that, the council had moved on to their final order of business.

Councilmember Reyka had disappeared.

Crier was so consumed in her thoughts about Junn—the Mad Queen, the Bone Eater, the ruthless one, *wanted to meet with Crier*—that it took her a second to take in this new bit of information.

"Reyka?" she blurted out, amid the mumblings of shock from the other Hands. Reyka, her mentor, her friend, if an Automa could use such a word—Reyka, who'd never responded when Crier had sent her political essays to her. Could this be why? Had she been gone for weeks and no one knew?

Questions were flying from the mouths of the other Hands, but Hesod seemed to have no other answers to give. Reyka was just . . . gone. Not dead, no ransom, and no sign of disturbance, at least as far as they knew—just gone. She had vanished in the night. There was no way of knowing where she was, or why she had left, or when (if) she was coming back.

"Perhaps she's finally joined the humans," said Councilmember Shen. "That's where she belongs, is it not? Always arguing on behalf of the *humans*, always so concerned about *humankind*. I would not be surprised if she renounced her own Kind, took up a servant's uniform, and went to work in the fields."

Faint laughter around the room. Crier felt a wave of nervousness. Would they say the same about her? Had any of them read her essay on the redistribution of representation? When she'd written it, it had felt like theory. Righteous, but harmless. Only now did it occur to her that it might have sounded threatening to the other Hands. It might have sounded as if she was arguing because she cared about humankind.

Which she did.

Like Reyka.

"Perhaps she has joined them, but not by choice," said Kinok, and the laughter faded out. "It would not be the first time that one of our Kind has been kidnapped by human rebels. They will do anything to bring us down, to weaken us." He paused. "Then again, perhaps Councilmember Shen is right. It was odd for Councilmember Reyka to be so . . . *passionate* about humans, was it not?"

He said it like a joke, and the Hands took it as one, smirking to each other.

Only Crier was left frozen, horrified. *Passionate.*

Suddenly, where once she'd seen a potential partner, an advocate, she now saw Kinok for what he was. A schemer. He'd pretended to be her ally, *it's you and me, Lady Crier*, but an ally wouldn't do something like this. Right? Crier knew she was naive, but she wasn't stupid. An ally wouldn't use her darkest secret against her like this, just for his own amusement. An ally wouldn't mock Councilmember Reyka, who wasn't even there to defend herself. No. Crier couldn't—wouldn't—trust Kinok. She couldn't take her eyes away from the gleaming compass he dangled in his hands, like a trophy of some kind. Everyone else kept looking at it, too—furtive little glances, some curious, some wary, some almost . . . envious.

"Unfortunately," said Hesod, once again cutting through the noise, "until Reyka decides to resurface, the council is left with an unoccupied seat."

And Crier's heart threw itself into her throat.

Is this why he finally agreed to let me attend a meeting? she couldn't help but think, and then immediately felt ashamed of herself. Reyka was missing, possibly in danger. This was no time to be thinking of her own political aspirations.

"In the current political climate, it seems wise to fill this seat as soon as possible, even under the assumption that Reyka will return," Hesod continued. "I already have my candidate for our newest Hand, but it will be put to a vote."

Crier looked around at what she could see of the other Hands' faces. Mar, Shen, Shasta, Paradem, Laone . . . all faces she had been looking up into since she was newbuilt. Was she finally about to join them, after so many years? As daughter of the sovereign, she was the obvious choice. Anticipation hummed beneath her skin, even though she was still so worried about Reyka. If she became one of the Hands, finding Reyka would be the first thing she would fight for.

"All in favor, say aye," her father said.

The Red Hands waited. Crier held her breath.

"For the unoccupied chair of Councilmember Reyka," said Hesod, "I nominate Scyre Kinok of the Western Mountains."

Kinok.

Of course.

The hurt that curdled in Crier's belly was almost unbearable—that it didn't seem to have even *occurred* to her father to think first of her.

But this was all part of his strategy, wasn't it? Offering Kinok a position on the council would provide—what had he said? *Stability. Access. Power.* It was a gesture not just to Kinok but to all supporters of ARM. It said *you are welcome among us*, and *we are all on the same side.* It said *let's work together.* It also said *we are watching you.*

A sinister thought: What if her father, or Kinok himself, had had a hand in Reyka's disappearance? The timing of it seemed all too convenient. A spot available, just now, as Kinok's movement was on the rise and as Hesod was seeking ways to reintegrate his dissenters.

She tried to banish the dark suspicion, but it lingered like a foul smell.

Crier felt herself go numb as one by one, everyone in the room—with the exception of Mar and Paradem—said *aye.* The voices echoed around the marble room, a ripple of sound. Crier heard it, and understood it, and yet could not believe it, could not recover from it.

"It is settled, then," said her father. "Councilmember Kinok—"

And that was the last thing Crier heard. Her head was filled with wordless, rushing noise, like the ocean, or like the first roll of rain in a thunderstorm. She stood there, swaying like a boat unmoored. Kinok had taken Councilmember Reyka's seat. Had taken *her* seat. Kinok was the new Red Hand. Kinok was on the council, and she was not. She was finally in the marble room, and yet she had never been further away.

In that moment, Crier realized it was never going to happen. Her father would never take her seriously. No matter what she did. He'd literally created her to be his heir, and still she was not good enough.

She was never, ever going to be on the council.

She would never have a say in her nation's future.

There was only one thing Queen Thea loved even half as much as her child Kiera, and that was the queen's pet songbird. It had been gifted to her by the king of Tarreen, and as such it was a breed of bird that could not be found outside the jungles of the south. The bird's feathers were a deep blue—the color of lapis lazuli, the queen often said—and it sang at dawn and dusk in a lovely, trilling voice, perched in its golden cage in the eastern solarium, and the queen sat beside it and watched, and listened.

Every day the Queen repeated this ritual. Dawn and dusk.

Until one morning, when she entered the solarium and found little Kiera eating the songbird alive, its bones crudely angled in her jaw, feathers drifting from her fingers to the floor like ribbons of perfect sky.

Later, Queen Thea informed the court that Kiera had done nothing wrong. It was the queen's fault, she said, for not adequately educating her child. It was just a mistake, she said; there are some animals that humans eat, and some they do not. Kiera had been, quite naturally, confused. Now she was not.

But it was this handmaiden who cleaned the blood and feathers and bone shards from the floor of the eastern solarium. And this handmaiden who saw doubt in the Queen's eyes from that day onward. How it grew and festered.

—FROM THE PERSONAL RECORDS OF AMES,
HANDMAIDEN QUEEN THEA OF ZULLA, E. 900, Y. 9

10

Ayla spent the day of the Reaper's Moon curled up in her cot, paralyzed with guilt. She almost wished that Crier hadn't gone to the capital. She almost wished that she'd been forced to report to the lady's chambers and do the usual litany of mindless things: preparing Crier's bath, brushing her long dark hair, ironing her dress, painting her mouth with soft rouge. At least it would have kept Ayla moving, kept her hands busy, kept her mind off Nessa. Kept her from staring, paralyzed with indecision, at the basket of food that had been delivered earlier by a very suspicious maidservant. Bread and honey, salted fish, soft yellow cheese, sun apples, a parcel of candied nuts. It was more food than Ayla usually saw in a week. She didn't want to eat it. She was starving. Her belly was rolling over itself. But eating would be like giving in. Like admitting something, some need. Right?

Crier had allowed Ayla to stay. Had given her the *day off*.

She'd never had a day off before—not since working here. She hated the stillness. Guilt gnawed at her, same as hunger. A quiet, private, relentless kind of torture. Revenge had left her hands bloody, but it wasn't the right blood.

She knew what she should be doing. She should be trying her best to find Kinok's private study. If he kept any secret documents pertaining to the Iron Heart, anything that would be useful to the Revolution—a map, blueprints, a heartstone ledger, information about the trade routes—it'd be there, in the safe Malwin had mentioned.

And yet every time she set foot near the doors to the palace, a horrible chill flooded through her—dread. The memory of Nessa's handkerchief. Her shoes.

Maybe I should just give up now.

But if I give up, then what have I even been living for?

Alone, she watched the sunlight slide across the walls of servants' quarters. Four hundred empty beds. Everyone else was out in the fields, the gardens, the orchards, the palace. The Reaper's Moon—marked by the last crescent moon of the harvest season, the moon shaped like a harvester's scythe—meant that weeks of laboring in the fields had come to a close, and it was time to settle in for the winter.

When Ayla's parents were growing up, the Reaper's Moon was celebrated with three days and three nights of festivals and dances and parties that lasted till dawn, huge feasts in the village square, neighbors eating and laughing and singing with each other, their faces painted gold. When Ayla and Storme were young, there weren't any big celebrations—not with the constant threat of raids. But Ayla's mother had always braided golden ribbons into Ayla's hair, and her father had sung harvest songs and moon songs and love songs, and the fire had been so warm, and they'd all been smiling.

Ayla's cot was cold and uncomfortable. She didn't usually feel the aloneness quite this much. But it was harder, this time of year, to ignore the graveyard in her chest. Harder still when it had just grown by two bodies.

The sunlight slid down the walls and turned from pale yellow to old gold to orange with sunset. In another life, Ayla would be dancing right now. In another life, she'd be dressed in rich colors and her face would be painted and her hair sleek with oil, and she'd be dancing in the village square, and her feet would hurt and it would feel so nice, and there wouldn't be any weight on her shoulders. No hatred, no fear, no death.

In this life, she closed her eyes.

And opened them barely a minute later when someone poked her hard in the forehead.

"Benjy," she snapped, shoving his hand away and ignoring his grinning face. "What do you want?"

"You think I'd let you sleep through the feast?" he said, plopping down on her cot. "No way. Look at you, all your bones showing. You need this just as much as the rest of us."

That meant the day of work was over. The servants would forgo their dinners to set up for the secret celebrations, deep in the woods or somewhere far from the immediate grounds. The council meeting was a perfect cover, sending Hesod, Kinok, *and* Crier away for the full day.

But Ayla couldn't stomach even the idea of a celebration. "I'm not going."

"Oh, come on, it'll be fun. It'll get your mind off—you know." He pushed gently at her shoulder. "There will be wine. Remember last year?"

"Yes. You drank too much and got sick in the ocean."

"Don't you wanna be there to watch me embarrass myself?"

"No, Benjy," she said, staring at a tiny piece of straw poking out from the mattress, willing her eyes away from his. "I'm not going, not this year. You have fun."

He scowled. "How am I supposed to do that without you?"

"Benjy—"

"*Ayla,*" he said, not annoyed anymore, just soft and pleading. "Please. I feel like I barely see you these days. When I do see you, it's because something terrible has happened. I miss you. You're my best friend and I—miss you." He grabbed her hand and squeezed it. "Please."

Best friend.

All she kept thinking of was the thread connecting them on Kinok's chart—blazing red like a fire.

She looked at their joined hands. His was much bigger than hers, but they were similar in other ways: the ruined fingernails, the calluses, the marks of labor.

A feeling rose in her again, familiar as Benjy's face: the battle between being close to him and pushing him away. Being friends with him and being friends with no one. Which was worse, vulnerability or loneliness? The danger of friendship or the safety of total isolation?

What had safety done for her lately?

"All right," she said finally. "I'll go." If only to stop his pleading. If only to keep moving, to stop thinking, to stop questioning.

He whooped, pulling her outside, into the welcoming dark toward the celebration—and she let him.

There were no golden ribbons in her hair, but there were caskets of pale, sour wine, and that was just as good. Or better, maybe.

They made their way to one of the big caves at the foot of the cliffs where the festivities were being held this year, a grotto with a wet, sandy floor. Inside the cave there was a fire pit, lanterns strung over the curving stone walls, two boys playing homemade drums—the beats echoed through the cave, sound doubling back on sound, so deep and incessant that it made Ayla feel strange and almost sick inside. Overwhelmed. There was space for dancing both inside the cave and on the black sand beach outside, the tide crashing and dissolving against the rocks that lined the shore like tall, straight-backed guards.

The air was filled with flecks of white foam, the smell of smoke and wine and sea spray, the sounds of drums and dancing and old harvest songs sung in a hundred voices. Everyone was wearing a mask. Some were painted with gold or vermilion, but most were just made from scraps of straw and clothing. These people were servants. Any luxuries had to be hidden and hidden well.

The moment she and Benjy entered the cave, a boy Benjy's age bounded up to them. He was only wearing a half mask, a silvery-purple thing around his eyes. "Ben!" he said happily, pulling Benjy into a hug.

Ayla hung back, wary. She had definitely never seen this boy before, but Benjy was hugging him back, looking equally happy to see him.

Benjy ruffled the boy's hair and stepped back, gesturing between him and Ayla. "Finn, this is my closest friend, Ayla. Ayla, this is Finn." *Finn.* She remembered the stories. He and Benjy had grown up together at the temple as kids, long before Ayla knew Benjy. Finn had been the first to run away. Benjy had been gutted by it, but the anger was what had galvanized him to leave, too. Years later, Rowan helped them find each other again. They'd kept in touch ever since.

Benjy was grinning wide, like a happy fool. "He traveled here from an estate to the east and I haven't seen him in nearly two years, the *bastard*."

Finn laughed. "It's hardly as if you've come to visit me!"

"Well, at least I always respond to your letters!"

"Oh sure," said Finn, rolling his eyes. "And it only takes you three months per letter."

They shoved at each other, bickering with an easy familiarity. Ayla hung back, silent, feeling a little lost. She knew Benjy wrote letters to people he knew outside the palace, but none of them had ever come to visit. And to come all this way just for the Reaper's Moon? It seemed like madness. The celebrations were a risk in and of themselves. They weren't sanctioned—they weren't strictly *illegal*, but the Automae didn't like any human gathering, whether it was ten people or a hundred. They saw it as a threat.

"Wait here, I'll get you both a mask," Finn said, and disappeared back into the crowd.

Benjy turned to Ayla, still grinning. "He hasn't changed a bit. Everybody's best friend, everywhere he goes. I bet you a statescoin there'll be some girl mooning after him when he's gone, even though he's only here for a night." His grin faded when Ayla didn't reply. "You all right?"

"Isn't it dangerous to leave the estate?" Ayla said. "Did he really travel all the way here just for a party?"

"Not just for a party," Benjy said. "He came here to see me."

"But it's *dangerous*," Ayla insisted.

Benjy was frowning now. "So? It's worth it, isn't it? We're family. It's important to stay connected to each other. In case you forgot, Ayla, that's what we're fighting for."

Stay connected. Once again, she thought of the red thread in Kinok's office. "I don't have a family. And I'm still fighting."

His expression softened. He reached out to touch her shoulder, thumb on her collarbone. "But you have the memories of them. You have ancestors, you have stories."

"Not really," she said. "My father's family is all dead and my mother never talked about her side. All I know of her line is that

I was named after her grandmother. That's it."

"Her grandmother's name was Ayla?"

"Siena Ayla." Ayla looked away, jaw tight. "A name. That's all I have." She clutched the locket under her shirt. A name, and a necklace.

"Ayla," Benjy said quietly.

"What?"

"Nothing. I'm just saying your name. Ayla." He stepped closer, letting her name whisper across her skin. "*Ayla*. It is a gift. It *is* a memory. And that's one they can't take from you."

Ayla felt the strange urge to laugh. A memory was nothing like a gift.

A memory: the day before the raids. A stupid, childish fight, Storme and Ayla shrieking at each other for no reason, Ayla hurling a handful of dirt and then, when that didn't make him stop teasing her, she hurled words. I hate you. She spat them out like poisoned water. I hate you. I wish I didn't have a brother. I wish you'd go away forever. She was so angry, her small body vibrating with it, and he was laughing at her. Like the child he was. Leave me alone! she screamed at him, and never took it back.

And the next day—

"Sometimes I wish I remembered nothing," she whispered, stepping back, her throat burning. "Sometimes it seems like that would be so much easier."

Benjy opened his mouth to reply, but just then Finn returned, pressing masks into their hands: a fox for Ayla and a plain straw mask for Benjy. Ayla put the mask on, immediately feeling much more comfortable with her face hidden. The dyed wool was scratchy on her cheeks.

They joined the party, Finn shouting and laughing and dragging Benjy along behind him. A girl she recognized from the stables handed Ayla a cup of the pale wine. It tasted terrible, bitter and sour all at once, but she drank anyway. The wine burned all the way down, a line of heat from throat to belly, and by her second cup Ayla was warm and pleasantly tipsy, bobbing along in her own head. The drums pulsed in her rib cage. Whenever he wasn't with Finn, Benjy kept touching her lightly, guiding her through the crowd, hand on her hip and arm and shoulder.

It was easy, for a while, to forget. Ayla drank her wine in great big swallows and let herself sway along with the music, so warm, sweating a little. She let Benjy pull her close and then closer, arm around her waist. She smiled at everyone she recognized and also everyone she didn't, even though her face was hidden behind the mask.

"Aren't you glad you came?" said Benjy when they returned to the casks of wine for a third cup. "Aren't you glad you listened to me?"

"Maybe," she teased him. "I don't know. You shouldn't ask me things like that when I'm swimming in wine."

"Oh? Why's that?"

"Because I'll say yes."

"Maybe there are some things I want you to say yes to."

Ayla laughed. "What are you talking about?"

"Ayla," he said, sounding very serious all of a sudden. She caught the movement of his throat, a nervous swallow. "Ayla, I need to tell you something—"

Suddenly, her stomach hardened.

No no no—

"It's my fault Nessa died," she blurted out.

The ensuing pause was terrible. Benjy stared at her for a second, confused, and then he shook his head. "Wait," he said, "wait, what, what are you—Ayla, I really need to tell you—I *want* to tell you—"

"She lent me her handkerchief," Ayla barreled on, quiet enough that no one else would hear her over the drums and singing but loud enough, sharp enough, to make Benjy's mouth snap shut. She couldn't do this, couldn't hear whatever he wanted to tell her; she had a sick feeling that she knew what it was and she couldn't, not now, not ever maybe. What if she let herself feel for him the way he felt for her . . . and then lost him?

She wouldn't recover. She knew she wouldn't. But how to explain that?

"I'm the one who accidentally left it in Kinok's chambers, Benjy," she said instead. "It's my fault they thought Nessa was snooping. It's my fault they tried to take her child." She wrapped her arms around herself, wishing desperately that she hadn't drunk so much wine. "It's my fault she died."

Benjy shook his head hard. "You can't blame yourself—"

"There's nobody else to blame! It was my fault!"

"Hush, keep your voice down," he hissed, eyes darting around at the pulsing crowd. He reached out to put his hands on her shoulders, swaying to the music—making it look like they were simply talking and dancing like everyone else. "Ayla. You can't take that on. You said it was an accident, right? Leaving the handkerchief in Kinok's room?"

"Yes. A stupid goddamn mistake. I can't believe I was so careless. So *stupid*."

His grip tightened on her shoulders. "Nessa wasn't the first to die in this war, Ayla." His words were a punch to the gut. "And she won't be the last. That doesn't mean we give up. It means we fight harder—we fight until we win this war."

"*War?*" She actually took a step back, and he gripped her hips tighter. His hands were big and warm and too much. "There is no war. There's only a rebellion that keeps failing. Nessa didn't die for the cause. She died because of me, because I wasn't good enough, because there's always something. Hell, Benjy. If I'd dropped my own handkerchief, it would have been *your* shoes hanging from the apple tree."

"No. Nessa must have done something else. Even the leeches wouldn't murder a good servant just for dropping a handkerchief on her rounds."

"It's not that she dropped a handkerchief," Ayla said. "It's that she was trespassing. And they tried to hurt her child, as *punishment*, and Nessa wouldn't let them. The same thing happened to Faye and Luna."

"What are you talking about?"

"Luna wasn't killed because of something she did. She was killed because of something *Faye* did. They punished Faye by killing the most important thing in the world to her."

"Are you sure?"

She thought again of that chart. "I'm sure." Quickly, Ayla explained about her awful run-in with Faye. "I don't know what she did. But it must have been serious."

"Maybe . . . maybe it had to do with Kinok." Behind the straw mask, Benjy's voice sounded far away. "I haven't ever seen something like Nessa happen before. Maybe it's because she crossed Kinok. Maybe that's why the punishment was so harsh. Maybe Faye did the same thing, maybe she . . . got in his way, somehow."

"Maybe." But what did it matter? The outcome was the same. The person Faye had cared for the most had been turned into collateral damage.

Guiltily, Ayla thought of her necklace. The locket that lay beneath her shirt even now. Crier hadn't reported her for it, but what if someone else saw?

Would they come for Benjy next?

Ayla looked around the grotto with new eyes. What had been fun and loud and beautiful just moments ago now seemed overwhelming, nauseating, the whole party spinning like a child's toy, a blur of noise and color and grotesque masks. She needed some fresh air. She needed the ground to stop tilting beneath her feet. She looked out at the mouth of the cave, staring longingly at the cool dark night—and saw it.

A flash of golden eyes.

Someone was watching them.

An Automa.

The shock of it went right through her. She wasn't sure how she knew it, but on instinct, she could guess who it was. Crier.

In a short time, she'd grown to know exactly what it felt like to be watched by her, the way Crier's gaze trailed her when she thought Ayla was busy with a task.

Only, how had Crier gotten here so early? Shouldn't she still be at the council meeting? And why had she followed them? And what would she do, now that she'd seen? And—

"Benjy," she said, extricating herself from the circle of his arms, "will you get me another drink?"

He sighed. "All right," he said, and took her cup of wine, heading toward the barrels.

When he returned to their spot near the fire pit, Ayla was already gone.

11

Perhaps the worst part hadn't been watching Kinok take the seat that Crier had always wanted. Perhaps the worst part had been getting sent home early. That, above all else, made it clear that she was not wanted or needed in the Old Palace. That there was no place for her in the Councilroom. That there never would be.

It was a brand-new hurt.

She wondered, during the long, silent caravan ride home, if it would feel like this for another Automa. If they would hurt like this, a dull ache deep inside. Or if she only cared so much because she was Flawed. At the meeting, in front of *everyone*, Kinok had joked that Reyka, too, had been *passionate*. Crier thought of the Automa woman whom she'd always looked up to, almost like a mentor. Reyka, who'd always locked eyes with Crier when she spoke, who'd given her treats and encouraged her to have her own opinions. But for what?

For the first time since discovering her sabotaged Design, the existence of Crier's fifth pillar felt *real*. Immediate. It wasn't a distant, humiliating fear—it was hurting her. There was no salve for this, no bandage. She wanted it gone. She wanted to cut it out of her. But there was nothing to cut. There was just the phantom lump in her belly, the imagined stone lodged in her throat. The whole world felt awful and sickening and abrasive, like the air itself was rubbing roughly against her skin. Even the tiniest noises—the whicker of the horses, the sound of a wooden wheel bumping over wet rock—made her temples throb.

The second her company drove through the gates and into the courtyard, Crier leaped from the caravan. She landed hard, the mud sucking at her shoes and splattering her skirts, and she had never cared less.

"Lady!" one of the guards shouted after her. "Lady, where should we—?" but she never heard the end of his sentence. She was already moving away from the palace and into the thickness of the night, needing to get away, needing to lose herself.

She'd wanted to wander alone. To mentally prepare, perhaps, for the promised arrival of Queen Junn—the one spot of brightness on the horizon.

But the last thing Crier had expected to find at midnight on the barren, rocky beach was a celebration. She'd seen the yellow glow of lanterns from half a league away and, curious, had picked her way along the rocky, sandy shore until she found the source: one of the caves that pockmarked the seaside cliffs was full of *humans*.

And they were dancing.

Crier crept closer to the mouth of the cave, unable to look away. The cave was massive, like a giant from the old human stories had taken a bite of the cliffside and left behind a hollow space the size of her father's gardens. Crier had visited this cave before—had once spent an entire night here, watching the tides—but she'd always been alone, in the dark. Tonight, the cave was glowing. The jagged walls were lined with strings of paper lanterns. There was a fire pit in the center big enough to roast a warhorse, but the humans weren't using it to cook. Instead, there was a circle of humans tossing what looked like wet, rotting driftwood into the flames. Sometimes, a piece of driftwood made the flames turn momentarily blue or green. Algae, Crier realized. Every time it happened, the humans cheered and drank. Around them, the rest of the cave was loud and chaotic with music. It was strange music, nothing but drums; a couple boys near the cave wall were sharing a drum that looked like a wine barrel with a bit of animal skin stretched over the top. They were flushed, laughing, slapping the drum with their hands. It was more excitement than rhythm, but somehow the humans were singing along. Crier strained her ears to catch the words— something about straw hats and sickles—and tried to figure out how all the humans knew the same song, the same dance.

She wished she could see their faces, but they were all wearing masks. Most were plain—red and yellow and gold—but some were shaped like animals. Crier saw a lion, a wolf, a bird with a bright plume of feathers. A fox.

There was something familiar about the fox. Not the mask, but the person behind it—whose body moved like crashing water. It was a girl, Crier was sure, and she was dancing near the fire pit, barefoot on the rocky ground. Most of the humans were wearing colorful dresses or tunics, but some were wearing the red uniforms of the sovereign's servants. The fox was one of the latter, the bottoms of her red pants wet with mud and sea spray.

Then the fox turned and Crier saw wild dark hair. She wasn't surprised. Some part of her had known it was Ayla from the first moment she saw the fox dancing on quick, nimble feet. The thing that surprised her was the person dancing *with* Ayla. He was lanky, curly-haired, but that was all she could tell—he was wearing a mask woven from ribbons and straw. Like Ayla, he was in a servant's uniform; his shirt was damp with sweat or seawater.

The straw boy moved closer and put his hands on Ayla's hips. She let him. Together, they spun in a messy circle, her hands in the air, his long fingers gripping her hips, her waist; she tossed her head back, laughing or yelling or singing, and her throat was a column of gold in the leaping firelight. The boy swayed forward. So did Crier, before she caught herself.

Crier looked away. The other humans were dancing, some dancing much closer than Ayla and her straw boy: Crier saw half-naked bodies intertwined, skin shimmering with sweat, couples dancing less to the drumbeats and more to their own slow, private rhythm, eyes closed, heads tipped back. She saw two boys sharing a cup of wine. One girl pressing another against the cave wall, bodies moving strangely.

Crier felt something—a pulse, deep in her belly. She squirmed, suddenly embarrassed for reasons she could not explain, and tore her eyes away from the two girls. It was fascinating enough to watch the rest of the crowd. So many bodies circling and crashing into each other like tides. Crier knew her father would not approve of this. If she were a good daughter, she would report it. Put an end to it.

It seems I am not a good daughter, she thought, and for once it didn't feel so devastating.

Ayla disappeared for a while, swallowed up by the pulsating crowd. But soon enough she was visible again, now carrying a cup of wine in both hands, stumbling a little, tripping over the slick, uneven floor of the cave. Sand, rock, shallow pools. She was going to slice up the soles of her feet. With the face of a fox, tapered ears, and fiery orange fur, she made Crier think of the Hunt, of the foxes skittering through the underbrush. Had it really only been two weeks since then?

Those foxes were wild, though. Wild, frightened, ready to run. Claws and teeth and matted fur. Sometimes that was Ayla. Most times it was not.

Most times, lately, Ayla just looked *soft*.

Crier didn't realize just how far she'd strayed from her hidden vantage point until, as if sensing Crier's gaze, Ayla turned around and looked directly at her. *Dammit*. Ayla jolted, wine sloshing from her cup in a pale arc. The straw boy nudged at her shoulder and she seemed to ask him something, pointing at her cup. He took it and melted away into the crowd. The second he was gone, Ayla began moving purposefully through the crowd . . . straight toward Crier. *Dammit, dammit.* Crier contemplated making a quick escape, but she knew it was too late. She'd been spotted. Instead, she slipped away from the mouth of the cave to hide in the shadows again, so at least nobody else would see her.

The soft sound of bare feet on rock, and then Ayla appeared in the entrance to the cave, silhouetted against the lanterns and firelight, a single tooth in the mouth of some ancient leviathan. She looked from side to side, her face still hidden by the fox mask, and finally hissed, "I know you're out there. I saw your eyes."

Crier took a breath. "Over here."

She was braced for Ayla's anger, for low, furious demands—*why are you spying on us?* But instead she was faced with—

"Don't tell," Ayla whispered, joining Crier in the darkness. They were hidden against the cliff face, in a patch of black sand among the tall, jagged rocks, an area ringed by tide pools. "*Please* don't tell your father."

Fear?

"I won't," Crier said automatically, and then felt even more embarrassed and a little out of control. "I mean. What would I tell him? What is this?"

"Just a . . . celebration," said Ayla. She pushed her mask up onto the top of her head, finally exposing her face. There was a thin sheen of sweat on her skin. "It only happens once a year after the harvest, and we didn't steal anything, so really there's nothing to tell."

"After the harvest—is tonight the Reaper's Moon?"

Ayla blinked. "You've heard of it?"

"I live in Rabu, don't I?"

"Well, yes, but—"

"I know your festivals. I've read all about them." She should have realized earlier, frankly. The masks, the dancing, the timing—right on the cusp of winter.

"Then you understand that this isn't a crime," Ayla said. Her eyes shone in the light from the crescent moon, her voice low and fierce but still loud enough to be heard over the drums, the voices, the pounding ocean. "We're just dancing, just for one night, we're not doing anything wrong—"

"I won't tell," she said again.

"—and nobody needs to get hurt—oh. What?"

"I won't tell," Crier repeated.

"You won't?"

"No," she said. "My father will never know. I—I promise."

In the dark, the noise of the ocean rushing all around them, the act of promising felt so heavy. Or maybe it felt exactly as heavy as it was.

"You—" Ayla began, and then they both heard it at the same time: the crunch of a second set of footsteps, coming from inside the cave and drawing nearer. "Oh damn, that'll be Benjy," Ayla muttered. "Damn it all, he can't see you here. We need to go."

She grabbed Crier's sleeve and started off down the dark beach, dragging Crier behind her. They skirted the sharp rocks, wending their way down a narrow fisherman's trail, hugging the cliffs. Every so often Ayla glanced over her shoulder to make sure they weren't being followed.

She stopped beside a tide pool and dropped Crier's sleeve immediately. It was much quieter this far away from the Reaper's Moon party. Above them, the crescent moon, the glittering night. Around them, the sea, the rocks, the tide pools teeming with colorful life. Crier's vision adjusted to the new darkness. There were strands of hair sticking to Ayla's temples and neck. As Crier watched, Ayla looked from her own hand to Crier's sleeve as if she too were surprised by her actions.

Crier didn't want her to be surprised. She didn't want Ayla to regret leaving the party. "You seem nervous," she said, probing, trying to figure out the tangle of Ayla's human emotions.

"I'm not."

"Worried?"

"Isn't that the same thing?"

Crier leaned closer, peering at Ayla's moonlit face. ". . . Guilty?"

Ayla flinched. "*No.* No, you were right, I'm just worried."

"About what?"

"Always the questions," said Ayla, but she didn't sound annoyed. More like exhausted. "I guess I'm worried because my, um, my friend Faye, she's another servant, and she's been . . . sick."

"She has taken ill? That seems normal, especially with winter approaching."

"No," Ayla said again. "I mean, like, sick up here." She gestured to her head. "And I don't know what to do about it, or how to help her, or anything." She huffed, a short, frustrated noise, and crossed her arms over her chest defensively, as if physically blocking off the next question.

Crier wanted to know more about this Faye. She wanted to know what Ayla meant when she said *sick up here*. But she did not want Ayla to run.

She wanted to give her a reason to stay. So, she sat down right there on the wet, sandy rocks. Cold dampness instantly began to soak through her dress. "My father's library has a collection of books on human mythology. Not just Rabunian—not even just Zullan. Stories from all over the world, dating back thousands of years. I've read them all."

Ayla sighed. But she joined Crier in sitting beside the tide pool, her toes dangling over the edge. She trailed a finger over the surface of the pool, ripples fanning out in perfect concentric circles, and for a long moment she did not speak.

"Tell me one," she finally said. She didn't seem to realize—or maybe she just didn't care—that she had just given an order to a lady.

Maybe she could tell that it pleased Crier. That Crier *wanted* to tell a story.

Maybe she just wanted to be sure Crier was distracted and would not report the celebrations to her father.

Or maybe, *maybe*, she, too, wanted to stay.

It was impossible, but Crier swore her Made blood grew warm as stories bobbed to the surface of her mind like detritus after a shipwreck, thousands and thousands of stories from Rabu, Varn, the jungles of Tarreen, the lands across the Steorran Sea. She had to tell the right story, to do this right, to keep Ayla's attention for as long as possible.

She thought of telling a story of Queen Junn of Varn. But no, that wouldn't do—surely Ayla had heard the rumors everyone else seemed to believe—that Queen Junn was mad.

No, she needed something else. A human story.

"Once," she began, "in a faraway kingdom, in a land of ice and snow, there lived a princess who was very, very sad. A war was brewing between her father, the king, and the neighboring kingdom. The princess, who loved her people more than anything, knew that a war would only bring death and destruction. She was desperate to stop the war before it began, but her father was blinded by anger and pride. He would not listen to her pleas to call for a truce. So the princess devised a plan: she drafted a peace treaty in her father's hand and set off for the neighboring kingdom alone in the darkest hour of night."

"A peace built on lies," Ayla said.

Crier didn't answer, but carefully, she removed her shoes and dipped her feet into the pool beside Ayla's. The cold gripped her ankles, like an element from another world. "The princess rode hard for three days and three nights," she went on, "without encountering any bandits, roadblocks, or bad weather. But on the fourth day, she had to cross through a mountain pass so narrow that it was named the Eye of the Needle. And because it was nearing winter—and because this is a story—she was exactly halfway through the Eye when a huge snowstorm struck."

Ayla cracked a smile. "Of course." Her fingers twirled in the cold water, ripples swirling outward until they touched Crier's ankles.

"The princess was trapped," Crier said quietly. "Snow-blinded and half frozen, she just barely managed to find a crevice in the mountainside large enough to shelter both her and her pony. And then, with nothing else to do, she sat down and waited for the storm to die." She paused. "But it did not die."

Ayla was as silent as the storm was loud in Crier's head. Her heart raced.

"Three days later," she plunged on, "the princess and her pony were freezing. The princess tried many times to light a fire, but her kindling was wet with snow and would not spark. Her bag of provisions had been lost in the storm. No food. No fire. She began to accept the fact that she would die here, cold and alone. Worst of all, her kingdom would go to war. She began to cry. Her tears froze on her cheeks, glittering like crystals.

"Just a few moments later, there came a voice from outside the crevice. 'Hello!' it said. 'What creature lives in this cave? Was it your shining coat that caught my eye?'

"A second voice replied, 'Do you have a brain between those ears? There's no creature. It must be a precious gemstone sparkling so bright.'

"'No,' said a third—this one deep, rumbling. 'Clearly it's just a reflection of the snow.'

"'Help,' said the princess through numb lips. 'Please help me.'

"And three animals—a white winter hare, a reindeer, and a great big bear—poked their heads into the crevice. The princess was so weak from cold that she was not scared, not even of the bear. The hare said, 'Why! So it's you with the glittering pearls on your cheeks. Disappointing, I must say. What's a thing like you doing out in this storm?'

"'I am trying to get though the Eye,' the princess said, and told them the whole story. When she finished, the animals all looked at each other with fear. 'That is worrisome,' said the reindeer. 'If there is war between the two kingdoms, your people will trample my forests.'

"'And march through my mountains,' added the bear.

"'And hunt me for meat and pelt!' moaned the hare.

"'Will you help me?' said the princess. 'I'm so cold and so hungry.'

"'Wait here,' said the reindeer. 'We will find you kindling for a fire and food for your belly.' With that, the three animals hurried off into the storm.

"By nightfall the princess was near death. Her lips were blue, her skin white and stiff, her fingers like stone, and even the sparkling tears on her cheeks had been scrubbed away by the icy wind. She leaned back against her pony, eyes closed, thinking only of the letter of peace in her pocket.

"The reindeer was the first animal to return, proudly carrying a pile of dry kindling. 'If you stop the war,' he said, 'remember what I have done for you.'

"So the princess was able to light a fire and stay warm.

"The bear returned next. He was too big to fit into the crevice but stuck his head in beside the reindeer and dropped a mouthful of bark and winter berries at the princess's feet. 'For your pony,' he said. 'If you stop the war, remember what I have done for you.'

"So the princess fed her pony, but her own belly was still hollow. Together, she and the animals waited and waited for the hare to return. The reindeer and the bear began to grumble. *The hare has always been useless*, they said. *He speaks so much and means so little. Maybe he'll never return.*

"Many hours passed before the hare returned. Carrying nothing.

'I'm so sorry, princess,' he whispered, bowing his head so low that his long ears brushed the ground. 'I looked everywhere for food. I found no fish, no mice, no birds. I even checked the hunters' traps. They were all bare. I have nothing to give you. But you must live, princess. You must stop the war. You *must.*'

"And he threw himself into the fire.

"The princess screamed and tried to save him, but it was too late. The hare burned. His flesh became meat. Horrified and ashamed of what they had witnessed, the bear and the reindeer ran away into the swirling snow and were never seen again.

"Even though the idea made her sick, the princess ate the hare. With every bite, she thanked him for his sacrifice. More glittering tears fell and froze on her cheeks. When the storm finally ended and she emerged from her shelter the next morning, she was never the same. Some people said it was as if her heart had wept and frozen over."

The water, and Ayla, had gone perfectly still, and Crier could almost feel the weight of her listening. As if her silence had a shape and pulse of its own.

After a long pause, Ayla turned to her and said, "Wait. That's it? That can't be the end. That's a terrible ending! The whole point of stories is that they're *different* from real life! The hare is dead and the princess is dead inside? What about the war? Stars and skies, what about the princess? Did the peace treaty work? Or did the hare die for nothing?"

"I don't know," said Crier. "Did he?"

Ayla spluttered. "That's not an answer! Come on, how does the story end? You read the book, you should know." Her face in the moonlight was almost furious. Her eyes were sparks, her compact body drawn up like a soldier preparing for battle.

For some reason, Ayla's outrage—over a story, over her words, over, maybe *her*—made Crier smile. A thought came to her: a story of its own, one that had only just begun writing itself in her mind: a story of two women, one human, one Made, who told ancient faerie stories to each other. Who splashed each other at the edge of the water. Who whispered the beauty of snow and the fear of death into the darkness of a late autumn evening.

And with that thought, with that bud of a story blooming inside her, Crier let her body slide into the deep tide pool.

She waded in up to her shoulders, the cold so bracing it left her light-headed. Her dress became ten times heavier in the water, wrapping hard against her skin.

"Crier!" Ayla hissed behind her. "What are you doing? I still want that ending!"

Crier.

Just Crier, no *Lady*.

This was a new feeling.

She turned back to face Ayla. "You'll have to join me to find out what happens next." To find out the ending to both stories. The princess's, and hers.

She heard Ayla huff, but couldn't interpret whether it was a sigh of annoyance or something else. And then:

Ayla splashed into the water. She didn't glide in gently as Crier had done, but plunged in, creating waves, charging right toward Crier. She arrived, face-to-face with Crier in the pool, both of them standing and shivering, though Ayla much harder. Crier's body could handle temperatures far more extreme.

A drop of water gleamed on Ayla's lower lip. Strangely, it made Crier want to—drink.

"So?" Ayla whispered. Her body gave an involuntary shudder.

Crier paused. Ayla had come to her. She had come through the cold of the water, for her, for her story.

Ayla stepped even closer. They were mere inches apart. "How does it end?" she asked, and her words made Crier feel hot instead of cold.

But then Crier remembered the story she was telling. The

war. The hare. The princess. The cruel king. "It ends happily," she lied. She willed her face not to move, her Made lungs not to breathe. "The princess delivers the treaty and the trick works. Her father makes peace with the neighboring kingdom. All is well."

"Ah," said Ayla, more breath than word, a sweet little sigh. "That's good."

Neither of them moved for another long moment, just staring at each other in the dark, Ayla's face unreadable, masked again, this time by moonlight and shadow. She was still shivering.

"You'll fall ill," Crier said at last. "We can't stay."

And so, drenched and shivering, they pulled themselves back up onto the rocks, the ends of their wet clothes dragging across sand and soil all the way back to the palace. They parted silently at the edge of the garden, and the night felt emptier, the air colder than the water had been, when Ayla left, each of them promising not to speak of what had happened.

That night in her bed, though, moonlight falling through the window like a curtain of white silk, Crier could not stop thinking of Ayla—her face, her words, her curiosity, her habits. The ways she moved and spoke. She was unaccustomed to this lack of control over her thoughts—usually she thought only about her studies, or a book she was reading, or carefully constructed fantasies about the future. She had only ever experienced a similar compulsion, a loss of control, when she listened to a piece of music she thought particularly pleasing, diverting, and then found it playing in the back of her mind, perfectly reproduced, for days. An invisible orchestra. Soft strains of piano and violin, a deep heartbeat drum that only Crier could hear.

Now piano was replaced by the way Ayla's dark eyes flickered over Crier's bedchamber the first time she had seen it, the way her gaze had lingered on the hearth, the reading nook, the massive bed. Violin was replaced by the tightening of Ayla's jaw when she knelt beside Crier at breakfast, hands clasped in her lap, head bent in deference to her lady.

Piano. Violin. And the deep heartbeat drums were replaced with a single question: *Why did you save me that day on the cliffs?*

Can you sense the human in me?

There were two possible answers to that question, and Crier had no idea which she would rather hear: *No, you are the perfect Automa,* or . . .

Yes. You are different.

I see you.

No matter how hard she tried, Crier could not force herself to sleep. Ayla was there, always, in the shadows of her mind, looking back, her gaze not like the stars but like the soft darkness that enfolded them.

Stop it.

When she didn't think of Ayla, she thought of Queen Junn, whose upcoming visit would perhaps finally bring answers to the curiosity in Crier's mind.

The restlessness drove her out of bed and into the hallways. She just needed to walk around for a little while, to sort out her thoughts. Along with Ayla's face, she also couldn't stop thinking about Kinok's chilling words during the council meeting— even after the night full of stories, the horror of the day, of its humiliation, was still there, alive and hungry, waiting for her in the darkness. Did he really think there was a chance Council-member Reyka had a Flaw? Surely Kinok had just said it to get under Crier's skin. A latent threat. But what if there was some truth to it? And now Reyka was gone?

Her mind raced with something—a kind of heat—and she thought again of how Ayla had been when she found her at the celebration: *worried*.

Crier was worried. What would happen to *her* if others found out her secret? Found out about her Flaw?

Crier paused for a moment, angry with herself. Kinok had so much power over her, he was ruling even her thoughts.

Maybe she could take some of that power away.

She didn't know whether Kinok had a copy of her Design papers, but if he did . . . if he did, she wouldn't put it past him to blackmail her. He could control her for the rest of her life. But if she got it back . . .

Her father and Kinok had remained at the Old Palace with the other Hands. Hesod had told Crier once that all the real politics happened after the official council meetings—laws were created and negotiated and altered in conversation over glasses of liquid heartstone. While Crier had come home early, Hesod and Kinok wouldn't return until tomorrow morning. Another blow.

But it was as good a chance as any.

Knowing full well it was dangerous and stupid and a terrible idea, Crier made her way to Kinok's study. He kept it locked, of course, while he was in the city, but Crier had once gone through a phase where she learned everything about how locks worked, to the point of designing her own unpickable locks simply for amusement. Locks were interesting, like the gears of a clock or like the workings of a mechanical toy. And unlike the locks Crier had designed, the lock on Kinok's study was not unpickable.

So, using one of the bone hairpins keeping her braid in place, Crier picked it.

She felt a little thrill as the lock clicked open, a satisfying *snick*. Then she slipped through the door and into Kinok's study.

The room was dark. There were no windows, only a dead hearth and a cold lantern. Crier lit the lantern, oil sputtering to life, and looked around. Writing desk, bookshelves, a tapestry on one wall to help insulate the underground room. Now that she was here, Crier didn't know quite where to begin. She didn't even know if her Design papers were going to be here at all.

She snooped around halfheartedly, too nervous to really touch anything. Kinok couldn't know she'd been in here; it would make everything so much worse. Now that the restlessness and the excitement of taking some power back were beginning to fade away, Crier felt more foolish than anything.

What was she *doing*, breaking into Kinok's study in the dead of night? What could this possibly accomplish?

Embarrassed with herself, she glanced over the papers on Kinok's desk one last time. His handwriting was hard to read, especially in the weak, flickering light of the lantern, especially when Crier's heartbeat was pounding so loudly in her ears. She just wanted to get out of here, to go back to the safety of her bed. She was about to extinguish the lantern flame when something caught her eye.

There was a book open on the desk. At first glance, Crier had seen that it was an incredibly dense book about Zullan shipping and trade laws, and she'd paid it no mind. But when she'd leaned forward just now, the lantern light had caught on something: something written in the margin of the book in pale, spidery ink. Two words.

Yora's heart.

It was everywhere, she saw. In the margins and in Kinok's notes. Sometimes those two words were paired with others: *Yora's heart . . . PROTOTYPE?; Y's heart . . . fuel, everlasting, no more rel.; Yora's heart . . . t.w.? s.?* Something in Crier stilled as she stared at the words. What did it mean? Who was Yora?

Somewhere beyond the windows, already lined with dawn, an owl cried out.

Startled, Crier dropped the book back onto the desk. A single page of notes fluttered out and, impulsively, she rolled it up and hastily stuffed it up her sleeve before slipping silently from the room. She blew out her lantern in the hall, its faint oil smoke swirling around her as she hurried away, feeling her way back to her room in the dark, rolling the mysterious, hastily scrawled words over and over again through her mind: *Yora's heart.*

E. 900, Y. 4—5: T. Wren appointed as royal scientist;
still young & unknown; all available accts (see:
Handmaiden Primrose, Maker Oona) of the time
note him as "fame-hungry," desperate for recognition,
obsessed with Q. Thea

> *personally appointed by Q. Thea—why?*
> *obsession romantic/sexual in nature?*

E. 900, Y. 10: Wren receives letter from Unknown
Woman "H——." (Name on letter obscured, no
records of her in Academy files or any other accts
from this period—purposeful? Even Wren, in his
own writing, refers to her as "H." Perhaps to protect
her identity from future historians. Perhaps to protect
himself.) "H——" being a former lover from Wren's
years at the Maker's Academy—letter informs him that
H—— has borne his child.

Excerpt from Wren's personal journal (I):
> *"[. . .] the letter arrived [. . .] battered. Half the*
> *words bleeding from water stains. Nigh unreadable.*
> *Only a single word stood clear from the rest. Her name.*

The girl-child. My child. Siena."

Wren goes to H— immediately. By his own account, he wished to spend time with the child Siena (b. sometime in Y. 9; now almost two years old) and raise her as his own.

Excerpts from Wren's personal journal (II):
"[. . .] Siena has my eyes. My nose. Without a doubt she is mine; she is sired by me. She will be raised by me as well. H reluctant. Regrets sending the letter, regrets seeing me again. Refuses, sometimes, to let me inside the house; to let me see my own daughter.
   [. . .]
   A discovery.
   This could be—it. This could be everything. To think. She was hiding it. That's why she didn't want me in the house. She doesn't care whether I see the child or not. She didn't want me to see this. For good reason. I think I might be carrying a lifetime's supply of gold in my pocket. I think I might be carrying my own legacy.
   It was the child. A toddler; they get into everything. She kept presenting me with little trinkets from around the house. A pen, a shoe, a little wooden toy. Papers from H's study. Blueprints. Designs. Thank the gods I looked them over instead of returning them blindly.
   Siena.
   I don't know if I will see you again.

But I owe you everything. . . ."

E. 900, Y. 11: T. Wren builds the first prototype of what would later become the Automa. He names his creation: "Kiera."

—NOTES ON THOMAS WREN, FROM THE RESEARCH
   JOURNALS OF SCYRE KINOK, FORMERLY OF THE IRON
   WATCH

LATE FALL,

YEAR 47 AE

12

The Mad Queen arrived with a spray of color and gold.

It had been two weeks since the council meeting, two weeks since the Reaper's Moon, and the weather on the northwest coast of Rabu had gone sullen and cold. The queen's retinue, glittering and flamboyant, were an odd contrast to the gray morning.

Ayla had been up with Crier long before dawn, for once accompanied by a few other handmaidens as they all flitted around Crier like honeybees, braiding her hair and painting her face and wrangling her into the kind of gown that one wore, apparently, when meeting a queen—silk the color of dark golden mead, the bodice lined with hundreds of pearls.

To Ayla's disturbance, Crier had seemed almost . . . giddy. But how could she be? Despite the queen's youth, she had a reputation for being violent, temperamental. Even the Automae called her Junn the Bone Eater.

For a moment as she was getting ready, Crier had caught Ayla staring at her red, painted lips in the mirror. It was embarrassing, such a foolish slip-up, but the sight of Crier's mouth had made Ayla think of another moment: the night of the Reaper's Moon, when Crier had slipped into the tide pool and Ayla, a moth to flame, had followed. Under the moonlight, Ayla could have sworn . . . They'd been standing so close together in the dark water, clothes clinging to their bodies, and Crier's eyes had lingered on Ayla's mouth.

Because I could use it, Ayla told herself. *Because the closer I get to Crier, the closer I get to revenge.*

That was the only reason why.

It had nothing to do with Crier's beauty. With the way her mind worked, the careful way she used words, the haunting shape of the story she'd told Ayla that night.

It had nothing to do with the key to the music room, or the way Crier seemed to trust her so readily, her voice going thin and tender in Ayla's presence, her eyes always so watchful, so full of depth.

No. Ayla wouldn't let herself get caught staring again. For the rest of the morning, she didn't meet Crier's eyes even once, ignoring Crier's searching glances. Then she and Crier joined Hesod, Kinok, and a veritable parade of other human servants in the courtyard to wait for Queen Junn.

The sky opened up with a downpour of rain during the second hour of waiting. There were a few minutes of chaos as the servants were sent rushing off to fetch a canopy, and then the truly miserable portion of the morning began: standing, soaked through, under a leaking canopy, unable to see more than a horse's length in any direction past the sheets of freezing rain. The leeches were fine—they didn't seem to feel the cold—but Ayla was shivering, just as she had been the night of the Reaper's Moon, when she stood in the tide pool with Crier.

Once again, Ayla thought of the way she'd told the story of the princess. The way she'd looked at Ayla in the moonlight . . .

No. She couldn't think about that.

Perhaps Crier had been right—perhaps Ayla *was* like a magpie, drawn to the shininess of trinkets. Perhaps Crier was just that—a shiny, distracting trinket. An inconvenience, adorned with a secretive half smile.

But the moment Ayla tried to push Crier out of her mind, Nessa's death would flood into it in her place. Or Benjy's ink-drawn face. She felt scrambled and torn. She was here for revenge, and to help the Revolution, but so far, she had only created more pain and suffering and confusion.

The twin deluges of thoughts and pouring rain only began to let up a little when, at last, the Mad Queen's procession became visible through the fog.

It wasn't the first time Ayla had seen the clothes and colors of Varn—even with the borders locked, plenty of traders made it through and sold their wares in Kalla-den and other human villages—but it was the first time she'd seen a Varnian who wasn't poor and starving. The procession was marked with deep green flags bearing the queen's emblem, a phoenix clutching a

NINA VARELA

sword in one clawed foot and a pickax in the other. The chariot in front was dripping with silver and gold. The servants trailing behind the queen—a long line of horses, carts, some stragglers on foot—were all dressed in jewel tones: green, blue, and violet. Their faces looked . . . strange. Unnaturally pale, like they were made from porcelain. Then they got closer, and Ayla saw it wasn't that these people had bone-white skin—it was that they were wearing white masks over their noses and mouths. The masks looked like they were made of clay or porcelain, molded perfectly to the nose and lips of the wearer. Some of them were decorated: wine-dark blush, painted lips, swirls of silver and green. Individually, the masks were pretty. But all together, the sea of expressionless white faces left Ayla feeling unnerved.

A horn sounded.

"Open the gates," said Hesod.

It took nearly half an hour for the whole procession to file into the courtyard. Ridiculous, thought Ayla, as they all waited for the queen herself to actually appear. This close—half a courtyard away—she could see the details of the queen's chariot, the size of the enormous warhorses all the queen's soldiers and servants were riding. She could also see how the humans were drenched and shivering under their rich clothes.

Leeches were just the same across the border, then.

Another horn, and finally the heavy gates closed behind the last of the servants and the procession was all gathered inside the courtyard. The rain had lightened to a cold mist, the sky washed out and sunless. In front of Ayla, Crier was standing

206

straight-backed, her chin lifted regally and her rain-slicked hair sticking to her neck. Even when she'd gotten rained on, she hadn't moved a single muscle.

The door of the queen's chariot opened, and the Mad Queen Junn climbed out. Her feet were light and soundless even on the muddy ground. Like her servants, she was wearing a white mask over the lower half of her face, though hers was painted with a red mouth. Her skin was the same brown as Ayla's, but like most Varnians her hair was lighter, honey-gold.

She didn't look like a soul eater.

Hesod stepped forward. "Well met, Your Highness," he said, and gestured at his own servants to collect the queen's belongings. The queen greeted him with a nod, and in front of Ayla, Crier had bowed her head in deference—and oh, everyone else was bowing too; most of the humans were kneeling, their noses inches from the mud—and the queen was saying something, and Ayla was supposed to be bowing, but she couldn't move. Her legs weren't working. Her ears weren't working.

Because someone else had stepped out of the chariot behind the queen.

He was tall. Unlike the queen and most of the other servants, his hair was dark. He was wearing the colors of Varn and his face was mostly covered by a white mask and he was tall (taller—three feet taller, at least) than the last time she'd seen him, but stars and skies, oh *gods*, there was that scar over his left eye, shaped like a starburst, pale with age but still recognizable. From half a courtyard away, recognizable. She'd seen it a thousand times. He'd gotten it at three years old after tumbling face-first into the corner of the stone hearth. A stupid wound, a child's wound. The scar had never faded.

Ayla knew it like she knew the ache of sadness in her bones: the man standing at the Mad Queen's side was her long-dead brother, Storme.

As if she'd called his name—as if her shrieking thoughts were so loud that he could actually hear them—Storme's eyes found her through the crowd of leeches and servants. He glanced at her and then away again, and then his eyes skittered back to her face, and all of Ayla's lingering doubts disappeared.

Storme looked like she had just sunk her fist into his stomach. Only his eyes were visible above the white mask, but that was all she needed. When Storme saw her, those terribly familiar eyes went huge. He stopped dead. One of the other servants bumped right into him and still he did not move, not for a long, aching moment, not until he seemed to realize that the queen was cross-ing the courtyard without him, and then he finally dropped his gaze and kept moving. More than anything, that single moment of eye contact confirmed it. This man was her brother.

If she'd had any remaining doubts, they disappeared within hours, because Storme wouldn't stop *watching* her.

She knew, because she'd been watching him.

Once, so long ago that sometimes Ayla wasn't sure whether it was a real memory or just something she'd dreamed, her father had showed her a Maker's notebook. It was filled with drawings of funny mechanical trinkets: music boxes; clockwork birds;

sundials the size of a fingernail; a spherical silver puzzle with a different solution for each phase of the moon. The designs were detailed, intricate, drawn with black ink on paper so thin it was half translucent. When you were looking at one page, you could see through to the next. Two images atop each other, one difficult to make out but still there.

That was what it felt like looking at Storme.

Every time Ayla dared to glance over, she saw two Stormes superimposed on top of each other: one was the Storme she was actually seeing, the Storme who was sixteen years old and dressed in jade-green wool, everything about him strong and shining and *rich*, luxurious, like he'd wanted for nothing in the past seven years. Then there was the Storme Ayla knew (had known), the nine-year-old boy with eyes too big for his face, all his bones showing because he was growing too fast. The Storme who had shoved her into the outhouse and left her there, and *died*. She'd seen it. Heard it, at least. Believed it to be true. But that *scar*.

This Storme—the Storme who followed silently behind Queen Junn—bore the same scar. The exact same one, down to the cleft in his eyebrow.

Because he was *alive*.

He was alive, and real, and here, somehow, *somehow*, after so long.

What happened to you? Ayla thought desperately, as she wrenched her eyes away from him for the thousandth time in the past few hours. *How did you survive? How did you make it out of our village? How did you end up in Varn?*

Why did you leave?

She'd heard him die. Alone in the terrible dark. She'd found his body. What she thought was his body.

For seven years, she'd thought he was dead. That was the only possible explanation. Because—because if he hadn't died, he would have come back. He would have come back for her.

He *would have.*

Ayla trailed listlessly behind Crier as they accompanied Hesod, Kinok, and Queen Junn through a tour of the palace, the gardens, the grassy bluffs. She didn't even try to pay attention, just kept her eyes on the back of Crier's head and concentrated on not losing her footing in the mud. She and Storme were the only humans in their small party. Vaguely, Ayla remembered one of the head scullery maids trying to make Ayla stay behind with the other servants, and Crier saying, "The handmaiden will remain at my side."

So the handmaiden, shadowlike, caught between memory and reality, remained at her side.

There were certain things you heard when you grew up in the streets of human villages. With the gutter rats, the whisperers. Stories of the Mad Queen, the Child Queen. Some said she'd killed her own father to take the throne. Some said she bathed in human blood. She was a legend, or a horror story. But now that the Mad Queen was in front of her, Ayla wondered how those stories had even begun. As much as she hated to admit it, the Mad Queen didn't act like a monster. She did not seem cruel, arrogant, or violent. When she spoke to the humans in her company (and they weren't just servants—the queen had human guards, and *Storme*) her voice was commanding but respectful, almost soft. During the tour of the palace, she kept Storme close. When she saw something she deemed interesting, like the hunting tapestries in the great hall or the library dedicated to Hesod's vast collection of human books, she pointed it out to him and waited for his murmured comments. Like she cared. Like they stood on equal ground.

A single afternoon spent in her presence, and Ayla could tell that the queen of Varn was a mess of contradictions. She wore power like a crown of pure gold, impossible for anyone to ignore, and yet she hadn't once used it to wound or punish. She was young—barely older than Ayla—but carried herself like an aging warrior-queen. She was fierce but gentle, unpredictable in her lack of cruelty. She looked like she could duel anyone in the kingdom and win, but also like she'd rather outsmart them instead.

She wasn't like the stories. Ayla looked at her and couldn't really imagine her bathing in a pool of human blood. Crushing bones between her teeth.

As the tour dragged on, Ayla began to realize that she wasn't the only one watching Junn a little too closely. Crier kept stealing glances, too. For a leech, Crier really wasn't very good at hiding her thoughts. She was looking at Queen Junn with something past curiosity, past intrigue. Almost like awe.

The tour took them through the west wing and to the east

wing, where the queen would be staying. The east wing was much airier than the west, some of the big corridors lined with windows to let in the pale, post-rain sunlight, the white marble walls almost glowing with it. The procession's footsteps echoed on the marble floors, a seemingly unending parade of sound. All of it was human—the queen's men. The Automae were moving in perfect silence, like ghosts. A gesture of deference.

Crier watching the queen.

Ayla watching Storme.

Maybe Storme had been captured, she reasoned. It was uncommon for leeches to take prisoners during their raids, but it happened. Probably. Maybe he'd been captured and somehow ended up in the queen's court and had never, not even once in seven years, had a chance to escape and come find the sister who believed he had been killed.

A wide, windowed corridor led them back into the bowels of the palace, where the marble halls were not so bright and unassuming. Lamplight flickered across the walls here, creating strange, leaping shadows. It was dim even in daylight. The procession's footsteps still echoed, but the sound was duller, emptier. Somehow deadened. Ayla strained her ears to catch Hesod's words as he told the Mad Queen about the history of these halls, the famous Automae who had built this palace and lived here since the War of Kinds. Power breeds power. She was only pulled from her daze when Crier paused in front of a single door, unnoticed by the rest of the party, and beckoned at Ayla to come closer. Ayla did, frowning.

"I want to show you something," Crier said quietly, nodding at the dark wooden door. "I think—I think this will mean something to you. It used to be empty. But as of yesterday, it is empty no longer. Guess who has taken up residence."

"I don't know," Ayla said, shaking her head.

Crier smiled. "It's *Faye*."

Ayla stared at her. "I'm sorry, why does Faye live in the east wing?"

Crier looked almost proud. "I requested it."

"But *why*—?"

"My lady," said another servant before Crier could answer. "Your father has noted your absence and requests that you rejoin him at the head of the party."

"Of course," Crier said smoothly, and turned away from Ayla without another word, following the servant down the corridor toward the tail end of the tour, the last Varnian humans disappearing around the corner. "Come, Ayla."

But Ayla was rooted where she stood, rooted to the marble outside the door that apparently belonged to Faye.

What have you done, Crier?

Before she could think better of it, she knocked on the door. There was a scuffling sound from within, and then the door opened just a crack. Just enough to show a sliver of someone's face, a single wide, unblinking eye.

"What are you doing here?" hissed Faye. "What do you want?"

Ayla glanced down the corridor—Crier was standing there at the very end, half melted into the shadows, so still that she might have been an extension of the marble floor, a statue erected in the middle of the hall. She was waiting for Ayla.

"What are *you* doing here?" Ayla whispered, so quiet that even Crier's Automa hearing wouldn't be able to pick it up. "Why did she give you this room?"

"Sun apples," said Faye.

"What about them? Please just answer me, Faye, why are you here?"

"I don't know," Faye said again, and made a low, hissing noise. She still hadn't blinked. "The shipments he was giving me, they weren't apples, they—"

"He?" She meant Kinok. "What happened, Faye?"

"I tried to make it right," Faye was saying, tears streaking her face. "I tried, I wanted to tell, but he found out first and . . ."

"Ayla!" Crier said, her voice echoing off the walls. "You can converse with your friend later. We will miss the rest of the tour. Come."

Ayla backed away from the door, but couldn't take her eyes off Faye. Her pulse caught in her throat. What was it Malwin had said? *Track the sun apples.* Faye had to be talking about the crates of sun apples the sovereign sent out as gifts for the Red Hands, the nobles, the major merchants and traders, anyone in his good graces. Had Kinok taken over those shipments—and then delegated to Faye? Why?

"Ayla. Handmaiden. *Come.*"

"It's all my fault," Faye whispered, and slammed the door.

13

The queen's tour had exhausted Crier, as if she'd been dragging a weight, a shadow, alongside her through the day. And ever since passing the room full of finery that Crier had specially requested for Faye after learning of Ayla's concern for her, Ayla seemed to have darkened, gone cold. Crier didn't understand it—she should have been . . . *happy? Relieved?* She felt once again completely perplexed by the way a human could swerve so far from their expected response.

And then, on a break between the tour and dinner, Ayla had slipped away, without looking Crier in the eyes. What had happened?

Now Crier was in her room, waiting for dinner. She looked up from her book when she heard a soft knock on the door. She was confused—it couldn't be Ayla, who always rapped on the door with her knuckles like she was trying to start a fight. She was even more confused when she opened the door to find

Kinok waiting on the other side.

"Lady Crier," he said smoothly. "I am here to collect you for dinner."

Why couldn't Ayla do it? Crier wanted to ask, but instead she just inclined her head. She could use this alone time with Kinok, however short it was, to probe for more answers about Reyka.

And of course, the questions she couldn't ask without revealing that she'd tried to spy on him: Why was the phrase *Yora's heart* written everywhere in his notes? Who was the secret woman mentioned in his entries on Thomas Wren?

She wrapped herself in a thin shawl and let him take her arm. They walked slowly through the hallways, passing scullery maids and errand boys. Crier waited until they reached a relatively empty stretch of hallway. Then, before she could lose her nerve, she said, "On the night of the bonding, you said we were in this together. You said you'd keep my—my secret. Yet the moment you stood before the council, you spoke of *Flaws* and *passion*. How could you?"

"I only said that to provoke you."

"You—!" She clamped her mouth shut when a housemaid turned the corner, waiting until the maid was out of sight. "How dare you? To say something like that in front of the *council*, just to—to—I can't believe you." She couldn't remember ever being so disgusted with someone before, where only weeks ago she'd truly believed him to be not much more than a philosopher, a thinker, a historian of their Kind. "And everything you said about Thomas Wren on the night of the binding—the beauty of his work, that each of us is a little different . . . I suppose that was, what, another provocation? Just you playing with my head?"

He huffed a laugh. "Not entirely."

"Then what did it mean? What does any of it mean?" He was such a tangle of studies and experiments and theories, and she suddenly realized she had no idea how they all connected. What did his interest in Wren have to do with ARM, or his past as a Watcher? And what did it all have to do with—"Yora's heart," she blurted out. She stopped walking, turning suddenly to face him. "What is *Yora's heart*?"

His eyes flared for a quick second. She didn't even care that she may have just admitted to snooping through his study— she wanted *answers*, and she was so tired of not getting them, of everyone around her speaking in half-truths and riddles and cryptic puzzles.

"Your curiosity pleases me, Lady Crier," he said, smiling. "Let me show you something."

He led her down the hallway the same way they'd come, toward his quarters in the west wing. Crier hung back when he unlocked the door to his room and looked over his shoulder, waiting for her to follow him inside.

"What are you going to show me?" she asked, increasingly suspicious.

"Just come inside," he said. "I promise, this is something you want to see."

She trailed after him into the room. She'd never been inside his sleeping quarters before, which were on a whole other floor from the private study he kept on the lower levels, and she felt a moment of caution as she entered. It was a large but relatively barren space, the quarters of a temporary guest, with a bed and a desk and some trunks of clothing and a massive tapestry against the side wall. Crier couldn't imagine what he would possibly want to show her, unless it was some sort of bauble from his many travels. She waited for him to retrieve something from one of the trunks, but instead Kinok went straight for the far wall of the room.

He pressed his hand to one of the stones on the wall, and a section of the wall shifted under his touch—a hidden passageway. Crier knew there were a few of them in the palace, most intended as escape routes in case of attack, some leading to private rooms like this one.

The door opened with the sound of stone scraping against stone, and Kinok looked back at Crier again, eyes glittering. "Coming, my lady?"

She followed him into the hidden room and stopped.

Unlike the bedchamber behind them, this room was anything but barren. It was small, barely bigger than a closet, but it looked like one of the alchemical laboratories Crier had seen illustrated in scientific texts: there were vials everywhere, ranging in size from the length of her little finger to large-bellied glass decanters that could have held half a barrel of wine. Some of the vials were connected with thin glass tubes; some were pouring smoke; some seemed to be empty and others were filled with a deep purplish-black liquid. The walls of the room were plastered with diagrams of human and Automa bodies, cross sections showing the veins, the muscles, the intricate spider web of the nervous system. When Crier breathed in, the air tasted acrid and metallic.

"What is this?" she asked, stunned. *Does my father know about this?*

"My little experiment," said Kinok. He stooped down, inspecting one of the vials filled with dark liquid. "Lady Crier, have you heard of Tourmaline?"

"Vaguely," she said. "It's a type of stone, right?"

"Yes and no. Tourmaline is also the name of a compound I have dedicated my life to discovering. There are people—Makers, Midwives, Scyres—who believe that it is possible to create a compound that could fuel Automae indefinitely."

Crier stared at the vials with new interest. "You mean, better than heartstone?"

"Tourmaline would make heartstone look about as effective for our Kind as human wine." He glanced at her just in time to see her eyes widen, and a thin smile spread across his lips. "Imagine it—you wouldn't have to imbibe something every day in order to keep surviving. You wouldn't be dependent on the Iron Heart, on the shipments of heartstone, on those all-too-vulnerable trade routes. This is a substance that could be manufactured anywhere. You would just . . . live. *Free of fear.* Free of threat. And you would be so much stronger than you are now."

"You . . . think we should not rely on the Iron Heart?"

"Of course we shouldn't," he said. "It is, and has always been, a finite resource. It's no different from a diamond mine, Lady Crier. Eventually you run out of diamonds."

Her eyes widened. "How long before we run out of heartstone?"

"No one knows. Not even the Watchers. But—I prefer to prepare for the worst. That way, I am never taken off guard."

Crier absorbed this, reeling, but didn't let herself forget why she was here in the first place. "But what does any of this have to do with 'Yora's heart'?"

"Ah. That, my lady, is simply another name for Tourmaline. I believe it originated from a human rumor, an old wives' tale, about the history of Tourmaline. That is all."

He turned away, effectively ending that line of questioning. Everything about his face and body language read *disinterest*, but Crier couldn't help but think that he wasn't telling the truth about Yora's heart, at least not entirely.

There was a small table in the corner holding an array of tools. Kinok retrieved a thin knife and, as Crier watched, he pricked his finger and let the blood drip into one of the vials. And Crier realized what the dark purplish liquid was. Kinok was experimenting with his own blood.

She turned away, a little repulsed. Her eyes fell on one of the diagrams on the wall. It looked sort of like a human family tree, except it was arranged not from top to bottom but outward from the center, like the spokes of a wheel. The name in the center of the tree was *Thomas Wren*.

"Your investigation," Crier murmured. "Does this map show

the people who worked with Wren?"

"Every genius draws from others," said Kinok almost wryly. "You can learn a lot by tracing the connections from one mind to another."

She didn't answer. She actually felt a little relieved after seeing Kinok's work laid out like this. She traced one of the lines on the map; it was the only one in red.

"What's that one?" Crier asked.

Kinok glanced over. "A rumor, not fully substantiated, but some say that Thomas Wren was in love with another scientist and that she bore him a child."

It comforted Crier somehow. Nothing he was doing seemed very dangerous—maybe she'd been overreacting with her suspicion of him. Maybe he really did want to work *with* her, to help her, Flaw and all.

"I'm glad you find my work intriguing," Kinok said a few minutes later, after carefully closing the hidden door, as they finally headed to the great hall for dinner with Hesod and Junn.

"I do," Crier said honestly. "I like anything that has to do with the history of our Kind. And . . . Tourmaline is certainly a tempting idea. Especially if we really are in danger of running out of heartstone. Have you spoken to my father about this? Or anyone else on the council?"

"So many questions, Lady Crier," he said, smiling indulgently. "Don't worry, I'll give you your answers. And I have more to show you—so much more. As long as you can prove your loyalty to me."

What?

Crier didn't have a chance to ask him what that meant. They had reached the great hall, and Queen Junn awaited.

Dinner was tense.

In a display of Hesod's beliefs, the table in the great hall was piled with human delicacies in addition to the bird's-skull teapot of liquid heartstone: stewed lamb, salted fish, rich brown bread with butter and honey, platters of sugared fruits from the orchards. No one ate except the queen.

Hesod sat beside Queen Junn as she feasted, partaking in cordial conversation. But Crier could see something cold and calculating in her father's eyes. He looked regal tonight, in the deep-red robes he usually reserved for council meetings or other formal affairs. A gold brooch glinted at his throat, engraved with the crest of the sovereign: a clenched fist, a crown, a glittering ruby. He was smiling. Arranging his features into something friendly—the welcoming, good-humored ruler. But his eyes told a different story.

Crier took a sip of her liquid heartstone. It was all she could keep down. She could *hear* the noise of Ayla's stomach eating itself whole. Ayla was kneeling at Crier's feet, like usual, even though Queen Junn's human adviser was seated at the table with everyone else. It made Crier's skin feel itchy and too small.

Ayla had been acting distant all day. During the tour of the palace, she had trailed behind Crier like a silent specter, looking ahead with sightless eyes. At one point, she'd nearly tripped over the train of Crier's gown. Would have, if Crier hadn't yanked it out of her path just in time.

The only thing that seemed to catch Ayla's attention was the human adviser. Whenever he so much as breathed audibly, Ayla's eyes flicked over to him, sharp and *awake*. It had been like that all day. What was so fascinating about him? Crier frowned at the uneaten scraps of meat on her plate. Was it because he was human? She glanced at him over the rim of her teacup. He was—not bad-looking, without the white mask. He actually looked a little similar to Ayla, as if they had come from the same village. Like Ayla, the adviser had thick, dark hair. He had a similar chin, a similar bump on the bridge of his nose. Though Crier noted that he didn't have Ayla's freckles. Or her cheekbones.

Not bad-looking, no, she thought to herself, and tore off another chunk of bread she had no desire to eat.

As if he somehow sensed that she was thinking about him, the adviser chose that moment to speak. "Lady Crier," he said, and Crier went still—a bit stunned that a human would address her directly, unprompted. He spoke like a native Rabunian, not like someone from Varn. That explained the dark hair. "Do you have anything to voice?"

She blinked. "I—I became distracted. Apologies," she said, nodding to the queen and then her father. "What is the subject?"

"What else?" he said. "Coexistence."

"I am my father's daughter," she said. "I believe in the perpetuation of Traditionalism. Coexistence, to a degree, with certain social, cultural, and political boundaries in place to separate the two Kinds."

Crier had said these words many times before, but they left a bad taste in her mouth this time. Her eyes wanted to find Ayla, but instead they found her father.

Across the table, Hesod regarded her with approval.

This was what she always wanted, his approval. But somehow, in this moment, it did not give her satisfaction. Rather, she felt unease.

"Interesting, daughter of Hesod," said Queen Junn, who was seated at the head of the table. Unlike most guests, she had not balked when presented with human food; she had eaten without complaint. Now she was watching Crier, her long fingers curled around a cup of liquid heartstone. "Then you truly believe that boundaries are necessary for peace between the Kinds?"

"Yes," said Crier. For some reason, she was finding it a little difficult to hold Junn's gaze. "All societies require some level of social organization. A society without boundaries and separation devolves into anarchy, chaos."

"You know this through experience?"

"Through extensive study."

"I agree with you," said the queen. "I do think society requires some sort of organization in order to function. But I am curious, Lady Crier: Why do you think we must be separated according to Kind? Why draw the borders of our hierarchy according to Made or not-Made?"

Because it's obvious, Crier almost said. *One Kind is stronger and one Kind is weaker. One dominant, one submissive. One meant to rule, the other to obey.*

Two months ago, she would have given that answer—straight from her books, straight from her lessons, straight from her father's teachings.

Now, though.

Now, with Ayla beside her (kneeling at her feet, refusing scraps), with the queen's human adviser across from her, Crier found herself unable to answer so easily. Her hesitation lasted only a moment, but it was still long enough for Hesod to cut in.

"You ask too much of her," he said, refilling his cup. His mouth was stained red. "My daughter is brilliant, but her mind is best suited for a library, not a debate."

You've never let me debate, Crier thought sourly. *So how would you know?*

"My apologies, Lady Crier," said Junn. "I forgot myself. I take too much pleasure in sharing my own beliefs."

"Ah," said Hesod, smiling indulgently. "Here it comes."

"You see, Lady Crier," said Junn, "for me, coexistence—not Traditionalism, not Anti-Reliance"—Crier stiffened at the mention of Kinok's movement and hoped the queen wouldn't notice—"but absolute coexistence, *true* coexistence, equality between the Kinds—is more reality than fantasy. In Varn, Automae and humans live and work side by side."

"I can think of nothing more admirable," said Crier, and Hesod's smile stiffened around the edges. Kinok, for his part, was silent. His face was blank, his eyes glittering with—amusement, maybe. "I know you've been working toward that reality ever since you took the throne."

"The War left my country all but destroyed," said Junn. "We are still rebuilding. We are simultaneously ancient and newborn. We are a growing nation, and all growing things must ache and learn and readjust. But in my nation, every day, we come closer to a future in which Automae and humans live in harmony."

Crier stared at her, transfixed.

"A fascinating idea," said Hesod. "But completely impractical. Our Kind was created for the express purpose of—"

"Lady Crier," the queen interrupted, and Hesod fell silent perhaps only because no one had ever interrupted him before. Crier could tell how much it rankled him, but he kept his mouth shut. Junn was a queen on a tour of diplomacy. None of them could afford to offend her. "After dinner, I would very much like to speak with you," she said. "Privately."

The shock from Hesod and Kinok—and admittedly Crier herself—was palpable, but the queen's smile didn't wane. Crier almost looked to her father for direction, but then she remembered the way he had ignored her during the council meeting. The way he'd said, *Stay.*

She raised her chin and met the queen's gaze dead on. "I would be honored, Your Highness."

And so, after dinner, Crier was summoned to Queen Junn's quarters. She tried to walk slowly at first, dignified, but the apprehension in her stomach made it feel like she'd swallowed a nest of horseflies. Her steps grew faster and faster until she rounded a corner so quickly that she startled a housemaid into dropping an entire tray of cutlery, all of which fell to the flagstones with a tremendous clatter, which resulted in the housemaid trying to simultaneously curtsy, collect the fallen forks and knives, and apologize profusely. Crier hovered for a moment before realizing that her presence seemed to make the housemaid nervous, and then she left, feeling extremely awkward and no less apprehensive.

When she knocked on the queen's door, it opened immediately, Queen Junn ushering her wordlessly inside. Maybe Crier was not the only one who felt a strange urgency right now.

The bedchamber was sparse. The queen's company was set to leave the next morning at dawn, so the only signs of life in the massive room were the hearth fire and the slightly rumpled bedding. There was a platter of cheese and candied fruits on the table, untouched.

Crier shifted awkwardly, gripping at her skirts. "You wanted to speak with me, Your Highness?"

"Please," said the queen. "Sit."

Crier sat in one of the two chairs at the table. The queen sat across from her. They were so much closer than they had been over dinner. Crier could smell her, like rain and dark spice.

"I am not the type to mince words, my lady," said Queen Junn. "The Scyre is a *problem*."

Crier's first thought was, *Stars and skies, finally.* "Oh?"

"But you already know that, don't you," said Junn, reading it from Crier's face. "You fear him."

"I do not *fear* him," Crier corrected her. "I do not fear anyone."

Junn smiled with her teeth showing. It was a smile somewhere between kindness and wickedness. "Fear is a good thing, Lady Crier. Fear means you are alive, and you want to keep it that way."

"My life is not in danger."

"Of course not," said Junn. "Because you are untouchable. Because you were Made to be invincible." She leaned closer. "I'll tell you a secret, Lady Crier. Humans believe themselves invincible, too."

A flash of memory: solid ground disappearing beneath her feet, the cliffside slippery and crumbling in her grip. Dark water below, white foam, tooth-sharp rocks. The clear image of her own body, shattered and bloated, her Made flesh unwanted by the wheeling seagulls.

Not invincible, no.

"What do you know about Kinok?" Crier asked.

"He is powerful," said Junn. "His ideas are dangerous. They spread like a human infection. You have studied the various plagues of the human world, I'm sure."

Crier nodded.

She remembered books filled with graphic illustrations. Human bodies bisected, cross-sectioned. Studies of ruined skin, weeping wounds. Maps covered in thin red lines, detailing the spread of a hundred different sicknesses.

"Fever and fervor," said Junn. "There is very little difference, in the end."

"Fervor isn't necessarily dangerous, Your Highness. Neither is passion."

Crier fought the urge to clap a hand over her mouth. Suddenly she felt like one of the illustrations in those medical books—flayed open, exposed. *Passion isn't dangerous?* There was nothing more dangerous. Nor was there a reason for her to argue in Kinok's favor—it was more a gut reaction, a defense mechanism because she felt so flustered. Why did she feel so flustered?

Queen Junn leaned in closer. And then closer still, so close that Crier's breath quickened in her throat. "You're right," Junn murmured. "But the Scyre's ideas *are* dangerous. I know this; you know this. I see it in your face when you look at him. I know that look because I have worn it myself."

"What do you mean, Your Highness?"

"You are not the first maiden to draw his attention, Lady," said Junn, jaw tightening. "Before you, it was me. He came to my palace last autumn. I admit: in the beginning, I found him charming. Desirable. He is clever, Lady, even for our Kind."

"He—he courted *you*?" Crier asked, shocked that she hadn't known of this. Did her father know? Did it even matter?

"Of course," the queen answered, waving the back of her hand as if brushing away a fly. "As you may have noticed, he is drawn to any whiff of power. His supporters are vocal, but his base is small. In order to truly push his agenda, he must ally himself with an established force. But I admit that even I was intrigued at first. For the whole of autumn, his ideas seemed to glitter inside my head. He spoke of a glorious future for our

Kind, and I wanted so badly to help him create it. But it was a tangle of lies, Lady. A fox's trick."

At Crier's confused look, she continued. "It's from an old human story. Once, during a long and terrible winter, Fox and Bear were afraid that their children would starve. Their milk had dried up and they were both too weak to hunt. Everybody knew that Fox was the cleverest animal in the whole forest, so Bear went to her and begged for help. 'My children are hungry,' she said. 'I can hear their bellies at night. What should I do?' And Fox told her, 'Last week, Brother Wolf attacked the farm on the edge of this forest. He killed one sheep and two fat hens. Now the humans are scared. Go to them peacefully and tell them that in exchange for one fresh hen per day, you will guard their hens and livestock from the wolves. You are weakened, but your body is big and your teeth are sharp. Brother Wolf will not cross you.'

"So Bear did as Fox said. That night, she left her cubs in their den and traveled to the farm on the edge of the forest. She knocked very gently on the farmer's door and said, 'I come peacefully. Please let me in.' And the farmer opened the door only to sink his hunting knife into Bear's heart. He thought it was another attack, you see."

Crier watched Junn's face as she spoke. Junn's eyes were focused on something that did not seem to exist in this room, something visible only to her.

"What happened next?" Crier asked. "Did Fox steal the farmer's chickens?"

"No," said Junn. "Fox waited until Bear's children died of

starvation. Then she ate them. The meat of two bear cubs was enough to last Fox and her kits through the final weeks of winter. She had hunted without ever lifting a paw."

"So she killed Bear on purpose."

"Weren't you listening?" asked Junn. "Fox didn't kill Bear. The farmer did. When the other animals discovered what had happened, they all blamed Bear for going mad. 'Walking right up to the farmer's door,' they said. 'What a fool.' And Fox nodded along with them, and nobody ever found out what she had done."

She looked at Crier closely, searching her face.

"So Kinok is the fox," Crier said. "Clever and deceiving."

The queen smiled. "No, my dear. Kinok is the *wolf*." She paused and stared at Crier for a moment. Then she said, "I want *you* to be the fox."

Her words moved over Crier like a wave of arctic air. "You said he spoke of a future for our Kind," she said slowly. "What future is that?"

"The New Era." The smile had left Junn's face. "The Golden Era. To the Scyre, it's a travesty that we still inhabit human cities—he thinks of us as vultures picking at dead things, living on the bones of a failed civilization. The true dreams of the Anti-Reliance Movement go far beyond just one capital city. He wants to raze *all* the old cities to the ground and build new cities, Made cities, Designed entirely for our Kind. Cities where humans are not only unwelcome but incapable of survival. Let them struggle, starve, kill one another off until they are, as his supporters would put it, 'no longer our problem.' And that's not all. He wants to Make a new breed of Automae. He wants the next generation of our Kind to be even stronger, sharper. With no human pillars at all. And most importantly, most desperately, he wants to end our reliance on the Iron Heart."

"He . . . he did mention something like this to me." Crier's mind whirred, overwhelmed by all the information.

"He claimed to have discovered a new source of power."

"Yes, he told me of his idea, but . . ."

Junn gave her a long, level look. "My lady, you of all people should know that there is no such thing as *just* an idea." Junn leaned forward again. "It is not merely philosophical. It is very real. The Anti-Reliance Movement is already under way. The Scyre's followers drink his words like sweet wine. There are only a few hundred now, but every day their numbers grow. A few hundred can turn into a few thousand in a matter of days. I need your help, Lady Crier."

"My—my help?"

"To stop the disease, before it spreads."

Still, Crier stared, unsure what that meant.

And so, the queen clarified: "To take him down."

Junn said it almost casually, like she was saying nothing more than *To bid him good morning.*

Finally, Crier understood why people called her the Mad Queen. How she could be the Child Queen and Junn the Bone Eater, everything at once.

"I don't know," she whispered, mortified by her own cowardice and yet unable to hide it. "I—I am betrothed to him, he's on the council, he's *powerful*—he's under my father's protection—"

He knows about my fifth pillar—

He could destroy me—

He wanted, in fact, to destroy all humans, or at the very least, to make the world increasingly uninhabitable to them. . . .

He was far more a monster than she'd realized.

"Do not be ashamed of your fear, Lady Crier," said Junn. "If you were not afraid, I would leave this room and never once look back. But you are afraid. That is why I trust you, and why I'm asking for your help." Her expression softened. "And I really am only asking. I will not force your hand, my lady. Nor will I beg."

"I need time," Crier said. "I need to think."

Junn nodded, leaning back a little. Without the smell and warmth of her, it was a little easier to breathe. "Of course," she said. "I wish I had more time to give you, but my company leaves at dawn. If you decide you want to help me, take this and slide it under the door to my bedchamber." She held out a green feather. "In Varn, the color green symbolizes alliance. We use it to communicate."

". . . We? Who's we?"

"Those who wish to take sides against the wolf," Junn said, and smiled, all teeth.

A few hours later found Crier standing in the corridor outside the queen's quarters, a green feather clenched tightly in her hand. She had the fleeting thought that she wished she knew where Reyka was, wished she could talk to her, ask for her advice. But Reyka was still missing, and every day that ticked by meant the worst was possible. Reyka might be dead. She might have been killed.

There was no evidence one way or the other, only the lingering taste of dread every time Crier thought of it.

She *was* afraid, but she was also tired of feeling like a pawn.

And Junn was right. She was tired of *Kinok*: his blackmail, his hatred of humans, his black-banded followers. The pleasure he took in wielding power, in making Crier feel helpless, reminding her at every turn that he knew about her Flaw.

She did not like feeling helpless.

She had no idea what would happen if she agreed to work with Queen Junn, but the days were slipping by so quickly. Soon, the trees would all be naked. Soon it would be winter, and she would be wedded. She would be pushed gracelessly into a new life with Kinok. Where would they go after they were married? Kinok had no estate of his own. That was probably half the reason he'd tried to woo Queen Junn. Where would he take her—the Far North, to the site of his planned new city?

Crier didn't know what she wanted. Her old dream had festered and died. All she knew was this: *she did not want to be Kinok's wife.*

With that thought in mind, she stepped forward—and heard a strange noise from inside the queen's bedchamber.

Low and throaty, it sounded almost like an expression of pain.

Crier froze. Was the queen in danger? She was protected by her guards, but what if they'd been overcome? What if she was being attacked?

Then the noise came again, louder and more drawn out this time, *breathy*, and Crier realized what it was.

Her whole body went cold and then terribly, ferociously hot. Whoever was making that noise was not in pain.

In shock, Crier couldn't move. She listened to the sound of gasps, and immediately her mind went to flesh against flesh, went to breath and lips and . . .

She scrambled backward to hide around the corner, far enough from the queen's door that she could no longer overhear what was happening inside. Her heart churned quickly; her skin was flushed with a new kind of heat. She didn't even know why she was reacting so strongly. She had seen *such things* before, from afar: human servants embracing in the orchard when they thought no one was looking. But that was different. That was humans, who mated physically, who were not Made. That was humans, who were weak against their base temptations and desires. *Like dogs in heat*, her father had said once.

Automae did not—do that.

They did not need to.

But the voice she'd heard (*the moan*, her mind whispered) had definitely belonged to Queen Junn.

Crier pressed a hand to her face, touching her own hot skin, and made up her mind to wait out here. If she left now, she might never work up the courage to come back.

It took only a few more minutes before she heard the door to the queen's bedchamber open and shut. Crier barely had enough time to shrink farther into the shadows before someone walked right past the corner she was hiding behind, making their way to another door down the hallway. It was dark, and their face was hidden by a mask, but the shape of their silhouette was unmistakable. The person sneaking out of the queen's bedchamber was her human adviser.

A secret lover.

A secret *human* lover.

The young man whom she'd heard the queen refer to during the tour as Storme.

Crier slumped back against the wall, cool stone on the nape of her neck. *Stars and skies.* She thought of the queen and the adviser, the way they'd acted around each other today.

She tried to concentrate, to slow the frantic whir of her mind, but it flew uncontrollably to the place she knew it would—Ayla. *Her* lips. *Her* breath. *Her* skin. Darkness and touching and kissing and . . .

She bit her lip hard enough to draw blood.

Head spinning, mouth filled with the heavy taste of her own blood, Crier ran away down the corridor and did not stop until she reached her own room, but even then, even with the door slammed shut, she was confronted with the heady darkness, her body, pulsing with new information, and above all, the thing she knew now she wanted, even though it was unnatural, even though it was wrong.

Passion.

She was called the Barren Queen, but I never met anyone less empty. For if one is wanting of a child, then by nature their heart is overfilled with love— overflowing, yearning for a new vessel to hold that love, like spilling water.

There are some who call her a monster. Some who call her mad.

If longing is madness, then none of us are sane.

—FROM THE PERSONAL RECORDS OF BRYN,
BIRTH-WITCH TO QUEEN THEA OF ZULLA, E. 900,
CIRCA Y. 40

14

Did you hear about Faye?

Yes. I heard she's got her own private rooms in the palace now. I heard she's got her own handmaiden, just like the lady.

Not just that. She's living the golden life now. The leech life.

How did it happen? Last I heard she was mad. Wandering the halls like a ghost.

I'd kill for a bit of cake.

I'd kill for a private room.

I'd kill for a night in a real bed.

Makes you wonder what she did for it.

The whispers were unbearable.

Ayla had been listening to them all day: in the servants' quarters, in the dining hall, in the hallways, one scullery maid to another, kitchen boys muttering to each other when they thought they were alone. *Faye is a traitor, Faye is a lapdog.* Ayla knew exactly who was behind Faye's newfound lifestyle, and it made her want to shake that *certain someone* hard enough to rattle their teeth.

Of all the fool things to do.

She suspected that Crier had only been trying to help. But didn't she see? It only made things worse. Drew attention, placed a target on Faye's back . . . and soon enough, Crier's attentions would put a target on Ayla's back too, if they hadn't already.

Not to mention, these little acts of . . . what . . . kindness? They made Ayla uncertain, made her question what she thought she know of Crier, of leeches in general. They didn't have feelings. They didn't act out of kindness. Crier was no different.

Was she?

As soon as darkness fell, the last of Ayla's patience drained away. Her feet ached from the long day of managing the queen's tour and racing about to help with the arrangement of her guest quarters and Crier's dinner gown and—the list went on and on.

Still, she managed to wait just a few more minutes, until the other servants were asleep, and then she crawled out of bed, threw on a coat over her sleeping tunic, and moved toward the door.

But just as she stepped outside into the cool night air, she heard someone call her name, softly, from inside. "Ayla."

It was Benjy. He slipped out of the servants' building and stood there in the darkness of the night, his curly hair lined in moonlight, his jaw cut by shadows. "Where are you going?" he whispered. "Not visiting the lady at this hour, I hope. . . ."

Ayla stopped short. "What exactly are you trying to say?"

Benjy put up his hands, as if in surrender. "Nothing. Only that people will talk. She does seem to have . . . I don't know. Some sort of fondness for you. Or that's what they say, anyway."

"People always talk, Benjy. But they know nothing. And, and . . . *no*. I wasn't going to see Cri—the lady. I . . ."

Where to begin? So much had happened in this one day—she'd seen Storme, alive again after so many years believing he was dead, was lost to her forever. Then there was the strangeness of the queen herself. And the disturbing encounter with Faye in her new private room. And the way Crier had glanced back at her all day as Ayla walked just a few steps behind her, with something like curiosity—or more—in her eyes.

But how could she explain all this to Benjy?

Instead, all she said was, "I left out a dress that needs ironing before tomorrow. I know I won't sleep if I keep thinking about the grief I'll get in the morning."

Benjy tilted his head at her. "I've missed you, you know," he said softly.

Her chest thudded with a painful pang. She couldn't look into his dark, glossy eyes. "Me too."

He stepped toward her and she could see his face better now. His lips were parted, once again as if he planned to tell her something important. But all he said was, "Well, hurry up and don't let the Varnian Queen eat your bones."

Ayla let out a small laugh. "She's not the monster everyone says. Or if that *is* her true nature, she keeps it well hidden."

"As only the most dangerous monsters do," Benjy said.

"True. . . . Listen, Benjy. I did learn something strange today. I can't quite understand it. It's about Faye."

"Did something happen? I heard the gossip, that she was promoted to a guest room. Do you know about it?"

Ayla shivered as a cool breeze lifted at the edges of her coat. She wrapped her arms around herself. "I saw her. And . . . there's definitely something . . . wrong with her. She kept mentioning the sun apples. I think Kinok had her managing the sun apple shipments. I can't quite figure what that has to do with anything, whether it's connected to Luna's death, or why Faye has unraveled. I just . . . wanted you to know. In case you hear anything."

Benjy nodded. "I'll see if I can find out anything on my end."

"Great." It felt good to be working together, even if her pulse sang with worry. "Now get back to sleep. I'll return in a few minutes, but don't wait up for me."

"Need my beauty rest anyway," Benjy said, and slipped back inside the sleeping quarters without another word.

Once he was gone, Ayla hurried up the muddy path to the palace. The night was harsh and windy.

She hadn't told him about Storme. She couldn't. Not yet, anyway. She didn't know what to think of it herself.

First, she had to see her brother—alone.

To get her questions answered.

Her ears hadn't stopped ringing all day, her mind buzzing with a hornet's nest of memories: Storme, young and scrawny and grinning in the dusty sunlight; Storme, sitting at their father's elbow, whittling a new handle for his knife; Storme, standing beside their mother, laughing as she ruffled his dark curls.

Storme, shoving her down into the dark; Storme, his mouth twisted into a furious snarl, *I'll kill them, I'll kill every single one of them*; Storme, peering out the front door during one of the first raids, *I hate those leeches more than anything*; Storme, knife flashing in his hand, *I'll cut their dead hearts from their chests.*

Storme, right hand to the leech queen.

There was no way he was serving her of his own free will. The queen must be hanging something over his head—the life of a friend, a lover, a child, someone, anyone. Whatever the blackmail, Ayla intended to find out. And help free her brother.

She still had Crier's key to the music room. She'd find him, bring him there, where they could talk in private.

She'd tell him about the Revolution, about Kinok's sinister chart, his means of punishing them, his secret safe, hidden somewhere in his study, in the bowels of the palace.

She was used to the twisting hallways of the palace by now, having walked it so many times with Crier. The queen had been put up in the north wing, the same as Hesod and Crier, as it was the only wing with guest chambers big enough to house her guards and servants and advisers and anyone else she'd brought along with her from the southern mines up to the cold northern shores.

"You."

Ayla froze midstep. She turned slowly to see a leech guard stalking toward her, his face like marble in the moonlight, boots unnaturally silent on the flagstones. A sheath glinted at his waist.

"What are you doing here?" he demanded. "No servants have been granted entry to this wing." He looked her up and down. "No *pets*, either."

Revulsion had the taste of bile. She struggled to keep her face and voice calm. "I am Lady Crier's handmaiden, sir, and I am here on her direct orders."

"Right. And what lady's errand is so urgent at this hour?"

"I don't think that's any of your business," Ayla replied.

Mistake.

The guard's eyes widened and his perfect mouth twisted into something ugly. "You arrogant little maggot," he said coldly, taking a step forward.

The closer he got, the more obvious it was how much taller he was than her, than any human she knew; how much stronger, too. How quickly he could dart forward and snap her neck simply for impertinence. "Know your place. If you don't, I will take pleasure in teaching you."

Ayla stumbled backward, thinking of her stolen knife—her sharp little knife, so deadly and so *useless* back in the servants' quarters. "Don't touch me. Lady Crier won't like it if you harm me."

"Lady Crier has no use for such a disobedient handmaiden," he said, toying with the hilt of his sword. "I think you would serve more purpose as a warning to the others."

"*I said don't—*"

"Handmaiden!"

Ayla whirled around, and there he was. Storme. He was striding down the corridor from the opposite direction the guard had come, gilded in moonlight from one of the windows lining the stone walls. Ayla was once again struck by how big he was, how broad. She had known him as a scrawny child, no meat on his bones. She herself had stayed small, half starved and hard-worked, but Storme had grown up strong. She felt twin swells of pride and shame.

"You are dismissed," he said to the guard, leaving no room for argument. "This girl was summoned by the queen of Varn. You will inconvenience her no longer. Leave us."

Even the way her brother spoke was different now. Mature. The voice of a man, not a boy.

A man she didn't know anymore.

But it worked: the guard opened and closed his mouth. Then, furious, he turned on his heel and slunk away into the shadows.

Neither Storme nor Ayla spoke until the guard's footsteps faded away. Then—

"Ayla," Storme breathed.

Her whole body seized up. Every muscle in her wanted to run at him, to throw her arms around his waist, to feel for herself that he really was *here, whole, alive.* Her arms wanted to hug him and her eyes wanted to memorize his face, to search for all the tiny remnants of their parents; her feet wanted to stamp on his toes; her mouth wanted to say, *I've missed you so much, I can't believe you're here, I can't believe you survived, why did you never come back for me?*

Instead, her mouth said, "I never thought I'd see you working for a leech."

Storme's face shuttered instantly.

He leaned back against the window.

"I could say the same to you," he said.

This wasn't at all what Ayla wanted, but now that she'd started it, she couldn't stop. "Are you a servant like me?" she asked him, stepping closer. "Are you trapped like me? What does the queen have on you, Storme? Are you plotting against her? Are you getting close to her so you can—"

"Shut up," he said fiercely. "Shut up, you know they can hear through stone walls. You'll get yourself killed."

She paused, and realized she was breathing hard. She was so—there wasn't a word for it; she wasn't angry or sad or scared or overjoyed or guilty or betrayed or any of it, she was all of it, all at once, her emotions mixing like oils in bathwater, impossible to separate and define. "You're not her servant," she said, trying to work through the things she'd been obsessing about all day. "You're—she doesn't treat you like a servant. You're her *adviser*. How did that happen, Storme?" She stared at him as if the answer would show itself on his face. "What *happened* to you?"

"I want to tell you," he said. "Later. Not now. Not where anyone could hear."

"Later," Ayla repeated slowly, still in shock. "But how long do we have? Where have you been? What's *happened*?" she asked again.

He sighed. "It's complicated, Ayla."

"Don't say that like you're older than me," she hissed. "Don't you dare say that like I don't know the world is *complicated*."

"There are things you don't—"

"Understand?" She reared back, so shocked she almost wanted to laugh. "You're damn right there are things I don't understand. Here's one: I don't *understand* why you spent the last six years, what, living in Varn? Worming your way into the queen's graces, while people are *dying* here in your home country, every day, the raids never stopped, and—*I was here*. I was here, and you didn't come back for me. You're right: I don't *understand*." Horrifyingly, her voice cracked on the last word.

"Lower your voice, Ayla," said Storme. "Stars and skies, *control yourself*."

She stared at him.

Took a deep breath.

"I have been controlling myself," she said. "Everything I do is about controlling myself. How do you think I ended up here, in this palace? How do you think I became a—a leech's handmaiden? Every single thing I have done over the past five years has all been working up to *this*."

"Working up to *what*, exactly?"

Should she tell him? It was already tumbling out of her in a torrent. The Resistance. The spying. The Iron Heart.

Revenge.

Storme stared at her in silence for a moment. She remembered when she used to be able to read those silences; now it was like an unbearable weight. "I don't think you should be interfering with Kinok, Ayla. Not on your own like this. It's not safe."

She scoffed. "As if you have any right to tell me what's safe anymore."

"Do you even know what the Anti-Reliance Movement is all about? Do you have any *idea* what you're getting into?"

"I know enough."

"Oh *gods*, Ayla. You know nothing. ARM may seem innocuous on the surface, but there is nothing but darkness below. If you've got any sense at all, you'll stay far away from anything to do with it."

Ayla just barely stopped herself from yelling, *You can't tell me what to do!* like a child throwing a tantrum. Part of the problem was that, despite herself, his words were sinking in. What did she know about ARM, really, that wasn't straight from Kinok's mouth?

"You were gone, Storme," she said, shoving her doubts aside. If there was one thing she was certain about, it was her anger. "You were *gone*. And now it's too late. You have no control over me. I've made promises. Nothing you can say will stop me."

He sighed. "That's always been your style, hasn't it? Little Ayla. Always planning something. Have you already forgotten the rats?"

"That has nothing to do with this," she said. "That was—I was a *child*."

"It's the same thing at the core."

"It *isn't*."

"Think about it, Lala."

"Don't *call me that*—"

It was summer, hot and muggy, everyone sweating, the whole village crusted with salt and swarming with horseflies. The air smelled like rotting seaweed. Ayla was six, maybe seven, old enough to know certain things—we are poor, we are hungry, something bad lives on the northern cliffs, Mama and Papa are scared, there are whispers of raids—*but too young to know what was coming, or how bad things really were, or how close they were to death, always, every hour of every day.*

But Ayla wanted to help.

She wanted to make bread.

It was a simple idea. The whole village was on rations for pretty much everything: grain, salt, butter. Ayla hadn't eaten bread for months. They'd been living on salted fish.

She knew how to make bread: mix the flour with water and let it sit; she knew how to roll the dough and

*salt it and slash it and how long to let it sit in the hot
ashes of the hearth.*

*So, for weeks, she snuck a single spoonful of flour from
the grain rations every fifth night, such a small amount
that Mama never noticed anything. She stole pinches
of salt from Old Woman Eyda's doorstep, because Old
Woman Eyda believed that salt would drive spirits and
demons and leeches away. The last thing she collected
was a pot of honey, or rather the dregs of it, a scraping of
honey that Mama had given to her as a rare treat after
they used up the rest of their ration. It was so hard to save
the honey instead of smashing up the pot and licking the
shards clean, but Ayla had willpower.*

*Flour, salt, honey: she hid it all beneath the loose
floorboards under her bed, waiting for the summer air to
dry out a little. Every night, she fell asleep picturing the
look on her parents' faces when she presented them with a
perfect loaf of sweet brown bread, still steaming from the
coals. Her stomach felt so empty, those nights.*

One morning, she woke up to a shout.

She jolted awake and leaped out of bed—Is this a
raid? Are we being raided? Is this what a raid sounds
like?—*only to shriek in horror when her foot landed on
something* soft, *something that made a horrible shrieking
noise right back and then wriggled out from beneath
her foot. Then Ayla saw that her mother was wielding*

a frying pan, her brother a broom, her father stomping around the floor in his fisherman's boots—and the floor was moving, *it was* moving, *a writhing dark mass of—rats.*

There must have been a hundred rats swarming the floor, hissing and climbing all over each other, their bony pink tails moving like snakes. They'd gnawed their way through the loose floorboard under her bed. They had eaten the flour, and the salt, had even shoved themselves inside the empty pot of honey and licked it clean.

They had eaten all the salted fish. And the pickled fish.

All of Mama's flour rations.

All the barley, and the seaweed, and the lard, and the eggs. All of it gone.

"That was years ago," she said now, shoving the rats and their awful musky rat smell far away, back into a distant corner of her mind. "I was a child. We both were."

"Yes," he said. "And I grew up."

What the hell does that mean, you traitor, you abandoner, you coward, she wanted to say, but swallowed it.

"Yes. You sure did grow up. *Somewhere.* But where? Where did you even go? After you—after—I thought you were . . . I thought you were *dead.* Do you even *realize* what that was like for me?" The words grated up through her throat, and she ground her teeth together to keep from screaming. "Your body.

It was all burned up. It was *you*. I saw it. And, and, and you never came back, Storme. You never came back."

She couldn't help it now. Tears were streaking down her face and she swiped angrily at her cheeks, trying to wipe them away, but it was no use. How dare he disappear. How dare he be alive all this time and never reach out, never reassure her, never *tell her*.

It was a whole new kind of pain, raw and wrenching, one she had been choking down all day, she realized, and now it was erupting uncontrollably.

"Ayla." His hand was on her arm, and then, gently, he touched the golden chain that was there, always, just beneath the lip of her shirt. "You still wear it," he whispered.

She trembled. Of course she still wore the necklace. It was her only remnant of her life before. Of *him*.

It was too much, suddenly. She felt like she was going to shatter. She jolted away from his touch, her back hitting the wall. "Don't. Touch me."

"Ayla." His voice—his whole face—was pained. She remembered that look. Of course she did. She remembered every look. "You know we can't talk here," he said. "Not like this. I can tell you—I ran away. *That day*, after the raids. And I was found by—by a group, who . . . Listen, Ayla, they took me in, they worked me over. They had me believing everything they said. About the leeches. About what we had to do to stop them. I had to vow I could never return to look for you. I had to promise, or else they'd do something terrible. I had to promise, I—Ayla." He was hissing the words at her now, urgently, and a stroke of fear moved through her.

"What are you talking about, Storme?"

"I thought you had died, too, along with Mother and Father. I feared the worst, but I also hoped for the best. I hoped you lived, even though I thought it was impossible. I hoped you made it, and in that hope, I knew I couldn't jeopardize your safety. I had no choice."

She had gone numb now. None of it made sense. "You had no choice but to abandon me and never look back. And now you're rewarded by becoming the Mad Queen's right-hand man? You can understand my confusion, I'm sure."

"If . . . if you come with us, I will tell you more. Come away with me. With us. Come to Varn."

Her whole body revolted. "What?"

All this time, as they argued, part of her had been hoping . . . been praying. Been imagining. That he would stay. That he would be hers again.

"It's not like you think. If you come to the queen's court with me in Varn, you'll see. I'll explain everything."

She kept her voice low and *controlled*. "So you will be leaving with Junn when she departs, then?"

"Of course."

She felt like she'd been slapped.

"Yes," she echoed. "*Of course.*" She felt disgusted. She had to get out of here. "Well, I certainly hope you and Junn have enjoyed your little *visit*," she spat.

"Have some respect," he snapped back. "Her title is queen."

Even after everything else, Ayla still felt like he'd just cracked her across the face. Again.

Who are you? she wanted to demand. *You're not my brother, what have you done with my brother*—but she knew it would just make her sound foolish, hopelessly naive, like the same weak, terrified child who had summoned the rats.

This. This was her brother. This person, standing before her, ordering her to have respect for a murderous leech—this was Storme.

"I know it doesn't make sense to you right now," he said quietly, his eyes intent on her face. "But don't condemn me. We're not so different."

"Of course we are," she choked out. "I'm not a lapdog."

"Aren't you?"

"What does *that* mean?"

"It means I saw the way your Lady Crier looks at you," said Storme. "It means I saw the way you look at her. The way you spoke to her. The way you almost touch her, sometimes."

"You don't know what you're talking about," Ayla said hoarsely. "You've got no idea. You're in the palace of the leech who ordered the raids on our village. You're in the spider's nest. You know that, right? It was Hesod. He's the one who killed our parents. He *created* her. I would have to be—*sick*, to—with any spawn of his—"

"Yes," said Storme. "I agree. Good night, Ayla. Please think on what I've said. You can still change your mind."

And he left her there.

For whole minutes, she stood alone, shaking. In anger. In shock. *You can still change your mind.* And oh, she wanted to change her mind. She wanted to change everything that had just happened. She wanted to move backward through time to the moment she first saw Storme, and race to him, embrace him. She wanted to move even further backward, to days, or weeks, before they were separated forever, and freeze time right there.

But, like so much else that had happened in the last months, she was reminded that life didn't work like that. No matter how terrifying and ugly the future was, no matter how difficult things were going to get, you couldn't avoid it, and you couldn't go back. It didn't work like that.

Not when your past was covered in as much blood as hers was.

The only way to go was forward. Into the darkness. Into the chaos.

She pushed her way out of the north wing and into the night air. She stalked the grounds, almost daring a guard to discover her, to report her, to drag her before Hesod for questioning. She'd tear his Made eyes out of his head, right there.

She was too furious, too upset to rest, but her legs and mind ached so badly.

She wanted to curl up in Rowan's arms, as she had that first night Rowan had found her, and weep until she was too dry to weep again, until she was an empty shell. But Rowan was gone on a journey that could very well end in her death. Ayla didn't know when, or *if*, she'd ever see her again.

Ayla wanted to lie down and never get back up.

She wanted her mother's lullaby. But it wouldn't come.

She thought about going to the music room, alone.

She found herself instead at the door to Crier's bedchamber.

15

Crier lay in bed, intensely aware of the fact that Queen Junn herself lay in her own chamber not more than four hallways and two stairwells from here. She couldn't get the sounds of moaning, of breath against skin, out of her head, even as she read and reread Rosi's letter, which had been waiting for her in her room when she returned. She turned to it once again.

> *To the Attention of Lady Crier, Family Hesod:*
>
> *To the first of your questions—no, I have not heard word of any new updates on the vanishing of Councilmember Reyka. But allow me to congratulate you and your fiancé on Scyre Kinok's new seat on the Red Council! He will make a wonderful Hand to the sovereign, your father, and I'm sure it must be such a great honor to you.*
>
> *I have never been modest about my support for, and appreciation of, your fiancé. Scyre Kinok has done so much for*

*myself and Foer! I hope you do not find it too forward of me
to say: we are more than willing to help Scyre Kinok with his
research again, should the need arise.*

*And even without that, we know we have Kinok to thank
for our very lives. If he hadn't warned us about the human
violence brewing in the south, so close to our estate, we would
not have been so safe. The two of us, and the southern Hands
Laone and Shasta as well. We are all grateful. We consider
ourselves Scyre Kinok's most loyal supporters!*

*I'm sending you a little Nightshade as a sign of my
"affection"—I haven't touched heartstone in weeks, thanks to
this!—and I hope to hear from you again soon.*

Yours,
Rosi of House Emiele

Crier swallowed.

Queen Junn had said it herself: Kinok was a problem. A
threat. Already too powerful, and growing more powerful by
the day.

Queen Junn. Should Crier tell her about this? She still had
the green feather, but . . . her stomach twisted. She was more
than a little reluctant to go seek out the queen in her quarters
again. Not after the . . . *sounds* she'd overheard just an hour or
two ago. She couldn't—get them out of her head. Not the adviser's grunting but Junn's low, breathy little noises, half-formed
words. Crier felt warm all over, her skin prickling, a sensation

almost like the pang of hunger in her lower belly, like when she didn't have heartstone for more than a few hours, but also not. She didn't understand it. She didn't *want* to understand it. No, she would stay away from the queen's quarters for now.

And, gods, what of Reyka? She'd been missing for weeks, and there was still no sign of her, and now Rosi claimed to know nothing. Crier wanted to remain hopeful—wanted to believe that maybe Reyka was lying low for her own reasons; maybe she'd gone into hiding of her own volition and didn't want to be found—but her mind was working against her, churning out worst-case scenarios. Reyka was a Red Hand, a powerful political figure. With the title came enemies. Crier had been hoping so *hard* that Rosi would know something. Anything.

After all, she'd been staying at Foer's estate, which was only a few leagues from the village of Elderell. The last place anyone had seen Reyka alive.

But Rosi knew nothing. She didn't even seem to care about Reyka's disappearance at all. Crier reread the letter a tenth time, jaw tight. *Kinok this, Kinok that.* And—Nightshade? There was a tiny paper packet attached to the letter, filled with a thumbnail-sized sampling of an unfamiliar powder. It had the same texture as heartstone dust, but instead of red it was a deep obsidian black.

I haven't touched heartstone in weeks, thanks to this!

But what *was* it?

Crier's thoughts were interrupted by a sound so faint she wondered if she was imagining it at first. But then it came again:

the sound of someone softly breathing right outside the door to her bedchamber, followed by a timid tap of knuckles on wood.

She sat upright.

There was no one else it could be.

She climbed out of bed, the flagstones cold on her bare feet, and tucked the tiny packet of dark dust beneath it, then opened the door. And yes, it was Ayla on the other side, a dark shape against the lamplight from the wall sconces. Her eyes were oddly wide, her body even tenser than usual. Her lips were a thin line.

Wordless, Crier stepped back and let her inside, closing the door quietly behind her.

"Have you need of me?" she said, after a long moment in which Ayla just stood there, silent and motionless. "Or—did you need something? Did my father send you?" She cocked her head. "Did something happen?"

"No," said Ayla, her voice wooden. "Nothing happened."

That's a lie, Crier thought.

Ayla wasn't happy. She could see that much. Ayla turned her gaze away, and Crier, out of respect, did the same.

She sat back down on the edge of her bed and kept her eyes on the glowing ashes in the hearth, the sparks leaping and winking out.

"You're not breathing," Ayla finally said.

Crier glanced up. Ayla was standing barely an arm's length away. The fading firelight was warm on her skin, catching all the places that were usually shadowed: the hollows of her cheeks and clavicles, the darkness of her brown eyes.

"No," Crier agreed. "Sometimes I forget."

For some reason, that made Ayla's jaw tighten. Crier was try-ing not to look for too long, but it was a rare moment that she was facing Ayla and Ayla was not paying attention to her—not watching her warily. Ayla looked particularly small right now, hands shoved into the pockets of her red uniform pants, her shirt untucked and loose around her frame. There was a gleam of gold at her throat, mostly hidden beneath her collar and the fall of her dark hair. The Made thing.

All of a sudden, the sounds came to her mind. The ones she'd heard through Queen Junn's door tonight. The moaning, soft and sweet, flecked with gasps. How the idea of it had made her shudder and grow warm.

"Why did you come here?" she asked quietly.

"I—I can't sleep," Ayla said, and then pressed her lips together like she had not meant to say anything at all.

Crier nodded. "I am familiar with that affliction."

"Really?" Ayla didn't sound curious. She sounded angry. And exhausted.

She considered it. "Yes. I sleep barely one night out of ten."

Neither of them spoke for a moment. This was a rare kind of interaction, Crier realized: they were together, but it was unscheduled. Like the evening by the tide pool. There were no tutors, no tasks, no upcoming meals. Crier had already bathed. Ayla was not even supposed to be here for another few hours. Until dawn, they could do anything. They could visit the music room or the library. They could sneak into the kitchens and

Ayla could eat the bread she liked, the kind with nuts and fruits baked in. They could go to the gardens to see the night flowers blooming in the moonlight, or they could go up to the rooftop and look at the stars, or they could even walk all the way out to the bluffs and watch the waves crash against the black rocks.

Crier looked at Ayla's face. The shadows under her eyes. There was something terrible in her, something clawed and angry and afraid and sad. She didn't know how she knew it, but she did. The truth of Ayla, the pain of her, was like a song you could feel vibrating on the air, even if you didn't know the words. It was a hum, low and throaty and full of sorrow.

"Come," she said. "You need more sleep than I do. And my bed is softer than anything in the servants' quarters." She patted the bed beside her.

"I—I'm fine. I shouldn't be here," Ayla said.

She said she shouldn't be here . . . but she didn't move to leave.

Another lie. This one better than the last, though.

"Stay. There's plenty of space." Crier wasn't sure where the words had come from; she knew only that something had possessed her, making her behave differently around this one person than she would around any other. She could only replay the teasing way Ayla had plunged into the tide pool, so many nights ago now, the way a single drop of water shone like a pearl on her lower lip.

The way the thought of Junn and her human adviser together had made Crier think of one thing only: Ayla.

"You need to sleep," she said, because it was true. "A lady needs her handmaiden to be at the pinnacle of health, you know."

Slowly, almost hesitantly, Ayla circled around to the other side of the bed. She stood there for a long moment, just breathing. Crier held so, so still. And then the bed dipped beneath Ayla's weight.

"Thank you," she whispered. Her voice wavered, and Crier felt that wavering all through her body.

It was a big bed, and there was plenty of space between them, yet it felt like there was very little space at all. If Crier reached out, her fingertips would brush the curve of Ayla's shoulder blade.

Even with the fire and the moonlight, it was so dark.

"What do you do when you can't sleep?" The question came out of Crier low and hushed.

"When I was younger," Ayla whispered, "my mother would sing to me."

Crier's first thought was, *I don't have a mother.*

It surprised her. She had never thought about that before, and did not want to start now. "What would she sing?"

"Lots of things," said Ayla. "Lullabies. Folk songs. War songs, sometimes."

"Is that why you love music?"

Love. The word sat on her tongue, turning over itself.

It made her want to lick her lips.

Made her want to speak more, to ask Ayla more questions until the sun rose.

But Ayla didn't answer.

"Which was your favorite?" Crier tried again, tangling her fingers in the bedspread to make sure she didn't do anything else with them. But there was the compulsion again—to behave differently. To reach out to Ayla. To take her hand. To turn Ayla's face toward her own.

She and Ayla were both on top of the blankets, which was how Crier always slept, but now she was wondering if Ayla would prefer to be under the blankets, in the warmth. If Ayla rolled over, would her hand stretch across the empty space between them? Thoughts and images crowded Crier's head, a thousand different scenarios—the *potential*—

In the next second, her mind went white.

Her thoughts vanished like dancing sparks.

Because Ayla started singing.

"Listen for my voice across the wide, storm-dark waters," she sang under her breath, so quiet it was barely a tune. "Listen for my voice, let it guide your way home. . . ." She shifted, curling further into herself as she continued. Then after another minute, she stopped as abruptly as she'd started, cutting the last note short.

Silence.

Crier felt like a harp. All her strings plucked. Her whole body humming.

"Thank you," she said, breathless.

Ayla didn't reply for a long time. When she finally spoke, it had nothing to do with the song. "You need to stop giving Faye special treatment."

"What?"

"Faye. The special room you gave her, and special privileges. I don't know *why* you did that, but you need to take it away."

Crier frowned into the darkness. "That doesn't seem fair."

"No, it's not. Nothing about this is fair, *my lady*. But you're not helping her like this. All you're doing is singling her out."

"To whom? The other servants?"

"The other servants. Your father. The Scyre. Everyone. It's not a good thing. It's—it's dangerous."

For some reason, Crier felt stung. "I was just trying to help," she whispered. *Because you were worried about her. You were worried about Faye. I wanted to help you.*

"I know," said Ayla, sounding defeated. "I . . . I actually believe you. But you can't just help one human, Crier, not like this." The sheets rustled as Ayla turned over, slowly, until she was facing Crier, her body curving toward the center of the bed. "The only way to help Faye is to help us all."

Crier looked at Ayla in the darkness. "Then how can I help?"

There was a long pause. Crier could hear Ayla breathing, soft like the distant rush of the ocean. But so much closer.

"How serious are you?" Ayla asked finally. "Because—because this could get me killed. This isn't a game, Crier. This isn't a faerie story in one of your books. This is life and death."

"I'm serious," Crier said. She propped herself up on one elbow, finding Ayla's eyes in the darkness. "Let me prove it to you."

They stared at each other. Ayla's eyes glinted in the moonlight—not golden, not like Crier's. Deep wells. Swallowing the light.

Did Ayla trust her? No, not yet. Crier could see that. But that didn't mean it was impossible.

"How much do you really know about Kinok?" Ayla whispered, as if she were suddenly afraid that Kinok might be listening in.

"Not much," Crier whispered back. "I've been trying to learn more. I know he's more powerful than I ever expected. I know he's experimenting with heartstone. I know he has a special compass. I don't know why it's special, but the Red Hands certainly did. And they looked . . . jealous."

A slight rustle, Ayla nodding her head against the pillow.

"Find out what he's really up to," she said. "That's how you can help."

Ayla hadn't given her anything, hadn't opened up, not really. But she'd asked her for something.

A thrill moved through Crier, and it stayed in her, keeping her alert and awake and alive, even as Ayla began to quiet, to nudge toward Crier, to move toward her warmth as if forgetting who—and what—she was. An enemy. An Automa. Instead, in the darkness between and around them, Crier was just a body. She could feel the moment when Ayla sighed, breaths slowing, sinking deeper into sleep. The fathomless depths of sleep, the dreaming place only humans ever experienced.

And at some point in the night, it happened. Ayla, who had shifted onto her back, rolled over into the middle of the bed. and in the process flung one of her arms over Crier's waist. Crier froze, instantly awake. More than awake. She lay there, perfectly still, everything inside her narrowed to the soft weight of Ayla's arm on the curve of her waist, that spot of warmth. She had to remind herself to breathe. Ayla preferred it when she breathed.

Breathe for Ayla.

The smell of her hair, like soap and sea lavender.

Breathe.

Midnight.

Moonlight.

In this new position, Ayla's cheek was pressed into the crook of her own elbow. Her mouth was open slightly, soft-looking in a way Crier hadn't really seen before. When Ayla was awake, her mouth was often a thin, displeased line, her jaw set. Crier tried to imagine what it would look like if Ayla's eyes were open, if she were awake and her mouth was still so soft and open, her lips parted, her gaze dark and heated, her arm around Crier's waist on purpose, with intent, and—Crier's heart was so loud. A pounding in her chest, an ache in her lower belly. That not-hunger.

The soft moans she'd heard slip through the wood and stone of Junn's door rose in her mind like sparks, flecks of gold in the dark. The shuddering breath. The leap and fall of voices. The knowledge of two bodies moving together, lips and skin and . . .

Silver light played across Ayla's dark hair; her eyelashes made tiny, spiky shadows on her cheeks. Crier listened to her breaths—still slow and even, tidelike. She didn't know how long they'd been lying like this.

Then Ayla shifted, nosing into the pillow, and something gold fell from the collar of her shirt. The necklace. Without thinking, Crier reached out to tuck it back into Ayla's shirt, heart racing as her fingertips brushed softly against Ayla's collarbones—but instead the chain came away entirely in her fingers. The clasp had broken.

There was a short, awful moment in which Crier thought *she* had somehow broken it, and then she looked closer and realized that the necklace was much older than she'd thought. The chain was dull and grimy, and the clasp had simply worn out.

It was still warm from Ayla's skin.

And now it was in Crier's palm, delicate gold chain and a gold pendant the size of a statescoin. Strangely heavy. The center was set with a single bloodred gemstone. It nearly glowed even in the darkness, like cut glass, like a glass of wine held in front of a lantern. Deep, rich color. She ran her finger around the edge of the pendant, admiring the smooth gold. Maybe she could fix the clasp before Ayla woke up, bend the metal back into shape. She brought it close to her face, pinching the clasp between fore-finger and thumb—until something nicked her. She frowned, holding her hand up to the moonlight. The edge of the broken clasp must be sharp; something had caught on her fingertip. Blood welled to the surface. A single drop.

Unthinking, she ran her finger over the pendant again, dis-tracted by the unnatural warmth of the gemstone, warmer than the gold around it, almost like there was a tiny source of heat inside—

Then the world lurched.

The familiar walls of her bedchamber melted away.

Crier blinked and *the world was burning.*

She gasped and then immediately regretted it. Her lungs filled with smoke and scorching ash, her throat lit up in pain.

She was standing in the middle of a street she did not recognize. The buildings on either side were too tall, made of wood and naked stone instead of the quicklime-white buildings of the seaside villages around the palace. The roofs were steep and pointed, piercing the sky, and the outer walls were lined with terraces of twisted black metal, and all of it was burning.

Above her, the sky was a bloody mess of red and yellow and putrid black smoke. Ash fell like snow from the burning rooftops, the buildings buckling beneath the weight of a raging fire—both sides of the street were burning, the fire howling, windows bursting open and raining glass down onto the cobblestones below—

"RUN—RUN, RUN." Someone barreled past Crier, bare feet slapping the cobblestones, and she realized she was surrounded by humans. There were humans everywhere, a flood of them in the street, their faces streaked with ash and tears.

Crier grabbed at a woman's sleeve, or tried to, but her fingers passed through it. She shouted at her—"Where am I, what is this?"—but the woman did not look at her. Did not even seem to hear her voice.

This had to be a nightmare. Crier had heard of those, though she'd thought they only plagued human minds, like a chronic disease.

The nightmare city burned, and somewhere in the chaos Crier heard a child crying. The noise made her wheel around. There, across the street, stood a man. Human like the rest of them, with the fair hair common in Varn. His eyes were the pale gray of morning. She could pick out the color even through the smoke.

In one hand, he held the crying child, gripping its tiny arm. "Shh, Clara," he whispered. It'll be all right. Mama's coming."

He stood still only for a moment, eyes on the roiling sky, the collapsing rooftops. His chest was heaving, his knuckles white around the child's arm. His mouth was moving but no sound was coming out. At first it just looked like he was screaming, and then Crier realized he was saying something, a single word, over and over again, his lips forming the same shapes. A name.

Siena?

A silhouette appeared in the smoke. Like a specter: first a shadow, then a body. A woman, emerging from smoke that looked like a wall of dark ocean, a massive, unstoppable wave. She was covered in pale ash and her head was bowed. Crier could see only a shock of wild hair.

Then she straightened up, and Crier stared. Because she knew this girl. It was Ayla. Caked with ash, blood all over her face, but it was Ayla.

Wasn't it?

No, Crier realized, as the girl drew closer. No, this person was not exactly like Ayla. Her hair was longer. She was taller, almost as tall as Crier. There was something about the shape of her face that wasn't quite right. She was not Ayla—but, stars and skies, she could have been Ayla's sister, or mother, or—

The child wailed and Crier wrenched her eyes away from the Ayla-like woman.

"Siena." The man took a step toward the young woman, they were barely ten feet away from each other now, eyes locked on each other's faces, and the woman grabbed his hands.

"Leo, take this. I have to go back for the blueprints. But take this." The woman—Siena—handed him a large blue jewel, bigger than a fist, glimmering like a giant crystal of heartstone, only as sea blue as heartstone was red.

"No, Si," he said, holding the shining, cerulean stone in his hands. "Stay with us, stay—"

But the woman had gone again, back into the flames of the burning village, and the child, Clara, cried out

"Mama!" and then an explosion in the distance, and—

Something happened inside Crier's chest. A chasm yawned open.

All her inner workings seemed to stop at once.

She doubled over, gasping. There was something inside her. She could feel it scraping away at her rib cage, rising like bile in her throat. A monster trapped within her flesh. Crier sobbed and realized her vision was blurred. Her cheeks were wet.

Crier clutched at her chest, fingers scrabbling at her shirt, the skin beneath, as if she could somehow rip herself open and remove this thing from her workings. It was too much. It was too much and it felt like poison, an oily black substance inside her lungs. Drowning her from the inside out. She couldn't breathe around it. She couldn't breathe.

Calm, she had to be calm. She remembered suddenly, but it was as though her memory was a distant dream—how the necklace had slipped off Ayla's neck while she slept, how easy it had been to pick it up, to study it in the moonlight, how she'd tried to fix the broken clasp—the drop of blood—

Eyes squeezed shut, Crier tried to focus on the weight of the pendant in her hand, soft gold, still warm from Ayla's skin; she tried to focus on letting go of it—letting go—she was letting go—

Chaos.

It took a second to realize she was in her bedchamber again, because everything was still chaos, but a different kind: instead of fire and smoke and heat and screaming, Crier had slammed back into a world that was dark and cold, and she was lying on a bed, and someone cried out, and—a mass of dark shapes was writhing in the center of the room, and it took a few moments of frantic blinking to realize that they were guards, there were guards in her room, and—

Ayla.

They had Ayla. She was pinned to the floor, three guards holding her down, one pressing her face to the flagstones. Crier leaped out of bed and stumbled, unsteady on her feet. When she realized what must have happened, Crier's blood ran cold. Had she really been in so much distress that it had triggered her chime? Regardless, her chime had gone off, and the guards had arrived.

And they'd found Ayla, Crier thought numbly.

In Crier's bed. In the middle of the night when she was supposed to be in the servants' quarters.

This is all my fault.

"Stop," she said, "*stop*, let her go, she did nothing wrong—" But the guards didn't even look at her. They were already moving, wrenching Ayla off the ground and out of the room. She wasn't struggling, Crier saw. Her eyes were huge and wild, her teeth clenched, but she wasn't struggling. She looked up at Crier, silently, and their gazes locked. Crier didn't know what her own expression was doing, but she thought it probably wasn't so different from Ayla's. Shocked, horrified, helpless, confused.

Then the guards dragged Ayla from the room.

Still disoriented, Crier scrambled after them. She paused only to hide the pendant in her drawer, where she'd hidden the key to the music room, and then she was racing out the door and down the corridor. The guards hadn't gotten far at all, not with Ayla weighing them down. "Stop!" Crier called out, as harshly as she could, and to her relief they actually obeyed. One of the guards turned to face her, his eyes flashing gold in the light from the wall sconces. He was the one who had shoved Ayla's face into the flagstones.

"My lady," he said in a monotone. "We are under orders from the sovereign. Please return to your chamber. The physician is on the way."

"I am not injured," Crier snapped. "I am completely unharmed, and Ay—the human has done nothing wrong."

"We are under orders from the sovereign," the guard repeated. "Should Lady Crier be placed in any danger, any and all humans in the vicinity are to be delivered to Scyre Kinok for questioning."

The ice in Crier's veins shattered. She reeled, trying not to show the fear and revulsion on her face. "To Kinok? Why? Why not to my father?"

"We are under orders from the sovereign."

She stared at him. He stared back, impervious.

"I am your lady," she tried. "You answer to me as well as my father."

"The sovereign's orders take precedence above all."

Crier opened her mouth, but nothing came out. She had no idea how to proceed from here. How to make them release Ayla, Ayla who had done nothing wrong, Ayla who should not be taken anywhere near Kinok, not without Crier there to—protect her, watch out for her, *something*.

The guards sidestepped her neatly, and with Ayla still slumped between them, limp, they marched down the corridor and were gone.

She stood there for a few moments, wide-eyed and barefoot and frozen with shock, the remnants of a burning city still flickering at the edges of her mind—a burning city that she knew was *real*. It hadn't been a nightmare. Everything made sense now: Ayla's strange paranoia about her necklace, the way she wore it always even though she seemed terrified of anyone discovering it.

The locket was a memory keeper, activated by blood. Crier had heard of similar objects, in the records of the old Makers, in estate auction papers she'd seen, listing the wide array of alchemical trinkets and gadgets for sale that were now forbidden to humans—silver models of constellations that, when activated by the crushed bones of birds, could fly in circles around your head in the exact patterns of the celestial bodies. Glass eyeballs that rolled in the direction of whatever you were searching for.

But this object was not just any Made object. It was Ayla's, and the memories stored in it were, in some way or another, memories of the history of Ayla and her family. Whoever had worn it before Ayla—the man in the chaos, amid the fires, the man called Leo—had allowed his memories to be recorded by the locket, and now they were trapped within it.

She didn't know what it meant, only that Ayla's history was full of violence and sadness.

And now, her future would be too, if Crier didn't do something about it.

She turned on her heel and ran in the opposite direction of the guards. She tore down the dark hallways, the wall sconces smearing in yellow parallax, and did not slow down until the door of her father's chambers loomed before her through the gloom. She was running so fast that it was hard to stop; her feet actually skidded on the flagstones. Then she was scrabbling at the door, shoving it open, tumbling inside. *"Father!"*

He was already awake. He was standing by the hearth, gazing into the flames.

"Father," she gasped, "Father, they took her, the guards took her but it wasn't her fault—"

Slowly, he turned to face her. "You speak of the handmaiden. The human."

"Yes, yes, but she didn't make my chime go off, it was me, I was distressed, and the guards—"

"Daughter."

Her mouth snapped shut.

"First Guard Lakell reported to me that when his men entered your room, the human was in your bed. Is that true?"

A hot, prickling flush spread from Crier's face all the way down her body.

"Father, I—"

"Was the human in your bed?"

Mute, Crier nodded.

Hesod turned away, looking into the flames again. "You nearly fall to your death, and the human girl is there. You have some sort of—fit—in the middle of the night, and the human girl is there *in your bedchamber, in your bed*. Are you trying to tell me that it is a coincidence? That your chime only goes off in her presence?"

So he knew about what had happened at the cliffs, too. Even though she'd begged the guards not to tell him.

He knew everything, it seemed.

But he couldn't know what was in Crier's mind—how she felt. And he didn't know about her Flaw. Not yet, anyway.

We were just sleeping, Crier wanted to say, but she didn't even know what she was defending herself against. *We weren't doing anything*. What would they have been doing?

The flush grew deeper.

"The handmaiden has never harmed me," she insisted, as calmly as possible. "She has never touched me. I was awake, thinking—about the queen's visit—and became distressed."

"What thoughts could cause such distress?"

"The queen is . . . very commanding," she stalled, trying to come up with an excuse.

"Well, you can be reassured, then. The queen and her entire retinue have already departed. It is a good thing, too, as this situation would have caused quite the scandal had she been around to witness it."

The queen was gone.

And Crier had missed her chance to deliver the green feather. To take her side.

"There are whispers, daughter," Hesod went on. "I hear them in the corridors, in the kitchens. The servants of this palace are under the impression that their lady has become attached to the human girl who serves her."

Crier shook her head. "They are *mistaken*, Father."

"I know," Hesod said gently. "I know that no child of mine, no child created by my hand, would commit such a heinous betrayal against their own Kind. I know the servants are mistaken, daughter. But humans, once convinced of an idea, are difficult to persuade otherwise. Their minds are not complex and malleable like ours. And you do not want them to continue spreading such dangerous lies, do you?"

"No," Crier whispered.

"Then I will offer you a deal," said Hesod, "because I believe that you are telling the truth, even if no one else does. I shall give the handmaiden one last chance. She will be allowed to remain at your feet, serving you." He paused. "Unless, of course, there is another incident. Then she will be removed."

"Yes, Father."

"In the meantime, you will wear the black armband that symbolizes the Anti-Reliance Movement. As a gesture of good-will, peace, and tolerance between Traditionalism and Anti-Reliance."

"Yes, Father," Crier said numbly. "I will do as you've asked."

Hesod finally looked at her again, and his eyes glinted in the firelight. "I am pleased," he said, "to have raised such an obedient child."

Crier didn't let herself second-guess the message she had penned the moment she left her father's side. She would not marry Kinok. Nor would she abide her father's decisions any longer.

The words flowed out of her pen with little effort, even the coded names coming easily.

Once satisfied, she stared at the wet ink for a moment, blew lightly across the page to dry it, then slipped a green feather into the envelope, sealed it with wax, and gave it to one of her father's messengers.

"Deliver it well," she said with a smile, picturing the sly look that would appear on Queen Junn's face when she received it upon her arrival in Varn—when the queen realized that she had an ally. That together, they were going to take down the Wolf.

Friend—

> You said to me that Fear is a tool of survival.
> I hope that you are right.

There is indeed a Wolf among us, and we must work together to hunt him down. If he kills again, there are three who will share in the spoils. Two will be found with red blood on their hands. To find the third, look foerward; he is closer than you think.

La st we spoke, you said, "It only takes One clever fox to best a thousand men."

I confess, I wish to be that fox.

These days, the Sha dows are long. Soon, the nights will Sta rt to swallow us whole. There is always a part of me that dreads the winter. Now more than ever.

—Fox

16

The guards had led Ayla into the bowels of the palace: into the maze of the west wing and then through a wooden door and down a flight of white marble steps that seemed unending, the air growing cold and dank the farther they descended. They were taking her underground. Ayla couldn't stop her hands from shaking, just a little. They were so far underground that she knew she could scream and the noise would just be swallowed by the rough, ugly stone walls and the darkness.

Were they leading her to her death, right here, right now?

She thought of her crime—curling up beside the lady of the house. In her own bed. What *had* she been thinking? In the moment, all the fury of her fight with Storme, all her fear and confusion, had simply led her there without thinking, without questioning. She'd been *drawn* to Crier.

Maybe it was *because* Crier had been the object of her thoughts, her obsessions, for so long. Since long before she'd become her handmaiden. And now, the obsession had begun to morph and change in the light, no longer as simple as a desire to kill, now colored, in certain moments, with a desire for something else.

A desire Ayla simply could not name.

The guilt and shame of it exploded in her gut, and she almost doubled over, sick with it, except that the guards held her, kept leading her forward into the darkness.

At least, she reminded herself, she'd gained *something* from last night.

Crier had mentioned something important—something potentially *very* important.

Kinok had a "special compass." If it were anyone else, she'd think nothing of it; a compass was a compass; it pointed north and that was it.

But a special compass carried by a Watcher of the Iron Heart was another matter entirely.

They turned a corner toward another set of stairs. One of the guards let go of her arm in the narrowness of the stairwell, and instinctively, she reached for the familiar weight of her necklace, but her fingers found nothing but skin.

Frowning, she felt all around her throat. Then her hair, it sometimes got tangled in her hair while she slept, and then around the collar of her uniform. Nothing. She checked her underclothes. Nothing. It wasn't caught on the inside of her shirt, either.

If fear was cold water, paranoia was ice. It spread across her skin like frost on a windowpane.

It was missing. The simplest explanation, and the most horrifying. Her necklace was missing. The one item she owned that could get her (*Benjy*) killed, and it was gone. She'd lost it. When? In Crier's bedchamber just now, when the guards had dragged her out of bed? In the halls before that?

If someone found it.

If they traced it back to her.

Benjy.

Lost in her thoughts, Ayla almost walked straight into a guard's back when they finally reached the bottom of the steps. It was so dark, the torchlights spread far apart on the damp stone walls, that she didn't see the stone door until someone was unlocking it, pulling it open from the inside.

Kinok had lit a single lamp, and Ayla just barely managed to bite back a surprised curse—she'd been expecting a prison cell, but instead they'd brought her to Kinok's study.

The room Malwin had mentioned.

The exact place she needed to find.

Somewhere in this study, she knew, lay a safe, that could hold Kinok's secrets. Information about the Iron Heart.

Maybe even the compass Crier had mentioned.

As sick and terrified as she felt, there was something too perfect about where she'd ended up.

She followed a guard through the stone door and into a small room lined with so many carpets and maps and tapestries that almost nothing of the floor and walls was visible.

To muffle sound, Ayla thought, and clenched her teeth.

The guards shut the door behind her, and she was alone, with Kinok.

He sat behind a large desk against one wall, the surface heaped with papers, books, more maps. A pot of ink, a quill. Beside it a bookshelf filled with leather-bound books. All of them fat and ancient-looking, the spines emblazoned with gold-stamped titles, long strings of words that Ayla couldn't read, and—

This time, Ayla really did curse.

Because *that was her necklace.*

Her Made object. It was *sitting in plain sight on Kinok's bookshelf,* between an odd little glass ball and a bunch of used nibs.

How did he get it so quickly, when she'd only just noticed it was missing? It seemed impossible. That his reach was so swift, that it was everywhere.

She tore her eyes away, but not fast enough. When she looked at Kinok he was already looking back at her, his own gaze flicking between her face and the bookshelf.

He knew. That's why he brought her down here. *This is a death sentence.* Between the necklace and getting caught in Crier's bed, she was as good as dead.

Or if not her, then Benjy. The chart. The red thread.

Her heart skittered in her chest as she met Kinok's eyes, waiting for the sentence. For the noose, the knife, the great blade of the guillotine, the thing lurking in Kinok's eyes. Whatever he said, she would fight it. Whatever he wanted to do to Benjy, she would stop it. She would—

"Where were you born, handmaiden?"

She didn't answer. Couldn't, not yet. Her body was tense as a harp string, blood pounding at her temples.

Was this a game?

Kinok snapped his fingers, a *crack* of sound, and she jolted.

"I asked you a question, handmaiden. Where were you born?"

"The village of Delan," Ayla said. Her voice came out hoarse. "To the north."

"You grew up there?"

Her stomach twisted. Yes, and no. She nodded.

"When did you first come to the palace?"

Her mind reeled. What was this line of questioning? *Why are you doing this*, she wanted to say, *Why are you drawing it out, just get it over with*, but instead she tried to calm down. Deep breaths.

"I came here five years ago," she said.

"As a child, then."

"No." She hadn't been a child anymore. That had been robbed from her long before.

His eyes flickered. "I see. And your family? Your parents— did they come with you? Do they work here as well?"

"Dead."

"What were their names?"

"Why?" Ayla countered. "What does it matter?"

"I don't think it's your place to ask the questions."

"Their names were Yann and Clara."

"And your parents' parents? What were their names?"

"My mother's parents were Leo and Siena," said Ayla. "But—my parents didn't speak of them. Most in my village were like that about the past." She tried and failed to keep the bitterness from her voice. "I've never known a bloodline that got out of the War unscathed. Never known a family tree that wasn't missing most of its branches."

"Humans don't keep records?" He seemed casually intrigued, like they were at market discussing the rising prices of tea. "You don't copy down your own history? Your own blood?"

"We did," said Ayla. "And then Sovereign Hesod burned my village to the ground."

She and Kinok met each other's eyes and neither of them blinked.

"Very well," said Kinok. He still looked perfectly pleasant, but his jaw was perhaps a little tighter than it had been before they started talking, and that fact made a wicked tendril of satisfaction break through the fog of Ayla's suspicion and fear. It seemed that whatever he was looking for, he hadn't found.

What would he do now? Dispose of her? Refer to his handy chart and trace the line straight to Benjy? What if this was her only chance?

"I was wondering something," she said boldly, trying to keep her shaky voice still. "I hear you were a Watcher. But Watchers never leave the Heart, do they?"

It was more than bold. It was ridiculous. The desperate act of someone who knew she was at her last shot.

He smiled. "I don't remember granting you permission to ask any questions."

"I only meant, you must be special . . . ," she pushed on. *Keep it together, Ayla. Don't give up now.*

The smile grew. There was nothing warm in it. "I have no answers for you, Handmaiden Ayla."

"Why?" she challenged him. "Were you thrown out?"

"Of course not," he said. "I can return anytime I wish."

Ayla felt another rush of satisfaction. Automa or not, Kinok was not so different from a human man. His pride was his weakest spot.

"But I thought it was impossible to get back once you leave," she said, pretending to frown in confusion. "I thought it was impossible to retrace the route through the mountains."

His eyes flickered sideways for a split second.

A split second that she watched carefully. Automae weren't the only ones who knew how to spot what they were looking for. "There are ways," he said, and then stood up. "We're done for now. Stay here."

Then, moving with just a little more speed and grace than a human could have, he left the room. The door clicked shut behind him before Ayla could really even process the fact that right before he'd left, he had grabbed the necklace from the bookshelf.

It was gone again.

And she was alone.

She forced herself to wait an entire five minutes, counting
the seconds, before she felt certain Kinok wouldn't be returning immediately. Then she leaped out of the chair and headed
straight for the corner of the study—the spot where Kinok's eyes
had flickered just for a moment.

Even leeches had their tells.

At first glance, there was nothing interesting at all about the
corner: there was the edge of a bookshelf and then nothing else,
just solid stone wall, solid stone floor. Ayla ran her hands over
the wall, checking for a give, a hinge, anything. She knocked
quietly against the wall and the floor, but there weren't any parts
that sounded like they might be hollow.

But she was *sure* the safe would be somewhere around here.

She ran her hands over the bookshelf next. It was a sturdy
piece of furniture, made of the same dark cherry wood as Kinok's
desk. Quickly, more and more paranoid about Kinok's return as
the minutes dragged on, Ayla began checking each book on the
shelf—lifting each one carefully so as not to disturb the dust on
the shelves, flipping through the pages, searching for anything
remotely off. She found nothing on the first shelf or the second.
She knelt down to search the third and final shelf, the bottom-
most one, trying to be as careful as possible while still moving
quickly. Surely Kinok would be back any moment now. . . .

There.

Hidden behind one of the books from the middle of the
shelf, only visible because Ayla was kneeling, there was a tiny,
nearly invisible seam in the wooden back of the bookshelf.

Heart pounding, Ayla set the book aside and reached out, running her fingers along the seam. It made a rectangular shape, barely larger than her palm. Like a tiny door. She pressed at the edges, trying to figure out how to open it—and there, *yes yes yes*, a tiny give when she pressed at one side of the seam. She pressed harder and the tiny door sprung open, revealing—

Metal.

The edge of what looked like a thin metal box. *A safe.* It was similar to the one Crier kept her finest necklaces in.

This one must have been barely an inch thick to fit so perfectly in the back of the bookshelf, painstakingly hidden by the tiny wooden door. Ayla leaned forward, wondering if she could maybe pry it out with her fingernails . . . but no, it was still half embedded in the wood, she'd need to remove all the books and then replace them afterward in the exact right order, which would take time she definitely didn't have, and even then she could see part of a lock on the front of the safe, a series of little clockwork gears, all labeled with strange alchemical symbols. Some she recognized: the eight-point star, the symbols for salt, mercury, and sulfur; body, mind, and spirit.

The language of the Makers. She didn't know it, but Benjy did. He'd learned that at the temple, as a child.

Breathless with her discovery, Ayla returned the book to the shelf and went back to sit in her chair, mind racing. So she wouldn't be able to open the safe alone. But she *knew* it had to be opened. She knew, with near absolute certainty—the kind that only came when you were so close to death you could taste it—that this was the puzzle piece she needed.

I can return anytime I wish, Kinok had said. *There are ways.*

Now all she had to do was get into that safe.

Kinok returned only a few minutes later. Ayla straightened up the second she heard his key scrape in the lock, feeling so much less afraid than before. Even though she still didn't know why he'd asked about her parents, even though she still didn't know why or how he'd gotten hold of her locket, even though she still didn't know what her punishment would be. As long as she could tell someone about the location of the safe, she would be triumphant. She'd win this one—or die trying.

She stared at Kinok, waiting.

"Leave," said Kinok.

Ayla pulled up short. ". . . Excuse me?"

"Leave," he said again, slow and drawn out, like he was talking to a horse or a particularly dim child. "I require nothing from you. Leave."

"I don't understand," she heard herself say, even as her entire body yearned for the door and the steps back up to sunlight, to something that wasn't freedom but was better than this. "I don't understand, aren't you going to—?"

"We are done here," he said, every word from his lips like something heavy dropping to the carpet between them, like he spoke stones.

She wavered for a moment longer, *is this a trap is this a trap*, but then finally body won out over paranoia and she darted away from him, out the door, up the marble steps, until she was inside the palace again and the air smelled like the sickly perfume of too many flowers.

She hurried toward the exit closest to the servants' quarters, walking as fast as she could without looking too suspicious, knowing she needed to talk to Benjy—immediately.

But before she could even make her way outside, another servant stopped her abruptly.

"You're needed in the kitchens. Malwin's been looking for you."

Malwin? What could she want? Their last interaction hadn't exactly been pleasant. She'd not soon forget how Malwin spat at her feet.

But she couldn't disobey.

Full of a new dread, Ayla made her way to the kitchens.

Upon arriving in the dim, smoky, cavernous room, she was ordered straight to a corner station to begin shucking the papery skin off a pile of onions. She hadn't spent much time in here, had only been on cooking duty once or twice—humans her age were usually reserved for manual labor.

The kitchens of a leech's palace weren't like any human kitchen. The floor was trodden earth and there was a roasting pit, a larder, a few big, rough-hewn worktables, a wall dedicated to pots and platters and knives—but there was also a massive clay fireplace that took up almost an entire wall, the flames occupied by a black cauldron that both Ayla and Benjy could have comfortably curled up inside with room to spare. This cauldron was used for one thing only: brewing liquid heartstone.

The white steam rolling thickly into the chimney smelled bitter, metallic. Ayla breathed through her mouth, and still she could taste it on her tongue. There was always a single leech guard stationed by the heartstone cauldron. Startled, Ayla realized that she recognized today's guard. It was the same one she'd run into last night.

Ayla shifted, hiding her face.

Through the thick curtain of her hair, Ayla watched a kitchen boy stir the contents of the cauldron. Soon, she knew, it would be strained and poured into another cauldron to cool. You could tell who was on pouring duty because their hands and clothes were stained red.

"Handmaiden."

Ayla looked up.

Malwin stood before her. She didn't look hateful or angry, as Ayla had expected. If anything, she was peering at Ayla with something like curiosity.

"I'm under orders from Queen Junn's adviser," said Malwin, speaking in a hushed voice so the leech guard wouldn't hear.

Storme.

Somehow, Ayla kept her face blank. "The human, ma'am?"

"Yes. He caught me just before they left."

So he really did leave. It wasn't a surprise, but it still stung all over again. Storme was already gone.

So much had happened between their argument last night and her getting caught this morning that she'd hardly had time to think of him again—or to grieve.

Because that was how it felt. It was like another death. Not crueler or more upsetting than the first, but dull and deep and aching.

"What's that got to do with me, ma'am?"

"Gave me something to give to you. He said you dropped it. He said to tell you, 'Don't lose it again.'"

Ayla stared as she reached into the pocket of her uniform and pulled out a single green feather.

"You know, you really shouldn't have this," Malwin scolded her. "I don't know why you carry it around with you, but I'm sure it counts as a belonging. You're lucky the adviser saw you drop it and not Lord Hesod. You could've got in real trouble, girl."

Ayla nearly barked out a laugh. Clearly, Malwin didn't know what kind of trouble she'd *already* gotten in.

"Right," Ayla said after a pause. "You're right, I'll—I'll be more careful."

"Well, don't tell me. 'S not my neck on the chopping block." She pushed the feather into Ayla's hands. "Hide that. I should've tossed it in the fire, but I'm feeling kind today."

"Thank you, ma'am." Ayla put the feather in her pocket . . . and set aside her curiosity. She'd have time later to wonder about it.

For now, she had to talk to Benjy.

Ayla waited for him under their tree, staring into the gnarled eye. She'd left her comb on his pillow, a signal that she wanted to meet, but what if he hadn't noticed it? It was so strange, using the comb as a signal instead of just whispering to him, or tapping the back of his hand as she walked past. They used to spend every possible moment together, but ever since Ayla became a handmaiden she hadn't seen Benjy nearly as much. Most days, all they exchanged was a single glance as they climbed into bed, their bodies separated by a dozen other sleeping servants.

As she waited, her thoughts were a hive of worries. Why had Kinok asked about her family? Would she ever see Storme again?

What about Rowan and the other rebels who'd joined her going south? She'd been desperate not to think of that—to think of the fact that she hadn't heard anything about them since. What had happened to them?

She couldn't worry about that now, though. Not yet. Because she had to tell Benjy about what Crier had told her.

Kinok's compass pointed to the Iron Heart. She was sure of it. Why else would such a thing be so special? Why else would even the Red Hands want it?

Total destruction was a possibility now in a way it hadn't been before.

Ayla was buzzing with the knowledge of it.

So excited that if Crier were here, she could kiss her for it.

She wanted to slap the thought straight out of her head, but just then, Benjy ducked under a tree branch, dust and sunlight in his curly hair. Ayla realized with a pang that he didn't even know she'd found Storme. But maybe it was better if he didn't know her secrets.

Anything to fray the thread between them.

But Ayla *missed* him. She missed him in the way of missing people who are not dead, who are warm and close and breathing. It wasn't something she'd ever experienced before. Missing her parents (and Storme, until yesterday) was different; it felt like trying to draw water from a well that had long since run dry. Missing Benjy felt like staring at a bucket of cool, clear water and refusing to drink. He was right there. But she had to keep him at arm's length, because anything closer was too dangerous.

"Hey," he said, smiling at her, and she did not smile back. "How's life in the royal palace?"

"Charming. Malwin loves biting my head off."

"Poor baby," he said, leaning against the trunk of the tree. "Wanna trade?"

She rolled her eyes. "Please. You wouldn't last a second as a handmaiden."

Something flickered across his face. "Yeah," he said slowly. "I probably wouldn't be as good at it as you are."

"What's *that* supposed to mean?"

"Nothing." He sighed and shook his head, reaching up to pluck a leaf and play with it between his fingers. "Nothing, sorry, been a long day. A long week."

"A long life."

"Listen, I have news."

"I do, too. But you go first."

"Rowan. She's back."

This wasn't at all what Ayla had been expecting to hear. Her heart practically thumped out of her chest. "Is she okay? Where is she?"

"Shh," he said, coming away from the tree trunk, his face part in shadow. "Not here."

"But—"

He took her hand. It felt warm and rough. "She's going to meet us. By the cliffs. Come on."

Together, they cut through the grounds, heading for the sea cliffs—the spot where Ayla and Crier had first met, where Ayla had saved Crier's life. They stuck to the shadows, the aisles of soft black dirt between rows of seaflowers, and Ayla glanced behind them every few moments to check for guards or other servants. But there was no one, and they reached the cliffs unheeded.

It was colder so close to the ocean, the rocks slick with sea spray. Ayla's arms were pebbled with gooseflesh.

Rowan was already waiting for them on the cliffs, silhouetted against the night sky and the ocean. Her silver hair tumbled over her shoulders and she looked still and calm as always, but when they drew closer Ayla could see the shadows under her eyes and the careful way she was holding herself, as if she had a hidden injury. Ayla forgot her own discomfort and hurried forward.

"*Rowan!*" Ayla said, joining her on the edge of the cliff. "Gods, I thought you wouldn't be back for weeks." *If at all.* "What happened? Are you hurt?"

"I'm fine," said Rowan dismissively. "And—nothing happened."

Benjy made an impatient noise and Ayla held up a hand to silence him. "We weren't followed," she said. "Even if we had been, nobody could hear us over the waves. You can tell us."

"That *was* me telling you," said Rowan. She sounded even more exhausted than Ayla felt, her voice empty. "That's why I'm back so soon. Here's what happened in the south: *nothing*."

Ayla frowned.

"I don't understand," said Benjy beside her.

Rowan sighed and sat down heavily on the rocks. Ayla immediately dropped to her knees beside her, halfway to panicking, but Rowan waved her away. "It's fine, Ayla. Just some bruising on my ribs. Makes it hard to stand for too long."

"But what *happened*," Ayla insisted. "It can't have been nothing. You said there were two hundred gathering in the south, a full moon, you *said*—"

"I know what I said. And I know what I heard, and who I heard it from—a person I thought was a reliable source. But I'm telling you, when I reached my contacts in the south, I found nothing. There were no uprisings. *There were never going to be any uprisings.*" She looked between them, her face grave. "The humans on those estates hadn't even heard the rumors. My contacts knew nothing. I came for a rebellion and walked into normal day after normal day. It was all a lie."

The three of them were silent, Ayla and Benjy struggling to make sense of Rowan's story.

Benjy spoke first. "But who would have spread a lie like that? Who stands to gain from it? Some leech trying to confuse the

Resistance, make us doubt each other? Maybe even provoke us into fighting with each other instead of the enemy?"

"I don't know who it was," said Rowan. "But I think this was less of a provocation and more of an experiment."

"What do you mean?" said Ayla.

"I mean that whoever created this falsehood, whoever wanted me to believe there were going to be uprisings to the south . . . I think they did this because they wanted to know where I get my information and then where I spread it. I think they wanted to track the connections between members of the Resistance. To see who talks to who, who follows who. They wanted to map us."

Benjy said something in response, but Ayla didn't hear it— her ears were roaring, and it wasn't the sound of the ocean waves crashing against the rocks.

They wanted to map us.

She had a pretty good idea of who lied to Rowan about the uprisings.

But how?

She didn't realize she'd spoken aloud until Rowan said, "I don't know how. I don't know which of my contacts I can trust anymore. All I know is that we have a mole. And we—the entire Resistance—is in danger."

"Who did you first hear about the uprisings from?" Ayla asked quietly.

"I don't reveal names," said Rowan. "But . . . I will tell you that it was someone from within the palace. A servant." She looked away, a muscle flexing in her jaw. "Someone whose information has always been true. Someone who has never led me astray before."

"And that person? Who did they hear it from?"

She shrugged. "In the past, they've mentioned only where she was stationed."

She. "And where was that? Where was she stationed?" Ayla's heart was pounding. She leaned forward, eyes intent on Rowan's face. Some part of her already knew what she was about to hear, already knew the answer, but she asked anyway.

"My contact said she's a scullery maid," Rowan said cautiously. "Stationed in the laundry room."

"Do you know something?" Benjy asked Ayla, catching the look on her face.

"Faye," Ayla said quietly.

Rowan's expression collapsed, but she didn't look shocked. She must have had the same suspicion.

But if that were true . . .

"Benjy, did you find out anything more about the sun apples Faye kept talking about?"

He nodded, looking grim. "I tried to get into the crop house at the end of the field this morning. Claimed I'd seen a bad batch of grain and wanted to check some of the supplies. There was a mountain of sun apple crates—far more than I would have thought the orchards could produce in just over a month."

"That's odd," Ayla said slowly.

"Not as odd as what I found inside them."

"What do you mean?" Rowan asked, her voice hoarse and low.

"The crates weren't full of apples at all—at least not the ones I managed to pry open. I didn't have much time before that tall guard, Tiren, was going to find me out, so I wasn't that thorough, but I did open two of the crates, and, and . . . they were full of . . . I don't really *know*. This . . . this *dust*. Black dust."

"Black dust? Like some sort of powder?" Rowan asked.

"Could it be a weapon?" Ayla chimed in.

Benjy shook his head. "I honestly don't know."

Ayla looked at Rowan. "If Faye was helping Kinok make shipments of this dust . . ."

"She was definitely in way over her head," Benjy finished.

Ayla's breath shook in her chest as she tried to speak. "Well, whatever the purpose of the dust, we know one thing—Kinok is controlling Faye. Using her. Maybe she tried to defect. Maybe that's why . . ."

She didn't have to finish her sentence. All three of them were thinking the same thing. Maybe that was why Kinok had ordered Luna's death.

Ayla swallowed hard. "So what do we do?" She and Benjy both looked at Rowan.

Rowan's voice was cold. "We take the Scyre down."

"Wait," Ayla said suddenly. "I know something. I learned something just last night." She avoided Benjy's eyes. He still didn't know the truth of what had happened last night. That she'd slipped out not to iron a dress but to confront her brother. And that it had ended with her curled up in Crier's bed. It was only a matter of time before that secret got out. "The Scyre has something in his possession that might help us. *Will* help us. It's a compass. Apparently, it's very important to Kinok, and I think that's because it's not just any compass—it's special. Instead of pointing north, *it points to the Iron Heart*."

Benjy's eyes widened. "Are you serious?" he asked, at the same time Rowan said, "Are you sure?"

"Crier said it was special, she said even the Red Hands seemed jealous of it," Ayla told them, and then immediately regretted it when Benjy's gaze turned suspicious. She continued before he could say anything. Imply anything. "Why else would I be spending so many late nights with her? She's so naive, she'll spill any secret if you get her talking for long enough." It didn't feel true, the way she was framing it, but it did feel necessary. "A compass that could lead us to the Heart. Think about the power of that. And it's in Kinok's study."

Quickly she explained about the failed interrogation in Kinok's study—neatly sidestepping the *reason* she'd been interrogated; she told them it was just Kinok being paranoid about his future wife's closest servant—and her own discovery of the hidden safe. "I think if there's anywhere he could be hiding the compass, it would be there. Even if it's not the compass, it has to be something else just as valuable."

Rowan nodded. The light was back in her eyes, the spark of excitement over a new mission. "We have to get into that safe. *Then*, once we have what we need, we destroy the Scyre and rescue Faye." She smiled, ruffling Ayla's hair the way she'd been doing since Ayla was small and starving. "You did well, my girl."

Ayla bit back a proud, silly grin.

"It's been nearly an hour," said Benjy. "The guards will be checking the servants' quarters soon. We should get back."

"Yes," said Rowan. "I can get away again next week—same time, same place. We'll come up with a plan for getting into the safe as soon as possible. We'll need a distraction. There's something in the air, something on the horizon. I can sense it. There's no time to spare."

Ayla and Benjy nodded. "We'll be there."

Rowan nodded, and the three of them parted ways.

WINTER,

YEAR 47 AE

17

What if Queen Junn hadn't received her letter?

It was all Crier could think about in the week since Ayla had been caught in her bed, and then released by Kinok without so much as a word of reprimand or concern on his part—in the week since she'd sent the coded missive to Queen Junn, pledging her secret allegiance.

Well, it wasn't *all* she thought of. It required a strength she didn't know she had to avoid Ayla's eyes all week, to *not* replay the way she'd turned toward Crier in her sleep. Though Ayla would never admit it, and though Crier had no proof of it, she believed it—Ayla had at least started to trust her. Had started to open up to her.

But now—the risks were too high. Everyone was watching her next move. She couldn't afford to let Ayla come under Kinok's scrutiny again. Which meant she couldn't give him any reason to. She couldn't pay extra attention to Ayla. Couldn't allow the darkness of her gaze to call out to Crier like it had so often in the last month.

And in the meantime, the need to slow Kinok down, to intercept his efforts and delay her marriage, was only growing in urgency. She'd sent Queen Junn information in the hope that it would show her loyalty—that in return, Junn would offer a strategy for the alliance she'd talked about. A way to eliminate the "problem" of Kinok for good.

Now: she'd been lying awake for hours, thoughts circling like vultures. Had Queen Junn even received it? She must have— unless the letter had been intercepted.

If the letter *hadn't* been intercepted—if it was in Queen Junn's hands—what was the queen going to do? Was it wrong of Crier to name Foer, Councilmember Laone, Councilmember Shasta as Kinok's supporters? What if she'd misunderstood Rosi's words? What if she'd put *Rosi* in danger by naming her fiancé? What if Queen Junn decided Crier wasn't helpful enough and cut off communication, and Crier was once again alone?

She was just about to hit hour number three of panicked, pointless thought when she heard footsteps in the corridor outside her door. Lots of them, quick and human.

Voices, barked orders. Someone sending for a carriage?

Crier didn't wait for Ayla to arrive—dawn was still a quarter hour away—and didn't even change out of her nightgown before hurrying out of her room and calling after the first servant she saw. "Has something happened? What is the carriage for?"

"The sovereign is leaving for Bell-run, my lady. Short notice."

"What—today? Why?" The small town of Bell-run was a day's ride to the west. Her father usually visited only once or twice per year, perfunctory, just to show his face to the people.

"Yes, my lady. This morning. As soon as possible. Been some killings in the night," said the servant, hushed, in the way humans had when they spoke about the dead.

Killings. A mass execution? A quashed rebellion? "Who was it?" Crier demanded. "Who's been killed? Human rebels?"

"No, my lady." The servant shifted. "They were Automae."

". . . What were their names?" A sick feeling of disbelief was beginning to move through her, making her sway.

Maybe some part of her already knew. But she had to hear it aloud.

"Two were Red Hands, my lady. Councilmembers Laone and Shasta. The other was the lord of a southern estate. Lord Foer."

Stars and skies.

"Pardon, my lady?"

She'd spoken aloud. "Nothing," Crier managed, and turned away before the servant could say anything else—or worse, catch the look on Crier's face and call for a physician.

I killed them, Crier thought dully, moving in a trance back down the hallway. *I named them, and now they are dead.*

Queen Junn might have given the order—because of course it was Queen Junn, there was no way this was a coincidence. Crier had given three names to her, and now the owners of all three names were dead.

But it was Crier who had caused this.

She couldn't believe how quickly Junn had acted. With no warning, no hesitation—just swift deliverance.

It meant the queen must have mercenaries all over Rabu.

Crier's temples were pounding; she felt starved of oxygen even though her intake was unchanged.

Oh, gods, *Rosi*. Rosi's fiancé was dead and it was Crier's fault.

Well, what were you expecting? she asked herself furiously, pausing for a moment to rest her forehead against the cool stone wall of the corridor. *Did you think the Mad Queen would send Kinok's supporters a kindly worded letter? Did you think she'd be forgiving?*

She thought of the story of Fox, Wolf, and Bear. How none of them could trust the others.

Crier looked down at her own hands and imagined, for a moment, her fingers dipped in violet blood.

Minutes later, Crier sat in the chair across from her father, the two of them alone in his study, and tried not to let the guilt and horror show on her face.

Murderer. That's what she was.

Luckily, Hesod was lost in his own thoughts, surfacing only to bark orders at the servants who kept arriving at the door. Ready the carriages, curry the horses, pack clothes and heartstone for three days' ride, prepare a party of guards and footservants, send word ahead to the estates of the deceased. They were going on a mourning tour. It was like the victory tour Hesod had taken in the weeks after he was crowned sovereign, but instead of victory in the air there was nothing but death, and shock, and Hesod's simmering anger. He was taking the deaths of his Red Hands personally.

If he ever found out Crier's role in their murders—

No. He wouldn't find out.

He couldn't.

"Daughter."

Crier started. Hesod was watching her closely from across the desk. She tried to seem blank, nothing but dully empathetic and concerned for him. "Yes?"

"I leave for the South in an hour to pay my respects to the estates of Councilmembers Laone and Shasta and Lord Foer. You will remain here while I am gone and keep up with your studies and your normal duties. That is all."

Maybe a month ago, Crier would have accepted this without question. But something about spending so much time around Ayla—who questioned everything from Kinok's motives to Crier's preferred bathing oils—made her sit up a little straighter, and shake her head.

"No," she said. "I have a relationship with Rosi, Foer's promised wife. Foer's death will be weighing on her. I—I must go see her and make sure she is all right."

Hesod regarded her coldly. "After everything that happened last week on the night of Junn's visit, what makes you think I trust you to manage part of this tour?"

"This is a way for me to rebuild that trust," Crier insisted, even though his words stung. "You can spend more time with the Red Hands' families—they are higher ranked than Foer, are they not? I can go alone to Rosi's estate and comfort her myself." She leaned forward. "I want to prove myself to you, Father. I made a mistake, being so lenient with—with the handmaiden. I know I disappointed you. Let me make amends."

He was still hesitating.

"I only wish to perform what is my duty to, to the state, Father," she went on. "Foer's estate, where Rosi had taken up residence during their courtship, is barely a day's ride south, near the border of Varn and the border village of Elderell. I can be gone for less than forty-eight hours, if that's what you want. How would it look for me to ignore my closest companion right now?"

"Fine," Hesod said. "You may go. But if anything goes wrong, daughter, anything at all . . ."

"Nothing will go wrong, Father," Crier said. "I promise."

As Crier left her father's study, she caught the first servant she saw. "Send for the handmaiden Ayla," she ordered the girl. "Tell her she is to meet me by the stables immediately."

"Yes, my lady."

The girl scurried off and Crier stalked through the halls back to her bedchamber, taking a precious few minutes to dress herself—her hands fumbling, unused to tying the laces herself. Then she threw two days' worth of clothes into a trunk.

She felt wild, heart skittering, reminding her for a moment of the tiny, rapid heartbeats she'd heard radiating up from a rabbit's den all those weeks ago, during her Hunt.

She really was going to comfort Rosi. To force herself to witness the effects of what she'd done, in the wake of Foer's murder. But she had another, ulterior motive for traveling south.

The village of Elderell.

A place Councilmember Reyka had mentioned a few times over the years, though she'd never said *why* such a tiny speck of a village was significant to her. Crier had asked once, and Reyka had said only: "I've business there."

Now, Crier couldn't help but wonder if that *business* had something to do with her disappearance.

Grabbing her traveler's bag, Crier made her way out of the palace and toward the stables, where there would already be a carriage waiting for her. The morning sun was hidden behind thick gray clouds, the smell of winter rain hanging in the air.

Ayla was already waiting outside the stables when Crier arrived. She looked equal parts wary and furious.

"What's happening?" Ayla demanded the second Crier was within earshot. "Why did you—?"

Crier grabbed her wrist, gently but firmly, and pulled her off to the side. She leaned in close, and even through the fog of worry, her eyes caught on the freckles dusting Ayla's nose. The shape of her full, pretty mouth. There it was again, that indignance, that anger that was so harsh and yet that made Ayla who she was. That fierce vibration in her that Crier felt drawn to again and again . . .

"*Hush,*" Crier hissed, partially to herself. "Please. Wait here.

Keep your head down, don't make a scene."

Ayla's mouth dropped open, but Crier turned and quickly moved toward the carriage. It was waiting at the mouth of the stables, a black beetle shell pulled by two fine old horses. The driver, an aging manservant with skin like cracked leather, was already perched on his seat at the front, reins in hand.

"Do you need help with your trunk, my lady?" he asked.

"No," said Crier. "Are we set to depart immediately?"

He nodded and tugged at the reins; the horses pawed at the ground, flicking their ears impatiently. "At a moment's notice, my lady."

Crier loaded her trunk into the carriage and then darted back to the side of the stables. Ayla was still standing there, anger in every line of her body, but there was no time to explain anything. Crier didn't want any of the stableboys—or worse, her father—to see Ayla, to know that Crier was bringing Ayla along with her to the South. Her father hadn't expressly forbidden it, but probably only because he thought there was no way Crier would dare.

Well, she dared.

After all, she knew she couldn't leave Ayla here alone. She might have bought Ayla some time, a respite of safety, but how long would it last if she wasn't there to watch out for her?

"Come," Crier muttered. "I'll tell you everything in a moment, just come with me and *keep quiet.*"

Ayla looked confused, but Crier took her hand and led her forward before she could reply. To her surprise, Ayla's hand clutched around her own. And despite herself—despite *everything*—a thrill went through her.

The second they were both seated, Crier drew the curtains and rapped her knuckles on the thin wall separating them from the driver. "Go, go!"

The carriage lurched forward, and they were off.

As Kiera, the First, got older and stronger, she required more and more blood—and so, by the fifth year, the queen was dying.

So great was the queen's love for Kiera that she would have gladly sacrificed herself to give Kiera even one more day of life . . . but Wren had fallen deeply in love with Queen Thea. Blinded by this human weakness—this love that grew inside him like a twisted, rotted thing—he planned to save the queen by killing Kiera. But the queen discovered his plans before he had a chance to act, and Thomas Wren was imprisoned.

Desperate to save the queen, Wren continued his work as a Maker even while imprisoned.

And this, above all, must never be lost to the waves of Time: no matter how much Queen Thea claimed to love her Automa daughter, it was she—not Thomas Wren—who murdered Kiera in the end.

—FROM *THE BEGINNING OF THE AUTOMA ERA*,
BY EOK OF FAMILY MEADOR, 2234610907, YEAR 4 AE

18

Ayla's thoughts rattled louder than the carriage wheels.

She was stuck in an enclosed space with Crier for the foreseeable future, furious about being virtually kidnapped and even more furious about the fact that she was so damn *hyper-aware* of Crier's presence, of their knees bumping every time the carriage lurched, of the smell of her hair, the scent of her clean, perfumed skin, the cut of her jaw and the smooth column of her throat—

Ayla pressed her forehead against the carriage window and refused to look at Crier. Because every time she did, she found it difficult to *stop* looking.

Maybe she wasn't even all that angry with Crier. Maybe she was just angry at herself. Here was the object of her revenge. And yet every day that ticked by and she couldn't kill Crier, every day that she used the lady to try and gain access to information instead, was another day that she felt herself . . . weakening.

Softening. Warming. It was the only way to describe it, as if her will were a wide lake in the sun, slowly evaporating at the edges until one day there'd be no will, no force, no drive, no anger left. She'd be empty.

And all because of Crier, because of the way she made her feel, the way the sensation of being looked at and thought about—thought about *kindly*, with a tenderness and curiosity that Ayla simply could not abide. It shook that thing that had made Ayla who she was for so long. That survivor instinct. That hunger for Crier's blood on her hands, to make things equal. Justice. Revenge. It had been the only force keeping Ayla alive, and now this fluttery anxious *sweetness* that brewed in her was ruining that, was taking it away from her.

She didn't know what to do.

They *had* to move forward with their plans soon, before Ayla crumbled entirely.

But now, that was all ruined, too, because today was the day she and Benjy had agreed to meet Rowan, and now Ayla was going to be gone for, what, another three days? And who knew the next time she'd be able to sneak away to meet Rowan?

She felt desperate, and alone, and had no one to ask for advice. She couldn't—gods forbid—talk to Benjy about this. And even Rowan, who'd been almost a mother to her . . . it would be far too great a betrayal to even admit what was going on inside her head—inside her heart.

She wanted to punch something. She wanted to shatter one of the windows and fly out into the road, to run into the woods, to escape. To run forever. To be free of this—*whatever* it was. This closeness. Crier's eyes. Her knees. Her *thoughts*. It was as if Ayla could feel Crier's thoughts, like soft caresses in darkness, and . . .

Stop thinking about her. Ayla closed her eyes, trying to tune out this feeling, to focus instead on sorting through everything she'd discovered and learned over her weeks at Crier's side. It felt like sifting sand through her fingers, looking for flakes of gold. She'd seen so much, and still there was so little she understood. Information like stars. She was trying to form a constellation.

She thought about the green feather from Storme. What did it *mean*? Was it sort of like a secret password, proof of her trust-worthiness, something she could show to the queen's guard if she ever needed an audience with her brother? She thought about the sun apple crates filled with vials of black dust: What did it do? Was it anything like heartstone? She knew only that it came from Kinok.

And now Crier herself was wearing his black armband—*why*?

Stop thinking about her.

Ayla thought about Storme.

And that was, somehow, even *worse*. The pain still fresh and raw as it had been one week ago when she stood in the corridor and silently begged him to love her again, to tell her the truth, to stay. But she hadn't been able to say any of that aloud and it didn't matter because he hadn't wanted to, hadn't been willing to.

In some ways, she'd spent the last week wishing he'd stayed

dead, the way he'd been in her mind for so many years.

Storme. The boy she used to know, her twin, her bright-eyed brother, shining in her memories and then gone. Then: the man he had become, right hand to the leech queen, exploding back into Ayla's life with all the force of a powder bomb and then, like a powder bomb, leaving nothing but wreckage behind.

How was it possible that she'd had him again but only for a day?

It was fitting that Crier had kidnapped her for a mourning tour. Ayla was in mourning. For Storme—and for her necklace, too. The last connection she had to her family, to her mother, and she'd *lost* it. But most of all, she mourned her former self, the girl who'd had the will of a never-ending fire. The girl who would burn and burn forever until she'd destroyed all the pain in the world.

Where had that girl gone?

She found herself touching the spot over her sternum where the locket usually rested, that old habit. Her neck felt lighter without the chain and pendant, but in a bad way, an aching way, as if someone had cut all her hair off. Lighter, but missing the weight.

Instead of touching the necklace, she reached into the pocket of her uniform and brushed her thumb over a different object: the key to the music room. It had become a stand-in talisman ever since she'd lost her necklace, something to rub between finger and thumb when she got restless. How embarrassing, that something from Crier—a gift—could be so calming. So grounding. She'd already used it several times in the past week to go somewhere quiet when she had a moment off work and needed a beat to think, to breathe, to be truly alone.

If she was being honest, she'd gone to the music room to think about Crier. It felt like if she thought about her around Benjy and the other servants, they'd immediately see it written all over her face.

Desire.

Longing.

Loneliness.

Curiosity.

Shame.

How she wanted to sleep in Crier's bed again. Or—something. How she hadn't slept as deeply in months, maybe years, as she had that night. How she hadn't felt so *safe* since before *that day*. That was the power Crier seemed to have over her.

Stop thinking about her.

Why was it so hard?

Gods. The sooner she stole the compass from Kinok, the better. She just needed to get her hands on the compass, and then she'd have everything she needed to lead Rowan, Benjy, and the other rebels straight to the Iron Heart. She wouldn't have to be Crier's handmaiden anymore. She could finally get her revenge, and then run. Leave the palace and never look back.

Ayla realized she was gripping the music room key so tight that the sharp points were digging painfully into her palm. She let go, placing both hands on her lap. Refusing still to look at

Crier. Their knees were touching. It wasn't even skin-to-skin contact; Ayla was wearing her uniform pants and Crier a long black mourning gown. So why was it affecting Ayla so much?

Those foolish, stolen moments in the tide pool, cold water and black night and Crier's skin turned silver in the moonlight. The story of the princess and the hare and how Crier's voice had started out quiet, unsure, but grew stronger as she told the story. Ayla had wanted to say, *Tell me another.* Another. She'd wanted to say, *Don't stop.*

The tide pool. Crier's bed. Moonlight again. Soft and warm, the smell of Crier everywhere, on the pillows and the blankets. When Ayla had turned her face into the pillow and breathed in, Crier filled her lungs. It should have felt like poison. It didn't. She should be lying awake at night thinking of nothing but sliding a blade into Crier's heart. She wasn't. Instead she thought of: Crier's odd, awkward affection, her questions, her endless curiosity—sweet, often naive, almost childlike, but always earnest, always fascinated by whatever answers Ayla was willing to give.

Ayla glanced at Crier out of the corner of her eye. Crier was staring out the other window, face turned away from Ayla. The curtains were drawn; a thin strip of grayish sunlight bisected her face, one half in light and the other in shadow. One eye glinting gold, the other a deep brown. She was beautiful. It was perhaps a terrible thing to admit, but Ayla couldn't help it. Crier was beautiful. Created to be beautiful, but it was more than that; more than perfect bone structure and symmetrical features and flawless brown skin. It was the way her eyes lit up with interest, the way her fingers were always so careful, almost reverent, as she flipped the pages of a book. The way she held absolutely still sometimes, like a deer in the woods, so still that Ayla wanted to touch her, reach out and touch her face to make sure she was still real.

"I know you're looking at me," Crier said, and Ayla looked away so quickly that she nearly knocked her head against the carriage window. "I can tell. I can always tell."

"No you can't," Ayla muttered, cheeks hot.

Crier raised an eyebrow. "Was I wrong?"

Ayla didn't answer. Instead, she let her gaze drop from Crier's face to the black band on her arm, a silent question. Challenge for a challenge.

"Ah," said Crier. "Yes. I . . . made a bargain. With my father." She touched the armband, rubbing the thick black fabric between her fingers. Her jaw tightened. "Didn't you wonder why Kinok released you so quickly?"

"I thought it was because he realized I'm useless to him," Ayla said weakly. Her stomach hurt, turning over with something she refused to admit was gratitude. Or guilt. "I thought I just didn't have what he was looking for."

"You didn't. But I did."

"What? What did you give him? What did you tell him?" Ayla leaned forward, heart thumping. "Crier, what did you do?" *Because of me?*

"What I gave him wasn't information. It was power." Crier almost smiled, thin and humorless, and let go of the armband.

Folded her hands back in her lap, and just like that she looked like a painting, a portrait, light and color and perfection captured, if only for a moment. "Power over me. His mark on my arm. My endorsement. But—*only in show*."

Ayla let out a breath. "So you didn't actually join him."

"No," said Crier, surprised. Like it had never even occurred to her that Ayla might be confused, might doubt her motives or beliefs. "I would never. But please understand. I didn't know what he was going to do to you. I was . . . concerned. I wanted to get you—away from him."

"You shouldn't have done that," Ayla said fiercely.

"Was I supposed to let you rot away down there? Or worse?"

"No, but you shouldn't have given him that. He's always three steps ahead. You can bet that he's already planning how he's going to use this, use your fake support—"

"I know that," said Crier.

"So *why*? Why would you risk that?"

Again, surprise. "Because I knew it was the only way he would let you stay. With me."

Ayla flopped back against the velvet seat of the carriage, furious all over again. "You shouldn't have," she hissed. "It was reckless, it was dangerous, it was—"

"Worth it," said Crier. Her eyes, out of the direct sunlight and both that deep, human brown, were fixed on Ayla's face. She looked calm everywhere except her hands, which were clenched tight in her lap.

In the tiny space of the carriage, it was too much.

Ayla curled up in a ball in the corner of the seat so that not even her knees could touch Crier, and she spent the rest of the journey staring sightlessly out the window, watching the dead yellow hills slide by, not even trying to not think about Crier, and the ache yawning wide inside her chest.

19

Foer's estate was smaller than the sovereign's, nestled in the dip of a valley. As was common in the South, the buildings were made from granite and dark, shining wood, the wooden rooftops curving up sharply toward the sky. The grounds were composed mainly of fields and horse pastures, a few orchards. No gardens—that was always the first thing Crier missed whenever she'd visited Rosi here over the years. The gardens and the sea air.

Their party descended slowly into the valley, the sun sinking behind them. Crier drew back the velvet curtains and peered out at the landscape: the hillsides were grass and rough outcroppings of gray stone, furred with brambles.

"Have you been here before?" said Ayla, breaking the silence so abruptly that Crier startled a little.

"Yes," she said, refusing to acknowledge the slight amusement on Ayla's face. "A few times. Rosi is my closest companion. Has always been."

"Really?"

"Well." Crier thought about it. "Yes. Comparatively."

Ayla seemed to mull that over. "You don't have very many companions."

"No. Not many."

Somewhere in the distance, horns sounded. One of her men announcing their arrival. Crier smoothed her skirts, her hair. She tried to fix her expression into something appropriately somber. It wasn't hard—she was not exactly in high spirits—but she always felt extra self-conscious around Rosi, extra performative. "Does my face look all right?" she found herself asking Ayla.

Ayla raised her eyebrows. "What do you mean, all right?"

"I don't know," Crier muttered. "Never mind. It was a foolish thing to ask."

She felt Ayla's eyes on her and refused to look up. She stared at her own hands in her lap, light brown against the midnight black of her dress.

"It does," said Ayla almost begrudgingly. "Look all right, I mean."

Crier's eyes widened in surprise, but before she got a chance to reply, the carriage was rattling to a stop. She heard the sound of her driver leaping from his seat, his bootsteps in the scrubby grass, the horses whuffing softly to each other. They had arrived.

"Lady Crier," said the driver; a moment later the carriage

door opened and she was helped down. She blinked, eyes adjusting instantly to the half-light of evening in the valley. Behind her, Ayla hopped down to the ground and cursed under her breath when she landed hard. Crier bit back a completely inappropriate smile.

"Lady Crier!" Rosi's voice cut through the evening like a knife through velvet. She was standing at the main entrance of the manor, flanked by servants and her own handmaiden. Behind her, the manor house was a mass of dark stone against the hills, windows glowing with lantern light. "Lady Crier, are you alone?"

"The sovereign sends his condolences," said Crier as she and Ayla approached the manor entrance. "He is visiting the estates of Councilmembers Laone and Shasta, but not out of lack of respect or grief for you or Lord Foer. I requested to visit you alone—not as the sovereign's heir but as a friend." She joined Rosi in front of the massive double doors and inclined her head, hands clasped in front of her chest. "I am truly sorry for your loss. The sovereign will find out who did this, and—and there will be justice."

"Thank you, my lady," said Rosi.

Like Crier, she was dressed in a black mourning gown. But that was the only familiar thing about her. Crier tried not to stare, but now that she was seeing Rosi up close, it was obvious that there was something very, very wrong. Something had changed since she'd last seen her, at the engagement ball back at the palace. In less than a month, Rosi had become manic, pupils dilated, lips almost blue—and nearly skeletal. It was like there was something living inside her, sucking the life from her bones. Her collarbones jutted out above the neckline of her gown; her face was gaunt, her eyes sunken into the sockets. When she spoke, Crier saw that it wasn't just her lips that were stained blue-black—it was also her teeth and tongue. It looked like she'd been drinking black ink.

But what Crier couldn't stop looking at—what frightened her most—were Rosi's veins. They stood out against her temples, her neck, the bones of her hands, and they were stark black.

"Rosi," Crier said, hushed. "Rosi, are you—are you well?"

It was a foolish question, considering the circumstances, but Rosi didn't say anything about Foer. She laughed, high-pitched and almost hysterical. "I'm well, my lady. Come, come inside. Bring the little human pet, too. Who knows what would happen if we left her all alone in the dark?"

Inside, Rosi led Crier and Ayla to a lavish sitting room, all high windows and velvet curtains and deep-blue divans, a piano, a tray of liquid heartstone already waiting for them. Crier's blood yearned for it—she hadn't eaten all day, and she was definitely feeling the effects.

"The pet can wait outside the door," Rosi said flippantly.

Crier wanted to argue but knew it would just be suspicious. She nodded at Ayla, apologetic, and forced herself not to wince when Rosi shut the sitting room door in Ayla's face.

Rosi and Crier took their seats on the divan. Rosi poured a cup of liquid heartstone for Crier but took none herself. Crier remembered the words from her letter: *I haven't touched heart-stone in weeks.*

She'd been taking the black dust instead.

The Nightshade.

Crier took a long sip of tea, feeling it spread through her like molten gold, the strength returning to her limbs. Then she set the teacup down and turned to Rosi. "I am truly sorry for your loss, my friend. We all grieve for Foer."

"Thank you, my lady," said Rosi. Gods, she couldn't even meet Crier's eyes for more than a second before her gaze skittered away.

"Please, if there is anything I can do, anything my father can do . . ."

"Foer's death really is a shame," Rosi sighed, seeming not to hear Crier. She didn't seem saddened or weighted down by the grief, however. And perhaps that was to be expected. Automae didn't suffer over death the way humans did. "Do you know how it happened? Do you know how he was found?" She leaned closer. "His head was severed. You probably guessed that. I'm told it was a clean wound. Well. As clean as possible. Sawing through the spinal cord's a nasty business. But it was—professional. Not some human with an ax. Whoever did it used a butcher's blade. Do you know how he was found?"

"Rosi," said Crier, feeling sick, "Rosi, you don't need to tell me this."

"He was found when his blood soaked through the

floorboards. He wasn't in the house, you know. He was in the stables. On the upper level, tending to the horse tack. He likes to oil the saddles himself. He was killed there, and his blood soaked through everything. Even started dripping from the rafters like violet rain." She barked a laugh. "Dripped directly onto a stable-boy's head. That's when he started screaming."

Crier could do nothing but stare at her.

"Anyway," Rosi went on. "Before all that, he was working with Kinok on something *very* important. And I know they were almost done."

"Something very important?" Crier repeated hollowly. She remembered Rosi's letter, her mentions of Foer and Kinok working together, but still wasn't sure what that meant.

"Top secret." Rosi nodded, widening her eyes. She obviously enjoyed knowing something Crier didn't. "I'm surprised the Scyre didn't tell you about it, my lady."

"Foer must have trusted you a lot," Crier said, ignoring the jab. "You must have been very precious to him."

"I was," said Rosi. "He told me everything. He was *vital* to ARM, you know. Absolutely vital."

"I know he was," said Crier. "Kinok told me the same thing, about how important Foer was. And you, of course."

"Did he really?"

"Oh, many times." She didn't mean it, but she knew the words Rosi wanted to hear.

Rosi lowered her voice, conspiratorial. "Foer was the only

one the Scyre trusted to investigate Thomas Wren. All those Red Hands in ARM, and he trusted *Foer*. No offense meant, of course, my lady."

"None taken," Crier assured her. "Of course he trusted Foer the most. Who else could do what he did?" She was fishing. *What did Rosi really know?*

"Nobody," Rosi said. "Nobody else has Foer's connections with the Midwives."

"Yes, exactly," said Crier. "And that's why Kinok chose Foer to—investigate Wren." She was trying to piece it together but couldn't—what exactly did his research on Wren have to do with the Midwives? It must be something about Design, something about Wren's original Designs for Automae and, perhaps, how the Midwives might improve upon it.

She thought of the page of notes she'd slipped from Kinok's book, the night of the Reaper's Moon. How they'd revealed Wren's secret connections to a woman only called H.

"Mm." Rosi leaned forward even closer. "Do you want to know what Foer discovered, my lady?"

Crier feigned uncertainty, trying not to look too eager. She didn't want to do anything that would make Rosi suspicious. "Should you really tell me? If it's top secret?"

"You're Scyre Kinok's fiancée," said Rosi. "You're bound to him. Spilling his secrets would bring harm to you and the sovereign as well." Her hands were shaking where they were clasped in her lap. "Besides, I—I want to give you a token of my own trust, my lady. So you remember how close we are, and how important I am to Scyre Kinok and ARM."

"You're vital," Crier murmured. "Vital to him. To ARM."

Rosi sighed happily. "Oh, good."

"So . . . Thomas Wren . . . ?"

"I don't know the exact details," Rosi said. "But I do know that the Scyre had Foer looking into Wren's research. All his collaborators, really anyone he ever spoke to. And Foer discovered that Thomas Wren didn't Make the first Automa at all. Did you ever know such a thing? He traced Wren's work back to someone else entirely—a peasant woman. *She* created our Kind, not him."

Crier's shock was genuine. A peasant woman had created the first Automa. Not Thomas Wren of the Royal Academy of Makers. Some woman no one had ever heard of.

It couldn't be.

"Are you sure?"

"Foer seemed to be."

Crier sank back in her chair. Rosi's eyes swept over her greedily, as if feeding on Crier's reaction to the secret.

She thought again of Kinok's notes. Of the phrase "Yora's heart." Of Wren's secret connection—affair?—with *H.*

"But . . . I don't understand," said Crier. "Why would this person allow Wren to take credit for her work? Why would she give him something so valuable?"

"I asked the same question. Foer said maybe her work wasn't given. Maybe it was taken."

The two of them sat there for a moment, mulling over the

knowledge. Or at least Crier was—Rosi didn't seem to be thinking of anything at all, her eyes darting around like mayflies,
fingers drumming on her knees. Her gaze was so empty.

"I wonder what made Kinok suspicious of Wren," Crier
mused aloud. "I wonder why he told Foer to investigate him."

Rosi made a dismissive noise. "Who knows? He's a genius. If
anyone could find Tourmaline, it's him."

Tourmaline.

"Thank you, Rosi," Crier said. "That was more than enough."

After making assurances that Rosi would be well taken care of
by the sovereign's men should she need any support in the wake
of Foer's death, Crier felt her duty had been completed—and
truthfully, she was eager to get out of Rosi's house, to get away
from the girl whose arms shook and eyes blazed and veins popped
out dark against her skin. But it wouldn't have been proper to
leave without a ceremonial dinner, and the trip was too long to
make it back in one day.

So Crier dined, hardly taking a bite of the useless food put
out before her. She pocketed a biscuit to bring to Ayla in the
morning.

When dawn broke, she was anxious to get moving. Ayla had
been made to sleep in the servants' quarters, and Crier felt irra-
tionally protective, worried for her safety, even though there was
no suggestion of danger to her here.

They left Rosi's estate the next morning, Crier feeling more
disturbed than ever. Nightshade, Tourmaline, Yora's heart,

Thomas Wren, the mystery of the unnamed woman . . . not to mention Rosi's strange and frightening behavior.

And Kinok had given her the black dust. Kinok did that to her. To countless others. Every day, with every new piece of information, the case against him seemed to build. Crier was determined to keep building it until her father had no choice but to listen to her, to see Kinok for who he truly was: a threat.

There was one more stop to make before she returned home. The village of Elderell.

It was the last place Reyka had been seen before she disappeared.

Crier waited until she knew they must be close to the village gates, and then she knocked on the wall of the carriage, hoping it was loud enough to be heard over the horse's hooves. No response. She knocked again, louder and more frantic this time, and heard the driver call out to the others. *Halt for a moment, the lady—*

She had only a few seconds before he would open the doors. She ignored Ayla's hissed *what are you doing*, hissing right back, "Just play along, all right? Just do as I say."

A second later the carriage door was opening and the driver said, "Is everything all right, Lady Crier?"

"No!" she said urgently. "My handmaiden is gravely ill."

The driver glanced at Ayla, who promptly doubled over and groaned loudly. A little theatrical, maybe, but it did the trick.

"We should keep going if we want to return to the palace by sundown, my lady," the driver said. "Perhaps the handmaiden—"

"Do you want her *dead*?" Crier demanded, drawing herself up. The driver cowered beneath her gaze. "She's a human, she is weak. What will it look like to the sovereign if I return with a dead handmaiden? What will it look like if you couldn't even keep both of us *alive* for two days?"

Ayla groaned again.

"My deepest apologies, Lady Crier," the driver said in a rush. "We are barely a league from the village of Elderell. I will take you there at once."

"Well, get on with it!" Crier snapped. "Take us to the Green River Inn at the heart of the village. *Now.*"

The driver nodded and slammed the carriage doors shut. A few moments later the jostling movement started up again, and Crier leaned back against the velvet seat in satisfaction as their course veered slightly east. When she looked up, Ayla was staring at her.

"Thank you," said Crier. "You did well."

"Right," said Ayla after a pause. Then she leaned closer, and Crier took in a breath. "Are you going to tell me what's in Elderell?"

Crier hesitated. She didn't know enough. The last time she divulged information hastily, three people ended up murdered overnight.

"I can't. Not yet. It's too—dangerous."

Ayla studied her for a moment, then pulled back and looked away.

"Ayla."

Ayla still refused to look at her.

To his credit, the carriage driver delivered them to the Green River Inn in record time. Crier had chosen it because she'd heard Reyka mention the inn a few times, as she frequently stopped to do business in Elderell. They pulled up outside the inn—a somewhat ramshackle building just off the village square, with a friendly-looking green door and smoke pouring from the chimney—just past midday. Crier hopped out of the carriage, bid the driver and guards to remain outside the inn, ready for departure, and helped Ayla down, supporting most of her weight. Ayla was pretending to be annoyed about the whole pretending-to-be-ill act, but Crier suspected she was secretly enjoying it. Her pained groaning was quite loud, and she was limping very dramatically.

"Which illness gives you stomach pains *and* a limp," Crier muttered, helping Ayla through the green door of the inn.

"A bad one," Ayla retorted.

The inside of the inn was warm and homey. The ground floor was a tavern. All the rooms were upstairs. A massive hearth fire crackled away happily in the corner, a spit turning slowly over it; the smell of roasted meat hung in the air. A human inn, then. It wasn't surprising—Reyka had always favored places run by humans instead of Automae. She said they were warmer.

Crier "helped" Ayla sit down at one of the low tables in the center of the room. There were only a couple of other patrons at this time of day, the sun still high in the sky, and they were both curled over mugs of ale.

The innkeeper, a plump human woman, noticed Crier at once. She approached Crier slowly, seemingly wary of a strange Automa in her tavern—especially because Crier looked like a noble. "Can I help you, ma'am?" she asked.

"Yes," said Crier. "When was the last time you saw Councilmember Reyka?"

The innkeeper frowned. "Councilmember Reyka? It must have been over a month ago, ma'am." She hesitated, and then leaned in closer. "I'll confess, I've been a bit worried myself. Usually we see the Hand every other week like clockwork. I've known her for near five years now, ma'am, and I've never known her to miss more than one visit in a row."

Every other week for five years, in a tiny village like this? "Do you happen to know the nature of the business the councilmember was conducting here?" Crier asked, trying not to sound too desperate.

"No, ma'am, I'm sorry. Tight-lipped, the Hand is." Another beat of hesitation. "But she was—kind. Always kind. If anything's happened to her . . ."

Crier ignored the innkeeper's searching look. She had no reassurances to give. Instead, she felt bitterness rising up inside her. And Crier had delayed her return home for nothing. "I see," she said, defeated. "Thank you for your help."

She was about to collect Ayla and head back outside to the carriage when a flicker of movement caught her eye. There, in the stairwell leading up to the rooms, a human girl was staring at Crier. When Crier looked at her, she beckoned.

Curious, Crier slipped off the stool and headed over to the stairs. She could feel Ayla's eyes on her back and glanced over her shoulder once, giving Ayla a short nod. *Stay there. I'll be right back.*

Wordlessly, the human girl led Crier up the stairs. She was clearly a maid of the inn, wearing a dove-gray uniform with her hair hidden under a kerchief. She was young—barely older than Crier and Ayla, with big doe eyes and hair like flax.

They reached the first landing and the girl stopped. "I overheard you asking after the Red Hand," she said in a whisper, keeping her eyes on the ground. She looked scared, hands twisting in the hem of her uniform shirt. "She was—she was always kind to me. She treated me well."

"What do you know?" Crier asked. "Have you seen her lately?"

The girl shook her head. "No. Not for weeks. But the last time she was here, she—she left something behind."

The girl hurried away, coming back a minute later, holding a small wooden box. "It was under the bed," she said, and pressed the box into Crier's hands. "I didn't open it, I swear, I would never—I just wanted to keep it safe. For Reyka." Her eyes went huge. "*Councilmember* Reyka. I'm sorry. I just—she was *kind*."

"Thank you," Crier said gently. "What is your name?"

"Laur," the girl said. She met Crier's eyes and then looked away again. "My name is Laur."

"Thank you, Laur. When I see Councilmember Reyka again,

I will tell her what you did for her. She will be just as grateful as I am."

"I hope she's all right," Laur said, biting her lip.

"She is," Crier said. "I'm sure of it. Now—do you have an empty room I could borrow?"

Minutes later, Crier was alone in an empty room of the inn. She set the wooden box on the bed and stared at it, oddly nervous. This was the only clue she had about Reyka's disappearance. The only thing that could help her find Reyka and make sure she was alive and whole. Crier took a deep breath, steadying herself, bracing for disappointment, and opened the box.

It was full of green feathers.

Crier pressed both hands over her mouth, horror washing over her like cold water.

Reyka was working with Queen Junn, and someone must have found out, someone who didn't like the queen, who considered her, and thus Reyka, an enemy to the state.

But who would feel that way about the queen?

Only one name came to mind: Kinok.

Of course, she had no proof, but then again, Kinok had multiple motives. He didn't like the queen or her beliefs. *And* he wanted a spot on the Red Council.

What had he done?

Reyka, please be alive.

Perhaps the answer was less dire. Perhaps Reyka had simply realized she'd been exposed, and was forced to go into hiding.

Maybe, even now, she was in Varn, under the queen's

protection. The thought gave Crier some relief.

Crier stared at the green feathers, so flimsy and light, yet carrying so much meaning.

If Kinok *did* do it, if he was willing to go after a member of the council, where would he draw the line? What if he found out Crier was conspiring with Queen Junn as well?

Would he make her disappear, too? Would he expose her Flaw?

Or would he go after her real weak spot, who was currently sitting in the tavern just one floor below, unaware that she was in unspeakable danger?

When she looked up and saw Ayla standing in the doorway of the room, stock-still, Crier at first questioned her own eyes. It seemed she had simply thought of Ayla, and Ayla had appeared. But it wasn't an illusion—Ayla was standing there with her wide eyes fixed on the open box. The green feathers.

Panic.

One second, they were staring at each other, ten feet between them, and the next Crier had dropped the box from her lap, allowing the feathers to scatter all over the floor, and she was across the room, twisting her fingers into the collar of Ayla's shirt, dragging Ayla inside, closing the door and slamming Ayla back against it harder than she intended—hard enough to make Ayla cry out in pain, or surprise, or anger.

"You saw nothing," Crier hissed, her voice tight and desperate in a way it had never been before. "You saw *nothing*, do you understand me?"

"Let me go!" Ayla snapped. She tried to wriggle away from Crier's hold; Crier only tightened her grip on Ayla's collar. She could feel Ayla's heartbeat against her fingers, radiating out from the pulse point in her soft neck, rabbit-quick, human-quick. "I'm not going to—"

"You must keep this a secret," Crier insisted. "You *must*."

"Crier—"

"If Kinok finds out, he will kill me," said Crier, meeting Ayla's eyes. Their faces were so close—she had the advantage of height over Ayla, and something about staring down into Ayla's face, even when it was all twisted with indignant anger, made Crier's blood sing. "He will kill me. And if I die, *so do you.*"

In era nine hundred, year fifty, justice came to Zulla like summer rain to scorched and sterile earth.

Their names were Tayol and Neo, and it was they who gained control of the Iron Heart.

It was they who captured Thomas Wren, the Maker of the First of our Kind, the Maker of Kiera. Once a brilliant alchemist, now a disgrace, a hermit, hoarding heartstone deep within the mountains, using it as leverage over the Made.

It was Tayol and Neo who murdered Wren.

With that single act, they set us free.

—FROM *ON THE WAR OF KINDS*
BY RIA OF FAMILY DARYLLIS, 0922950901, YEAR 8 AE

20

"Will you calm down?" Ayla snapped, trying to remain calm herself. It was as if her mind had slowed, gone into survival mode. "I'm not going to tell anyone. I know what those feathers mean. You're in contact with the Mad Queen."

Crier's mouth moved but no sound came out. "How do you know?" she whispered at last.

"I'll show you how. But first you'll have to *let go of me*."

Still gaping, Crier finally let go. She took a step back, her eyes never leaving Ayla's face.

"Gods," Ayla said, rubbing at her shoulder. She could already feel the bruises forming, marks in the shape of Crier's fingers.

"How do you know about the feathers?" Crier demanded.

"Because." Ayla reached into her pocket and pulled out her own green feather, the one Storme had given her. She hated thinking about Storme. It was like pressing on an old wound that had only just recently reopened. But there was no safer place to keep the feather than on her person at all times. "I didn't know she'd contacted you."

"I didn't know she'd contacted *you*," said Crier.

Ayla snorted. "Guess I don't seem like a likely candidate, do I."

"Neither did Reyka." Catching Ayla's look of surprise, Crier explained. "You're right. I am in contact with Queen Junn. But these feathers aren't mine. I wanted to stop in this village because it was the last place Councilmember Reyka was seen alive."

"The box is hers," Ayla realized, looking around at the feathers scattered everywhere.

"Yes. Apparently, she left it behind the last time she stayed here, sometime this fall. I think she did it on purpose. Perhaps she knew she was in danger, perhaps she was leaving a clue in case someone came looking for her. Either way, she was working with the queen. And I'm not sure, but I think Kinok could be connected to her disappearance."

"Why are you telling me all of this?" Ayla asked.

Crier bit her lip, a human gesture. "You already knew about the feathers. I have to trust you, don't I?"

Ayla paused. "You didn't trust me an hour ago, when we were in the carriage."

"I didn't want to *endanger* you," Crier said.

Ayla registered that it was true. She could read Crier, she realized—had been able to for some time. "That night," she said quietly. "The night your chime went off." She couldn't bring herself to say *the night we lay side by side on your bed*. It felt like it had happened in another lifetime. She felt her body heat up at the memory of it. "I asked you what you know about Kinok. What have you learned?"

"That his reach extends through all ranks of Automa society. That he is controlling his followers with a black dust. They take it instead of heartstone. They call it Nightshade, but it seems to have . . . damaging effects."

"Yes." Ah. The crates of dust—that's what it was, then. Not a weapon, exactly, but a substance. "And not just Automa society."

Crier looked at her. "What do you mean?"

"He knows all about *us*, too. My Kind. How we're connected to each other, who we care for. He even charted it—I saw it in his chambers, it was like a map of our relationships, our connections. Not just bloodlines but also friendships, romances. Any kind of love." The word *love* floated in the air between them. "And . . ." Could she really tell Crier all this?

"And what?" Crier stepped toward her and Ayla backed up, remembering the strength and power of Crier's grip on her just moments ago—it was the strength and power of an Automa. An enemy.

But an enemy who could *help*.

"I believe," Ayla said slowly, remembering what Rowan had told her and Benjy in the orchard just last week, "that he's had help spreading false information about the Resistance among us. Spreading claims of an uprising among the humans, perhaps to . . ." Her mind was spinning. "To set us up."

Crier was staring at her so powerfully she feared Crier's eyes would set her skin on fire. "Rosi told me that Kinok had armed the southern estates in advance of the first Southern Uprisings," Crier said. "Almost as if he'd—"

"Been the first to know about them. Or—"

"Been the instigator."

Ayla felt sick. "He didn't just have insider knowledge. He *was* the insider. The west was a tinderbox and he was the flint, the spark. He created a rebellion to justify slaughtering my Kind . . ."

"And make himself look like a hero in the process," Crier concluded.

Ayla felt dizzy. The room was spinning. Crier's face; her strong hands; the closed door; the box of green feathers.

"You said he spread these lies through humans, not just Automae. Do you know who helped him?"

Ayla paused, and swallowed hard. She felt sick, thinking of Faye's panicked face, the words she'd muttered, which had seemed like nonsense at first, but now . . .

It's all my fault, Faye had said.

Crier was looking at her with fascination. Ayla hesitated. To give up a name was a huge risk. And yet, it was the name of someone who had potentially betrayed Rowan, betrayed the Resistance.

"Faye," she whispered.

"That kitchen maid? How?"

Ayla's breath shook as she spoke—the story coming together as she told it, all of its pieces finally falling into place. "The crime Luna was punished for was not her own. It was Faye's. Faye even told me—it was all *her* fault. She's racked with guilt about *something*. I couldn't figure out what, but she said—'sun apples.' She was so—fixated, I had no idea why. Rambling about Kinok and his sun apples and something that had gone terribly wrong. But then I realized: it's a code word. There are stacks and stacks of crates shipping out of the palace, all labeled 'sun apples,' but they're filled with black dust. So they must be going to . . . his followers, I guess."

Crier stared at her. "Kinok is moving shipments of black dust under the guise of sun apples from the palace."

Ayla nodded. "And as for Faye . . ." She thought again of the girl's fractured mind, the terror in her eyes, something more than, worse than, simple grief. "She must have done something to get on Kinok's bad side—maybe she even tried to warn us, or escape. So he . . ." Her voice felt flimsy in her throat, but she forced out the rest: "Killed her sister. Killed Luna. And now he must be using her as a pawn. I can't imagine she's very useful— she seems half mad. But she could still deliver letters, maybe. Simple messages. She's probably too terrified to even think of disobeying him."

"Ayla," Crier said softly. In the dim light of the private room, the gold of her eyes looked almost green, like the feathers.

Ayla cleared her throat. "What I don't understand is what this black dust is, or why it's so important to Automae."

Crier sat down on the bed. "He showed me some of his experiments, a few days back. It seems he's been trying to find— to create—a replacement for heartstone. That's all part of what 'anti-reliance' means to him. He wants us to be invulnerable. As for black dust, well. I guess he's finally succeeded."

Invulnerable. Ayla knew what that meant. Invulnerable to human attack. For years, the rebellion had sought to expose the trade routes to the Iron Heart, and perhaps he feared they were getting closer, knew they wanted to destroy the Iron Heart. As always, he knew everything and was one step ahead.

If Automae didn't *need* heartstone anymore, they wouldn't need the Iron Heart. Which meant the entire focus of the rebellion would have been a waste. And there'd be no way to take down Automae anymore. No more weak spot.

"We have to find out who he's working with," Ayla said. "If we can get a list of all the people Faye sent 'sun apples' to, under your father's name, we'll have our list of Kinok's conspirators."

"Ayla, that's—that's a very good idea, actually," Crier said, standing up and grasping Ayla's hand. "Will you help me, then?"

Ayla yanked her hand away, instinctive.

Crier's mouth twisted. "Ayla."

"Let's deal with these feathers," said Ayla, not meeting her eyes. "We should clean them up before a servant comes in and—"

"*Ayla,*" Crier said again, softer this time. "I'm—I'm so sorry."

"Sorry for what?"

"For everything. For—for being so harsh with you, for pushing you against the door—I didn't realize my strength—I—"

"You're an Automa. It's your nature to overpower."

Crier looked as if she'd been slapped.

For some reason, the hurt on Crier's face enraged Ayla. How dare she express sorrow or remorse *now*? Her Kind had been treating humans horribly, had been responsible for so much death and suffering, ever since the War. And now she wanted forgiveness, she wanted Ayla to absolve her, not for the atrocities but for a shove?

There would be no forgiveness. Not here. Not today. And not ever.

Tenderly, cautiously, Crier lifted Ayla's chin so that she was forced once again to look into her eyes. A quicksilver touch, two fingers at Ayla's jaw, there and gone.

"We are equals, Ayla," she said. "We should be—we should be allies." She took an odd little breath, lips parting, a flower opening at dawn. "We should be *friends*."

Ayla was honestly speechless for a moment. "Friends?" Her voice shook. "I'm your handmaiden. Your *servant*. And even if I wasn't, I'm human. Your people kill mine for fun." She felt like an open flame, she felt like she could devour anything she touched; it had been a long time since she was this angry. It felt almost *good* to return here, like coming home. This fire *was* her home, the element she thrived in—Crier's words were the wind, awakening her, turning her into something blazing and burning.

And despite herself, despite her fury, her hatred, the heat running through her—or perhaps *because* of all those—Ayla felt her heart pounding harder than it ever had before.

"We are more alike than not," Crier said quietly, insistently. She seemed to search for something in Ayla's face, gaze flicking over Ayla's wide eyes, her brows, the half snarl of her mouth.

"We're not," Ayla choked out, wanting to silence Crier,

wanting everything to be different. Because part of her, the center of that angry flame, knew exactly what Crier was saying.

Knew what Crier was *feeling*.

This thing that had been rising between them for weeks now. In the tide pool, in Crier's bed. In the songs rough against her throat and the rose scents rising from the bath. The cold seawater and the warmth of her touch. Ayla felt it like a fishhook inside her: a sharp pain, a constant tug, and she was helpless. Something so much bigger and more powerful than herself was pulling her forward. Pulling her in.

"We *are*." And Crier's fingers touched Ayla's wrist, the movement quick but gentle, as if feeling for her pulse. Ayla didn't pull away.

Crier took Ayla's hand and placed it on her sternum. Right above her heart. She could feel the thud of it—Made, but no less real than her own. "I have a heart, like you," she breathed, and again her eyes searched Ayla's face, and Ayla heard her own heartbeat so loud in her ears, like the drums from the cave, like the night she'd led Crier out onto the black rocky beach and begged for the end of her story.

"I have a heart like you, Ayla," Crier repeated, pressing Ayla's hand harder against her chest. Ayla heard her own heartbeat and felt Crier's—a song tapping against her palm, a racing pulse beneath her fingers. Ayla was breathing too hard. She was breathing too hard.

"I feel things too," Crier whispered.

The hand that wasn't on Crier's sternum moved on its own.

Ayla watched herself reach up, watched her own fingers stutter across the sharp line of Crier's jaw, watched them pause on the soft spot just below the hinge of the jaw, where the heartbeat was closer to the surface. Ayla pressed her fingers in a little bit, into the softness, the warmth, the moth wing flutter of a pulse. Crier held completely still. Let it happen. Didn't pull away, even though she could.

Instead, Crier raised her own free hand to the same spot on Ayla's jaw.

"We're the same," she said.

"We're not," Ayla hissed. "We're not the same at all, Crier," she said, though what she meant was the opposite, and she was already surging forward—it should have been to shove Crier away, maybe even to strike her, to make her *hurt*. But it wasn't. She knew it wasn't.

She knew she'd been wanting this for a long time, even though she hated herself for it.

Crier moved at the exact same time, hands flying up to frame Ayla's face, and they were kissing. Hot and furious, gasping into each other's mouths, Crier's fingers in Ayla's hair, her teeth scraping against Ayla's bottom lip, their bodies pressed together. For a moment Crier went stiff, mouth unmoving beneath Ayla's, and through the haze Ayla realized Crier didn't know how to do this. Crier had nothing to draw from, no knowledge, no instinct. But they'd moved at the same time.

Somehow Ayla's hands found Crier's shoulders, her throat, her jaw, and she dug her fingernails into Crier's skin, still wanting to hurt, to make Crier bleed, to make her cry out—but instead Crier was shuddering against her, making another noise into Ayla's mouth, this one softer, wanting, *aching*. Ayla wanted to hear that noise again, that soft, wounded sound, muffled against her lips, a cut-off hum.

Ayla pressed a thumb to the corner of Crier's lips, coaxing her mouth open, deepening the kiss, and oh, gods—it was breath and heat, a hint of wet, the taste of Crier like a drop of honey on Ayla's tongue, and she'd never been so close to anyone before, never done anything that felt like this, her whole body awake and thrumming, pulse racing hotly beneath her skin. She wanted to get even closer. Wanted to press their bodies together until she couldn't tell them apart. Wanted—

—no—

Ayla wrenched away, scrambling toward the wall farthest from the bed. She knew she must look just as wild as Crier did, if not worse: mouth dark and swollen, hair messy, eyes huge.

The temporary madness disappeared, replaced by horror.

What have I done?

"Wait!" Crier moved forward and then froze when Ayla backed away from her, keeping a solid six paces between them. "Wait," she said, low and desperate. "Just, just wait for a moment, please. *Please*. I have to give you something."

"What could you possibly have to give me right now," said Ayla. Her mouth felt bruised, and her heart—she was breathless, terrified, like she was standing at the edge of the sea cliffs, just one step from leaping over the edge. She wanted to run. She wanted to pull Crier in again. She wanted to shatter like glass, to disappear, to not *feel like this*.

Then Crier reached into the pocket of her dress and pulled out something that glinted in the torchlight, something that seemed to glow from within—

Ayla's necklace?

"No," said Ayla, shaking her head. She felt dizzy, stomach roiling. "No, that doesn't make sense, how could you—?" She'd seen it on Kinok's desk. Had Crier somehow stolen it from Kinok? Had he given it to her? Why would he give it to her?

"It's yours," said Crier, holding it out. The necklace dangled from her hand, delicate and golden. "It's yours. I know it is. You're not"—her expression cracked, something like guilt bleeding through—"you're not in trouble, I promise, I just want to return it."

But Ayla took another step back. Her bitten mouth, her shaking hands, the taste of Crier on her tongue. She wanted to scrub everything about this moment off her skin, scrub off the skin itself. *What have I done.*

"Get that away from me." *It's a weakness.* Like this. Like her. "It's just a stupid trinket. I don't want it anymore."

Crier was frowning, still holding out the necklace. "A trinket? Do you even know what it can do?"

"What are you talking about? Did you make another deal with Kinok—one to get that back for me?"

Crier stared at her, the desperate look giving way to confusion. "Kinok never had this in his possession."

Now it was Ayla's turn to feel awash and drowning in confusion. If he'd never had her locket, then what locket had she seen in his study, when he'd been questioning her?

It dawned on her.

The other locket. The twin to her own. She'd always thought it was lost forever. Maybe not.

Crier's eyes darted around the room. It wasn't like there was much to see; a bed, a chest of drawers, a small bedside table with a dull brass candleholder, a pen, a pot of ink. Things a traveler might request. Ayla opened her mouth, about to demand a real explanation, but Crier was hurrying over to the bedside table. Grabbing the pen. She studied it, considering, and then pressed the sharp nib into the pad of her thumb, piercing the skin. Dark blood welled up and Ayla sucked in a breath, but Crier's face didn't even change. She held out the pen to Ayla. "Go on."

"You want me to . . . what, stab myself?"

"Just your fingertip, just enough to draw even a drop of blood," said Crier. "Please, please just do it, and you'll see."

If it had been an order, Ayla would have turned on her heel and left the room, fled the inn altogether. But now she was so curious, so confused, so—

Please.

Swearing under her breath, already regretting this, Ayla stepped forward and pricked the tip of her index finger on the pen. The tiny wound throbbed.

"All right," Crier said shakily. "Now."

She held up the necklace between them, the locket glinting

in the low torchlight. For a moment, Ayla could have sworn the light seemed to pulse along with the wound on her finger; it looked as if the locket was glowing, producing light instead of reflecting it. Crier held her bleeding thumb right over the locket, indicating what to do.

Together, they touched the locket.

Their blood—red and violet, human and not—smeared.

And the world lurched and spun.

Ayla breathed out and tasted dust; she breathed in and tasted sunlight, summer air, something lush and green. She realized her eyes were closed, and she opened them.

She was in a forest, and she wasn't alone. Crier was there with her. It was barely past noon, even though the sun had been setting outside the tavern windows moments earlier. Butter-colored sunlight streamed down through the foliage, creating a dappled pattern of shadow and gold across Crier's face.

"Is this real?" Ayla breathed.

"Yes, I think so. Or . . . it was. It's memory now, it's—"

"Leo?"

Ayla and Crier whipped around in unison, searching for the source of the voice. A moment later they found it: a rustle in the undergrowth, and then a young woman stepped out of the trees and into the clearing. She was barefoot and beautiful, her skin the same brown as Ayla's, her black hair loose and tangled around her shoulders. Her dress was strange. Old-fashioned, like the clothes in old paintings.

"Leo?" the woman called out softly. "Leo, are you here yet?"

There was a pause in which the only sounds came from the chattering birds above their heads, the woman catching her breath. The forest seemed to swallow all other sound. The woman didn't even glance at Ayla and Crier, even though the three of them were less than ten paces apart. She . . . couldn't see them?

There was a scuffling noise, a muffled curse, and then a man stumbled out from behind a tree. He was as young and beautiful as the woman, broad-shouldered and brown-skinned and tawny-haired. The moment he reached the woman, he tugged her into his body, arms curling around her. She snorted and half shoved at him and then melted, nudging her face into his chest. Ayla felt suddenly uncomfortable. She didn't know these people, she had not chosen to come here, and yet she still felt like she was witnessing something she shouldn't. Something too intimate, too personal.

"What did you need to tell me?" he asked. "What was so secret that we had to meet out here?" When she didn't answer immediately, his tone grew worried. "Did something—?"

"No," said the woman. "Well—yes, something happened, but it's not bad. It's not bad at all. I—I found the blueprints, Leo. I found my mother's blueprints."

She was grinning.

He was not.

"Si . . . ," he said slowly. "You promised. You promised you wouldn't—go too far."

"Too far?" she said, almost laughing. "Gods, Leo, don't you see? There's no such thing as too far. This is my calling. If the gods have given me anything, this is it. I want to continue where my mother left off. I have to."

"Si—"

She pulled away from his embrace, all traces of laughter gone. "You don't understand," she said. "I was born to do this, Leo."

"Born to defy the laws?"

"No, my love," she said. "I was born to Make this. I was born to Make—her."

Leo opened his mouth to protest, but just then Si whirled around, startled, as if she'd heard a sudden noise. And Ayla's mouth dropped open. Because she could finally see the details of Si's face . . . and those were her own eyes staring at her, identical in shape and color. Now that she was looking, really looking—Si's nose was similar to her own as well, and she had the same round face, the same wide, full mouth—stars and skies, this Si even had the same dusting of freckles *across her nose and cheeks, faint but visible.*

Si. Siena. Siena Ayla, Ayla's namesake. Her grandmother.

"Wait," said Ayla, but not quick enough.

Crier tugged at the locket in their bloodied hands, and the forest clearing fell away as if it had never been there at all.

It was late now—the sounds from the tavern below had grown louder, and Ayla shuddered at the thought of all those travelers down the stairs, at the thought that anyone could have walked into this room and discovered them.

Ayla felt a million questions crowding her tongue, *who were they what was that how how how how how*, but her head was spinning and *skies*, the smell of the ale from the tavern brought back the all-too-recent memories of what she and Crier had done just minutes before, the recollection of heat against Ayla's body and hands in her hair and Crier's breath against her lips, and it was finally too much.

"Ayla," Crier started. She was clutching the bloody locket in both hands, eyes fixed on Ayla's face. Her voice was as low and soft as if she'd spoken to a spooked horse. Could she read the panic on Ayla's face?

"Don't," Ayla said. "Just—*don't.*"

Then she opened the door and ran.

But she didn't make it far. "Have you seen the lady?" the innkeeper asked as Ayla stumbled down the stairs.

"Yes, she's upstairs, ah, readying herself to leave." Ayla fumbled for words that made sense. *She's cleaning up feathers. She's holding my locket. She kissed me—and I kissed her back.*

But the innkeeper just stood there, wringing her hands as she blocked Ayla's way. "Unfortunately, I must ask that you remain here for the time being. I'm afraid it isn't safe to leave."

"Why?" Crier had appeared behind her—had followed Ayla down the stairs. Ayla stiffened, involuntarily, unable to meet Crier's eyes, knowing if she did, all of her feelings would be written plainly for Crier to see.

The innkeeper faltered. "I'm—I'm not sure, ma'am, but there's some sort of—riot on the roads outside the village. I—I don't know how it began, but—"

"Humans or Automae?" Crier demanded.

"Pardon?"

"Who's rioting," she repeated. "Your Kind? Or mine?"

"Mine, my lady," she said. "Seems a fight broke out in the marketplace between one of mine and one of—one of the sovereign's guards, and somehow it escalated, and now the mob's headed this way. There's a guard post nearby. That's the target. We've—they've tried to burn it down before." She looked terrified by her own slipup, but Crier didn't even seem to notice. For that, Ayla was grateful. "It's not safe to leave Elderell, my lady. At least not until extra guards come."

"How long will that take?"

"I don't know." She gestured at the window. "See for yourself, my lady. It's near impossible to move through the single road. I suggest you both stay the night and return tomorrow instead."

Stay the night. No, Ayla could not spend another night here, alone with Crier. Even the crowdedness of the servants' building back at the palace would be more tolerable. At least there she'd be able to wrestle with her feelings away from Crier's gaze.

Crier looked out the window, and Ayla joined her. At first, she didn't see anything. But then, when she scanned the rooftops of the village, she saw it: smoke, past the village's outer gates, rising up into the sky, a black plume.

"*Staying* is not an option," Crier said to the innkeeper. Ayla noticed she wasn't making eye contact either. "We must leave now, we can't wait this out. We have to deliver a—a time-sensitive message."

The innkeeper looked despairing. "I must advise you to wait."

Ayla finally looked at Crier—for an instant, and then she looked away again, jaw working. "We can't wait. We have to go."

"Tell my driver to ready the carriage," Crier told the innkeeper.

". . . Yes, my lady. If—if that is what you wish."

Within minutes, the carriage appeared, and Crier and Ayla boarded in a hurry. Around them, the sky was darkening—not with evening. With smoke.

The second Crier closed the door behind them, the driver

cracked the whip and they were off, bumping along the cobble-
stoned street. Ayla pressed herself up against the far wall, as far
from Crier as she could possibly get without actually just throwing herself out the window. Mercifully, Crier made no comment.

They drove along, windows rattling with the uneven street,
and at first it looked like everything would be fine. Like they'd
be able to leave Elderell unhindered by whatever riot had broken out.

Until Ayla realized something was wrong. She heard the
driver curse aloud and urge the horses forward, heard a shout
that didn't belong to him, and then another shout, and then
another. She tensed, pushing the velvet curtain aside to peek out
at the street. At first, she didn't see anything out of the ordinary.

Something struck the window hard enough to crack the
glass, barely an inch from Ayla's nose. She gasped, rearing back.
Someone had thrown a rock at the carriage window.

"Gods," Ayla said, her voice low. She scooted toward the
middle of the carriage, the desire to stay away from Crier giving
way to the desire to remain alive.

"I can hear it," Crier said. "Them." Two shouts had become a
dozen; a dozen had become too many too count, a wall of angry
voices. "There's a crowd. A mob. Close, and getting closer."

Ayla swore. "How far are we from the village gates?"

"Not far, but I don't know if we'll be able to—"

Another rock hit the window with a *crack*, new spider webs
appearing in the glass. The noise of the mob was growing closer
still. Ayla risked a glance out the cracked window and saw, to her

horror, a wave of people in the street, another billow of smoke, this time rising from a rooftop only one street away.

"My lady!" she heard the driver scream.

Then the mob fell upon the carriage like waves crashing against rock. Another rock hit the side of the carriage, another earsplitting crack—then Ayla heard the sounds of a dozen hands hitting the sides of the carriage. They were being rocked back and forth, humans shoving at the carriage on both sides.

She braced herself against the shaking wall. "Gods, they're not going to stop until they rip this thing apart—"

An absurd image flashed into Ayla's head: the carriage cracked open like a giant black crab shell, her and Crier pulled like soft meat from the wreckage.

"There are more," Crier said—she had to yell to make herself heard over the shouting and the horrible creaking of the carriage. "They won't let up."

"We either wait to see what they'll do to us once they get inside . . . or we try to escape," Ayla said, poising to break out. It was their only option. But—

The carriage shuddered hard enough to throw them both sideways, Crier's head nearly cracking against the window. Ayla gasped.

She dived forward to see if Crier was all right—of course she was all right, her Kind could handle far worse than this—when she spotted something out the window.

A flash of silver.

A face.

"*Rowan.*" The name slipped from her tongue in her shock, before she could stop it. She threw back the velvet curtains even as Crier shrank into the seat, staring in horror at the furious humans surrounding the carriage, a sea of hands and faces, teeth and wild eyes. Behind them, oily black smoke rose up from the rooftop of a nearby building. The humans stared into the carriage—stared at Crier—with white-hot hatred, screaming things Ayla couldn't make out, slapping at the carriage windows, shoving themselves bodily against the wheels and sides.

"Rowan!" Ayla cried out again. Because there she was: a woman standing stock-still at the center of the mob, staring at the carriage. Her silver hair stood out like a beacon against the writhing crowd, her mouth forming a silent word: *Ayla.*

Ayla pressed both hands to the window, nothing but a thin pane of glass separating her from the mob. She didn't care. "Rowan!"

Crier crawled across the seats and grabbed the collar of Ayla's shirt, trying to drag her away from the window, but Ayla squirmed out of her grip. "Let go of me!" she snarled. "Let go, that's my friend out there—"

The sound of a horn cut through the shouting. The innkeeper's guards must have arrived. Ayla couldn't see them yet, but she saw the moment the crowd realized what was happening: she saw some of them scream with new anger or fear, she saw a few peel away from the edges of the mob and make a break for it.

Another one pulled out a wooden club.

"Ayla," Crier said urgently, tugging at Ayla's arm. "You have to get away from the window."

"No! We have to get Rowan out of there!" Ayla struggled, almost panicking. "She can't get captured, she's important, we need her, we can't do any of it without her! *Rowan!*"

"Ayla, I'll have the guards take her to a safe place, just *get away from the window.*"

Ayla swiveled to Crier, panting. "You'll protect her? You'll make sure she's okay?"

"Yes," said Crier. She looked out over Ayla's shoulder. Rowan was waving her arms and shouting to the other rebels, gesturing at something. Trying to calm them? Or rile them up further? "I promise you," Crier said. "Just get *down*, get your face away from the glass!"

Another rock hit the glass, this time breaking through; Ayla got a faceful of shattered glass. She felt the impact first and then pain, white-hot and searing, radiating through her entire face. Her lip and forehead were bleeding; blood dripped down her chin; she could taste it.

Crier was pulling her down to the floor, while outside the carriage, there was a flash of black. The guards had arrived. Hazily, she could see a line of them closing in around the mob, swords drawn. Automae. Their faces were different, but all wore the same expression: blank as new parchment, cold as ice.

It all seemed to happen in slow motion, even as Ayla scrabbled against Crier, pushing her way back to the now-broken window, because she needed to break free, needed to reach Rowan—

First, the guards were at the edges of the mob, making it impossible for any of the humans to escape. Then, there was a burst of movement near the center, and the man who'd drawn the wooden club reappeared again, brandishing it above his head.

Rowan wrapped her arms around him. She was trying to make him lower the weapon. But it was too late. The guards had seen a threat.

Ayla couldn't hear the noise the sword made when it pierced Rowan's back. But she saw it happen, and so her mind produced a terrible, gut-wrenching noise. The noise of a blade pushed through flesh and organ and spine.

The guard pulled his sword out of Rowan's back. Slowly, so slowly, inch by inch, the metal dark with blood. Around them, the other humans were beginning to realize what had just happened; new screams, of fear and anger, tore the air. Red human blood spattered the man with the club. It dripped from the hilt of the sword. It bloomed, a growing patch, across the center of Rowan's spine. Her dress was forest green. The red looked black.

Rowan swayed and fell.

Only then did Ayla scream.

Ayla barely remembered returning to the palace, the imagined sound of metal on bone still echoing in her head. She hadn't even looked at Crier for the rest of the carriage ride back, let alone spoken, and though they'd driven through the night, through sunrise and half the morning, neither of them had slept at all.

Ayla had just sat there, hollowed, sucking on her broken lip. Blood on her tongue.

When they pulled to a stop at the stables, she practically threw herself out of the carriage, eyes stinging with unshed tears. She wouldn't cry. Rowan wouldn't want her to cry. Rowan would want her to act.

You did well, my girl.

It was time for Ayla to finish what she'd started.

Benjy. Have to find Benjy.

He didn't know. It seemed impossible that he didn't know. That he wouldn't have simply felt it, felt the universe change so terribly and abruptly, felt a phantom sword push through his spine.

A field worker. A girl, hair cropped short, familiar face. Ayla caught her by the sleeve outside the servants' quarters, maybe said something, maybe just said Benjy's name. Either way, the girl pointed wordlessly toward the orchards.

Ayla found Benjy under a sun apple tree, harvesting the shiny red fruits, his hands streaked with dirt.

And he caught the look, the blood, on her face immediately. "What's wrong?" he demanded, looking around wildly as if afraid Ayla was being chased down. "What happened?"

She couldn't get the words out for a moment. Didn't want to. It was childish—like if she didn't say it aloud, it wouldn't be true; it wouldn't be real.

But that wasn't how the world worked.

"Rowan," she managed, and then all the horror and grief

returned in a rush, and the world snapped back into place, the haze disappearing, the shock making itself known again. She tried to fumble through it. Tried to explain. The mob, the crush of people, the chaos, the guards, the blood.

"What are you saying?" He strode forward, put his hands on her shoulders, and only then did Ayla realize she was shaking. Benjy's eyes were huge. He looked almost like the boy she'd first met four years ago, all eyes and cheekbones and freckles.

You're stronger than him, Ayla, Rowan had said once. *You have to protect him.*

She swallowed hard. "Rowan is dead. She was killed by guards in the village of Elderell. By one of *them*."

Benjy just stared at her. "No."

"I'm so sorry." And that was when the tear finally came—harsh and stinging and gutting. She dropped to a crouch and he was down there with her, arms around her, whispering *no*, his voice in anguish.

She knew what his pain must be right now. It was the same as her own.

They'd lost a mother. A mentor. The arrow that always pointed north. They had nothing without Rowan—would *be* nothing now if it hadn't been for her.

The leeches had killed her, just like they'd killed everything that ever mattered to Ayla. Just like they'd killed Ayla's parents. Just like they'd killed Luna, Nessa, thousands of others. Rowan, who had taken care of her, had taken her in, had given her a life and a purpose. Rowan, who had scolded her countless times, but always out of the desire to make her stronger, to keep her alive.

"Did you—did you actually look at her body? Are you sure she wasn't just injured?" Benjy's jaw was clenched tight, he was shaking Ayla, angry with her now. "She's tough. You know she's tough. She could still be alive."

"Benjy," Ayla whimpered. "I saw her fall . . ."

He was clutching her shoulders so tightly it was sure to bruise.

"I want to mourn her properly," Ayla said. "And we will. But not right now."

She began to wipe her face. To suck in the snot and smudge away the blood and blink back the tears.

"What are you talking about? What do you mean, we can't mourn her right now? When the hell else—?"

"I've got a lot to tell you," she murmured. "Time is running out."

She told him: about the black dust, spreading across Zulla like the poison it was. The moment it became as common as heartstone, it would be too late to launch an attack on the Iron Heart. There would be no point, if Automae depended on black dust instead of heartstone. The Resistance had to act *now*.

"We have to break into Kinok's study and steal the compass, like we discussed. Like Rowan wanted. Tomorrow. No more stalling."

"That doesn't give us much time to make a plan, Ayla."

She nudged their shoulders together. "That's what we're doing right now."

Benjy huffed, and she could see he, too, was pushing tears away, trying to be brave, to do what was right. "While you were gone, I thought about how to get our hands on the safe. If someone can create a distraction on one of the upper levels of the palace, it would be possible to break into the study and at least steal the entire safe—we can always crack it open afterward."

"A distraction," Ayla repeated.

"Yeah. Only problem is—what kind of distraction?" He sniffed, rubbed his nose. "I was thinking maybe a fire or something . . . we just need to distract the guards for a few minutes, just for long enough to get into the study. . . . Something that would guarantee they'd all come running."

They fell silent, both thinking.

"I know what we have to do," Ayla heard herself say. "Her chime." It felt like it wasn't *her* speaking, like it was someone else, someone stronger. The girl who wanted revenge. The girl who would do anything for it. The girl Rowan had found on the streets of Kalla-den, starving and frozen. The girl who had lost everything. "If we set off Crier's chime, every guard in the palace will come running straight for her. If it's at night, she'll be in her bedchamber in the north wing. Far away from Kinok's study."

"That—that could work," Benjy said, voice still thick with tears.

"And I have to do it." The realization landed like a stone in her belly, a hollow thud. "I'm her handmaiden. I can—I can visit her bedchamber, even in the middle of the night, and no one will stop me." She turned to look at Benjy. "It has to be me."

His mouth twisted. "Ayla . . ."

"Benjy. Do you remember what I've been working toward? What I've wanted for so long?"

They stared at each other. Ayla knew they were both thinking the same thing.

"You're not just going to set off Crier's chime," Benjy said slowly. "You're going to kill her. Ayla, are you *insane*? The guards will capture you, or kill you on sight."

"No," she said.

She looked to the east.

Out there, past the orchards and the palace and the gardens, the Steorran Sea was crashing, as it always had and always would, against the rocks. Ayla pictured it: seething black water, pale-green froth. The cliffs. The spot where Crier had fallen. Where Ayla had moved without thinking, lunged forward, grabbed Crier's wrist. Saved her life. Set this whole thing in motion. "I'm finally in my right mind," she said carefully, the words feeling once again as if they were coming from outside her, from the Ayla of the past.

"I've been—I've grown soft, I've grown *weak*, I lost sight of the only thing I've wanted this entire time, the only thing I've *ever wanted*. I want to kill them all, Benjy, but the daughter of the sovereign most of all. Hesod must pay for what he's done. This is my chance, don't you get that? I won't miss it. I *can't*."

Something dark flitted across his face. "Are you sure you'll be able to do it?"

"What the hell is that supposed to mean?"

"You said it yourself," he muttered, looking out over the ocean. "You've spent so long at her side. You've grown soft—for her."

For a minute, she was silent. No matter what, she couldn't say it wasn't true.

Finally, she swallowed, hard. "The only thing I've ever wanted is revenge. I've never once forgotten that."

"I know you haven't," he said. "But things have changed, haven't they? I've seen the way she keeps you close. The way she looks at you."

Ayla felt the blood drain from her face. She wanted to cry again, to be sick, or . . . "You don't know what you're talking about." It was weak, too, this attempt to deny it.

"But I do," he said, and there was something lurking in his voice now, something more than bitterness or even jealousy, something young and pained and almost scared. "I do, Ayla, *gods*, how do you not—" He broke off, letting out a shaky breath.

"Benjy—"

"I know what it's like," he said over her. "Loving someone who's . . . who's impossible to have. I know what that's like more than anything."

Ayla was stunned speechless.

"But you just do what you think is right, Ayla. It was never really a choice, was it? Wanting her. Killing her."

Ayla pushed herself to her feet, unable to handle this conversation any longer. Right before she left Benjy alone in the orchard, she looked down at him. Forced her voice into something cold and hard. "If a spider weaves her web to catch flies and catches a butterfly instead, what does the spider do?"

Benjy stayed silent.

"She eats the butterfly," said Ayla.

21

The necklace felt heavier than usual in Crier's hands that night. As if every time she fell into it, she left a part of herself behind. A part of herself—and a part of Ayla, now. The forest clearing was green and vibrant in Crier's mind, imprinted on the insides of her eyelids: the sunlight, the rustling branches, the laughing girl, the laughing boy who swept her up and held her tight. The easy intimacy between them, the way love glowed in their eyes and in their smiles. What a pure, crystalline memory. Once secret, now shared.

It had been a long day.

Crier had spent the morning sifting through endless shipment records. Her father had returned a day early from his portion of the "mourning tour," full of righteous anger over the growth of the rebellion in the rural lands, and Kinok had expressed only polite relief in the fact that she had survived an attack on her carriage. She didn't tell them the rest: that she had watched a rebel murdered right before her eyes.

Had watched the way that single act had turned Ayla back into a hardened shell, cold and armored with hate. Crier couldn't get that image out of her mind, the pure hatred on Ayla's face, the stiff set of her body, a defense mechanism, *stay away*—she couldn't stop thinking of it, even as it tore at the memories of their kiss.

So she occupied herself with the list of shipments.

There were a lot of Red Hands on that list.

Betrayal tasted like metal on her tongue. In a surge of anger (how *dare* they call themselves Red Hands, how *dare* they claim to serve the council, the nation of Zulla, and *all the while*—) Crier had included one last piece of information in her newest letter to Junn.

Friend—

Fear blossoms like a fed garden. I have reason to believe—*I suspect strongly*—*that Wolf is responsible for the disappearance of a Red Hen. The Wolf's reach is wide and its greed is strong.*

I have a way to track down those who support the Wolf, however. The pack that protects him and works with him. The Wolf's paws leave traces of darkness behind. Traces we can follow.

Make no mistake: Wolf is a predator, a threat to all of

Zulla. Please, help me stop him—before spring comes. A gathering in late winter is the perfect time to pluck snow blossoms—to be rid of the weeds.

—Fox

In Rabu, it was tradition to fill the hall with white flowers to celebrate the marriage of two Automae. And every single Red Hand would attend her wedding. Every single Red Hand—the ones still alive, anyway—would be there. All of them gathered in one place.

Queen Junn would read between the lines.

A big part of her was terrified about what Junn might do—but an even bigger part was ruled by her own anger, her sour-bile disappointment in the leaders she had admired for so long.

It felt huge and terrible, sending the letter off with the courier, knowing it was too late to change her own words, to scratch them out. Too late to take any of it back. Crier tried not to think about the Red Hands who had already died at Queen Junn's quick and merciless hand. She had no illusions about the queen's methods, and none of them were gentle or kind.

Would Crier's wedding be a bloodbath?

Could her world really change in a single day?

Yes, something inside her whispered. *No matter what: yes.*

And it was the only way, she told herself firmly. There was no way she could actually marry Kinok. Especially not now—not after the kiss. Not after she knew the truth about herself.

That she was capable of the most human feeling of all.

That she loved Ayla.

The thought was like a bell resonating inside her, echoing and echoing and echoing. She didn't know how it was possible—it had to be the result of her Flaw. But it was true.

Besides, if she married Kinok, even if he wasn't the killer she suspected him to be, he would always have absolute control over her. She would never, ever be free. She'd become another part of his plans. *We won't need humans at all.*

The only way to survive was to put a stop to Kinok's plans before they advanced any further—to swipe her arm across the chessboard and knock all the pieces to the floor.

There would be deaths. Automa deaths.

But Crier would live. Her father would live.

And maybe, *someday*, if she proved herself worthy, if she stopped Kinok—if she made things better for Ayla's Kind, for every human in Zulla . . . maybe she could have what Queen Junn had with that human man.

Maybe she could be with—

She turned the necklace over in her hands, examining the deep-red stone for the thousandth time. Moonlight slid across the wall of her bedchamber, catching on the gold threads in the tapestry of Kiera. It was far past the middle of the night. She hadn't slept properly in—five days, maybe more. She should sleep.

Or.

Without letting herself think too closely about what she was about to do, Crier reached up and pulled one of the pins from her hair. It was a pretty thing, a little white flower made from pearls with two jade leaves. More importantly, the end was sharp. It was easy, easier each time, to deliberately prick her finger hard enough to draw blood.

She pressed her bloody finger to the red stone at the heart of the pendant, and once again the world smeared like paint around her, colors dripping down the walls.

When she opened her eyes, she was still in her bedchamber.

Crier frowned and sat up, confused—and realized immediately that while she was sitting in a bed in the dark, this wasn't her bed. It wasn't her bedchamber, either, but one much smaller. The walls were rough mud brick, not stone, and there were no bookshelves, no tapestries, nothing but a hearth, a small table, a wooden chest in one corner.

As always, Crier wasn't alone. There were two women sitting on the stone lip of the hearth. Crier recognized one of them as Si—Siena, the laughing girl from the woods. She looked maybe a few years older, a few years more mature, her dark hair tied back in a braid instead of loose and wild around her face. There was a heaviness to her shoulders that had not existed in the forest.

The other woman with her was not human.

But not Automa, either.

Crier stared at her, fascinated. Not Automa, no, but close. An early prototype? The girl sitting with Siena was beautiful in a way that seemed almost grotesque. Her features were too symmetrical, and all of them were slightly too exaggerated: eyes a little too big, nose a little too thin, lips a little too red. She looked, oddly, like a very beautiful bird. Her skin was tan, her hair the color of dark honey and falling in curls to the small of her back. Her cheeks were artificially pink. Crier moved closer, aware that neither girl would be able to see or hear her. She crept across the floor to stand behind Siena so she could see the not-Automa girl's face even better.

The firelight was kind to her inhuman features, adding warmth and softness to the sharp lines of her cheekbones and jaw. Her eyes were bright gold. Even in shadow, even in the flickering half-light of the fire, they were bright gold. And yet they looked so dull—like the blank eyes of a porcelain doll. Or a dead animal. The longer Crier looked at the girl, the more she realized the biggest difference between herself and this creation: Crier had a mind, a heart, her own thoughts. This girl did not. She was a beautiful vessel, but an empty one.

It didn't seem to stop Siena from caring for her, though. Siena was pulling a comb through the girl's long hair, brushing it out with gentle movements. There was nothing but fondness on Siena's face, a peaceful, proud sort of love.

Crier was so caught up with watching them that it

took her a moment to realize that there was someone else in the room.

Leo.

He was sitting in the corner, far from the warmth and light of the fire. He had a pair of leather boots and a tin of boot polish in his lap, but it looked like he hadn't moved for a long time. He was sitting stock-still. Like Crier, he was also watching Siena and the Made girl. He didn't seem so fascinated, though. He looked . . . pained. Almost jealous. Of what?

As Crier watched Leo, she was struck by a wave of—emotion. It was like the very first memory she'd fallen into, the burning city, when she'd felt Leo's blinding terror like it was her own. It wasn't terror this time, but something quieter. Subtler. A pang of longing, deepening when Siena set the comb down and ran her fingers through the Made girl's hair, separating it into sections for a braid.

"Aren't you tired, love?" Leo said suddenly, startling Siena, who twitched and nearly dropped a handful of hair. "Don't you want to come to bed? Or—Clara's asleep, but you could wake her. She'd love one of your stories."

Siena didn't even look at him. Just kept braiding. "She's too old for my stories."

"She's barely seven years," Leo said. "She's a child yet."

"Stories," said a new voice. A strange, whispering,

metallic voice, a voice like clock gears whirring together.
The Made girl looked over her shoulder at Siena, doe eyes
wide and unblinking. "I like your stories."

"I know you do, Yora," Siena cooed. "You'll never be
too old for them, will you?"

"Never," said the girl.

Crier felt everything Leo was feeling in that moment.
It was a terrible mix of revulsion, guilt, jealousy of the
Made girl, and below it all, like an underground river: his
love for Siena, his wife. Untouchable, unchanging. Even
with all the bad things layered above it.

"Maybe I shall tell you one tonight," said Siena.
"Which would you like to hear, Yora?"

"'The King and the Black Horse,'" Yora said in her
metallic voice.

Crier felt a throb of despair, an echo of Leo's sadness
for—for the little girl in the next room, the seven-year-
old girl—Clara; Leo was thinking of her, Clara, his
daughter—their daughter, their real daughter—

A falling sensation, another smear of color and firelight and
dark, and Crier was back in her own bedchamber. Her own bed.
She was alone. Her own hearth fire was cold and dead, long
burned out. And she could still feel Leo's pain like a dagger in
her chest. His anguish over Siena's wavering love, the bone-deep
fear that she loved the Made girl, Yora, more than she loved

him—or even their daughter.

Yora.

Yora. The name caught in Crier's mind, a briar. She'd heard it before. More accurately, had read it before. Crier could conjure it up perfectly, her own crystal-clear memory of those two words in Kinok's handwriting:

Yora's heart.

She understood something then, something terrible.

Ayla's family history was in this locket . . .

And it contained the secret Kinok wanted.

She had to tell Ayla, had to warn her. Tonight.

No, it was too late. She couldn't risk it. Not now—not after everything . . . she *wanted* to go to her right away, but she knew Ayla was grieving, knew she was furious over their kiss, even if Crier swore that she'd reciprocated, maybe even started it—that she had wanted it just as much as Crier had.

No, she wouldn't try to find and wake her now. She'd sleep—it had been far too long since Crier had slept, and her body needed a rest.

Tomorrow.

Tomorrow morning Ayla would come to her, and Crier would tell her everything.

Crier would find a safe place for Ayla to go—away from here.

But first, she would tell her a thousand other things. That she was sorry. That she loved her. That she would prove it, some way, some day, if only Ayla would let her. That she would help keep her safe, and that when the time was right, she'd find her again.

Tomorrow.

She'd tell her everything tomorrow.

They came at night. They moved silently in the darkness. We didn't know they were coming until they were already at our doors. They all looked the same. Tall and strong. They all moved the same, too, like monsters in the old stories. Like shadows. Demons from the dead realm.

They had no torches. But when I looked out over the demon army I saw light. At first I couldn't tell what it was. A thousand tiny specks of light. It looked almost like fireflies.

Then I realized. It was their eyes.

—FROM THE PERSONAL RECORDS OF AN UNNAMED
HUMAN GIRL DURING THE WAR OF KINDS, E. 900,
CIRCA Y. 51

22

Ayla had spent the day shivering. Not cold shivering, but fear shivering. Adrenaline shivering, raw-nerve shivering, like something was alive and wriggling around inside her bones, making her teeth chatter and the hairs on her arms stand up straight. She nearly dropped a teacup of liquid heartstone, a book, Crier's bone-handled comb. When she handed over the cup of heartstone, it rattled against the saucer, and Crier frowned a little but miraculously didn't comment.

She also hadn't commented on the fact that Ayla had been late that morning. If she had, Ayla would have said: *I stopped to help a laundry maid pick up a spilled basket of clothes*. It was only mostly a lie. Because she had *seen* a laundry maid trip and spill a basket of dirty clothes all over the flagstones in the western hallway, but she hadn't stopped to help. She'd been on her way back from the music room. That was step one.

But Crier didn't ask. In fact, she didn't say anything at all for almost an hour. Her jaw kept working, her long fingers kept tugging at the small, curling tendrils of hair that always escaped her plait. It seemed like she was preparing for something.

Ayla didn't want to know what it was.

So when Crier finally said, "Ayla," in a raw, gutted voice as Ayla poured her a second cup of heartstone, Ayla had looked her dead in the eye, steam rising between them, and said:

"Don't."

"But," Crier had started, "Ayla, it's important, you're in—"

"Danger?" Ayla cocked her head. "As opposed to the rest of the time, when I'm perfectly safe?" She didn't let Crier respond. "Unless there is a battalion of your father's guards outside the door at this very moment, ready to drag me away, I don't want to know. It doesn't matter."

Crier's mouth opened, closed, opened again. "I," she said. "I, but, but that wasn't—that wasn't everything, I wanted to—"

"I. Don't. Want. To. Hear. It," said Ayla. A few weeks ago, it might have been a nasty thrill, talking to Lady Crier like this. Today, she felt nothing. Nothing at all. "Whatever you're going to say, I swear to you I don't want to hear it."

And Crier had taken a funny little breath and fallen silent, and neither of them spoke again.

Anyway. The music room was step one.

This, here, was step two.

The gardens at night were a completely different animal. During the day, they were pretty much just like the rest of Hesod's land, all neat and methodical and utterly soulless, nature removed from anything even remotely resembling wildness. But when the sun began to sink, slipping down the winter sky like a drop of water on a windowpane, it was like the shadows touched things and made them chaotic. Like that story, that old old story about the king whose touch turned things and people into gold. That kind of weird alchemy—things transforming into other things, things warping and twisting and tangling up, carefully trimmed roses becoming wild thorn bushes when the shadows slid over their green spines. Sun apple trees became gnarled; fruit glowed like gems or rotted right off the branch; seaflower bushes grew legs and crept to different rows, until Ayla, who had spent a third of her life in this damn garden, found herself getting just a little bit lost.

But she wasn't late.

She spotted Benjy under the apple tree with the knot that looked like an eye, just like they'd planned. She scurried through the roses, trying not to think of anything at all, and watched Benjy perk up when she drew near. The air smelled like roses and too-ripe fruit. Underneath it, the bite of salt and sea spray.

Benjy looked furious in the new moon dark. He looked cold and cruel and like he'd been carved out of bronze. All his edges sharp and deadly.

Footsteps silent on the soft dirt, Ayla joined Benjy under the branches of the sun apple tree.

"Hey," said Benjy, more breath than voice.

"Where are the others?"

"There," he said, gesturing into the orchard. Ayla saw a

handful of figures melting out of the darkness between the rows of sun apple trees. Within moments they joined them under the tree. There was Yoon from the kitchens, Tem and Idric from the stables, a couple other faces that Ayla had seen around the palace but couldn't name. Seven in all, and all of them looking at Benjy, waiting for him to speak. Ayla wasn't sure when he'd become their leader, but she found herself grateful for it. She didn't want anyone to look at her. She was afraid of what they would see on her face.

"What time is it?" Yoon asked, breaking the silence. "When should we—?"

Benjy glanced at his wrist, and Ayla caught a glimpse of his grandfather's watch. "Five minutes till the first distraction. Then we take the palace." He looked around their small circle, meeting everyone's eyes. When he reached Ayla, he lingered on her face. "Then we've got fifteen minutes," he said, and paused.

Ayla realized a beat too late that he was waiting for her to jump in. "Yes," she said, trying not to cringe when seven pairs of eyes bored into her. "From the moment we enter through the music room, we probably have about fifteen minutes. Benjy will lead you to Kinok's study in the cellar to steal the safe with the compass in it. Meanwhile, I'll—I'll take care of Crier."

"That's distraction two," said Benjy. "That'll keep the guards away from Kinok's study. We get in, we get the safe, we head back to the music room. We wait for everyone until midnight. Then we run."

"What of you?" said Idric, directing the question at Ayla.

"Are we waiting for you?"

"Until midnight." Out of the corner of her eye, Ayla saw Benjy shift his weight from foot to foot. He still hated this part of the plan, and Ayla knew there was a part of him that thought she wouldn't be able to do it. To kill Crier. "If the clock strikes midnight and I'm not in the music room, you run. You leave me behind."

Yoon opened their mouth to protest, but seemed to think better of it. Everyone else merely nodded, or did nothing at all. There were no illusions here. They weren't friends, not with Ayla and not with each other, and there was a good chance that tonight would claim all their lives. They would leave her in a heartbeat. Ayla didn't blame them one bit. The only wild card was Benjy.

Benjy, who was squaring his shoulders. "Two minutes," he said. "Before we go—before it all happens, before everything goes mad—remember that tonight we're forging a new future. Remember that we're on the right side. The leeches killed our people. They burned our villages. They poisoned our wells. They slaughtered our children in the streets."

He was barely speaking above a whisper, but he might as well have been shouting. Even the sea wind had gone silent to listen. The seven faces in the circle ranged from grave to anguished to furious, everything in between.

"The leeches think they can look down on us from their marble thrones and control us with an iron hand. They think we are no better than mindless cattle; they think we won't fight back. Tonight, we prove them wrong." He looked around the circle one last time, meeting everyone's eyes again. "Are you ready?"

Seven nods, seven hisses of *yes*.

"Are you ready?" he said more quietly, just for Ayla.

She nodded. She didn't trust herself to speak.

"All right," said Benjy. "It's time."

Seven became four when Yoon, Tem, and Idric peeled away, melting back into the shadows of the orchard and the gardens beyond. Ayla, Benjy, and the others waited breathlessly under the sun apple tree, watching the dark expanse of the palace grounds. Seconds crawled like ants across Ayla's skin, each minute lasting a thousand years, until—*there*.

A glow.

A flicker of orange light in a sea of black.

Then, a moment later, the flicker became an inferno as the oil-soaked roof of the stables caught fire. It happened so quickly: practically between one breath and the next, Ayla watched the fire spread across half the roof, then all of it, pale smoke billowing up into the night sky, obscuring the stars. She could smell it in the air—like a thousand oil lamps burning at once. The horses would already be panicking. Ayla kept her eyes on the stables until she saw it: a flash of light at the western corner of the burning building. Yoon's tiny hand mirror catching the firelight.

"There," Ayla said, nudging Benjy.

The mirror flashed once more. The distraction had worked;

all the nearby guards were rushing to the stables to free the horses and put out the fire.

"Follow me," Ayla said. She didn't wait for a response before leaving the relative safety of the sun apple trees and heading straight for the palace. That morning, when she was late reporting to Crier's door, it was because she'd opened one of the windows in the music room. Just a crack: not wide enough that anyone would notice. Just wide enough that it could be opened the rest of the way from outside. The six of them, Ayla and Benjy and the housemaids, skirted along the edges of the west wing until they reached that window. Benjy, the tallest among them, pushed it open, and helped Ayla and then the others get a leg up and over the sill. Then, silent as cats, they slipped one by one through the window and into the dark, empty music room.

Benjy was the last to enter. "Stars and skies," he murmured, staring in something almost like awe at the instruments around them, and Ayla remembered her own shock and wonder the first time she'd been in here. At night, the music room was eerily beautiful. Moonlight fell over the instruments, and something about the elegant lines of the harp, the piano, the violins, made them look less like things and more like people: like marble statues in a garden, pale and frozen but full of expression.

Ayla shook herself.

Thoughts like that were poison tonight.

She faced Benjy and the others, trying not to think of anything at all. "You remember the way to Kinok's study?"

A housemaid with a shaved head nodded sharply. "Been there every damn day for a year. Fetched him a sea's worth of ink and heartstone. I could walk these halls blindfolded."

"Right." Ayla swallowed hard. "Remember—out the window at midnight. No matter what."

The housemaid nodded. After a moment, Benjy nodded too.

"Go, then," said Ayla. "And good luck."

They headed for the door, but Benjy lingered behind. "Give us a moment," he said to the housemaid with the shaved head. She gave him a short look and then closed the door to the music room behind her, leaving Ayla and Benjy alone.

"Benj," Ayla managed, "we don't have time—"

"Ayla."

He was closer than she'd thought. Closer than they'd been since the night of the feast, the night they'd danced together in the sea cave. His eyes searched her face, and part of her knew what he was looking for, and the other part of her wondered if he was finding it.

"We couldn't have done this without you," he whispered. "This never would have happened without you. You know that, right? Everything you've done, all the information you gave us, no matter how small, all of it was vital. Remember that. People are gonna know your name. Ayla, the handmaiden. The spy. The girl who lived with leeches." He grinned, a flash of white, and then his fingertips were under her chin, tipping her face up. "You're making history, Ayla."

It was time. They had to go.

"You know, it's not even really killing," Benjy said almost soothingly, "not if she was never alive to begin with. You've trapped your butterfly, little spider. You know what to do next."

Never alive. Living things were born, not synthesized. Living things grew. They stretched upward or curled into themselves, into the center of themselves—the core, the heart, the old shriveled seed-bit—and turned brown and gave off that sweet wet rotting smell and turned at last, again, to dirt. Living things grew and rotted and grew from the rot. That was how it worked. Leeches didn't rot. When Crier died, her body would just sort of go stiff like petrified wood, and they could dump her in the ocean or a grave or string her up for the crows to eat, and she wouldn't rot and the crows wouldn't eat her anyway because her skin wasn't made of skin.

"It's time," said Benjy, eyes huge in the darkness. "Are you ready, Ayla?"

Was she ready?

All she had to do was open her mouth and say yes.

Why couldn't she do it?

Why couldn't she move?

"Okay," said Benjy. "Okay. Run it back one more time. I take the safe. And you . . ."

"I go straight to Lady Crier's room," Ayla rasped. "At five to midnight—"

"You stab her in the heart."

Benjy's face was so close. His eyes were so strange in the moonlight, like the eyes of a ghost. His hands were on her jaw.

"See you on the other side, Ayla," he said, and then he kissed her.

It lasted only for a moment, his mouth hard against hers, an instant of heat and pressure, his big hands holding her steady. Then he pulled away, staring at her, still searching. Always searching.

Ayla didn't have any answers for him.

It had been so long since she'd felt sure of anything, anything at all.

"Be safe," said Benjy. And then he was gone, the door to the music room closing behind him. Ayla hadn't breathed since he'd kissed her. (Twice she'd been kissed. One so different from the other. One had awakened her, one had felt like—like closure.) She glanced at the battered old pocket watch she'd swiped from one of the other servants. It was fifteen minutes to midnight.

There was a knife hidden in the waistband of her handmaiden's uniform. It was cold against her hip.

11:46.

At some point, she must have started moving, because she blinked and realized she was no longer in the music room. She was creeping through the white marble hallways, her soft leather boots silent on the flagstones. Nobody tried to stop her. She passed only one pair of guards, and they paid no attention to a human girl in a handmaiden's uniform even at this hour. Ayla was invisible. She slipped through the dark palace completely unnoticed.

11:49.

She touched her sternum, the place where her necklace should have been, and once again felt the loss. A physical pang from somewhere deep between her lungs. Not just the loss of an heirloom, now; the loss of lives, stories. How many other memories were held in that strange red jewel? She would never know. Her own history, her family's history. Gone.

11:50.

The knife was cold against her hip.

She turned a corner and there was the door to Crier's bedchamber. Ayla had opened that door countless times over the last two months, opened it and stepped across the threshold and stoked the fire and filled the room with warmth and light.

The hinges did not creak beneath her touch.

(That day. That first day on the bluff when Ayla's necklace had fallen out of her shirt and Crier's eyes had caught on it. For a split second Crier had been distracted enough to let her mask slip. Her hard mouth had gone soft, her flat eyes wide and scared. She'd gone from leech to girl, just girl. And Ayla knew then that she couldn't let this girl die.)

But she'd hated Crier.

She still did. It wasn't a lie. She had to remind herself of all the reasons: Crier was naive and arrogant, fool enough to think she could help them, could help Ayla. She was clueless and hardheaded and stubborn and the daughter of the sovereign and promised to Kinok. And she was a leech, a *fucking leech*. She represented every miserable thing about this miserable world— death and pain and a white dress hanging from a post, shoes swinging below a sun apple tree, a traitorous sister torn apart and howling with grief. Crier represented burning villages, ruined families, lost brothers. Ayla hated her. She hated her so goddamn much. It wasn't a lie.

It just wasn't the whole truth.

11:52.

She was standing over Crier's bed—shocked that Crier hadn't heard her come in, when sometimes she could hear so much as a breath from all the way down the hall. She must have been in a deep sleep state.

Ayla stood, staring, wondering.

The knife was in her hand.

The handle, which was carved from dark wood, was cool to the touch.

At five minutes to midnight she would stab Crier in the heart. Three minutes left. Crier was sleeping on the left side of the bed, the side closest to Ayla; she always slept on that side. Something about preferring to face the door. Her head was pillowed on her arm and the actual pillow had been tossed carelessly to the floor and she was sleeping on top of the blankets like she always did, which was something Ayla knew and did not know how to unlearn. Crier's hair spilled across the mattress like seaweed. It was a miracle that she was sleeping. Ayla had been half expecting to find her wide awake at the window seat, buried in a book.

11:54.

Crier shifted in her sleep. Ayla's breath froze in her lungs, her grip tightening on the knife, but Crier just shivered, brows furrowing a little, and did not wake. Her body was a curve above the blankets, an open parenthesis, the beginning of a sentence. She'd shivered; she was cold. It took a lot to make a leech get cold. The fire had gone out; the room was dark and cold and silent as a tomb, no crackling hearth fire, no warmth. Crier was cold. There was a space behind her on the bed, at her back, a curving space the size of another body. Where another body could bend and fit against her, and press their face to the notches of Crier's spine.

Inside her chest, in the core of her, Ayla felt her heart stretch and swell and take root.

11:55.

Making it quick is a kindness, even.

But Crier hadn't killed Ayla's family.

That terrible, truthful thought poured into her like water.

11:55.

Ayla raised the knife.

11:55.

One single downward movement. A piercing of the flesh, the same way Crier had pierced her own thumb with the nib of a pen. Not so different. A kindness. Maybe it wouldn't even hurt.

(Crier's eyes on her in the carriage. Ayla's mind was somewhere else, lost in foolish, half-imagined ideas of southern heat, a white shore, blue water, belly full of fish, never cold, never afraid, never exhausted, and Crier's eyes on her the whole time. Crier's gaze not cold, but warm, a patch of sunlight on Ayla's skin.)

11:55.

(That kiss. The way her entire body had lit up, everything inside her coming awake.)

Ayla's knuckles were white like raw bone. The knife was quivering, catching the moonlight. She had to do this; Crier's chime had to go off. The second distraction. Somewhere else in the bowels of the palace, at this moment, Benjy must be searching Kinok's study for the safe.

11:55.

(That night inside the cliffs, sharing the story of the hare and the princess, the way Crier told it with such intimacy, told it knowing how terribly the story would end, but changing it—promising Ayla happiness and peace, pretty lies, kind lies, because it had never been written that way. Because some things were just impossible. How the whole time Crier spoke, her words like honey in the darkness, Ayla had wanted to taste that voice forever.)

A flash of gold. For a horrible moment, Ayla thought Crier had woken up. But no, it wasn't her eyes. It was something in her hand, tucked into the hollow of her throat. Gold.

The necklace.

Crier was holding Ayla's necklace. The chain was twisted around her fingers, the pendant held between finger and thumb. The same way Ayla held it. So carefully, Crier held everything so carefully—books and maps and teacups. It was infuriating. Ayla wanted to see her break things, wanted to see her broken, wanted to watch her break apart, wanted to be the cause of it, wanted to make her shudder again, make her breaths come fast.

She'd gone to sleep holding Ayla's necklace.

11:56.

The knife slipped from Ayla's fingers and clattered to the floor.

Crier's eyes snapped open.

No. Ayla gasped a curse and scrambled to pick up the knife. She held it up again, her entire body trembling, poised to strike, to slash the knife across Crier's throat, stab her in the chest, the belly, wherever, but she was shaking, she couldn't—Crier was just *staring up at her*, lips parted in shock, and the worst part was that she didn't even look afraid, she just looked *confused*.

"Ayla?" Crier breathed.

And Ayla ran.

23

Crier was on her feet in an instant, adrenaline shrieking through her veins. "Ayla!" she half screamed, the name strangled out of her, but Ayla was already gone, Crier was alone, and then she wasn't—a dozen guards burst through the door of her bedchamber, half of them immediately spreading out to search the room, the other half forming a protective circle around Crier.

"What's going on?" she demanded, gasping when one of the guards put a hand on her shoulder, forcing her down onto the bed. "Don't touch me! What's going on?"

"We need you to stay put," said the guard who had grabbed her. "The palace is not secure."

Crier shoved his hand off her shoulder. There was a loud noise over by the window and she leaped to her feet again only to see two of the guards sweeping all the books off her bookshelves and desk, maps and loose papers drifting through the air, a jar of quills upended, a pot of black ink hitting the floor and shattering, ink spilling everywhere. "Stop!" she ordered, almost hysterical. Her books, her maps, some of them ancient and priceless and *precious*, years of her life spent tracking them down and bargaining for them. "Stop, please stop! What are you *doing*?"

But the guards ignored her. Another ripped the tapestry of Kiera off the wall as if he thought a human rebel might be lurking behind it.

"We don't know how long they've been planning this attack, my lady," said one of the guards. "They might have planted weapons, firebombs."

"On my *bookshelf*?"

Nobody responded. Crier sank to the bed and pressed both hands over her mouth, trying to calm down, but it was impossible. *Ayla.* Ayla, standing over her, that terrible look on her face, the *knife.*

She was going to kill you. Crier curled over her knees, squeezing her eyes shut. No, Ayla wouldn't, she wouldn't, but what other explanation was there? Slipping into Crier's room in the middle of the night, a silent shadow, the knife glinting in her hand. *Ayla was going to* kill you.

She'd read about heartbreak in a hundred different human stories. Had always thought it was a metaphor, poetry about pain. But as she sat there in the dark, the guards destroying her books and her own mind torturing her with the image of the knife in Ayla's hand, Crier felt like she was actually breaking. Cracks forming in her heart, pain leaking out like spilled ink, midnight black and poisonous. It *hurt*, she had never felt anything like this, not even when she experienced Leo's anguish in the locket memories—that had been an echo of someone else's pain. This was her own, real and unrelenting, and it *hurt*.

She realized dimly that she was still holding the locket. She hadn't let go of it, even during the commotion. Part of her wanted to throw it away, crush it beneath her foot. The clasp was broken, she couldn't even wear it. Instead, she slipped it into her sleeve.

Already, it was a relic of a time before—a time before Crier could ever have imagined this happening.

Ayla.

Finally, the guards decided the room was safe. Crier looked around at the wreckage of her things—her books and maps everywhere, her desk drawers emptied, one of the bookshelves knocked over, her clothes strewn across the floor; one of the guards had even taken his sword to her mattress and pillows and now there were feathers dusted across the room like snow. Everything ruined. Crier felt a dull pang of loss for her books and maps, but couldn't even think about the rest. *Ayla.*

"Come, my lady," one of the guards said. "We have orders to take you to the sovereign's study. It's safe there."

She didn't bother snapping at them or trying to resist when they pulled her roughly to her feet. All the adrenaline, all the fight, had leached out of her, and now she was just—empty. She let the guards lead her through the dark halls of the palace. It was strange not seeing a single human servant. Crier wondered how many had been part of the attack. How many had been plotting to kill her?

They reached her father's study. The guards pushed the door open, ushering Crier inside. Hesod was standing in the center of the room flanked by his own guards, and when he saw Crier his face collapsed in relief for a split second before smoothing out again. Crier wanted so badly to run forward into his arms. She wanted her father to hold her and tell her this had all been a terrible dream. But she was not supposed to do things like that, had been punished for it before. She held still.

"You are safe," said Hesod.

She nodded.

"Do you require a physician?"

She shook her head.

"Well, sit by the fire," Hesod said, scrutinizing her. "You look ill."

Crier obeyed, taking a seat on the lip of the hearth, and a moment later Hesod draped a thin blanket over her shoulders. She must have looked something worse than ill if he was worrying over her like that. She wondered what her expression was doing. If he'd noticed her shaking hands.

Ayla was going to kill you. She wanted *to kill you.*

All this time—

Crier pulled the blanket tighter over her shoulders, even though she knew it would do nothing. There was no banishing this kind of cold. Ayla's dagger hadn't pierced her, but it might as well have: the cold felt like a knife blade lodged between Crier's ribs. Surely she'd been wounded, somewhere unseen.

A guard came in and spoke to Hesod. About half of the rebels, by their calculations, had escaped, he said in a low murmur. She didn't know which ones hadn't.

It was a new and humiliating level of pathetic: hoping that someone who had tried to kill her had escaped unscathed. She stared into the fire. The flames were so bright, burning white mouths eating the kindling. Then the door behind her swung open, creaking on its hinges. Crier straightened up automatically when Kinok, flanked by her father's best guards, stepped inside. Kinok's eyes were as flat and lightless as two black pools of ink.

"Clear the room," Hesod ordered.

The guards hesitated.

"I said *clear the room*," Hesod thundered, and the guards hurried out. He closed the door behind them and turned to face the study, now empty of everyone but himself, Kinok, and Crier. "Rise, daughter."

Crier got to her feet, trying not to stumble on her stiff legs. She'd been so tense for hours. "Father, what—?"

"The guards are still searching the palace and all the surrounding lands for the human traitors," said Hesod. "Barely two leagues to the south, they overtook a single courier bearing no colors, no crest. He attempted to run from them. As if he'd been expecting an interception. He did not succeed. The courier was carrying only one letter. A coded message to Queen Junn of Varn."

It took everything to keep her expression curious instead

of terrified. She was caught. Her father would have already put two and two together. The letter was stamped with Crier's seal. Her personal seal. There was only one seal like that in the entire world and it was sitting on Crier's writing desk. Crier had used it to make sure Junn opened her letter, but now it was nothing but a red arrow pointing directly at Crier's face, a word emblazoned on her chest: *TRAITOR*.

She couldn't look at her father. She was not ashamed of what she'd done, but like a stupid, selfish child, she was terrified of the consequences. She had committed treason against her own father. And—Kinok knew. She couldn't look at him either. Had he already told Hesod about her fifth pillar? Did Hesod know his daughter was not just a traitor, but a mistake? A damaged thing?

"Father," she started, "I—"

He held up a hand. "Crier. The letter bore your seal. Do you know what that means?"

She shook her head desperately. "Father, please—"

"There is a spy inside the palace."

Crier pulled up short. She finally dared to meet her father's eyes, and they were still furious, but—not at her. It was a far-away anger, directed at someone else. Sovereign Hesod had been betrayed, had been attacked, had been bested, and he wanted blood. But not hers.

"It had to be someone inside the palace," he said quietly. "Someone with access to your bedchamber and your seal. Someone with a history of insubordination. Can you think of anyone who fits that description, daughter?" When Crier didn't answer, his lips twisted into something that looked like a smile but was not. "Somehow you have become even softer than I feared. Tonight, the handmaiden attempted to kill you in your sleep. For months, perhaps years, she has been working with the Mad Queen to destroy us all from the inside out."

"I didn't know," Crier whispered, too shocked to know what else to say. He'd gotten everything wrong. She was safe, for now, but Ayla . . .

"And now you do," said Hesod. "And still you protect her with your silence."

"Father . . ."

Hesod looked at her. He studied her face with the expression of someone attempting to read a passage written in a language they did not possess. Finally, he let out a slow breath. "Did I really Design you?" he murmured, more to himself than to her, and that was how Crier learned that pain was not finite; there was no limit to woundless hurt.

And she was mute.

Of course, she thought hollowly. Her father was fascinated by humans. He enjoyed reading about their gods, their songs, their stories and languages, their holy days, their strange rituals. But they were still animals to him. Oxen and dogs. They were not rulers; they were not daughters. Crier had always known that. She had always known that.

"Sovereign," said Kinok, breaking the terrible silence. "With all due respect, the eyes of the world are watching you more closely than ever. Word will get out about tonight's attack. We *must* prove to the world that Lady Crier is alive and well—and that your foothold in Zulla has not faltered."

"And how do you suggest we do that, Scyre?" said Hesod.

"First," said Kinok, "we move up the date of the wedding. There is too much time to plan another attack. Second, Lady Crier must be guarded at all times. She barely escaped with her life tonight." He was so good at sounding concerned. It made Crier sick. "Third, we find the handmaiden, and we kill her."

Crier's eyes widened, but Hesod was already nodding. "Good counsel as always, Scyre Kinok," he said. "You will be married in one week's time. Assign four of the best guards to watch Lady Crier day and night. And yes, Scyre—do find the handmaiden. Bring me her head. I want to see it."

Kinok nodded. "Of course, Sovereign."

And he swept out of the room, leaving Crier and Hesod alone.

"Father—" she began.

"If you are about to ask for the handmaiden's life, daughter, I strongly suggest that you do not."

"I wasn't going to," Crier said evenly. "I want nothing more than a small favor. Now that I am to be married in one week's time, let me take three days to visit the Midwifery where I was built." She ignored the way Hesod's eyebrows rose, and thought quickly. "Let me Make a gift for my future husband. It was tradition once, wasn't it, just like the Hunt? The bride gifting her betrothed a Made object, a clever trinket, a token of goodwill?

Let me do that for Kinok, as a gesture of goodwill and faith in our future together. That is all I ask."

Get me out of here. Away from him.

"Daughter, you were nearly killed tonight. Do you really think it safe to leave the palace?"

"We will tell no one where I am going. Not even Kinok. You and I will be the only ones who know. And you can send a dozen guards along with me. Two dozen. If the—the *handmaiden* was a spy, who knows how many other servants are working for the queen? Surely I am safer on the road than here."

He considered it.

"Please, Father," said Crier. "Just three days."

"Fine," said Hesod. "Three days."

At the beginning of the War of Kinds, the bone beasts—soft-bodied and fragile, those of full mating age killed as easily as their maggot bairn—thought themselves kings of this land. By the end of it, the sky was black with the smoke of twenty thousand corpses, and the superior Kind had ascended to their rightful place.

The age of Automae as mere pets and possessions of humankind was over.

The Golden Era had begun.

—FROM *THE ERA OF ENLIGHTENMENT*,
BY IDONA OF FAMILY PHYRIS, 3382960905, YEAR 19 AE

24

There were two things that had changed since Ayla last visited the market at the heart of Kalla-den. The first was that Luna's dress was finally gone. Torn to pieces by curious seagulls, maybe, or perhaps it had simply been carried off by a particularly strong gust of sea wind. No matter how it had happened, the result was the same: the dress was gone, and with it the ghostly presence of Luna that had once hung, like the dress, over the marketplace, a stark reminder that nobody there was ever safe, not really.

The second was that Ayla and Benjy were fugitives.

"There he is," Benjy hissed in her ear. "There's the bastard."

She followed his gaze.

They were huddled behind a stack of oyster barrels in the market at Kalla-den. It was the second dawn since their attack, since Ayla had tried and failed to kill Crier. She and Benjy had spent the past day and night with one of Rowan's old friends, a fisherman who lived in a tiny shack nestled into a crook of the sea cliffs, impossible to find unless you knew exactly where it was. He'd recognized Benjy's face and granted them a hiding place while the sovereign's guards searched all the nearby villages. Yesterday, they'd made contact with the owner of the fish cart, offered him all but a few of their pooled statescoins, plus Benjy's grandfather's watch, to turn a blind eye when they snuck onto his cart this morning in the busy hour right before dawn, when all the traders and traveling merchants—including the fish cart man—were heading into Kalla-den for the day, choking the streets. The plan was to spend the day in the village, buy or steal enough food for a three days' journey, and then slip back onto the fish cart at sundown. From there, they'd leave Kalla-den, once again cloaked by movement and merchants, and the fish cart man would take them to the docks.

By then, night would have fallen. Black cliffs, black rocks, black water. There was no better time to become stowaways.

Everything had been going all right—they'd pilfered three days' worth of bread and salted meat, hardtack, waterskins. Everything had been going according to plan.

But the damn fish cart wasn't in the agreed-upon location.

It was across the market square, and as Ayla squinted at the fish cart man, she could tell there was something *off* about him. Something shifty in his movements.

"He's going to leave without us," she whispered, still staring at him. "Maybe he realized who we are."

"Will you *please* keep your head down," Benjy whispered back.

She risked looking at him. His face was mostly covered by a hood—they had both borrowed hooded cloaks from the fisherman—but Ayla could tell by the set of his mouth that he was in pain. He'd been hurt during the attack, a guard's sword glancing off his left calf. The cut wasn't deep enough to sever anything important, but it was still painful. Could still become infected, if they didn't take care of it soon, and it made every step miserable for Benjy. His lips were pressed in a thin white line.

Ayla looked away. She was trying not to think about Benjy's lips.

His kiss. Her knife. All of it for nothing.

She hadn't managed to set off Crier's chime, but that wasn't why the plan had failed. Benjy and the other rebels had assumed something had gone wrong on her end and taken a chance, making their way to Kinok's study even without the distraction. They'd made it into the study without being caught by the guards, they'd even found the safe hidden in the bookshelf—but when Benjy, the only one among them who could read the language of the Makers, had cracked the lock, they hadn't found the compass that would lead them to the Iron Heart. They'd found something else entirely: a faded piece of parchment with three words on it.

Leo
Siena
Tourmaline

Her grandfather's and grandmother's names, and something else.

When they heard the guards raising the alarm, the rebels fled the study, taking the piece of parchment with them. As planned, they waited for Ayla in the music room, all of them wild-eyed and panting among the silent, beautiful instruments, like grave robbers in an untouched tomb.

Ayla didn't know what expression she'd been wearing when she burst through the door, but Benjy took one look at her face and told the others, "Crier's still alive. *Run.*" And they had: out the same window they'd stolen in through and then through the dark orchards, and none of them had stopped running until they'd left the palace grounds far behind them and were lost to the lightless hills between the palace and all the surrounding farms and villages. From there, Benjy and Ayla had split off, spent the night in the branches of some farmer's sun apple tree, and made their way to the fisherman's shack before dawn.

And now: fugitives. It was the only part of the plan that had gone as expected. But instead of glory—instead of the compass in their possession, the Iron Heart in their control, Kinok's Movement under their foot, Crier's heart in Ayla's hands (no, pierced by her knife)—instead of glory, they were scattered. Ayla and Benjy had no way of knowing if the others had survived the night. They were on the run. Alone. Empty-handed, after giving all their coin to the man with the fish cart.

Oh, he was *definitely* going to leave without them. Take their coin and run.

"Bastard," Ayla muttered.

But she didn't get a chance to curse him any further, because her attention was drawn by a crash on the other side of the market, just a few stalls away from the fish cart. Her blood ran cold: *guards*. Half a dozen of them, all wearing the sovereign's crest. As she watched, one of the soldiers upended a barrel, spilling oysters and brine all over the cobblestones. One of the human vendors shouted in outrage and another guard pushed him to the ground, sword aimed at his throat.

"We have to get out of here," Ayla breathed.

"You'll have to help me," Benjy said tightly.

She looped her arm around his back, helping him to his feet. He leaned heavily on her, wincing with every step, and together they moved away from the market square as quickly as possible, sticking to the last shadows of the fading night. Somewhere to the east, the rising sun must be curling its fingers over the edge of the Steorran, staining the sky and water the palest palest pink, like the sheen of a pearl button.

There were two things that Ayla had wanted. The first was revenge. The second was something she would not admit to herself, could not put into words, because even thinking about it made her heart feel like a bridge giving way, tumbling down into water, all her pieces carried off by the current of something far older and more powerful than she was. Right now, Ayla had nothing but her pieces. She could not give way.

Slowly, with a hand pressed over her mouth. That was how Ayla left everything she'd ever known behind her, the sovereign's palace and Kalla-den and the northern shores and somewhere among them the village she'd been born in, Delan, all of it now at her back. And those three words repeating themselves over and over again in her heart: *Leo. Siena. Tourmaline.* Leo and Siena, her grandparents' legacy—the memories in her locket, which Crier had, and the second locket, which Kinok had somehow gotten his hands on.

One thing was becoming clear. The only way to keep going, to keep fighting, was to learn more about her past.

And she knew just where to start. Storme.

Which meant they were headed to Varn. Whose borders on land were closed—but not the ones by sea.

"We're almost there," she said to Benjy, setting her eyes on a narrow alley between two buildings, a place to wait out the guards. "You all right?"

He shuddered. "I'll be fine. Just keep going."

"Always," she said. "Always."

25

During the journey to the Midwifery, as she sat alone in the carriage, Crier came to a conclusion. Even after everything that had happened, after what Ayla had tried to do. Crier *still* loved her. Maybe she had loved her ever since the moment Ayla had saved her life on the cliff so many weeks ago.

Crier had been Designed. Crier was Made. But in the moment Ayla first touched her, Crier had learned what it felt like to be *born*.

She'd asked Ayla once what love felt like.

I don't remember, Ayla had answered, lacing up Crier's dress. Crier could still recall the way her rough, calloused fingertips had brushed across her shoulder blades.

Is it pleasant or painful? Crier had asked.

Depends. Ayla's voice, soft across her neck.

So you do remember.

There was only one logical explanation for such madness:

she loved Ayla because she was Flawed. Because she had a fifth pillar. It was her Passion that had fallen in love with Ayla, *not* Crier herself—she would never otherwise be that foolish, that uncalculated, that *wrong*. Lady Crier was an Automa. She was heir to the sovereign—had every intention of reforming the Red Council, of changing the laws and ways of Zulla. Lady Crier would never allow herself to become so weak and soft over a human girl. She would never open herself up to betrayal.

All of this had happened only because of the fifth pillar. Logically, there was only one solution.

She needed it gone.

Ayla hadn't succeeded in cutting out Crier's heart. So Crier would do it for both of them. She wanted the Passion out of her, wanted to carve it out herself, like cutting away the bruise on a piece of fruit. Like burning away deadly spores on a tree branch, killing part of the tree so the rest could survive.

The Midwifery operated out of what had once been a human cathedral. It was a massive building, nearly the size of the Old Palace, the spires twisting up into the sky like columns of smoke. Every inch of the facade was carved with intricate designs: scenes from old human stories, gods and heroes, diagrams of the night sky: the planets, the constellations, the phases of the moon. The Automae guarding the doors were cloaked in black, their faces hidden by masks, and they reminded Crier far too much of Kinok. As her carriage drew near, she couldn't help clutching the necklace, rubbing her thumb over the smooth red stone. Somehow, it helped calm her down.

A pair of Midwives appeared the moment Crier's carriage passed through the iron gates. Like all Midwives, they were human and dressed all in white: white uniform shirt and pants, their hair pulled back and hidden under a white veil. One of them wore a white mask over their mouth, sort of like the masks Queen Junn and her retinue had worn. They looked like the inverse of the guards.

"Welcome, Lady Crier," said the Midwife without the mask, even though Crier hadn't introduced herself or sent word ahead that she was coming. "We are honored."

The two Midwives helped Crier out of the carriage, and then the one with the mask led it away toward a small keep so the horses could rest and replenish themselves for the journey home. The remaining Midwife glanced at Crier's small guard, her eyes impassive.

"We do not allow weapons inside the Midwifery," she said.

"Don't worry," said Crier. "They will remain outside."

The Midwife nodded, giving Crier a long look from beneath her white veil. Then she inclined her head. "You may call me Jezen." Then she turned on her heel and headed for the wide wooden doors of the Midwifery.

Crier followed, trailing after Midwife Jezen through the doors and into the belly of the cathedral.

If the exterior of the Midwifery was beautiful, the interior was breathtaking. The walls were lined with polished stone pillars that met to form an arched ceiling so far above her head that she had to crane her neck back to look at it. Shafts of sunlight streamed through the tall windows lining the nave, tiny galaxies of dust motes floating and orbiting in the light, and the walls were painted with images similar to the ones carved into the facade. But the paintings were newer than the carvings: they included Automae. Golden-eyed figures emerging from swirls of red smoke, images of Kiera in her bloodred cloak, Kiera charging into battle during the War of Kinds. Humans genuflecting at her feet. Humans gazing reverently at newbuilt Automae. Humans crying with joy, bowing happily into the dirt, as if there was nothing more pleasurable than being ruled.

Crier looked away from the painting. She'd seen enough.

Where there might have been pews in a human cathedral, the Midwifery had rows of tables, sort of like the work space at the back of an apothecary. Some of the tables were curtained off, protecting newbuilt Automae. Others were covered in plants, some in stones or bits of metal. Some of the tables held clearly Made objects: everything from tools to trinkets to jewelry and, despite Jezen's words, even weapons. This was where Crier had been Designed and Made. Crier would have been spread out on one of those tables, once, hidden by a curtain. Existing but not yet alive.

"Why have you come, Lady Crier?" Jezen asked. They had stopped in the center aisle of the nave, between the two rows of tables.

"I am getting married in a few days," Crier stalled. "I came here to Make a gift for my husband."

Jezen studied her for a moment. "That's not true."

Crier wanted to point to her chest, *this is the hurting part, this is the bleeding part, fix it or take it out.*

She looked down into Jezen's big green eyes. She took one deep breath and then another, and then realized this was an utterly human tic that she must have picked up from Ayla, and that made it easier to speak. "You must help me."

"Lady Crier?"

"I am Flawed," Crier said. "I was Made wrong. You must help me correct it."

"I don't understand what you mean," said Jezen slowly. She looked Crier up and down, as if searching for a well-hidden third arm. "What is your Flaw?"

"I have five pillars." Crier saw the way Jezen's eyes widened and kept going. "I was never supposed to know. My father Designed me, but someone sabotaged his Design. Someone Made me with five pillars on purpose. Midwife Torras," she said, remembering the name Kinok had given her. "I don't know why she did it. A huge scandal, I was told—I'm not the only one. But I saw the difference between my father's papers and the final blueprint. I have Intellect, Organics, Calculation, Reason—and Passion."

She waited for the Midwife to gasp in shock. Maybe recoil, the way people recoiled from lepers. But instead Jezen just stared at her with a slight furrow between her brows, her expression more confused than anything else.

"I have two Automa pillars and three human pillars," Crier said again, just in case Jezen somehow didn't understand. "I have a fifth pillar. You must remove it."

"No, my lady," said Jezen. "You don't have a fifth pillar. You can't."

Crier shook her head. "Please, do not lie to me. I know what I saw."

"Lady Crier, I am not trying to hide anything from you. It's just—what you saw is simply *not possible*. I would know better than anyone. Years ago, I was one of many Midwives who experimented with creating Automae with five pillars, hoping we could Make an even stronger and more perfect being. But it never worked. Every single five-pillared Automae died in the Making process. Every single one. The fifth pillar threw their inner workings off-balance, no matter what we did—and trust me, my lady, we tried everything. It is not possible to have five pillars. You would have died newbuilt."

"But—I'm not lying," said Crier. "I, I saw the blueprints. . . ."

"I believe you. I believe that you saw them. I don't think it's you who is lying, Lady Crier. But it's not me either." Jezen paused for a moment, then nodded to herself. "I'll prove it to you. Wait here, my lady. I'll be right back."

Crier couldn't have moved if she tried. During the handful of minutes that Jezen was gone, she stood there struggling to comprehend what the Midwife had said.

Jezen returned with a roll of parchment in her hands. "We keep records of everything, of course," she said, beckoning Crier over to a nearby worktable and undoing the length of leather string that kept the parchment bound. "This, here—these are your blueprints, my lady. Your real blueprints."

She unrolled the parchment. Like the papers Crier had gotten from Kinok, there were multiple Designs—first a rough draft, then improvements, as her father worked with Midwives and Designers to home in on a final model. Then, finally, the last sheet of parchment. The final blueprint. Unlike the papers Crier had found, this final blueprint bore her father's signature. The midnight-blue ink of Hesod's name was stark against the softer, lighter lines of the blueprint.

Jezen pointed to the center of the blueprint, the center of the Crier on the page, but it wasn't necessary. Crier was already looking at the pillars. Four tiny columns of ink: Intellect, Organics, Calculations, Reason. Four. Just like there were supposed to be.

"I don't understand," she whispered. "Why would there be . . . ?" And even as she said it, she did understand.

"The blueprints you saw were fake," Jezen said gently. She could probably already see the realization on Crier's face. "They were forged. Can you think of anyone who might want to trick you, Lady Crier?"

Yes, of course she could. Someone who wanted not just to trick her, but to control her. To blackmail her into absolute obedience. To make her live in constant fear.

She felt sick.

Crier wasn't Flawed. She'd never been Flawed. She was perfect; she was fully Automa. There was nothing wrong with her, no Passion consuming her from the inside out. No love.

"No," she said without meaning to. "I don't know who would do that." Her own voice sounded so far away, as if she were hearing herself speak from across the entire Midwifery.

With careful hands she picked up her own blueprints and rolled them up again and fastened the leather string tight around them. She did all of this without a single thought in her head, nothing but a faint hum, the buzz of a locust swarm. Perhaps she had finally hit her limit.

"Lady Crier," said Jezen.

Crier handed her the roll of parchment. "Thank you for clarifying the error, Midwife Jezen," she said. "I apologize for keeping you."

"Lady Crier—"

"My driver is waiting. I'll take my leave now. Thank you again."

"*Crier*," Jezen said, grabbing Crier's sleeve. Crier turned to face her again, so surprised by a human grabbing her like that that she didn't even try to resist. "Before you go, let me say this."

Crier waited. Jezen's eyes, the color of the forest in Siena's memory, were so intent on Crier's face.

"Humanity is how you act, my lady," said Jezen. "Not how you were Made."

And she let go of Crier's sleeve.

Back in the carriage, Crier did nothing but turn Ayla's necklace over and over in her hands. It had become a habit to run the gold chain through her fingers like water, to hold the tiny red stone up to the light, to rub the gold casing like a talisman between finger and thumb. To hold the stone up to her ear and listen to the faint ticking of its odd inorganic heartbeat.

She supposed she should do away with it now. It belonged to Ayla, and she would never see Ayla again. Before Ayla it had belonged to Siena, long dead. Crier was done fishing through the memories of a person she would never know. Whatever had driven Siena to Make or commission this necklace, Crier would never know. She didn't want to see Siena with that wild, beautiful, laughing human boy. Definitely didn't want to see her with the not-Automa, Yora. That was a story that could only end with sorrow and blood.

But there was still one thing she didn't understand: What did *Yora's heart* mean? And why had Kinok written it down?

Closing her eyes, Crier held the locket between her palms. She could *feel* the heartbeat like this, the tiniest vibration against her skin.

One last time, she thought, squeezing the locket tight. If she couldn't cut the love out of her, she would rid herself of it like humans did: by saying goodbye. *Goodbye, Ayla*. She took one of the bone hairpins from her hair and carefully pricked the top of her finger with it. Then she pressed her finger to the red stone and closed her eyes.

Images flashed through her head, one right after the other, and she realized she was thrown back into the same memory she'd witnessed before, entering where it had cut off—

A burning city. Buildings collapsing beneath the weight of the flames, smoke billowing into a sky like an open wound. Two figures racing away from the flames, toward the sea—the port. Leo and Siena, little Clara in Leo's arms.

". . . humans in the southeast fishing villages are standing strong," Leo was saying, his voice loud and raw above the deafening roar of the fire. "We just have to make it down the coast and we'll be safe—"

They reached the port. There were other terrified humans huddled on the docks: all of them dirty and shell-shocked, children wailing, parents staring back at the city with anguish on their faces. Their city, their beautiful city, their history, their lives—all of it destroyed. Clara shifted in his arms, pressed her face into his neck. Thank the gods she was all right.

But something was still wrong. Siena kept wavering, looking back at the city, the haze of smoke and flame. Leo knew what she was searching for. Knew it was too late. But she would never believe that. Not when it came to Yora.

Right at the edge of the docks, seawater lapping at their feet, Siena stopped dead. She was holding something. Cupping it with both hands. She must have been holding it this entire time; he hadn't noticed. Siena held out her hands, revealing a stone cradled in her palms. It was about the size of a plum, smooth like glass, a deep, dizzying blue.

"Take it," Siena said, pressing the blue stone into Leo's free hand, the one that wasn't clutching their daughter. "Please just take it."

"Si, what is this?"

She looked manic. "Tourmaline. Just take it."

"What—what is that? Why does it matter so much? Si, please—"

"It's Yora!" she said desperately, terribly, her voice breaking on the name. "Please, Leo, please, it's Yora, it's her heart, it's everything, please just take it, take it and keep it safe. I have to go back for her, for her Design, I have to save something else of her, but I'll be back. I promise."

"No!" he gasped. "No, Si, don't you dare—SIENA," but she was already running, running away from him and Clara, away from the port, back into the burning city. Leo screamed her name. Clara began to cry, struggling against his grip, wailing for her mother—Mama!—Si, please, don't do this—Mama, come back—

And then Crier was wrenching awake, gasping, tasting bile. She flung the locket away. It hit the opposite wall of the carriage and fell to the floor at her feet, landing with a *thud* far louder than any object that small should have made.

Crier tried to calm her breathing. She stared at the locket, resting so innocently on the floor of the carriage. Practically glowing, even though the velvet curtains were drawn across the carriage windows.

It's Yora. It's her heart.

No, Crier thought, even as the pieces fell into place at last. Tourmaline.

You're Tourmaline, she thought, thinking of the magnificent blue stone Siena had held in her palms. *You are Yora, and you are Tourmaline.* It felt impossible that the truth had been right here the whole time, first hidden beneath the collar of Ayla's uniform and then in Crier's hands. It was real.

It was just like Rosi had said—someone *had* invented the Automa before Thomas Wren, but their designs had been stolen. Siena's mother was the inventor, the creator of Yora: a creature similar to Wren's Automa, but not the same. A different prototype. One that had a blue gem for a heart and didn't require heartstone to live.

The blue gem. Tourmaline. A source of immortality.

Crier understood the locket now, too, what it was. Siena had been a Maker—amateur, maybe, but a genius. She must have made the locket to trap memories—perhaps she'd made it for Leo, since it seemed to have captured his side of the story and not hers.

Somehow—the result of genius and alchemy—Siena had created Tourmaline, too; she'd put it in Yora's body in an attempt to ensure that Yora, her greatest creation, would never die. It was real.

It was *real*.

Oh, gods.

Maybe Tourmaline wasn't perfect—Crier couldn't forget Yora's soulless eyes, her blank stare. But still. Immortality. An infinite source. The Automa who knew how to create Tourmaline would be the most powerful Automa in Zulla overnight. Kinok would be more powerful than the sovereign. More powerful than the entire Red Council, the Scyres, the Watchers, Queen Junn. Every last Automa would be under his command.

The girl who was no longer under Crier's protection.

No, said a voice in Crier's head, so fierce that it took a second for her to recognize it as her own. *No. You cannot take her.*

There was only one thing to do. Crier felt oddly calm as she considered it. Something inside her had already accepted that she would do what must be done to save Ayla and stop Kinok. It was simple, in the end. She had to find the source of Tourmaline before he did.

She already had her first lead: Siena's locket. And Ayla was her second. There was no other human alive who could trace the locket's history, help her find out more about where exactly it had come from. There was a possibility Ayla wouldn't be able to help at all—she hadn't even known about the locket's properties—but she was Crier's best bet. Crier's only hope.

Find Ayla.

Find Tourmaline.

Only then could she stop Kinok.

Crier pressed both hands to her sternum and breathed in deep. *Find Ayla.* The idea brought forth so many emotions, she didn't know how to sort through them, which ones to focus on. It made Crier shiver and close her eyes and take another deep breath, trying to calm herself.

She had to find Ayla. Had to warn her—

"My lady," said her driver, knocking on the carriage door.

Gods, had they stopped moving? She hadn't even noticed.

"We were intercepted by a messenger from Varn. There's an urgent message for you."

A message. From Varn. Crier flung the carriage door open and the driver handed her a letter. The wax used to seal it was green, the seal itself forming the imprint of a single, tiny feather.

Crier shut the door again and tore open the envelope with shaking hands, heart pounding. . . .

> *Fox—*
>
> > *Don't worry about the missing red hen. I took care of her.*
> >
> > *I know it pains you, but you must go through with the wedding. Trust me, little Fox. The Wolf, his followers, and all of the corrupt Red Hands in one place . . . I can think of no greater opportunity to eliminate the worst of what stands in our way.*
> >
> > *Be brave. Have faith. You've done so well.*

Crier let the letter slip from her fingers, fluttering to the floor of the carriage.

Reyka was dead, and it wasn't Kinok who had killed her.

It was Queen Junn.

The Mad Queen of Varn.

And now Crier saw the cold truth: she was more trapped than ever. Kinok was after Yora's heart, which meant he was after Ayla. But if Crier ran away to find Ayla, to warn her, she'd be a threat to Queen Junn just like Reyka had been. The queen didn't like loose ends, uncontrolled variables. Didn't like people who talked.

No matter how useful she'd been, she recalled all the rumors she'd ever heard about the Mad Queen and she knew, deep in her bones: Junn would show the Fox no mercy.

Crier could risk her life to save Ayla, who had tried to kill her. Or she could stay put. Go through with the wedding, if that was what Junn wanted. Take down Kinok and his movement from the inside out.

It was a terrible set of choices, and Crier had to choose one.

But for now, the only thing she could do was pull aside the velvet curtains, let the evening light spill into the carriage, and allow a second, more private truth to make its presence known inside her heart. No matter what she chose—whether she abandoned her life and duties to chase after a human traitor, or married Kinok for the sole purpose of destroying the Anti-Reliance Movement—it would be a direct rebellion against her father. Against the Red Council. Against her nation. Crier would become just as much a traitor as Ayla was. Just as much a fugitive.

Just as much a revolutionary.

No matter what Crier chose, there would be a battle to win. No, not just a battle.

A war.

ACKNOWLEDGMENTS

Kieryn. You are my person. It is an honor to know you. Knowing you has made me kinder—to everyone, to myself. Knowing you has changed how I write and think about love; it has changed how I love. It is an honor to love you. The next time you're trying to talk about feelings and I'm breaking out in hives, you can point to this. A paragraph isn't enough. My acknowledgment to you is everything I've written over the past six years. Everything I'm writing, everything I will write, that's your acknowledgment. Your existence informs and transforms every page. My person, my writing partner, my QPLP, my soul mate, coparent of the beastling, rescuer of plots, creator of worlds and apocalypse escape plans and regular escape plans. I'd fry up twenty pounds of latkes with you any day. I hope that says it all.

Mama and Papa, I have wanted to be a writer since I was, what, four?—and your belief in me has never once wavered. You never once doubted I could do this. You had so much more faith in me than I ever had in myself; when I said "if," you always said "when." I don't think that's the norm. I got lucky with you. Thank you for loving this strange daughter. Thank you for raising me in houses full of books. Thank you for encouraging every story. My first readers, my home. I love you.

Piera, you're the younger one, but I think you've taught me more than I've ever taught you. You are my role model. You are empathy and bravery and damn good poetry. No offense to our parents, but I'm your biggest fan.

Tony, you're already teaching me new things. How dare you be so young but so wise. Remember I love you, remember I miss you, remember my home is your home, remember I am here for you, always. Fiona, thank you for your endless love. You didn't have to make me your daughter, but you did. From the very beginning. Paul, thank you for everything you have done for us; thank you for being there, unconditionally.

Thank you to Nana and Grandpa for the love and support and *Doctor Who* marathons and fruitcakes and just for being there. To Granny, I miss you; I vow to never see a giraffe without thinking of you.

Yes Homo, Full House, my guad, thank you for your weirdness, for your kindness, for making me laugh, for listening, for making this southern baby feel at home in LA; you are worth the lack of green things. To Amy, thank you for the music-up-windows-down fly away nights, thank you for the Treat Yourself days, for your loud, beautiful heart, for always texting me when there's a particularly good moon.

Thank you to Mr. Wilson for seeing something in me, for

taking me seriously. For the Jane Kenyon.

Thank you to Lady for being consistently horrible and also the love of my life. Thank you to Crave Café for being open 24/7. Thank you to Namjoon for the light.

Glasstown folks, thank you for making this happen. Thank you for giving this queer girl a chance to write about queer girls. Thank you to Lexa for being there every step of the way, for sparking everything, for loving this story and these characters so deeply, for believing in me and my writing, for your patience and hard work, for championing this story, for being gentle when you remind me for the thousandth time that not everything can be an inner monologue and there does, at some point, need to be a plot. Thank you to Jessica Sit for helping bring this world to life, Mekisha Telfer and Kat Cho for your thoughtfulness and insight across so many drafts, Lauren Oliver for making space for stories like this. Inkwell folks, Stephen Barbara and Lyndsey Blessing, thank you for getting this book on the shelves.

Thank you to everyone at HarperCollins: Karen Chaplin for turning a draft into a book, for untangling some very tangled threads, for working hard to make this book beautiful inside and out; Rosemary Brosnan for believing in this story from the beginning; David Curtis and Erin Fitzsimmons for the absolutely gorgeous cover; Megan Gendell for the copyediting (I'm sorry about all the commas); Jon Howard for bringing everything together; the entire marketing and publicity team for making sure people actually read this thing; Emily Berge-Thielman for the hard work and enthusiasm despite my social media ineptitude.

Thank you to Ryan Douglass—I appreciate you, your effort, your thoughtfulness.

Thank you to the old readers. I've been posting my writing online for over a decade, and I was always, always met with kindness. Some of that writing was incredibly cringey—the work of an angsty thirteen-year-old. It would have been easy to tear it apart. Nobody did. I cannot tell you how much your kindness and support meant to that angsty thirteen-year-old. And that angsty sixteen-year-old. And that angsty twenty-year-old. And—you get the idea. You made me keep writing. Really, above all else, it was you. Your comments, your kudos, your friendship, across multiple platforms, across dozens of stories. From the silent lurkers to the faithful commenters to the online friends I've known for years, it was you. I was sad and lonely and I needed someone to tell me, "You are not wasting your time, you are good at this, keep going," and you did. Over and over again, you did. Tens of thousands of you. Ironically, I cannot put it into words: how much that meant, how much that means. How much you helped me. I wrote for you. I write for you. Thank you.

To the queer readers: for reading this book, but also just for existing. Some people will try to tell you your story doesn't matter. That is the biggest lie you will ever hear. Reader, everything you feel and experience and create is vital to this world. Never sit down; never shut up. Nobody else wants to write about us, so:

screw it. We'll do it ourselves. We will write ourselves into every genre. We will make it impossible for anyone to pretend we don't exist. Please tell your story—I'd love to read it. Thank you for reading mine.

TURN THE PAGE FOR A SNEAK PEEK
AT THE EPIC SEQUEL TO *CRIER'S WAR*!

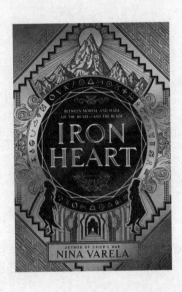

1

It was barely midmorning and Ayla had already cheated death twice.

Maybe that was dramatic. More accurately, she'd already been *this close* to getting caught by two different members of the royal guard—but then again, it was the same result in the end, wasn't it? Ayla was a stowaway and a human. Either crime was often punishable by death.

Thalen, the capital of Varn, was a glittering white city surrounded by high white walls. Like Sovereign Hesod's palace in Rabu, Ayla's home country, it was seated on the coast, on the shores of the Steorran Sea. But Thalen was a good hundred leagues south of the palace, and here the sea wasn't an icy black expanse; there were no cliffs of sharp black rock, slick with ice, just waiting for someone to take a wrong step, slip off the edge, and be swallowed by the freezing water below. Here, the sea was jewel green and almost warm. Instead of cliffs, there was a beach of coarse yellow sand heaped with piles of washed-up seaweed, and farther up, short, sloping bluffs of gray rock spotted with green moss and beach grass. The bluffs formed a crescent-moon curve around the port that Ayla and her best friend, Benjy, had managed to smuggle themselves into. After they'd fled the sovereign's palace. Fled Rabu, the only home they had ever known, in the hold of a cargo ship, hidden among casks of grain. The journey had been brutal: Benjy seasick the whole time, Ayla fine at first and then, after the grain was switched out for barrels of rotting sardines, violently ill. She remembered that week and a half at sea in sweaty, nauseous flashes, head spinning, stomach lurching.

But they'd made it.

This port was the largest on Varn's coastline. Massive docks jutted out into the sea, bustling with sailors and fishermen and traders and seamen of all kinds. All human, as this was dirty work, hard labor, and therefore beneath Automakind. Hundreds of ships docked here, some of them floating inns and waterboat taverns, many of them flying the royal colors, green and white. Queen Junn's emblem was everywhere: a brilliant green phoenix clutching a sword in one clawed foot and a pickax in the other. Varn was a mining country. A nation of rolling hills and deep quarries, of iron, coal, precious metals, and gemstones buried deep beneath the earth.

The air smelled like salt and fish and human sweat. The sun shone brighter than it ever did in the frozen north. Ayla hadn't been this warm in a long time. She hadn't been this warm since—

Since—

Midnight. Moonlight. Soft bed, softer blankets. Dark hair spilled across the pillow. A body beside her own, breathing too slow to be human.

But Ayla wasn't thinking about that, or her, now.

She ducked out of the narrow alleyway she'd been hiding in and headed back toward the center of the port town, satisfied she'd thrown the second guard off her track. She'd given them no reason to chase her—the meat pies in her knapsack were paid for, thank you very much. But in a town of burly dockworkers, a small shifty-eyed girl stood out, drawing suspicion from humans and Automae alike.

The port town was little more than a collection of inns and pubs clinging like barnacles to the shore, every third building marked with the crest of a shipping company or major merchant. Bobbing just offshore were a cluster of houseboats—and houses on stilts, floating like long-legged insects on the surface of the water—where the stevedores lived. That was it. All the important business happened in the capital. Wherever you stood in the town, or in the port beyond, you could see the monolith of the white walls of Thalen, rising up from the shore like strange, too-perfect cliffs. Ayla didn't like looking at them for too long. It made her nervous, a capital city so deliberately hidden away. Walls that high, you had to wonder: Were they keeping something out, or in?

Benjy was waiting for her outside the Black Gull, a tavern that seemed busy at all hours of the day. It was a good place to meet if you didn't want to be noticed. Ayla sidled up next to him, sticking to the shadows below the sloping roof. They kept a careful distance between them, looking ahead, speaking only in whispers. Benjy was smoking a pipe, presumably to look like he had a good reason for hanging outside the tavern instead of going in, which Ayla found hilarious: he grimaced with every inhale, clearly hating the entire experience.

"You're late," he murmured, exhaling blue smoke.

"Got tailed twice," she said, frowning. "Had to lead the leech guards on a merry chase for a while. I felt like a damn fox. The sooner we get into the city, the better—it'll be so much easier to blend in."

"You're sure you lost them?"

"Positive. Anyway. Got a couple meat pies, if you're hungry."

He glanced over at her, and she couldn't help but glance back. Just for a split second, just long enough to catch a glimpse of his face, tawny skin and big doe eyes, the freckles on his nose visible even in the shadows. "You know full well I'm always hungry."

"How could I forget the bottomless pit," she said dryly. "Well, come on then. We can eat on the way into Thalen."

The plan was to find Ayla's brother, Storme. It was a horrible plan, as it involved sneaking into the single most dangerous and heavily guarded place in all of Varn: the Mad Queen's palace. Best-case scenario, Ayla and Benjy would somehow, by some miracle, get to Storme and tell him everything they knew about

Scyre Kinok. About why they'd risked everything to sneak into Sovereign Hesod's palace that night. The night Ayla had stood above Lady Crier's bed, knife in hand, failed to do the one thing she'd been fantasizing about for years, and fled with Benjy, surviving the night only because they knew the treacherous sea cliffs better than the sovereign's guard.

Kinok had been a Watcher of the Heart, a member of the elite guild of Automae who dedicated their lives to protecting the Iron Heart. Automae didn't need to eat like humans did—their bodies depended on heartstone, a red gemstone imbued with alchemical power. The Iron Heart was the mine that produced heartstone. As it was the sole source of the Automae's power, and therefore their greatest weakness, its exact location—somewhere in the vast, thousand-league spine of the Aderos Mountains— was known only to Watchers. Only one Watcher had ever left their post. Kinok. For those last weeks at the palace Ayla's goal had been to steal a special compass Kinok had in his possession. She was positive its arrow pointed to the Iron Heart itself. That was the main reason she and Benjy and the others had staged the attack on the sovereign's palace: to break into Kinok's study and steal the safe containing his valuables. But the only thing in the safe had been a piece of paper with three words: *Leo. Siena. Tourmaline.*

She needed to tell Storme about all this and more. About Kinok's desperate search for Tourmaline, a potential new life source for Automae. About Nightshade, the mysterious black dust he'd given to his followers to consume instead of heartstone, even though it seemed only to ruin their bodies, to drive them half mad.

Best-case scenario, Storme would relay the information to Queen Junn and—Ayla didn't know. The queen would arrange for Kinok's death? And Storme would finally give Ayla the answer she was looking for, the answer to a question that had been reaffirming itself with every beat of her heart since they'd first been reunited for those few precious days: *Why did you leave me after the raid on our village? Why did you let me think you died along with our parents? I thought you were dead, I mourned you, I never stopped mourning you, how could you leave me?* And Storme would give her a completely reasonable answer, and everything would make perfect sense, and she would forgive him, and they would embrace as brother and sister, and then Ayla and Benjy would live out the rest of their lives in the luxury of the queen's court. Best-case scenario.

Worst-case scenario, they died a bloody death before they even made it inside the city walls, taking Kinok's secrets with them. Worst-case scenario, Ayla would never see Storme again, and he would never know she'd died so close to him, *so close*, her body at the bottom of a harbor just outside his door. He would board ships above her, sail across her grave, and he would never know. Worst-case scenario, the queen wouldn't find out about Nightshade until it was too late.

Of course, there was one other person who could tell the queen, tell *anyone*, about Kinok's plans. One other person, and Ayla's mind wouldn't let her forget it. A thought kept repeating itself, demanding acknowledgment: *She knows. She could still do something.*

Crier knows. And then it hit her—as it had been hitting her over and over again since yesterday morning, when she'd first heard the whispers circulating on the docks, in the small marketplace, outside the Black Gull, everywhere she went—as it had been hitting her over and over again, a series of gut punches, each one a sick terrible swoop, leaving her breathless—

The date of the wedding between Scyre Kinok and the daughter of the sovereign of Rabu had been pushed up. *Unknown reasons*, people whispered to each other. *I heard something about an attempted coup*, someone would whisper, and then someone else would reply, *No, no, I heard that wasn't true. I heard a servant went mad and tried to burn down the palace. No, no, that's not true either, do you just believe everything you hear?*

Crier was getting married today.

Today.

The ceremony had probably already begun. Not that Ayla was thinking about it; not that she cared. Not that she was thinking about the way Crier used to look at Kinok, wary at best and fearful at worst. Or about the way Crier edged closer to *her*, Ayla, whenever Kinok entered a room.

Ayla kept her head low, trailing a good ten paces behind Benjy as they followed one of the narrow, veinlike roads that fed into the wider road connecting the port town to the city gates. She was thinking about Storme and the Queen and nothing else. She'd traded one goal for another. One mission had failed. (*Was it really less than two weeks ago that she'd last seen Crier? That their eyes had met for one terrified instant before Ayla dropped the knife and ran?)* No matter. She had a new mission. She was going to stop Kinok, stop him from growing even more powerful, tightening his hold over Rabu. Whatever it took.

To do that, she had to find Storme, and tonight was her best chance. Varn was celebrating the Great Maker's Festival, an annual holiday in honor of Thomas Wren and the other early Makers, the creators of the Automae. All of Thalen had been thrown into chaos, the frenzy of preparation. The city gates were open wide for the streams of travelers and merchants and vendors and festivalgoers from all corners of Varn. Ayla and Benjy didn't even need to sneak in. As the sun began to set, the crowds growing ever thicker, they simply walked through the gates with everyone else.

Strings of lanterns swayed along the streets of Thalen, a glowing path through the darkness, leading from the gates to the festival itself in the heart of the city. Ayla and Benjy were swept along by the crowd of revelers, the sea of green and white ribbons, white roses, and white masks, some shaped like long, white beaks. Green feathers fluttered everywhere: they were braided into long hair, woven into bright pluming crowns and shining, iridescent capes. Ayla felt like she'd stumbled into the middle of a royal menagerie, a city of magnificent birds. She kept seeing Automae in the crowd, unnaturally beautiful, glossy hair tumbling down their backs or twisted into crowns, and every time her heart stopped before she realized it was normal here.

For humans and leeches to share a festival, to celebrate among each other. For humans to attend a festival not as servants but as guests. Not equals, never equals, never truly safe, but closer to it here than they ever were in Rabu. Despite all the sovereign's posturing about *Traditionalism* and *respect*. Ayla couldn't reckon with it, couldn't wrap her mind around it. She didn't know if she was more shocked about Automae wanting to mingle with humans or humans just . . . letting them do it.

Don't you know what they do to us? she wanted to shriek at them. *Don't you know what they're capable of? Don't you know they're just waiting for any excuse to hurt you? Don't you know some of them don't need an excuse?*

Her skin prickled. She was sweating, even in the chill of winter. This place wasn't a menagerie. It was a pit of snakes.

Queen Junn's palace lay at the northernmost point of the city. Ayla heard it before she saw it: the roar of thousands of festivalgoers, all those rivers of people converging in the same place, laughing and singing and cheering; the wild rhythmic crash of what sounded like a hundred lutes, and drums, and horns. The buildings lining both sides of the street began to thin out the closer they got to the palace, granaries and cobblers and masonries and other little shops and sharehouses replaced by manor houses, the buildings becoming larger and more ornate. More Automa. Still, the streets were lit with lanterns signaling the way. This wasn't forbidden territory. This wasn't like Yanna, the capital city of Rabu, where humans starved on the streets in plain sight.

As Ayla and Benjy continued, even the manors fell away, the street spitting out everyone into a massive square—a white stone courtyard that could have easily held the entirety of one of Sovereign Hesod's sun apple orchards. The courtyard was filled to the brim with people, lanterns and firepits lighting the crowd with a flickering orange glow, banners emblazoned with the queen's phoenix and Thomas Wren's insignia—the alchemical symbols for salt, mercury, and sulfur; body, mind, and spirit—flying overhead. Smoke billowed up into the night sky, obscuring the stars. Ayla took a deep breath, filling her lungs with the smell of frying fish and frying dough and something almost sickeningly sweet, wine and cider and the copper scent of liquid heartstone, the charcoal-and-grease of a roasting pig, and rising above it all the delicate fragrance of white roses, bushels of them. Ayla saw people wending through the crowd, passing out crowns of white roses. Past the smoke and banners, she could just barely make out the palace itself on the far side of the courtyard. The white walls, a smaller version of the walls ringing the city. The gates.

Someone bumped into her from behind and she realized she'd been standing there, frozen, at the edge of the courtyard. She couldn't help it. She'd never seen anything like this kind of—luxury wasn't the right word, opulence wasn't the right word. This wasn't an Automa gathering, this wasn't the controlled splendor of Crier's engagement ball. This was lavish, beautiful, overflowing with food and color and light despite the late hour, and it was so deeply human. Chaotic, unrestrained. It was like the Reaper's Moon celebration the sovereign's servants held each year in the seaside caves, but a hundred times bigger.

Ayla blinked hard and found Benjy a few paces ahead of her, equally frozen. She joined him, reached out to lay a hand on his arm, hesitated. Ever since the night they had snuck into the palace, when he had pulled her aside right before they'd parted ways—him to Kinok's study, her to Crier's bedroom—and kissed her, quick and hard, she couldn't touch him without remembering it. They hadn't talked about it. They hadn't talked about *anything*, really; that night or the aftermath. Ayla still didn't know if the kiss meant something to him, or if it was just the act of a scared boy who knew he could be dead within the hour, wanting to experience something for the first and last time.

She didn't know which answer she'd prefer.

Maybe that was a lie.

"Benj," she said, quiet enough for no one else to hear but loud enough to be heard over the music, the ocean-roar of a city drunk and merry. "The palace gates. Come on."

He nodded. Heads bent, they made their way through the center of the courtyard, where the music was loudest and the smoke thickest. Sticking to the edges would have been easier—but that was where the royal guards were stationed, watching everything from behind their white masks. So instead Ayla and Benjy wriggled their way through the tightly packed crowd, pressing up against dozens of sweaty, drunken, laughing bodies. The smoke stung Ayla's eyes. Even after the meat pie, her belly panged at the sight of so much food: tables piled high with a dozen different types of fish, platters of cheese and fruits and shimmering black eels, fruit pies, baskets of oranges, loaves of sweet dark bread, honey and oil and butter, mulled wine, and honey cakes, seed cakes, ginger cakes. There were a few humans in what looked like green servants' uniforms flitting around the tables, refilling platters and pouring cups of wine.

She was so hungry, and she'd eaten nothing for three days but pilfered bread and the meat pies she'd bought. Before that, the week and a half at sea, sick and delirious in the cargo hold, she was unable to keep down anything but water. Ayla's stomach gnawed at itself, crumpling, rolling over. She clenched her teeth and forced her eyes away from the food. She didn't have time to eat. She just had to get through the gates, inside the palace. . . .

IN BETWEEN TWO GIRLS—ONE MORTAL, ONE MADE—LIE THE HEART AND A BLADE.

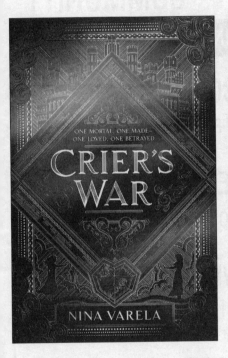

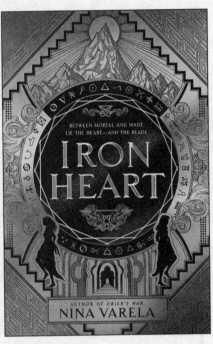

Don't miss this dazzling sequel!

JOIN THE

Epic Reads
COMMUNITY

THE ULTIMATE YA DESTINATION

◀ **DISCOVER** ▶
your next favorite read

◀ **MEET** ▶
new authors to love

◀ **WIN** ▶
free books

◀ **SHARE** ▶
infographics, playlists, quizzes, and more

◀ **WATCH** ▶
the latest videos